THE WINSTONS

BOOK ONE

BECKA'S AWAKENING
&
MATT'S DILEMMA
ROWENA DAWN

SCARLET LEAF
TORONTO
2019

ROWENA DAWN

Table of Contents

BECKA'S AWAKENING
BOOK I

ROWENA DAWN

I dedicate this novel to two couples that fell in love at first sight and whose love is always as strong as ever after many, many, many years of marriage:
Dafinka and Giampaolo Scatozza
Diana and Aurel Botorog

THE WINSTONS

REBECCA'S CHILDREN

    Adam (m. Anna)

    Evelyne (deceased)

    Adam's children

    Marjorie (Twin, m. Jonathan) – children: Matt (34), Maggie (28), Jay (28)

    Michael (Twin, m. Amelie) – children: Josh (26), Lily (26)

    Gabriel (m. Emilie) – children: Ariel (32), Alex (32), Becka (19)

ROWENA DAWN

PROLOGUE

"COME ON, MAN, THIS is so not right!" Josh exploded.

He threw his fork back onto the plate and made his aunt, Marjorie, frown. She loved that set of dishes and feared that the young man's frustrations would sooner or later put a crack in them.

"You're complaining, huh?" Maggie waved her fork at him in mockery and rolled her eyes. "You're still fairly young compared to some of us, and you have enough time ahead of you, so you shouldn't be the one complaining," she replied angrily.

"He has the right to complain, Maggie, as well as anyone of us," Becka replied in support of her cousin. "So what if we are younger? We're all in the same boat," she punched the table with her little fist. "Auntie, can't we do something about this?"

"I know you want to, pumpkin, but there's nothing you can do about it," Aunt Marjorie stroked her arm in an attempt to soothe her. "What must be done must be done!"

"So, we have to pay for something that happened a hundred years before we were even born? How does that make any sense at all?" Alex snapped and joined the others in voicing his outrage, though it didn't stop him from scarfing down another piece of the pie.

"It's less than a hundred, you nitwit!" Lily replied with disdain and punched his arm.

"Who the hell cares?" Alex retorted with his mouth full.

He never did learn not to talk with his mouth full, try as his parents might. Anyway, he wouldn't have given a rat's ass on such things, especially at home.

"One hundred, two hundred, same shit, pardon my French. You know what? I don't feel like paying for some jackass's mistakes!" he ended his heated speech, his finger still pointed at Lily.

"So, what do you propose to do, then?" Matt, who had kept his mouth shut until then, asked with nonchalance.

He had been sipping from his glass of whiskey quietly, with a detached expression on his face that suggested that nothing they discussed could affect him.

"Don't tell me you're okay with this!" Alex answered back in disbelief. "Come on, Matt! You're the oldest, man, and you've only got one year left. You've got to be as angry as I am, if not more! Don't pretend it doesn't bother you because that's not possible!"

Matt took a few moments of silence, sipped a little more from his glass, then looked at Alex, and shook his head.

"Angry? Maybe. Can I do something about it? I don't think so," he replied to his cousin with his usual coolness, his eyes gazing steadily at him. "So why should I bother?"

No one had anything to say to that. They were all aware they had to fulfill one stipulation. Only then they would get their trust funds and reach their full potential. The worst part was that they had to do so before turning thirty-five. Once one of them had turned thirty-five without satisfying that condition, their share of the trust fund would be divided among the remaining younger ones, who still had time to succeed or fail.

"You know what? I don't really care about unlocking my powers," Ariel said pensively without addressing anyone in particular. "Although, it would be nice to see what you can do if you use your full potential," she continued, lost in her thoughts, as always.

Her cousins gave her time to get to the point. They knew that she had the bad habit of rambling on and on or getting lost in her own thoughts only to leave everyone hanging. Yet, sometimes, if not most of the time, she would come up with some quite interesting solutions if they had the patience to listen to her.

"But I want to do something for myself. I'd like to open a little business," Ariel finally said with longing in her tone of voice.

"Keep dreaming," Maggie snapped. Ariel's way of talking irritated her, and Maggie wasn't a patient person, which regularly brought unpleasant consequences in her life. "Until you take care of your part of business, Ariel, you won't open a shed."

"Why are you always so mean to her?" Alex snapped at Maggie. "If she wants to dream, let her dream. What else can she do? What else is there for any of us?" he asked. His angry eyes scanned each of them to see their reactions.

"Beat the curse?" Marjorie asked softly, trying to diffuse a potentially explosive situation.

"Not so easy, auntie," Ariel said with sorrow in her voice. "I've tried, you know. Do you remember? I thought that guy, Eric, the one I met two years ago, would be the one. It wasn't meant to be, you know. It's not so simple, and you know it very well. You see how things are now. There's no real romance left in this world, I'm afraid. If there's no romance left, where can one find true love?"

Marjorie nodded. She did know it. Finding true love wasn't easy-peasy. She had been in the same situation when it was her turn. She had nearly lost everything because of her own stubbornness and family's meddling.

"It's never easy, my dear, I know," she answered and stroked the young woman's arm with love again. "But, Ariel, sweetheart, you have to keep trying. You can't merely give up. Think about it! You will be able to use your powers and get your money, but only once you find your true love and commit to it. You'll be genuinely happy then."

Ariel turned her gaze to her plate on the table. She knew that everyone would read in her eyes that she had already resigned herself. She was sick of hearing platitudes and encouragements whenever her family got wind of something like that.

Everybody around the table kept silent for a few seconds. No one believed that they could offer a solution.

Jay cut another piece of his mother's incredible pie. Marjorie was the best cook in their family, and that was why they always chose to meet at her house. In Jay's opinion, they could get to terms with everything when there was a good pie or cake on the table.

"I think we should see if there's a legal way to get out of this situation, guys. We need the money now, don't we? It's not like we can wait around forever," Alex broke the silence when the idea came to him suddenly. His eyes analyzed his siblings and cousins carefully, and the people nodded their approval. "Look," he continued. "I'm already thirty-two. I don't have time for stupid things, games, and idiotic attempts at love. I want to do something for myself, as Ariel said. Now, while I still can."

Almost everybody found themselves in agreement with him, but they still looked at Matt. He was the smartest guy in the family, and they knew that any solution should come from him. Matt's eyes shifted around the table, feeling their expecting gazes on him, and in the end, he shook his head.

"There's no way out, buddy," Matt put his glass on the wooden table, and at the same time, he rose off the bench. "If you called us here just for this discussion, then I'm out of here. I've got real things to do, places to see..."

"You don't even want to try," Becka cried out, jumping out of her seat. "You've just given up because you have so little time left, and you don't care anymore."

"I tried, sweetie," Matt told her with a sad smile on his lips.

Becka was his favorite cousin. Maybe, because she was the youngest, wholesome, and playful, and had a big heart. His fingers stroked her cheek in a loving, yet sad caress, and he kissed her forehead.

"Becka, I tried hard to find a loophole in the wording of the trust fund papers. Believe me. There's none. If I couldn't find one, sweetie, then no one can. And you know it. There's a reason I'm one of the best attorneys in the country, and all of you know that this isn't merely my vanity talking. Anyway, honey, these days, I content myself with making my own money the hard way and enjoying as much as possible the little spare time I have left. I've stopped chasing such dreams. It's not in the cards for me, and that's it."

His cousins looked at him in shock. Only his sister, Maggie, understood Matt very well. She didn't have any patience, especially with fools, but Matt was something special.

Maggie had always looked up to him, and she knew that he wasn't the guy to give up on anything without a fight. Hearing him say that he had resigned himself made her understand the depth of his anger, even though he hid it from all of them. She felt like taking Matt into her arms and never letting go. However, she knew that he wouldn't like that. Her brother didn't like very big on displays of affection, so she merely petted his hand and left it at that.

"Matt, you should try to use that time you have left to find a girl," his mother said reproachfully, and everyone's attention turned to Marjorie. She continued, "You still have a chance, son, and I'm not talking about the money here, you know it. I know that sad affair with Velma's left you afraid to commit again, and I don't like that in the least. That's not the Matty I know. That wasn't love, son, and you know it. If it had been true love, you'd have had your full powers by now even if you hadn't gotten the money."

"Mother, Velma's been out of the picture for a decade already. She's in the past. What's the point in bringing her into the conversation?" Matt retorted curtly, shaking his head. He couldn't understand his mother's reasons for bringing up bitter memories.

"Because she was the reason you stopped looking at women with hope," Marjorie pointed out, shaking a scolding finger at her firstborn. "You think that all women are like her, and that's why you only take everything you can from them and move on. Another woman on the list! It's like you're keeping a score. How many women can Matt score?" she reproached acidly.

The young people had never witnessed something similar before, and wide-eyed, they stared at her.

"It's not good for you, Matt. Even if you've already given up on the trust fund, which is stupid, by the way, you're still alive, and you still need a reliable woman in your life, as I've already said over and over again. You'll grow old, and alone, and bitter," Marjorie ended her unusual tirade by punching her son's chest with her finger.

"Thanks for the heads up, mom. It's always good to know what your future will look like," Matt replied sarcastically and removed himself from the path of her pointy finger. Yet, he didn't leave. He seemed undecided and glanced back at his cousins.

Marjorie shook her head bitterly but chose not to continue that line of discussion. She knew her son quite well, and she knew she couldn't make him change his mind when he was like that. It was like talking to a rock.

The silence stretched for a few minutes. Everyone seemed busy eating their pie or playing with their drinks, pretending that nothing out of the ordinary had happened between Marjorie and her eldest son. They avoided each other's eyes, worried that someone would say something hurtful again. In the end, Alex, the most outspoken of all, couldn't stand the heavy silence anymore. He glanced around the table, gauging everyone's mood. He wasn't sure that it was even worth it but shrugged and decided to try a new line of conversation.

"You are the old lady's favorite great-grandson, Matt. Can't you convince her to stop this nonsense? She can change the papers if she wants to. The words aren't carved in stone, after all," Alex said and waited anxiously for his cousin's answer.

"I tried that too, Alex." Matt sighed and shook his head. "She said that she did it for our own good whatever she means by that. So I can say I've tried everything, and it's time to limit my losses."

Again, no one said anything for a few moments. They couldn't bring themselves to look at each other in the eye. So, the silence stretched on.

The cousins' get-togethers were fairly chatty and loud affairs, and the odd silence prompted Matt to take his leave. He waved to them and started down the path to the kitchen door, whistling softly.

Dreamy, as always, Ariel gazed after Matt until he was out of earshot. Then she said, "It's sad. He's the oldest, and he's already given up."

For a few moments, everyone stared at her speechless. It was as if she grew a second head during the last hour.

"Well, we're close to that too, Ariel," her brother, Alex, retorted after a moment of disbelief. "We don't have much time left. Only about three years, you, dimwit! Once we turn thirty-five, everything will be gone: the money, the powers, everything. And we can't do anything to stop this."

"We can't even cheat," Jay intervened bitterly for the first time, and the others burst into laughter.

"Oh, yeah, I remember," Lily said. "You tried to pose as a fool in love and came with that simpleton. Camilla, I think her name was."

Jay nodded, smiling. He had already forgotten the ridicule he had suffered at the time. His easy-going nature didn't allow him to keep a grudge for long.

"Yeah, but it didn't work, did it?" Josh said matter-of-factly. "Those two fossils sniffed you out."

"Well, they can read minds, so it was a piece of cake to sniff him out," Aunt Marjorie pointed out with an enigmatic smile on her lips. "That's why they've been appointed trustees, you know. No one can fool them. You shouldn't have tried to cheat, Jay. The old lady hasn't forgiven you for that yet."

Jay shrugged. He knew very well where he stood with his grandma those days, and he didn't think that she would ever forgive him.

Resentful and bitter, the old bat was a real piece of work. Only a few of them could steal a smile from her. Lately, Jay hadn't been part of that group. After the stunt with Camilla, she didn't notice Jay at the family dinners anymore. She pretended that he didn't exist.

Jay looked around and noticed that all the others had gone quiet. They seemed to be thinking about the implications of what had happened to him. He hoped that he wouldn't go through a new period of veiled jokes or innocent teasing. Becka was a master at that, so he flinched when she started talking. He expected the worst.

"So, we only have to wait for them to die..." Becka began to say tentatively, her gaze passing from one to the other.

"Not so fast," Marjorie interrupted her hastily. "The rule says that if they pass away, two others will take their place. The same type of power, pumpkin, so there's no way to fool them either. You have to understand that you can't go around this. You have to play by the rules."

"Damn it," Alex swore. "All this drama only because great-grandpa had the nerve to abandon great-grandma for another woman, and then another idiot left aunt Evelyn at the altar, and she killed herself," he shook his head. He still couldn't understand why he had to pay for someone else. "So, now, generation after generation has to pay for those two idiots. Where the hell is the justice in that?"

"Well, I also think that grandmother had reached a radical conclusion," Marjorie replied in a mollifying tone of voice. "Nevertheless, there's never been a way to change grandma's mind, unfortunately. I know that my father tried hard at the time, but she wouldn't listen to him. He tried again when my happiness was at stake, and still nothing. He didn't have any success. She wouldn't give in. Not even a bit. Since the money was still hers, she had the right to decide what she wanted to do with it."

"But why the curse on our powers? I really don't understand it," Becka wondered.

"Same reason. Grandpa was a witch himself, so he used those powers to entice a very young woman, leaving grandma afterward. And another witch seduced the man who left Evelyn at the altar. So, grandma didn't want any other witch to misuse their powers."

"I wouldn't," Becka cried out.

"I know you wouldn't, pumpkin," Marjorie patted her hand tenderly. "Not all apples are rotten. I know that much. But grandma didn't want to hear a thing, so here we are. Now everyone in my generation paid for that, and yours must pay, as well. However, if you succeed in finding your true love and get your trust funds, then at least the money problem will end. The next generations will have only the curse to defeat," Marjorie looked around the table and tried to lift the young people's mood, but with little success.

"Oh, only that," Lily sighed and put her chin in her hand, fixing her dreamy gaze somewhere in the distance.

"I did want to open that nursery," Ariel whispered inconsolably, and her brother stroked her fingers, his eyes shining with a deep concern for his sister's dreams.

"Nothing is lost, sweetheart," Marjorie said and caressed Ariel's hand at her turn. "You'll see. You'll find your soul mate, Ariel. Everything will be fine."

"Where? Where could I find my soul mate, auntie? The people I deal with every day are not even lover material, believe me. I wouldn't let them touch me with a ten-foot pole. So, finding a soul mate is quite out of the question. There's no chance for me out there. I've looked around for years and nothing," she said, and this time tears welled in her eyes.

"Wait and see, Ariel. These things have a way of working out," Marjorie whispered to her and then started picking up the plates on the table to show that the conversation ended.

There was no point in debating something they couldn't fix. There wasn't anything more to add, and whining wouldn't help. The older woman knew it well. Whining never helped. You had to roll up your sleeves and do something.

Although the others jumped out of their seats to help her, they were still thinking about the discussion and a none-too-rosy future. It looked pretty hopeless for them at that moment.

CHAPTER ONE

BECKA LEFT THE COFFEE shop in a hurry. She held a hot coffee cup in one hand, and at the same time, she tried to stick a muffin and a toasted bagel in her handbag with the other.

She had forgotten to ask for a hot sleeve for the cup. On top of that, she had also neglected to take a napkin. Her head was high in the clouds that morning. Now the searing heat burned her fingers through the paper cup.

Nevertheless, she couldn't go back to the coffee shop. She was already late for her morning classes, and the last thing she wanted was to miss the entire lecture on her favorite subject. So, Becka kept struggling. She tried to make the muffin and bagel fit in her handbag, at which point she wondered why she had left the house with such a tiny purse that morning.

The people and things around her became a blur, the more she wrestled with the bag, and the more she rushed toward the bus stop.

No more than a moment later, just as she turned around the corner, her eyes still on the tiny handbag that wouldn't cooperate with her, she ran into a tall man. As luck would have it, the lid of the coffee cup came loose, and all the hot liquid spilled all over the giant's pristine, white shirt.

Becka thought that things couldn't get any worse. Not only did she scald him, but the damn shirt had to be white. Why not black? No one would notice a coffee stain on a black shirt.

"Oh, my God, I'm so sorry! Really, really, sorry!" she blabbered and tried to clean the man's shirt with her bare hands. She forgot about the cup lying on the pavement, discarded like yesterday's news, all but empty. She had also forgotten about her coveted breakfast, which was leaning precariously on one side of the handbag, ready to fall out as well.

Her hands shook the man's shirt as fast as she possibly could. Her meager attempts hoped to limit the burns at the very least.

Becka knew that the hot coffee must have already penetrated his shirt, and she didn't even want to think of what had happened to the skin beneath it, badly burnt by the freshly boiled brew.

"I think you'd better take your shirt off!" she cried out, but she didn't take her gaze off the task at hand.

Remorse drove Becka's actions now. Images of the emergency room flashed at the back of her mind. Focused to a frenzy on her nearly catastrophic mistake, Becka never noticed the rest of the man to whom the chest belonged, much less the eyebrow that shot up as soon as she ordered him to strip.

"May I ask what exactly you're trying to do?" the man finally asked in a deceptively mild tone of voice. Until then, shocked by the actions of the little woman, he had stared at the top of her head.

At the sound of his voice, Becka finally looked up and blinked. Not once or twice, but three times. The man under her gaze wasn't the regular polished and polite man she had encountered in her life before. He was a far, far cry from that.

A long, pale scar on his left cheek set off the man's rugged face. It began somewhere close to the corner of his eye and continued to nearly the corner of his mouth, giving him a dangerous allure. He looked like one of the mercenaries Becka had seen in one of the documentaries about the civil war in former Yugoslavia. That wasn't reassuring at all.

His brow still rose scornfully, and for a moment there, Becka wondered how he did it. She imagined that it wasn't easy to pull off that move for long. The woman just about forgot her curiosity when she met his eyes, colder than the Arctic Ocean. His brow still rose scornfully, and for a moment there, Becka wondered how he did it. She imagined that it wasn't easy to pull off that move for long. The woman just about forgot her curiosity when she met his eyes, colder than the Arctic Ocean. She swallowed hard and forced herself to be brave. She refused to be a scaredy-cat. Becka would always face danger, and it wasn't the moment to change her ways.

"Hmm.... I was thinking...you know...your shirt..."

"I heard that bit about my shirt, don't worry. But I don't know what difference would make if I took it off now. With or without the shirt, my skin is still scalded, my morning still ruined, and I'm still pissed off," he said in a level tone of voice. He didn't show the slightest hint of anger, but that made her even more fearful.

While it was true that he didn't sound mad, the complete clash between his words and his tone made her nervous. Becka couldn't even begin to think of how to talk to him.

She swallowed again and bravely said, "Yes, I know that. But the coffee is mostly on the shirt, so if you take it off..."

"Now?" he mused when he saw she stopped without finishing her sentence.

"Well, yes," she nodded and stressed her words. She wanted to lend them more confidence than she had.

Becka pretended to know what she was doing, although her face burned in embarrassment and shame. She had asked him to take the shirt off, but it was the first time she said that to a man. Besides, his tone and attitude made her uncomfortable, and she worried that everything showed on her face. Becka didn't have a poker face worth a damn. Every time she played cards with Jay, he would laugh at her best, yet failed efforts to bluff.

The man stared at her for a few seconds, but then, with a bold move, he took his shirt off. "Do your worst," he said and handed her the ruined piece of clothing.

However, Becka didn't take it. She didn't even notice that the man was holding the shirt for her to take. She couldn't find her voice to answer back. Her eyes were too busy taking in the expanse of a chiseled chest peppered with curly coarse hair, still wet from her coffee. She had forgotten what she wanted or was supposed to do entirely.

"Earth to the moon?" he mocked her in his grave voice and waved his hand before her eyes.

Finally, his gestures pulled her out of her reverie. Becka's gaze shot up to his eyes in an instant.

"Sorry, just lost in thought for a moment there," she mumbled more than a little disappointed with her silly admiration of the male figure. She had thought herself above such trivial endeavors.

Finally, she took the shirt from his waiting hand and used it to dry his chest more vigorously than it was necessary.

The coffee was already a dry sticky stain. However, that wasn't on Becka's mind. Neither was the fact that her vigorous brushing might take off a layer of the man's burned skin. Upset with herself for her carelessness and every reaction that followed, she was brimming with embarrassment. Not only had she poured her coffee all over a stranger, but he also caught her staring at his chest like a lustful, simple-minded woman.

"Yeah, I noticed," he replied, amused, watching her expression while she cleaned his chest. The man enjoyed the young woman's train of thought. He could read it on her face with no effort whatsoever.

It was refreshing to see someone so unspoiled as the woman before his eyes. He was tired of all the games played in society and wanted something new.

After a few moments, he decided to ask, "Does any man's chest have this effect on you or just mine?"

A little malice sneaked in his voice, and that made Becka straighten up and look directly into his eyes. Then, she replied sulkily, "I'm only trying to help, you know. Why are you acting like a jerk?"

At her snapped reply, the man's eyes became colder than they had been before, and he yanked the shirt out of her hands.

"Yeah, with such help, I wouldn't be surprised if I'm dead tomorrow," he observed.

She tapped her foot in frustration, raised her voice a notch, and replied to him with her usual self-confidence, "You're just pissed off because I ruined your shirt."

Her voice mustered all the determination she could, and she added a nod for good measure. She hoped that it would give her more of a knowledgeable air.

"But it was a mere accident. You must understand. It wasn't like I wanted to spill my coffee all over you. I'd have preferred to drink it," Becka scoffed and shrugged her shoulders.

Becka stood tall before him, matching his confident, dominant attitude with her own. However, she spoiled everything when she continued in the tone of a stubborn and willful child, "I really could have used that coffee."

The sudden change in her attitude fascinated him, and he watched her more thoroughly. Only now, he noticed her chocolate eyes, and especially, her small mouth with rosy lips, arched like a bow. A part of him was practically begging and pushed him to grab her already and have a taste of her sweet, sensual mouth.

The longer she talked, the more his interest in her lips grew. An agonizing need compelled him to lean in and claim what he wanted. He found them more tempting when the tip of her tongue came out and licked her upper lip anxiously. Something stirred inside him, and suddenly, his interest changed entirely.

"You owe me," he said so abruptly that it charged the atmosphere in an instant.

Shocked, Becka opened her mouth to reply. Yet, too stunned by his sudden outburst, she couldn't make a sound for a few moments.

The man didn't clarify his statement or expand on it. He just waited for her to process his words and get back to him with a bold retort. From what he had seen so far, he was sure he would get one. He didn't have to wait for long.

"What are you talking about?" Becka eventually contrived to say with thinly concealed indignation in her tone of voice. Her rounded eyes stared at the man intently.

"What you heard," he brushed off her harmless furor and continued, "You owe me."

"For this shirt?" she asked incredulously, showing the shirt she held in her hand.

"Among other things."

His wolfish smile ran shivers down her spine, as her mind started dreading the worst and conjured unsettling scenarios.

"What other things?" Becka asked, although more than a little hesitation and uncertainty delayed her question.

Her eyes seemed to grow wider, and the tip of her tongue touched her upper lip nervously again to torment and make him more aware of his increasing desire for her.

He couldn't understand that irrational, unlikely desire for a clumsy woman he had just laid eyes on, but something in him wanted her. He needed to have her, just like that.

She looked a little young. Maybe very young. However, he knew that looks deceived sometimes. Still, he made a mental note to ask about her age. Although she drew him agonizingly, he didn't want to get involved with jailbait. He had a strict policy about not going to jail.

"You poured your coffee on me. You scolded my skin and ruined my shirt. Of course, I can't go to an appointment half-naked. And, please, note that it's a significant appointment. I'm already late because of you," the man explained patiently to her as if he talked to a small child.

Of course, it was a ruse. He only wanted to see what kind of reaction he could draw from her.

Becka felt the blood rush to her face, and she cursed her creamy complexion. It revealed too much, and in the most inappropriate moments. No matter how much she tried to appear sophisticated or cool-tempered, she always failed. Her skin betrayed her. It was the curse of her life. Maybe not the unique curse she had to contend with, but it made the top three.

Becka thought of going a different way with him, to get herself out of the trouble that seemed to be brewing, and very politely, she said, "I'm very sorry for scalding you and ruining your shirt. Of course, I'm sorry about your appointment as well, but I don't see how I could..."

She never finished her sentence. A naughty smile flourished on his lips, and that made her lose her train of thought again. This time she was afraid of what he would say.

"I think you owe me something, and you can set it right by going on a date with me," he finally specified his conditions in a tone that implied too many things that would better remain unsaid.

"A date with you," she repeated as if she couldn't grasp the concept.

"Yes, princess, a date," he repeated in a tone of voice that showed that he meant it. "You know, that thing where we go somewhere, have something to eat, talk, that sort of stuff. It's usually called a date. So, that's what I want. A date with you. Today. Not right this moment because I certainly can't go anywhere without a shirt, but immediately after you go into that store over there and buy another one for me.

Don't worry about it, though. I won't ask you to pay for it. I'll give you the money," he waved his hand magnanimously as if the price of the shirt were the problem.

"That's not a problem. I can buy it. You need a new shirt because of me, after all," Becka replied, offended by his condescending attitude.

"It' not necessary," he refused. He took his wallet out of the back pocket and pulled a few bills out.

"Here, that should be enough," he said, giving her the money. "Now, go in, buy me a white shirt. Keep in mind, a white shirt, not blue, not black or green, or striped or whatever. Just white. Then we can go on our date."

"No, I can't," she said stubbornly and shook her head.

"Why not?" he asked, his face so rigid and stern as if it were set in stone. He didn't seem to take her rejection well. "As I said, you owe me. You know I can say that you attacked me."

"Ha, good try," she scoffed at him. "Attack by coffee! A deadly weapon! Don't make me laugh. No one would believe that stupid thing, and you know it full well. Everyone will see that it was a simple accident and nothing more."

"So then, am I to understand you're too good for the likes of me?" he frowned.

Becka scoffed again and dismissed his silly, inconsequential words with a wave of her hand.

"Get serious! I haven't even considered that. But since I don't know a stitch about you or your life, it would be difficult to make such assumptions, don't you think?"

"Is it my scar?" he asked peevishly now. "Do 'stitches' make you uncomfortable?"

She scoffed at him again but refused to answer a question she considered quite stupid and not worthy of her attention.

"You're not legal, is that it?" the man tried again, determined to get her to admit to something. He didn't understand why, but he couldn't just let go.

"No, I'm legal. You don't have to worry that I'm underage. I'm three months over nineteen already," she replied, and this time she smiled warmly at him.

That puzzled him a little more than her former, vague refusals. "So? You have a boyfriend then, and you won't cheat on him," he tried again. He had already reached the point where he just wanted to find out the reason, end the conversation, and walk away if she kept rejecting him. He had no explanation for that, but finding out why she wouldn't go out with him was still a priority.

"No, I don't have a boyfriend. However, I do have a class right now, and a couple more later on. The point is that I really don't want to miss any of them, and I'm already so very late. But, if you still want to, I can see you in the afternoon," she said and noticed that he was astonished that she agreed to go out with him. "And not because I owe you, or anything stupid like that. But because I'd like to see you again. I don't owe you a thing. Just so we're clear."

His gaze searched Becka's face. He wanted to make sure that Becka didn't try to string him along but brushed the thought off after a second of thought. He was nearly positive that she wouldn't show up. Nonetheless, he didn't have anything to lose, and he couldn't force her to go on a date with him, either. Everyone would have laughed at him if he had claimed that a girl attacked him with a Styrofoam cup of coffee.

"All right," he accepted. "When?"

"If you want it to be today, then it will have to be after four," Becka answered cheerfully, visibly keen on the unexpected date.

"Dinner, at six?" he asked her.

"Why not? I do need to eat dinner."

"This spot here, where we are now?" he asked again.

She nodded, a little amused by his way of asking questions and turned to leave.

"Hey, you forgot my shirt," he cried out after her.

"I'm buying it now," she turned her head back to him.

"Take the money, then," he insisted, stretching his hand out to her. "I don't want you to pay for it."

Becka was stubborn enough to go against his wishes. She did want to have it her way and leave him with his hand outstretched. However, she took note of the dogged expression on the man's face and realized that he wouldn't give up so easily. He seemed more stubborn than she was, so she gave in and took the money.

CHAPTER TWO

THE MAN PACED BACK and forth on the corner of the street. In the beginning, when he got there, about five minutes earlier, he had decided to wait patiently. However, he was almost sure that she wouldn't show up and had used her classes as an excuse, so she wouldn't have to go on a date with him at all.

The young woman seemed delicate and sheltered. That led him to believe that she would avoid any further contact with him.

He had seen that type of woman before, those sheltered flowers, living in a polite world, where everything was covered under several layers of paint to deflect reality. Well, in his experience, those innocent flowers would run away like scared rabbits once they took a good look at him and his scar. None ever stuck around for a second chance.

He didn't harbor any illusions about romance or anything like that. He had left such baggage aside some time in his past. He knew that a girl like her wouldn't dream about a man like him. He didn't fit the mold of a man she would bring back home to meet mom and dad.

Thank God, he didn't have such aspirations. He was too much of a realist. Besides, although he didn't want to admit it, he was too terrified to put himself out there in the open and reveal what was in his soul. It wouldn't have been smart. Someone would assuredly stomp on it.

He glanced at his watch as he continued pacing around. Surprised, he noticed that he had arrived too early for their meeting. There were about three minutes left until six. Anyway, he knew that he would wait, not only until six o'clock but probably even ten or fifteen minutes past six, although he didn't expect the woman to keep her promise.

Somewhere, at the back of his mind, there was the knowledge that he had partly set up that date only to punish himself. He was very good at teaching himself, repeatedly, not to reach for someone as innocent and wholesome as the girl from that morning.

He had been warned against such wishful thinking many times in the past. Nevertheless, he still found a masochistic delight in challenging fate as if his turn would surely come one day, and then he would win for once. He liked beating the odds.

He was still striding on the sidewalk nervously when, suddenly, he saw the woman rushing toward him. She was pushing past the moving crowd in a hurry, much like she had done that morning.

It occurred to him that probably, being late was one of her habits. It wasn't the worst habit in the world, anyway. He had seen worse things than that, and after all, he could live with that.

This time, at a second, more appraising, glance, the first thing he noticed was the woman's honey-colored hair, thick and full of curls. It flew freely over her shoulders. In the morning, she had it gathered in a thick ponytail. He had liked her hair that way too. That mass of hair was too deep and lively not to like it. However, right then, with that wild mane set free, the young woman was much more enticing than he remembered.

A slow smile flourished on his lips, and he wasn't even aware that he was smiling, although it was out of the ordinary for him. The longer he watched and admired the woman, the more he realized that he would fall for that girl, and in a dangerous way. The thought troubled him enough to make him frown for a second, and any trace of his earlier grin disappeared.

The young woman stopped a few steps away from him and smiled shyly.

Her smile reached her eyes and colored the chocolate of the iris in a warmer nuance than the one he had liked so much only a few hours before. At that very moment, he was sure he would give her anything she wanted only to enjoy her sweet eyes a little more.

"Hi," she said out of breath when she reached him, and her lips arched a little more, tentatively. "I'm really sorry that I'm late, but I had a bit of a problem at home, and I had to take care of that. That's why I couldn't leave earlier. My kitchen flooded. Again."

"It's all right. You're not late. But It looks like you're not having a very good day today, though," he replied with a smile. Her way of talking amused him. Her voice was low.

It didn't sound like the voice of some of the women he had dated. He appreciated that it didn't chime like tiny bells in his ears every single time she opened her mouth. He hated the high pitch of an all too sweet, dishonest voice.

"I think we should introduce ourselves. I'm Bryan," he said, smiling at her.

"Becka," she extended her hand to him enthusiastically, and the man's smile grew wider. She didn't seem reluctant at all to go out with him, and that got his hopes up. His perpetual smile hinted at the change in his expectations and his opinion of her.

"Hello, there, Becka. Nice to meet you." He took her small hand and shook it gently. "So, aside from nearly sending a stranger to the hospital this morning and the flood this afternoon, how was your day?" he continued, and without letting her hand go, he turned her toward the strip of shops.

"Well, I was too late for my first class this morning, which annoyed me. Immensely," Becka said. Then, she rolled her eyes in frustration, and she fell into step with him. "I really like that class, you know. Worse, now I'll have to figure out by myself everything I missed. That means a lot of work and at least an entire afternoon wasted," she complained.

"So now you resent me," he replied in a low and flat tone.

"Why would you say that?" Becka turned to him, surprised at his odd reaction. "I was late even before I bumped into you. It's not your fault at all. It's just that I didn't sleep much last night. Too many thoughts, you know how it is. And this morning, I had a bit of a slow start to my day. That's all."

Bryan nodded. He understood that she didn't blame or begrudge him for it. However, more than anything, he was content because Becka still allowed him to hold her hand.

"What kind of thoughts could keep a young girl like you awake?" he asked in a condescending tone of voice.

She scowled at him, turned her nose up, and said peevishly, "The kind of thoughts I can't share with you."

"Hmm," Bryan mumbled but let the subject drop. The woman seemed determined not to say anything, and he didn't want to push his way in too forcefully and scare her away.

"By the way, I know an Italian restaurant by the lake," Bryan told Becka and squeezed her fingers. "They have a delightful terrace overlooking the lake and a gorgeous view. I should also mention that they serve original Italian food. I've heard it's an unforgettable experience."

"I'd love it," she looked up at him, and a broad smile appeared on her lips. "But are you sure we can get a table at this hour? If the view and the food are so great, wouldn't it be packed now?" Becka worried.

"Don't worry, sweetie," he waved her concern off. "I've already made reservations for us."

"So, you were very sure about you or rather about me. You were sure that I'd come," Becka murmured to herself, but Bryan heard her anyway.

"No, not at all," he contradicted her. "Actually, I didn't think you'd show up, but I'd have gone out for dinner anyway so...," he shrugged.

"Do I seem so unreliable?" Becka asked touchily. She pulled her hand out of his, and that made him laugh.

He liked those little, illogical contradictions in her nature and found her funny.

"No, Becka, you don't, but you do look too sweet and young for a man like me," Bryan answered unapologetically even if her words amused him. He chose to be direct whenever he could.

"I am not so young," she frowned at him. "I've told you I'm already nineteen, haven't I?"

"Yes, you have. I know. But I'm almost thirty-two, practically a lifetime away. More importantly, I've seen much more of this life than you, and not all of it good," he replied, and then he took her hand back into his and entwined his fingers with hers, making her shiver for a moment.

Both felt something like an electric shock run through their intertwined fingers, but neither dared to say anything. They glanced at each other briefly before Becka looked away, trying to mask what she was feeling.

After a few moments, she looked back at him, "I wouldn't have thought you were so old." Bryan's brow rose doubtfully, and she hurried to correct herself. "Not that you're old. You aren't. But..."

The man started laughing heartily, and she stopped her explanations, turning her nose up childishly again.

"You're so funny! And your fuse is so short! Amazingly, you get upset so easily. It's refreshing to see someone so natural, not faking every emotion," he said and squeezed her fingers gently.

"You should know it's not a good idea to annoy me," she started in force but left her statement at that.

"Or what, sweetie?" he asked a bit steely.

She stopped suddenly, glanced behind them, then back at him again with nervous eyes, and whispered, "I can't tell you."

"Now, you've made me curious. Really, really, curious. Are you with the mob or something?" Bryan asked her, only half-joking.

Nothing truly shocked him anymore, and he had learned to take everything in stride. However, he liked to know what he was up against, and the sooner, the better. His hide might not have worth too much, but it was his, and he had some attachment to it.

"What?" Becka cried out and stopped in her tracks for a second. His idea was so outrageous that her eyes widened to what seemed the size of small saucers.

Becka couldn't believe her ears. She wouldn't have ever imagined that someone would ask her such a question, and she was afraid Bryan was making fun of her.

"Well, you just threatened me..." he started speaking, but she interrupted him at once.

"I didn't threaten you, you, blockhead! I merely warned you," she replied with real anger in her voice this time, but he didn't seem to care.

"The same thing," he shrugged nonchalantly.

"No, it isn't," she insisted. "That's not the same thing. And I haven't said anything about the mob. Where did you get such an idea?" she asked in a biting tone of voice.

He glanced at her and saw her face was turning purple. "But you warned me not to annoy you," Bryan tried to approach the matter logically and calm Becka down at the same time. Her temper was rising.

"Yes, but that doesn't mean..."

"I understand a threat when I hear one, Becka," he interrupted her forcefully this time. There was no trace of playfulness in his voice anymore. "So, what are you going to do to me? Murder me in my sleep?"

"Are you mocking me?" she scowled at his questions and the tone of his voice.

"No, I'm dead serious. I might have a worthless hide, but it's still attached to my back, you know," Bryan replied in a matter-of-fact tone of voice, echoing his earlier thoughts.

"Wait! What do you mean when you say that you have a worthless hide?" Becka asked, confused, and for a moment, she forgot the subject of their discussion entirely.

"Just something someone told me," Bryan replied softly, avoiding going into details.

"You know you shouldn't trust people who say things like that," Becka advised him wisely. "I might not know you, but you don't seem worthless to me. At least, this is one thing I can do well. I'm a good judge of character. I can tell you're much more complicated than you seem, and I would guess that you have a very speckled past. But you're not worthless at all," she said pensively, kindlier than she had been in their argument just moments ago.

"Wow, you do like to talk," Bryan exclaimed when she finished delivering her lengthy speech. Mostly, her words humbled him, and he didn't want to let her see it.

"You want me to shut up?" she replied, upset. "I can shut up. If it bothers you so much, I can stop talking altogether. It's not a problem for me."

"No, not at all," he pulled her closer to him and squeezed her fingers tenderly. "I actually like the sound of your voice. It's not one of those voices that sounds like a chime and grates my ears. It's got a low pitch, almost throaty, sexy, I could say. Although, I'm pretty sure that mouth of yours would be good at other things, too, not just talking," he added with measured nonchalance. At the same time, he watched her. He wanted to see her reaction to such a blunt suggestion.

Shocked, Becka looked up at him for a few moments, and her eyes widened again. Then she started walking faster, to leave behind what he had just said, but she forgot about their laced fingers that wouldn't allow her an easy escape. Bryan laughed and matched his stride to hers.

"Come on, don't act like a little virgin. No one is so innocent these days," he tried to smooth her ruffled feathers.

"It's not about being innocent, you ass! It's our first date," Becka snapped back and rolled her eyes.

"So? Do you follow the rules? A kiss on the first date, a longer one and first base for the second, and sex on the third?"

"I don't follow any rules. I don't know any rules. But if there are any, then you can forget about getting any kiss today or tomorrow or the day after," Becka replied furiously.

"Why? Am I being punished?" he asked, a quiet chuckle betraying his teasing interest.

Becka scoffed at his words, "As if I cared to punish you. It's about what I feel and what I want."

"And you feel nothing when it comes to me. Is that what you're saying?" Bryan asked her, more curious about her opinion of him so far than at all disappointed with the thought. It wasn't as if he'd gotten his hopes up for a relationship only to find out that he didn't measure up.

"I didn't say that, so, please, don't put words into my mouth."

"Then what did you say?" he insisted.

"That it might be a possibility. I actually don't appreciate what you said. It was coarse, and you know it. I think you did it on purpose only I don't know why."

He waited to see what else she had to say. He found her more fascinating than he thought she would be, especially for someone so young.

"You know what? Let's have dinner, change the subject, and maybe you'll get that kiss," she replied cheerfully, trying to appease both of them and save the evening.

"I'm not a child to bribe me with candy, Becka," Bryan replied evenly, scowling at her.

"Ugh!" she growled. "You're impossible. You choose to misunderstand everything I'm saying."

"Why? Because I don't let you treat me as you'd treat the children you normally date?" Bryan retorted.

Becka stopped and turned to him in disbelief yet again. "You know what, Bryan? I think you've got a complex, and it's a big one. You have a big chip on your shoulder, don't you? I don't understand, though. If our age gap stresses you so much, why did you ask me out? You should have played it safe and spared yourself the trouble of putting up with a child," she ended her tirade almost shouting, and a slight breeze ruffled the leaves in the trees.

Bryan didn't say anything for a few moments. However, he had to admit that the woman had a point. He decided not to let her see that she touched a nerve, afraid that she might guess what he thought. So, Bryan continued to stare her down, but his action didn't have the desired effect. Becka didn't back down.

"I don't have a complex," he replied stubbornly after a few seconds. "But I don't like to be patted on the head like some five-year-old, either. I don't like to hear that if I'm a good boy, I'll get a cookie."

"Oh, really? And you think I'm going to believe you?"

The man let her comment hang in the air for a few moments, unsure what to believe of her. She seemed in challenging mode, and that didn't seem plausible.

"You're a little hellion, Becka. I'm almost twice your size..."

"What's that got to do with anything? Unless you intend to fight me?" she asked.

She seemed to want to know how the dispute would end, and considering her tone of voice, the woman half-challenged him and half-warned him off.

Bryan laughed heartily, brought her hand to his lips, and kissed her fingers.

"Of course, not. Don't be silly. You only astonish me. Usually, women are more careful around me," he replied, amused.

"How come?" Becka asked.

"Well, if you want to know, most of them avoid me. But no woman has ever threatened me or provoked me as you do," he said, watching her as if she were an odd exhibit in a museum.

"Oh, for God's sake," Becka snapped, throwing her hands into the air dramatically. "I haven't threatened you. Can't you get it through your thick skull?"

Bryan opened his mouth to say something, but she reached up and covered his mouth with her palm. At the same time, she shook her head to stop him from adding anything else to what he had already said. He obeyed mutely and merely watched her.

"Could we leave it at that, Bryan? Believe me. It was not a threat, okay. Maybe, one day, I'll tell you what's all that about, but not today, okay?"

"Okay, not a threat," he said after Becka took her hand off his mouth.

THE HOSTESS SHOWED them to a table close to the lake. There, Bryan courteously pulled Becka's chair and helped her to sit at the table.

After she took her seat, Becka looked at the lake wistfully. A dozen boats had set sail out on the lake that day, and white sails, canoes, and all kinds of other boats peppered the shiny surface of the water.

Becka was crazy about sailing. Yet, she had rarely had the chance to go out on the lake lately. Matt was the only one who owned a boat, and busy with his work all the time, he hadn't had enough time to take her out sailing that summer.

Bryan sat down at his turn and gazed at Becka. He noticed the wistfulness in her eyes and understood what she wanted. Bryan took her small hand in his, and his fingers brushed over her skin with tenderness. He hoped to make her forget about her longing. Bryan said softly, "If you want, we can go sailing on the lake tomorrow morning or in the afternoon. I understand that the weather will keep, so we'll have another fine day with no clouds. I have access to a little pocket cruiser you might like."

"Really?" Becka's entire face lit up with excitement. Bryan's invitation meant that the summer might not go to waste, after all.

Her reaction fascinated Bryan again. Yes, he had liked her beautifully arched lips enough to ask her out on a date. However, now he saw much more than that in Becka.

She was a beautiful woman indeed, and she didn't have any use for artifices. That puzzled him. Most women would wear a lot of makeup to be attractive, especially when they were very young and wanted to appear sophisticated.

Becka's makeup was subtle to the point of nonexistence. She might have used something on her eyelashes, but he couldn't be sure. He could be sure, though, that she didn't wear any lipstick and not even a trace of perfume. And yet, she smelled like wildflowers. Leaning in, closer to her, he realized it was her hair that smelled of flowers.

"Hmmm..."

"What?" she asked, startled.

"Nothing. Nothing," Bryan waved her concerns away. "I was only wondering about your shampoo. I've never smelled anything like that," he explained to her.

"Really? My shampoo? We were talking about sailing," she scolded him for such a silly side-note, and he could tell that she was disappointed.

"Yes, we were," he reassured her. "My offer still stands, even if you don't want to go tomorrow. My question about your shampoo was just curiosity. That scent is amazing," he specified.

"All right, then. Let's satisfy your curiosity. It's a shampoo that one of my cousins had made especially for me. That's why it's so unique. She chose some flowers that go well with my skin and hair. But that's not important now, Bryan. Yes, I want to go on the boat with you tomorrow. I'll skip my classes, not a problem."

"Just like that?" he wondered.

Bryan wasn't ready to accept that it had been so easy to get her to go out with him again. It wasn't usually that way with other women. He had to work a little more.

"Yep, just like that," she replied, smiling at him. "I'm truly crazy about sailing, you see, and I haven't had any chance to go on the water this year. That's why I actually took classes this summer. I knew I'd die of boredom otherwise. At least, having to go to school takes my mind of what I've missed," the young woman explained to him.

"Who takes you sailing usually?" Bryan asked, feeling the sting of jealousy rising in his throat. He had known he must have had some competition but had preferred to push the thought aside.

"Matt, but he seems to be busier than ever this summer. Every time I tried to ask to go sailing, he never had the time," she said with regret in her voice.

"Who's Matt?" Bryan asked, now quite envious of the unknown man. "You said you didn't have any boyfriends, sweetie," he pointed out.

"Oh, no. Matt's not a boyfriend. He's just one of my cousins," Becka answered to him hastily, but she didn't add anything more when the waitress interrupted them to take their order.

Bryan waited patiently until the waitress left with their orders and then asked, pretending to be absent-minded, "You have lots of cousins?"

"You might say that," Becka replied, turning her gaze back to him. She had been watching the lake again. "I have five cousins and two siblings. You?"

Bryan shrugged and replied, "I might have a cousin somewhere in the west of the country, but I haven't seen him in ten years at least. No siblings."

"Oh, that's bad. Aren't you lonely?" Becka asked, feeling sorry for him. She couldn't imagine how it would be not having someone with whom to plot or quarrel. She had always counted on someone to turn to if she needed company or help.

"Not really," he mumbled and leaned back to let the waitress who had returned with their drinks to put the glasses on the table.

The beer was cold and felt good after that hot afternoon. After a few moments of indolent silence, while Becka watched the boats on the lake, and he gazed at her, Bryan said, "We can leave in the morning if you want and return in the evening, take a picnic with us..."

"I'd love that," Becka jumped at Bryan's proposition. Then she continued talking fast, with enthusiasm, she couldn't even begin to restrain. "Let's do it! How early do you want to leave? I hope it won't be at the crack of dawn. I can't function very well early in the morning," she said in a cheerful tone of voice. She was earnest, though. She avoided waking up early when she could.

"No worries, not so early," he replied with a smile in his voice. "We can wait till eight-thirty or nine. What do you say if I come and get you at eight-thirty? Or are you afraid to tell me where you live?" Bryan asked when he saw her reflect upon his words.

"Ah, no, no, it's not that," Becka waved his concern away as not significant. "I don't mind if you know where I live. You don't give off that serial killer vibe," she said, and Bryan's brows instantly rose at her odd opinions. "I was only trying to decide if eight-thirty would be too early or not, but I think I can survive if I get up at seven."

For a moment, Bryan only stared at her. He wasn't even able to think of a reply. The serial killer reference still stumped him. The man had never heard that a vibe specific to a serial killer existed. After a few moments of shock, he shook his head, trying to clear his mind. Only then registered what else Becka had said.

"You do like your sleep," he laughed.

"You don't even know the half of it," Becka merrily replied. "I'm a bit of a night owl, you see. I like to go to bed late at night, so it's no wonder that I can't get up early in the morning," she shrugged.

"How do you manage school?" Bryan asked, taking another sip of his drink.

"Oh, that's another story altogether," she waved her hand dismissively and sipped from her beer, as well. "Actually, it's not that much of a mystery," Becka suddenly decided to answer. "I choose my courses with two things in mind: they can't be too early in the morning, and of course, they have to be interesting. You know," she said with a conspiring air, "I can't even declare a major. I don't know what courses to focus on. I like too many things, you see, and..." the woman circled her hand to fill in the blanks.

"So, you're undecided about your future," he concluded, stroking her long fingers with carefully manicured, short nails. Bryan didn't think that her indecision was too much of a problem at her age. She still had the time to choose what direction to follow in her life.

"Actually, I do know what I want to do in the future," she corrected him. "Not that it would do me any good," Becka mumbled grudgingly.

His strokes were playing havoc on her sensitive nerves and confused her thoughts, stealing away her senses toward a drowsy concentration on the soft, pleasant caresses.

It wasn't as if she never met a guy who tried to play doctor with her, but this man was different. Bryan was entirely unlike the guys who asked her out before.

Becka had been unresponsive to her dates in the past and even convinced herself that it was her fault that she couldn't feel anything. She had concluded that she was probably a cold person.

What happened now contradicted her beliefs. Her body reacted very strongly to this man, and without the usual annoyance, she felt whenever someone wanted to touch her.

"Why not?" Bryan asked. The chain of emotions passing over her expressive face mesmerized him. He was positive that Becka had to be the worst poker player in the world. Virtually everything she thought was visible on her face for all to see.

Becka looked at him startled as if she didn't expect him to talk, and then, she realized that she had said too much in her pleasure-induced near-trance.

"It might not be possible to do what I want," she said after a while. "There are some conditions...and even people that are much better than I didn't succeed...so...."

"Don't sell yourself short," Bryan cut her hesitation short. "You might succeed even if others have failed. You want to elaborate, though, so that I understand and probably help..."

"Oh, no, I can't," she interrupted him. "It's not something I'm supposed to say, you see?"

"Why not?" he frowned. He didn't like foggy matters, and apparently, the young woman was involved in a lot of such things.

"Because I can't," she pleaded for his understanding.

"Are you mixed up in something?" he scowled at her, and not because he didn't want to get involved with a woman tangled in nefarious affairs. Nonetheless, he felt a sudden urge to get her out of trouble.

Bryan wasn't a particularly helpful man, but the young woman had wormed her way into his heart. That troubled him.

"Oh, no, not that, of course. Don't be silly," Becka laughed with carefree cheerfulness, dispelling his dark thoughts. "It's just a family thing. Can we talk about something else?" she waved the subject away.

"People date so that they can get to know each other, Becka. If you keep secrets...." Bryan shrugged, trying a different way to get to the heart of the matter.

"Oh, come on. Like you've told me your secrets," Becka cried out frustrated. "I won't fall so easy for that thing."

"You haven't asked me anything," Bryan answered, and a grin tugged at the corner of his mouth. "But I have asked, you see, so, of course, I expect answers," he nodded to put more weight on his words.

Pensively, Becka traced the contour of the glass with a finger. She tried to figure out some way to turn his expectations against himself.

"But why do you get to ask first and not me?" she glanced at him with suddenly sharp eyes.

"All right, ladies first," he generously gave in as if he were doing a favor to her. "You ask your questions first, and then I'll want my answers," Bryan said. A finality sounded in his tone of voice and promised that he would offer her no reprieve from holding up her end of the deal.

Becka took a few moments to think about it, but finally, she admitted with disappointment, "I don't know what to ask or how to ask," she said, glancing back at him.

"Then I don't know what answers you want," Bryan mused at her, unwilling to say anything without being specifically asked.

She frowned for a second, then smiled as if she had just discovered the secret of life, "All right, tell me everything about you."

"Huh, you don't ask for much, do you?" he laughed at her ingenuity.

"I think my question covers everything, so start talking," Becka gesticulated. "I'm afraid you might not even finish today, and you'll have to continue tomorrow and the day after tomorrow, and so on," Becka laughed, happy that she found the perfect solution to elude his questions.

"You're something else," Bryan said. He shook his head and chuckled. Then he grabbed the woman's hand. He looked at her fingers and stroked each of them gently until he realized she was shivering. "Do I make you nervous?" Bryan asked, glancing at her face.

"No...no, you don't. I'm just...not used to that," she tried to explain.

"Hmm, you make me wonder how many boyfriends you've had, and how inept they were," Bryan said under his breath, but Becka still heard him.

Before answering, she took a few seconds to think, tilting her head to the side in a gesture he had noticed earlier and found endearing. "I think there were four, and yes, they were clumsy and went directly for the kill."

"And what did you say?" he asked, holding her gaze with interest. He could imagine his little hellion crush the laughable attempts of horny teenagers.

"Of course, I said no," she answered haughtily.

"But not always," Bryan surmised. He was a realist, after all.

"Why not?" Becka shrugged. "Believe me, they didn't worth the bother," she replied and scowled at the same time. Becka didn't understand where he was going with his line of questions, and she wasn't very comfortable with them.

His sharp gaze held hers before he let go of her hand. Leaning back on his chair, Bryan analyzed her for a few moments. His disbelief was palpable. Then he asked her in a voice full of awe, "You want to tell me that you've never been with a man...or a boy before?"

"It's not that I want to say so, but it seems I've already had. Is that a problem for you, Bryan? Do you prefer experienced women? You don't date a little bookworm like me?" Becka asked him snappily. She hated labels, especially when they were attached to her.

"Where did that come from?" he asked, puzzled by her sudden outburst.

"You said..."

"Wait a minute, sweetie. I haven't said anything about you being a bookworm," Bryan interrupted her by putting his hand up sharply to stop her from talking over him.

She waved his concern aside and replied, "It's not a big deal. Others said it, so I'm not surprised that you might think the same way too," she shrugged his excuses off.

"Don't lump me in with the others, Becka, all right?" Bryan leaned toward her, stressing his words so she could get his message loud and clear. "I'm not a stupid teenager, who's looking to score with a different girl every night and add notches to my belt. And besides, you don't strike me as a bookworm," he clarified, always fixing her with his firm eyes. "Not even a little."

"Well, to be honest, I am a kind of a bookworm," Becka admitted sheepishly, her gaze shifting aside to avoid his eyes. Despite it being the truth, it was a particularly raw button for her. "I prefer reading than spending time with my classmates. Some of them can't share a thought between them and..." Becka shrugged again. "Look, I tried, okay...but it was so damn boring to be around them all the time," she protested with broad gestures.

Bryan burst into laughter and said, "Let's hope that I'm not as boring as them, and you won't get sick of me too soon."

"You know I've never said anything like that," Becka said reproachfully, a little concerned about them being at odds all the time. She'd never been so snappy and contradictory with anyone before. She didn't understand what made her react so strangely when it came to Bryan.

"No, you haven't, I admit it," Bryan agreed with a nod of his head. "Anyway, I'm sure I can show you some things neither of those kids could," Bryan replied with a wolfish smile that made a shiver trickle down her spine.

His words, as well as his meaningful smile, stunned for a few seconds.

Bryan was as blond as a Viking or rather the way she had always imagined Vikings. His icy blue eyes seemed to shoot arrows her way now and then, and she felt each one of them somewhere in her belly. It was like a constant attack on her senses.

Whenever he would touch her hand and stroke her skin with those long, thick, and calloused fingers, little sparks ignited in all her nerve endings. It made her feel strange. She found herself wanting something more from him, and at the same time, she was afraid of what she might get in the end.

Becka was aware that Bryan wasn't the kind of man with whom she could play games. She only hoped that he would stop if she said no in the end. He didn't look like he would take anything like that kindly. Bryan was too hard and seasoned for something like that. One thing was clear to her. A relationship with him involved a lot of risks, and yet, she didn't want to back out of it.

Becka also had the unsettling feeling that Bryan was aware of what he was doing to her and enjoyed the results immensely. Since she wasn't sure whether he was serious or only having a little fun with her, she hated herself for being so transparent and offering everything to him on a silver platter.

What bothered her more was the fact that she was painfully aware of what was going on. That didn't mean that she could do a thing to change the way she reacted.

Becka was just stunned that she would experience such intense sensations merely because he stroked her fingers. It wasn't like she had never dated, and she hadn't had any experience on the scene. Nevertheless, Becka knew that none of the guys she dated in the past had made her feel a tenth of what she was feeling now, and Bryan didn't even make a lot of effort.

Becka picked up her glass with beer and drank slowly. She needed time to think of something to say. Becka thought hard, but she didn't find anything worth mentioning.

At the same time, she was staring at the tablecloth as if she could find some inspiration there. However, her mind was blank, which only made her more furious with herself. She was acting like a fool. She couldn't bear the thought that a man could make her forget everything in a matter of seconds. That woman there wasn't anything like her. Where were her witty spirit and her deflective skills?

Bryan touched her hand gently again and made her snap out of her thoughts and look up at him. He was smiling at her.

"Don't try too hard," he advised her in a soft voice. "It's not rocket science. It's just a date. We can talk about anything and everything. It's up to you. No one can make you say or do something you don't want. All right, Becka? Let's find a neutral subject. For instance, why don't you tell me about those classes you're taking," Bryan suggested.

Becka pulled her hand away and let it fall into her lap to cut off the flux of emotion. Then, she cleared her throat and said, "I'm taking some art classes this summer. They're just optional courses, you know. I just needed something to do," she said, shrugging her shoulders, and Bryan noted that the gesture seemed to define her.

Becka continued, unaware of his thoughts, "Everybody in the family is busy with something right now, and I was feeling a little... left aside, if you know what I mean."

Bryan, who knew very well how it felt to be left aside, nodded and, glancing at her left, said, "It looks like our food is here."

They both kept silent while the waitress laid the food on the table, and then they said their polite 'thank you' and attacked their plates.

Happy that she finally had something to do, Becka started cutting into her juicy steak with enthusiasm. It seemed to be precisely the way she liked it. She hoped it would also taste as good as it looked.

She hadn't eaten much that day. She had lost the muffin and the toasted bagel when she went to buy the shirt for Bryan. Because of the flood in the kitchen, she hadn't had the time to eat that afternoon. So now, she was hungry and didn't fake her interest in the food.

"It was refreshing to hear you wanted a steak and not a salad with the dressing on the side," Bryan told her after he swallowed his first bite. "I hate seeing women go hungry just because fashion says they have to be skinny with no curves. I, for one, can't understand why anyone would want a woman with no curves."

"Huh... you won't see me doing that," Becka replied, glancing at Bryan. At the same time, she cut another piece of steak. "I mean skipping meals or eating only salad," she specified. "Of course, I enjoy a salad as much as the next person. Don't get me wrong. But, I do enjoy a good meal, especially if I don't have time to eat all day, like today. It's not like I'll ever get skinny anyhow, and I don't think it's worth crying about something you can't have," she said, and this time, she lifted one shoulder.

Bryan's gaze lingered on her silhouette for a few moments. Then he said matter-of-factly, "I don't think you have any reason to complain. You're just the right size."

"Thank you, you are so kind," she retorted sarcastically. Becka was sure he was either trying to be polite or was making fun of her in a covert way.

"No, really, you are. Believe me. I can't wait to trace the shape of your body with my hands."

At his words, she just dropped the fork on the plate. She didn't register the clank, which resonated far enough to make people turn their heads towards their table. Her mouth formed a perfect 'o,' which prompted him to laugh heartily.

"Come on. Don't tell me that you didn't expect me to go in that direction," Bryan said in a playful tone of voice, trying to make her feel at ease. He failed.

Becka tried to say something, swallowed hard, and tried again. Nothing came out. She was speechless.

"Are you all right?" he asked her, concerned by now. If the situation had amused him for a few seconds, now it worried him and seriously. Bryan was afraid that he had pushed too soon. Becka seemed entirely overwhelmed. He knew that he would hate himself if he pushed her away with his hastiness. She was the first woman that had attracted him in months, and he didn't want to lose her before they had a chance to begin something.

Becka nodded hesitantly, and then, standing up abruptly, she said, "Will you excuse me for a moment?"

He stood too, setting his fork and knife down on the plate. Now the man was worried, and his worry showed in the frown between his eyebrows.

"You're coming back, aren't you?" he couldn't help but ask her.

"Yes, of course, I will. Where do you think I'm going? I'm just going to the ladies' room, not fleeing the scene," she glanced at him and nodded.

Then, Becka hurried in the direction of the ladies' room without looking behind. Inside the ladies' room, after checking to see if she was alone, she leaned heavily on the first sink, which didn't seem wet, and looked carefully at herself in the mirror.

Her face was flushed, and there was a new shine in her eyes, which worried her a little. Becka closed her eyes for a moment, breathed deeply and thought, "All right, I think that this is the one. Maybe not tonight, but soon, definitely. The first man who made me feel like doing it. It makes sense..."

Becka made her choice and then threw some water over her face. She straightened up and dried her face and hands thoroughly. She weighed her decision for a few more seconds before leaving the washroom to go back to the table, where Bryan was waiting for her, sipping slowly from his beer.

His eyes found her at once, and he watched her until she got to the table. When she was close enough, he stood up respectfully to help her sit down.

That was something she hadn't seen anywhere else but in movies until then, and she felt flattered he would go through all that trouble. Becka also admired the fluidity of his movements, which showed he was a man who would go through rigorous training, maybe every day.

Becka sat down with an encouraging smile and picked up her glass of beer to wet her lips in the bitter liquid. Bryan still could see her smile over the rim of the glass. It was bolder now, and the look in her eyes made Bryan feel that pull towards her stronger.

His pants became tighter, and Bryan felt uncomfortable. Nevertheless, he became aware of two things. First of all, he was happy that he was sitting down, and the tablecloth hid his awkward state. He didn't want that Becka noticed her effect on him, especially because she hadn't reacted well at his naughty suggestion at the beginning of the evening. The second was that the thought that he would definitely have her sooner or later. Bryan made a promise to himself. He couldn't just allow Becka to pass by and out of his life too soon.

He needed her at a visceral level, and not only in his bed. He needed to spend enough time with Becka and see what that pull between them meant. Bryan was determined to steal that time if necessary.

"Are you up for a stroll along the lake after the meal?" he asked her, nodding toward the promenade busy with people. "It's not too windy, and it's still warm out for this hour of the evening."

Becka nodded and added in a playful tone, "I hope you'll buy me some dessert as well, though."

Bryan laughed heartily and shook his head as if he couldn't believe her.

"I have to say you're the first woman in years who's asked me for dessert. I wasn't even sure women ate cakes or ice-cream anymore."

"This one does," Becka told him, leaning toward him as if she was confessing a sin. "If possible at the same time, the better. You know, a hot chocolate cake with a scoop or two of ice-cream on top. However, for future reference, it's not a good idea to mention your previous relationships to a woman," she winked at him as if she parted with a secret. "We have this thing, you know," Becka waved her hand. "Maybe it's a quirk, but we prefer to think we're the only one that ever existed in a man's life."

"Duly noted," Bryan replied with amusement and grinned. "I'll refrain from making comparisons from now on, although I'd have thought you'd be flattered by the comparison."

She shook her head at him, and with a big wave of her hand, she replied, "Not really. You're far, far, from the truth. You see, I might conclude that you think I'm a glutton, and that won't do. No, it won't do at all."

"Oh, no, baby, I wouldn't think anything like that. I've always wanted to see a woman with a healthy appetite, and here you are. It seems I've finally found one. You might be entirely unique," Bryan retorted and enjoyed some more of his beer without taking his eyes off her.

"Of course, I'm unique. Everyone is unique, Bryan. There aren't two people alike," Becka said a little too loud, and one head or two turned to them, but neither Becka nor Bryan noticed.

"If only you knew," he said wistfully, shaking his head. "Too many people try to emulate someone else, and in the end, you just end up with so many copies of the same person that you're sick of them," he continued and something like regret registered in his voice.

"Wow, Bryan, I don't even want to know what kind of women you've dated if you have such a good opinion about my sex," Becka replied with awe in her voice. "Luckily for you, I'm here now. And as you mentioned, I'm one of a kind," she joked.

"Yeah, you are, Becka, and I mean to keep you," he answered, and his voice became suddenly serious. His words sent a shiver down her spine. Becka understood then that is sincerity showed that he wasn't a man with whom she should trifle.

"Should I be worried?" Becka tried to joke, but he could see that the intensity of his statement brought a little glimmer of concern in her eyes.

"I'm not a stalker, Becka. Don't worry about it. I meant only to say that I wanted everything to go fine between us. Then I could have more time with you. That's all," Bryan explained patiently, to ease her anxiety.

"Ah, all right then. We'll see then, won't we?" Becka stated matter-of-factly.

Bryan nodded. Then he noticed that Becka had already finished her steak, so he waved for the waitress.

"So, what would you like for dessert?" Bryan asked Becka and handed her the dessert menu, which the waitress had left on the table.

Becka opened the menu and perused the dessert choices at length until she found something to suit her desires best.

Becka opened the menu and perused the dessert choices at length until she found something to suit her desires best.

"I think the triple chocolate brownie with ice-cream. I told you already. I love chocolate cake and ice-cream. My favorite. You?"

"Decadent, I like it. I'll take the same. Something more to drink?"

Becka looked at the lake, then at the approaching waitress, and only then, found the courage to meet his eyes, and say, "I don't really drink, Bryan. I think that even this beer was too much."

"Damn it. You're only nineteen. You're barely legal to drink. I completely forgot. I'm sorry, Becka. Would you like a soft drink?" Bryan asked her. He was angry that he had missed something so important.

He kicked himself mentally for letting himself so engrossed with her that he would make such a mistake. Usually, he would let nothing slip past him.

Bryan knew he couldn't afford to make mistakes if he wanted that relationship to last. It wasn't as if she hadn't had her choice of men. He was just one in a sea of tens, probably.

"Yes, I'd like a soft drink or maybe just sparkling water. I think sparkling water is perfect."

"Sure?"

When she nodded, he gave their order to the waitress. After the waitress left, he took her hand and kissed her fingers. He seemed obsessed with her fingers, and she didn't know what to believe.

"I'll keep in mind not to have alcoholic beverages around you, all right?"

She laughed merrily and eased his worries.

"Come on, Bryan. You can drink, it's not like the law forbids you to drink around me," she laughed. "I like a glass of champagne now and then. That I like when there's something to celebrate. I'm not too fond of anything else. The taste is not for me."

"So, I'll buy you only champagne, Becka. The best kind, of course. I'm sure I'll be able to afford it if you drink only on special occasions," he said, laughing.

They spoke of everything and nothing in particular for the remainder of the dinner, and after he paid, he took her hand and led her to the shore of the lake for a romantic evening stroll.

The sun was setting, but the promenade was still bustling with people, which Bryan resented deeply. He wanted to have her only to himself, and the people milling around intruded on his time with her.

Becka felt the shift in his mood and wondered what had brought such a change. The man looked light-hearted and in a cheerful mood, only a few minutes ago. Now Brayn practically brooded.

"Is something wrong, Bryan?"

"Too many people, that's all, Becka. I'd have liked to be alone with you," he admitted openly.

Becka seemed to have a peculiar effect on him. She made him reveal things that he wouldn't usually tell women, and especially on a first date. Bryan had a strong conservation sense didn't make such mistakes.

"Well, this place is full virtually all the time, you know," Becka dismissed the people around with a big wave of her hand. "It's a favorite place for strolls, especially in the evening," she said, trying to appease him.

"I know, of course. That doesn't mean that I have to like it, do I?" Bryan replied tersely, although he knew that wasn't her fault that the place was so popular.

"Well, if we go sailing tomorrow, we'll be alone for some time," she pointed out, in another attempt to cheer him up.

"We are definitely going," Bryan said. "I hope you haven't changed your mind," he turned to her to see the answer in her eyes.

She shook her head and squeezed his fingers reassuringly, a gesture he enjoyed. In the spur of the moment, he leaned towards her and kissed her lips softly.

That first kiss didn't last more than a few seconds, but the pleasant, electric tingle he felt when he touched her lips was stronger than he'd expected.

Both of them stopped, still close enough to feel the warmth of each other's lips, and Becka stared at him with eyes full of wonder. It was barely a kiss, but she felt it as if it had been much more than that. The tingling she had felt earlier seemed like a pale reminder now.

When he pulled her to him tightly, she went along. She didn't even think of resisting. She was impatient to taste more of those low vibrations that made her body hum. She found herself completely stretched along his body, every hard plane of his chest and abdomen burning through her dress.

Bryan kept her very close as if he'd wanted to leave his mark on her, and she didn't mind. His lips touched hers, traced the shape of her mouth unhurriedly. His mouth was trying to learn the texture of every cell in the sensitive skin he was tasting. His hot tongue touched the delicate surface of her lips, stroking them slowly as if they had all the time in the world to indulge in each other.

The world outside ceased to exist. Becka and Bryan deeply immersed in each other, and nothing else mattered but what they shared. The people strolling around them became invisible, and any noise drowned in the background. They listened only to the rhythm of their hearts and the blood pulsing in their ears.

Their lips touched harder and sought a way to become one. Their tongues dueled and caressed one another, at times slowly, unhurriedly, tasting one another, exploring and creating sensations. At times, they dueled violently, as if they feared that they had no time left, and every second mattered.

Bryan bit sharply on her bottom lip, and she exhaled with a whimper. Then he nursed her abused lip, swallowing the moan that escaped from her throat and making it part of himself. His greedy fingers played with the skin covered by the flimsy cloth of her dress and pressed harder whenever he expected more from her.

Becka tried to find support and keep her balance, and her fingers dug into the hard muscles of his shoulders. A violent storm ravaged her senses, and she teetered on the edge of the unknown. A whirl of sensations fogged her mind. She couldn't think of anything else but Bryan's devouring, demanding mouth that taught her the meaning of a real kiss ruthlessly.

The young woman had the feeling that she had finally left her teen years behind, and now she was on the brink of maturity. She was in the arms of a man able to give her what she had longed for over the last few years when she felt so restless. That wasn't just about the conditions her great-grandma had put on the trust fund. It was much more than that.

When they finally came up for air, Becka was panting heavily, and she was trembling. Even Bryan had to gulp a mouthful of air. Then, he smiled wolfishly at her with that smile that seemed to belong exclusively to him. He tilted his head and bit the spot between her neck and collarbone but stroked it quickly with his tongue when he heard her sharp intake of breath at the unexpected pain. Bryan kissed Becka then, and she forgot about the bite. She went from pain and fear to magical joy.

Becka was throbbing everywhere. She knew now that she wanted his touch all over her body. She needed that ruthless mouth of his on her, on her most sensitive spots. Becka opened her mouth to say something along those lines, but Bryan put a finger over her lips and stopped her.

"Becka, we have an audience," he said and pointed to the left.

He glanced at the left as well, and when she turned her eyes in that direction, she noticed several teenage girls clustered together. They watched them with curiosity and laughed as if they had never seen a woman and a man kiss before.

Becka couldn't hear their words, but she imagined that she wouldn't have liked to know them anyway. At a loss for words, she looked up at Bryan, waiting for his opinion.

"I think we should move on," he said softly, and after stroking her cheek with his rough, calloused knuckles, he took her hand in his and slowly started towards the other end of the promenade, where the lake was shimmering in the sunset light.

CHAPTER THREE

BRYAN ARRIVED AT BECKA'S house five minutes earlier than the time they had agreed for their date, so he decided to wait until eight-thirty before he rang her bell. He remembered quite well how particular Becka had been about the time of his arrival, and how much she loved her sleep. He assumed that she would also need time to get ready, and he was determined to give it to her.

Bryan didn't want to start his day with Becka on a sore note. Spending his entire day with Becka, as well as developing a relationship with her, seemed very promising, and he wanted to cling to his chance.

On top of that, he had his own expectations for their second date. He knew that he was probably hoping for far too much, and his expectations were maybe too high, but he still wanted to fulfill them or at least a part of them.

At eight-thirty precisely, he rang the bell at the door. The sound of her doorbell stirred the butterflies in his stomach to life, and they churned with anticipation and anxiety. At the same time, a grin flourished on his lips as the theme from Jaws beamed in his ears.

Bryan wouldn't have expected to hear that song playing on her doorbell. Had it been something else, like We Wish You a Merry Christmas or the theme of Love Actually, for instance, he would have understood. Every time he discovered that there was more to Becka than met the eye and that was what made him so adamant not to lose her.

Bryan could hear the echo of the thrilling theme fill the house. That sound made him more anxious to see Becka open the door and beam widely at him with that bright smile of hers, which always reached her chocolate eyes. So, Bryan stretched his ears and listened carefully, eager to catch the sound of Becka's quick steps coming to the door. Unfortunately, that didn't happen. In the absence of that, the man hoped to hear Becka throw a shoe into a wall at least. To his disappointment, no sound came from inside the house, and his hopes plummeted hard.

The thought that she might have just made a fool out of him and had no intention of seeing him again flashed through his mind, and Bryan frowned and gritted his teeth.

He was sure that he had walked her to her door the previous night. He had even watched her go inside. He hadn't seen her use a key to open the door, but she had waved at him and closed the door behind herself.

It wasn't like he had left her standing on the steps of a house of her choice so she could walk to another door after he had left.

The thought that Becka had duped him was unbearable. He had been there before and didn't have any desire to revisit the experience. However, this time, the hurt ran deeper.

Bryan had positively believed that they had had a great time together, and it worried him that what he had felt might have been one-sided.

Bryan didn't want to travel down that path. However, he had to admit that Becka might have just visited a friend, although she had gone inside the house the night before as if she owned it. That friend might have left earlier that morning, before he arrived, or who just kept quiet like a mouse, waiting for him to give up and leave.

His anger increased more at the thought of having been played like that. Bryan choked under the pressure of his fury. He wasn't mad only at her because she had made a fool out of him. He was furious with himself, as well, for falling for her act.

Furious, he punched the door frame with such force that the hardwood scraped his knuckles, and he started bleeding.

He swore and cursed himself viciously. Damn it, he wasn't a green, young man and he should have known better. Much better.

Becka had seemed too refined and beautiful for the likes of him, and he shouldn't have hoped anything. He didn't have that right. After all, Bryan had been told that often enough during his life. He thought that he had learned that lesson. However, it seemed that he had only lied to himself.

The man glanced at his watch again and noticed that almost five minutes had passed since he rang the bell the first time. Still, there wasn't any sound coming from inside the house.

That was the last drop and convinced him that he had been wrong, and his worst fears had turned out to be true. Becka had just played him.

Bryan turned his head and glanced at the car he'd parked in the driveway that morning. He hesitated for a few moments, but then thought he'd better leave since there wasn't anything else for him to do there. If she didn't want to see him, then he couldn't do anything to force her.

In that instant, something hardened inside him and shaking his head, Bryan stubbornly decided to try his chance again. He rang the bell once more. He listened anew to the musical sound, bouncing off the inner walls of the house, but he still couldn't hear any movement from inside.

That was the final straw. Bryan had to admit defeat. He leaned in and pressed his head on the front door in a moment of weakness. His shoulders stooped.

A slip of a girl had tricked him, and he had to live with that. Well, it wasn't the first time, and it probably wouldn't be the last. Weak consolation!

Furious, he gritted his teeth, clenched and unclenched his fists, and then, finally, he turned around and made a beeline to his car. His stride was determined, and his anger showed in every big step he took.

Bryan opened the car door when Becka's breathless shout reached his ears.

"Bryan, wait! I'm coming. Don't leave now!"

The man sharply turned to the sound of her voice, and astonishment glimmered in his hard eyes. His puzzlement increased more when he spotted Becka running down the street towards him on wobbly legs.

Her face was nearly blue because of the effort, and she was close to exhaustion. However, that didn't stop her, and Becka tried to smile at him.

Becka held her hand on the right side of her body. A stitch had been bothering her for the last ten minutes. Becka hadn't believed that she would arrive at home on time, although she ran as quickly as she could.

Bryan waved at her to slow down and stop running. A bright, wide smile spread on her lips. She was grateful that she could finally stop. That was the smile he had been waiting impatiently for that entire morning.

Becka stopped abruptly and bent, and her hands pressed desperately on her knees. Then she started panting, gulping noisily for air. It was clear that she had no training for jogging.

Becka was only at about three houses far away, but Bryan hurried to her and reached her in no time. Worried, he slipped his arm around her waist to support her and brushed the thick hair away from her face.

"What are you trying to do?" Bryan asked Becka, seeing the traces her sustained effort had left on her face and feeling her tremble in his arms. "Are you training for the marathon or what? Don't you know you should take it gradually?"

"I...had...to...do...something," Becka replied with difficulty, gasping the words and trying to catch her breath at the same time.

Bryan allowed her to recover and didn't press further. He was content only to have her there with him. For the moment, it was enough. It was much more than what he had had a few moments before when he thought that she had deceived him.

"When I saw I was going to be late for our date... I had to run to make it here in time," Becka finally said when she could breathe easier.

There was still a strain in her voice, and Bryan stopped her, touching her lips gently with his fingers.

"Okay, baby," Bryan told her, "just breathe now, and you'll tell me everything later."

Becka nodded and started to walk towards her door, but her legs chose that very moment to start shaking violently, and she almost fell on her face. Luckily, Bryan was still there and had one arm around her, ready to save her from diving on the hard pavement.

He shook his head, then picked her forcibly up into his arms, and without a word, he carried back to her house. His long strides were eating the distance with ease. With a faint yelp of surprise, Becka slipped her arms around his neck.

"How long did you run?" he asked when they made it in front of her house, and he stopped to look at her.

Becka had her head comfortably resting on his shoulder, and her nose was close to his neck. She was merely enjoying the smell of his skin when she heard him speak. His voice startled her, and Becka felt a vague hint of guilt but shoved it aside without much anxiety. She needed to take a moment to understand his words.

"Well, about ten blocks, I think, or maybe more...," she answered uncertainly. She couldn't remember exactly.

Bryan looked down at her with astonishment. "Why the heck would you run such a long distance? Especially if you don't have the training? What went through your mind?"

"How do you know that I don't have the training?" Becka pouted, choosing to deflect only a part of his questions.

"Well, the shaking legs and the cramp you have on your right side are clear indications, Becka. I don't need to be an expert to see that you don't usually run such long distances," Bryan replied, laughing, although his concern was far from appeased. "If you run at all," he specified, and his right brow rose inquiringly.

"Ah! Right...," her voice trailed off as she lost herself in thought.

"Still with me, baby?"

She looked up at him and smiled.

"Yes, still here, of course. I was only thinking."

"Yeah, I noticed that," Bryan replied, amused, gazing into her eyes. "What were you thinking about?"

"All right, then," Becka said. "I was wondering whether I should come clean or not."

At that, Bryan's left brow rose. He didn't expect a confession from her. He didn't expect her to have something to confess.

"I don't have any training, and I actually hate jogging," Becka continued, making him burst into laughter.

He had expected to hear something else, and the innocence of her confession was music to his ears.

"No, you see, I had to leave this morning, and since I didn't get your phone number to let you know I wouldn't be here when you came, I had to hurry back," she explained after she slapped his shoulder for laughing at her.

"That's very considerate of you," Bryan answered quietly after a second, uncertain of what he should say.

It was the first time in his life that someone had thought to show him any consideration. People either feared him and avoided him from afar or didn't give a damn about him. Either way, no one had ever considered his feelings before that day, and he felt humbled.

The cynic in him was a bit stumped and didn't know how to react. He was deep in uncharted territory there, and he felt as if he had to act out a part in a play, but he didn't know his lines.

"If you want, you can put me down so I can open the door," he heard Becka's voice and turned his eyes to her, taking in her disheveled appearance, bright eyes, and her cheeks still violently red.

"If you give me the key, I'll open the door without putting you down," he said with a hint of playfulness and a smile to match.

"Oh, fine by me," she answered. "No need for a key, though. The door is not locked."

Stunned, Bryan could only stare at her. He couldn't form a sentence or even move. He had never heard of someone who didn't lock their doors.

"What happened?" Becka asked him. "Why are you staring at me like that? Is there something on my face, and I should know about?" she asked and touched her face to check for herself.

"You didn't lock your door," he said in a flat tone, which conveyed how foolish he believed that to be.

"No, I didn't. Why should I?" Becka asked, baffled both by the suggestion and his reaction.

"Why should you?" he asked in disbelief, then repeated more forcefully. "Why should you?"

"No need to get so upset over such a little thing," she patted his shoulder and continued in a tone meant to calm him down. "Believe me, there's no need to lock the door," the woman reassured him.

"Are you for real?" he burst out. "This is not a small village, where everybody knows everybody, Becka. Even in small villages, things happen. We're in a big city, for God's sake!" he finished his speech, almost shouting. "People lock their doors, Becka."

"Come on, Bryan. What's the worst that could happen? You know that what's meant to happen, it will," she said wisely.

"Spare me that bullshit. Don't go quoting shit to me," Bryan replied angrily. "You have to be more careful and start locking the damn door!"

Furious with her foolishness, Bryan kicked the door open with his foot as if he wanted to emphasize his statement.

Becka looked at him in silence, unsure of what to say, seeing how worked up he had gotten. She thought to diffuse the tension and spoke calmly, hoping that that would make him calm down as well.

"Are you upset because I said what I said, or is it because you think something might happen to me?"

"What the heck do you think?" Bryan barked again. "If you start locking the damn door and you're more careful from now on, you can quote me as much crap as you wish and whenever you feel like it!" Bryan snapped at her.

"Okay...," Becka dragged the word out. "So, you're saying that you're concerned about me?"

"What kind of question is that, Becka? Of course, I'm concerned. What's wrong with you, woman?" he inquired with a grown and frowned at her.

"Nothing, nothing," she said quickly to take his mind off his anger. "By the way, you might get tired, holding me, Bryan. I'm not so light. So, either you put me down if you want to continue the conversation on the stairs or we could go inside. It's your choice, really," she said while looking at him as if completely glossing over his mood.

Bryan felt frozen in place as if he couldn't believe her levity. He shook his head, closed his eyes in defeat before the strangest woman he had ever come across, and then carried her inside the house, closing the door with his foot.

Once inside, he looked at her questioningly, waiting for her directions.

"I suppose we could go to the kitchen first and have a cup of coffee," she answered his silent question. "I'm dying for a cup of coffee after the morning I've had," she groaned and continued, "I understand you don't feel like letting me stand so... The kitchen is right ahead, through the living room. It's the last door on the right," she pointed.

Bryan nodded curtly and carried her to the kitchen, where he put her on a padded chair in her breakfast nook, which overlooked the garden. The entire wall to the garden was an expanse of glass framed by yellow curtains bound with thin silk ribbons.

Becka's garden sported an explosion of colors. Patches of all sorts of flowers bathed in the morning sunlight, joyful and full of cheer.

At first sight, Bryan had the feeling that a madman had designed that garden. It was the oddest garden he had ever seen. He couldn't remember to have ever noticed so many colors and such undefined shapes in a garden.

His mother's flower garden presented flawlessly rectangular flowerbeds of petunias or roses, each of them with a well-defined place. That strict setting was a far cry from Becka's otherworldly garden. It was nothing like those whirls of all sorts of flowers, tumbling off the pots, scattered throughout, without a distinguishable order to them. Many of the specimens were probably wildflowers because he hadn't ever seen them in a garden before.

He shook his head in disbelief at first, but after a few moments, he finally understood that that garden was Becka entirely. It was wild, unpredictable, with sudden moods and surprises.

"So, what do you think of my garden?" Becka's soft voice came from behind.

Bryan turned around, and his gaze fell on Becka. An eager light in her eyes, the woman stood a few steps away from him. She tried to sound indifferent, and only a little curious about his opinion, but the gleam in her chocolate gaze told him that she was quite fond of her garden.

"I think it suits you," he answered honestly. "It's exactly like you, Becka."

"Don't you think it's just crazy, and I should change it, maybe tame it a little?" she asked, never taking her eyes off him. He wouldn't have been the first to find the disorder of her little garden unsettling.

"Why would you change it? It's exactly the way it should be, I think," Bryan answered her with a shrug of his shoulders. "I don't think you should change anything, baby. It really suits you," he said, stroking the side of her face with his thumb.

Becka beamed at him with happiness, pleased that he saw her garden the same way she did. She squeezed his hand appreciatively before she turned to the kitchen counter, where she started to prepare the coffee.

"I suppose you'd like to have a cup of coffee with me," she asked him while she was busying herself with the cups and saucers.

"Yeah, I'd like a cup of coffee," he replied, watching her small hands arrange the cups and saucers on a tray. "Becka, who told you, you should change your garden?" he asked with curiosity.

Becka shrugged it off as inconsequential but answered his question to satisfy his curiosity. She remembered well that they had decided to get to know each other better, after all, even if it was about such small matters.

"Well, actually, everybody but you. At least my sister Ariel is a real pest about that garden. She has a knack for gardening, and she thinks I should take every piece of advice she has in stock for me when it comes to it. She doesn't understand that I want to express myself, not some rule book. I don't want a geometrical garden with straight rows of flowers and individual flowerbeds. Anyway, that's a sore subject between the two of us, so I prefer to avoid it."

The man came up behind her, slipped his arms around her, and pulled her gently to him.

"You're a smart girl, Becka. You shouldn't change for anybody," he said, kissing the crown of her head first, then resting his head on the top of hers.

They stayed like that for a few moments that stretched on in silence. None of them wanted to pull away and end it.

Becka felt content in his embrace as if she always belonged there. She loved being held in Bryan's strong arms that had carried her to the house and inside. She wondered if she could make Bryan stay. Becka hoped that he would give her more time. She wanted the time to discover the contradictory man, who hid behind those sometimes-abrasive words. She had already noticed that Bryan was generous in his gestures, and he made her feel contented and cherished.

The shrill of the coffee maker startled them apart, and both burst into laughter at their silly reaction.

"Well, it seems we both spaced out," Bryan tried to joke, but the humor didn't reach the serious, longing gaze he kept trained on her as if he didn't want to let that moment end.

She smiled at him, her thoughts still on the comfortable, dreamlike embrace, but finally pushed him away, "Go and sit down. I'll bring the tray to the table."

"No, you go and sit down, and I'll bring it to the table," he refused, giving her a little nudge to make her move. "You've just run the better part of a marathon, Becka, and you need to rest. Do you still feel up for going on the lake today?" he asked, worried about the intense workout she had had that morning.

The woman nodded and went to the table, enjoying the fact that he didn't expect her to wait on him. She could still feel his eyes on her and wondered what he actually saw, and if he liked the way she moved or how she looked.

Becka became aware of the path of her thoughts, and she admonished herself. She almost shook her head. Becka had never considered herself a simpleton who put a lot of stock on her looks. She wanted that Bryan liked her for more than that. However, she had to admit that, in spite of what she thought, she had some vanity inside her. Because of that, Becka needed that Bryan appreciated her for her looks, and not only for her intellect.

The distant sound of Bryan's words snapped her out of her daydreaming, and she realized that she had nearly missed what he was asking.

"Do you take your coffee with sugar and milk, Becka?"

"Oh, yes, I forgot to put the sugar bowl and the milk on the tray," she jumped out of her chair, ready to go back and correct her mistake, but he stopped her with a gesture.

"No need to bother yourself with that. Just tell me where you keep the sugar and milk, and I'll take care of that," Bryan assured her.

"The sugar dish is in the cupboard above the coffee maker, and the milk is in a little spout in the fridge," she told him, happy to sit tight and let him serve her.

Becka couldn't stop thinking, happily so, about his concern for her well-being and his willingness to make coffee in her home. It made a smile tug at her lips every time she thought of it.

Bryan opened the cupboard and took the sugar dish out. He examined it for a moment and noticed how small and delicate it was, a white piece of thin porcelain with small, dainty, blue flowers painted here and there, so lifelike that they seemed almost real, yet nearly a blur at the same time, much like an illusion. The man shook his head slowly.

Taking out the milk spout from the fridge, he discerned the same delicate and thin porcelain and the same painted motif, which made him smile. He had the feeling that he had uncovered another side of Becka. She seemed to lean toward the fragile and artistic in her dishes. Bryan had already noticed the coffee cups and saucers. Lace encircled the rims, and they presented a motif of tiny fairies, dancing with their veils flying in the wind. Bryan liked that side of her. He even thought that he hadn't found anything he didn't like about her. Even her moods were refreshing.

The wild garden couldn't be more at odds with the elegant tea sets in her cupboard, but he couldn't help but feel that the contradiction was perfect for Becka. She wouldn't fit in only one category. She was a free spirit, ready to express her opinions, and didn't let anyone intimidate her, or at least she didn't let him intimidate her, and that said something. He had a real talent to intimidate women.

Becka was fresh and young, but she wasn't rambling on and on about irrelevant things that would made him feel old and left behind or put him to sleep. He had been afraid that she would bore him to tears the other evening, and he had been surprised when it didn't happen.

Becka had been so lively and entertaining that he hadn't wanted the evening to end. When he drove her back home the night before, Bryan had only regretted to let her go inside. The door had closed behind her, and he instantly felt lonely.

The man loved that she didn't try to pass for a fairy, only nibbling on some green leaves, enough not to lose consciousness. She wasn't obsessed with reaching the size dictated by the fashion of the time, and that was something. He had encountered that rare quality only in some women past sixty. All the others were determined to be a size under ten, and they were doing everything they could to get there, including starving to death. He couldn't understand what was wrong with a size twelve or fourteen or eighteen. The size didn't matter, but what was inside the package. That was more important.

He eyed Becka and appraised her to be a size fourteen, but that only meant that she was the way nature intended. She was gracious, but she had curves in the right places, especially in the areas he appreciated most.

Bryan had been drawn to her looks at first, but now he kept discovering new things, and his attraction to her deepened. He liked the Becka inclined to the fantastic, who used the Jaws theme as a doorbell. However, he also fancied the Becka, who had designed a garden out of a fairy tale.

The man brought the tray to the table and placed it in front of her. He let his fingers brush a strand of hair away from her face, and then he sat down, too.

"I thought to take a shower after we drank the coffee. Then we could leave for our sailing adventure. What do you think?" Becka asked, smiling at Bryan in excitement and poured the coffee in her whimsical cups.

"Works for me," he shrugged.

After a few moments of comfortable silence, he asked, "Where did you have to go this morning?"

At first, Becka waved his question away as insignificant, but then she realized that it was significant for him, so she decided to tell him the truth.

"I told you that I have some cousins... Well, my cousin, Jay, is a sort of a...gambler, you could say," Becka said with some hesitation. "Last night, he got involved in a game with some shady guys. They thought that Jay was cheating, so they roughened him up."

Bryan looked at her in disbelief.

"It's not like that," she said, reading the thoughts reflected in his eyes. "Jay doesn't cheat, but he has a...particular talent, let's say," she explained with broad gestures.

"What kind of... talent?" Bryan asked her, staring at her intently.

"Well... he knows what cards the opponent has in his hand," Becka rushed with the explanation, hoping she wouldn't have to say more than she was prepared to reveal.

"So, he's counting the cards...," Bryan started to say, but she interrupted him with a shake of her head. "No?"

"No," she answered.

"Then what?" Bryan insisted.

Becka hesitated a few moments, then she replied unwillingly, "He only knows what cards you have in your hand. You shouldn't ever play with him. He doesn't cheat, but... you wouldn't stand a chance."

"It's not possible, Becka," Bryan retorted. "He either counts the cards, or he cheats."

She shook her head eagerly again. "No, he doesn't. I'm sorry, but it's not really for me to say. Still, don't play cards with him. Okay?"

Bryan shrugged. He was sure that she didn't want to admit that her cousin was a cheater and that he got beat up for it.

"So, you went to take care of him, or what?" he asked, sampling his coffee.

"Well, when I got there around 3 a.m., he was in pretty bad shape and didn't want to go to the hospital... God, he hates hospitals more than I do."

"So, you played Florence Nightingale for him, or what?"

She nodded and poured some more coffee in her cup, adding plenty of milk and sugar. That made Bryan smile. It wasn't coffee anymore. It looked more like milk with a touch of coffee.

"So, you slept only a few hours last night," the man concluded.

Becka nodded but rushed to say, "Don't worry, Bryan, I still want to go on the lake. Maybe I'll sleep a little on the deck. Who knows?" she shrugged.

Bryan didn't say anything for a while. He sipped his coffee and watched her, assessing the shadows under her eyes.

"We can go out on the lake some other time, Becka, if you don't feel well enough. It's enough for me to see that you want to go."

"No, no, no," she jumped up from her seat. "No way! You promised that we'd go today," she shouted at him.

"Easy, love, easy! Of course, we'll go if you want to. I only thought that you looked so tired," Bryan said but stopped when he saw her shake her head. "We're going. We're going. Go take your shower, and then we'll go," he rushed to mollify her.

Becka enthusiastically kissed his lips and rushed out of the room only to be stopped by his question.

"Becka, do you have a travel mug or something? Your coffee's great, and I think we could use a batch with us."

"Oh, yeah, there's one, I think... You know what, you should check those cupboards there," she pointed to a row of cupboards, "and you might have a chance at finding it. When I get back, I could prepare some food to take with us," she told him joyfully.

"No need, Becka," he shook his head. "I've already taken care of the food. I told you we'd have a picnic on the lake, so I have everything we need in my trunk."

"All right, then. You take care of the coffee, and I will go shower. See you in ten minutes?" Becka said, and Bryan could hear the joy in her voice.

He started laughing heartily.

"What's so funny?" Becka asked.

"You're funny, Becka. Ten minutes? Come on. I've never seen a woman ready to leave the house in ten minutes, and you still have to shower."

"Yeah? All right, let's make a bet," she challenged him, putting her hands on her hips.

He grinned and accepted her challenge.

"So, you like to bet even when it's not smart to do it?"

"You'll see, mister," she scoffed. "I bet you ten bucks that I'm back here in ten minutes, ready to go."

He stared at her, thinking the joke had gone on long enough, but saw the mutinous expression on her face and found himself nodding.

"You have a bet, Becka, then. Now, go, scat," Bryan push her along and smiled, seeing her flee the room as fast as she could.

CHAPTER FOUR

BRYAN STEERED THE YACHT carefully with an eye out on the lake, where lots of sails crowded the horizon. He wanted to avoid any problems and close calls due to inattention.

He kept his other eye on Becka, who was sleeping soundly under the canopy he had mounted on the deck that morning for her before setting sail.

A gentle breeze soothed his warm skin. The sun was high in the sky, and the air was hot. Now and then, the echo of a shout or a burst of laughter over the water reached his ears. Otherwise, everything was silent. He felt wrapped in another world, all by himself. He enjoyed it every time he went out on the lake.

When they left the harbor, they worked together, although he didn't need anyone's help to sail his small yacht. Yet, he found out that he enjoyed working in a team with Becka, whose enthusiasm was contagious.

The woman knew her boats, and she wasn't afraid to get a bit dirty and use her muscles. She might have been small, but she was a bolt of energy.

Bryan admired her knowledge about sailing and navigation, but more so her determination not to let her small size stand in her way. For such a slip of a girl, she had enough strength in her arms. Even though she was tired because of what had happened earlier that morning, she was still energetic enough to work shoulder to shoulder with him before falling asleep under the shade he'd created for her.

They had been sailing for about two hours already, and his mind was still on the bet he had lost to Becka. Anyway, it wasn't like he had too much to do while she was sleeping. Minding the yacht wasn't too big a deal since he knew the drills by heart and could drive the boat and let his mind wander somewhere else at the same time.

That bet was bothering him, but not because he had lost money to Becka. The amount was ridiculous, although she had jumped up and down with glee when she took his money. The thought made him smile again. It was a moment Bryan had enjoyed immensely.

The man couldn't explain why, but he felt a certain sense of fulfillment whenever he knew he was the reason behind that beaming smile on her face. It was as if her joy were his own, and he felt the need to give her more reasons to enjoy herself.

What puzzled him, though, was the fact he had never seen a woman getting ready to go out under ten minutes flat, even if it was only about going sailing, rather than clubbing or something else.

In his experience, women needed much more time before setting foot out of the house, and Bryan had had his share of waiting over the years. Of course, that waiting had come with a lot of frustration.

To his bewilderment, Becka hadn't even needed the whole ten minutes she had demanded. She had used only eight minutes. Bryan had timed her, and how stupid did that seem now? In exactly eight minutes, she had already been downstairs, ready to go.

It was true that her hair was still wet from the shower. Becka had only taken the time to pass a comb through the thick locks of hair in a rush. Then, she had put on a pair of khakis and a t-shirt. That was the sum of her efforts. She hadn't wasted a second of those tiny eight minutes.

Becka was a bundle of contradictions. Altogether, she was shy and daring, whimsy and realistic, with a penchant for the horror, while living a fairy-tale in her eccentric garden with shapeless flowerbeds and the explosion of colors and wildflowers.

Bryan kept discovering new things about her, and everything made him shake his head in wonder. Nevertheless, he understood that Becka had a complex personality, and there were many other aspects to explore, but Bryan hoped to have a lifetime to do it.

Bryan was thrilled that he had been so lucky to have her stumble over him and pour that hot coffee all over his shirt. It had been a chance that he wouldn't get more than once. He wasn't afraid to admit it to himself, despite the tinge of desperation that crawled into his heart. The man lived with the permanent fear that Becka would disappear one day, and then his life would go back to what it had been before meeting her. It saddened him. He knew his life would be bleak again, and he didn't even know if he could go on as he had done before when things occurred and changed his path.

It was one thing if he didn't know what he was missing, and another to have something fabulous in his life and lose it. He was sure he wouldn't be able to forget her the same way he had forgotten the string of women before her.

In less than twenty-four hours, Becka had touched him like no one before, and that was scary. Bryan was a realist, and he couldn't discount the possibility that something so good wouldn't last forever.

Immersed in his thoughts, Bryan still paid attention to Becka's every movement. He couldn't take his eyes off her for very long, so he noticed when she woke up. She rubbed her eyes like a child, and the gesture made him grin. The woman looked very innocent and young. She hadn't put any makeup on, and there were no smudges under her eyes. He liked that. He dreaded seeing smudges under women's eyes in the morning.

Becka's hair stuck out in every direction, and she looked like a porcupine. Bryan had to stifle his laughter, afraid that she might misinterpret his amusement. She was very young and very touchy.

The man slowed the yacht down but kept his eyes always trained on her. He saw her look around with a faraway look on her face. She didn't know where she was, and she was taking her bearings.

He noticed when she finally understood where she was and became aware of her surroundings. Then, she turned and looked for him. When her gaze found him, her face lit up as if she were sincerely happy to lay eyes on him.

That happy smile on her lips touched him profoundly. It was completely unexpected. It squeezed his heart and made him hope for impossible things.

Bryan believed that Becka liked to be with him, at least for a while. She acted that way. Yet, he hadn't even dared to hope she would beam at him with so much joy just because he was still there. The contentment her gesture gave him winded him like a punch in the gut.

He wanted to say something and let her know how much everything meant to him, but words couldn't pass by the knot in his throat. If he had been a lesser man, he would have cried of joy, and that would have spoiled everything. No woman would stand a man weeping, no matter what she said. And why the heck would he feel like that? He gave himself a stern nudge to put himself back together.

"You have a good sleep, Becka?"

Becka stood up with a nod and walked over to him with a dreamy light in her eyes. He watched her lazy stride and admired her long unclad legs, covering the spread of the deck.

When they got on the yacht, she had taken off her capris and t-shirt and remained in a two-piece bathing suit. Bryan couldn't stop himself from noticing again how the bathing suit hugged her curves enticingly, and he felt his pants tighten a little more.

Becka wasn't tall by any means. She reached only to his chest, and that if she had her shoes on. Despite her height, her legs were long, and her ankles were supple and gracious, although her thighs were not on the thin side.

In Bryan's opinion, she couldn't complain about anything. The entire package was there, and it was damn tempting for a man who lost more ground every minute.

Becka stopped near him and leaned on him. She slid one arm around his waist and let her head fall on his chest with a natural movement as if she were doing it for ages.

Bryan looked at the crown of her head for a few moments, and then, he brushed some of the strands around, trying to bring some order to her disheveled hair. He abandoned her tousled hair and raised her chin with his thumb. He looked at her for a couple of seconds, and then, he leaned down to kiss her.

He lingered for a few moments, just a hair away from her lips. He wanted to give himself the time to inhale that sweet and fresh scent, which was unmistakably Becka's.

It was only after a few moments of panting expectation that Bryan took her mouth into a searing kiss. The man put into that kiss all the longing that had churned inside him for the last two hours. He had been watching Becka sleep in the nest he had made for her on deck, and he had been thinking about how it would feel to have her in his arms and know that she belonged only to him.

When Bryan raised his head and looked down at her, she still had her eyes closed. Becka was still clinging to his arms as if she couldn't find her balance. Her mouth was rosy, and her lips slightly swollen. Satisfaction welled up in his chest.

It was gratifying for Bryan to see that his kiss had such an effect on her. He had to accept that the little woman held his thoughts and heart in her small fist.

Her mouth still beckoned to him, and he found himself unable to refuse it. Bryan leaned in again and brushed his mouth over hers flittingly. Then, he bit her bottom lip lightly and made her moan, which increased his desire a notch. His mind was already racing ahead, thinking about taking her right there on the deck, when he heard her whisper.

"I'm hungry, Bryan."

Her words felt like a blow to the head. The man just blinked and stared at her. Becka didn't even open her eyes, and her fingers were still digging into his arms. Bryan was fired up like a rocket, and Becka seemed oblivious to everything. He shook his head as if he couldn't believe her.

"Are you sure?" Bryan asked her, squeezing her hip, unaware his fingers were digging firmly in the soft curve and could have marked her.

His actions made her nose twitch, and she opened her eyes wide. Her mouth formed a perfect 'o' and just looked at him for a few seconds. Becka seemed unable to say anything at first, but she regained her gumption soon enough.

"I said I'm hungry, and that means I'm pretty sure, Bryan," she scowled at him.

"We were just kissing, Becka..." Bryan started to object, but she interrupted him, pressing a delicate finger to his lips.

"So? Can't I kiss you and be hungry at the same time? Or everything must be on a specific timetable with you?" she raised her voice a little, which made him look at her with stunned eyes.

"Wow, that's a good way to ruin the romance, baby," Bryan chastised her.

He was hurt because he had hoped she would feel the same way as him, and her reaction was like a cold shower over his feelings.

Becka shrugged with indifference and finally let go of his arms. She stepped back and looked him straight in the eyes.

"Romance is great, Bryan, even for me, but I can feel romance even if I eat, you know," she replied with practicality.

"Okay, Becka, hold your horses, we'll eat soon enough," Bryan conceded with resignation.

He put aside his dreams of a little lovemaking on the deck. Becka was full of surprises, and he needed to adjust his thinking to her if he wanted their relationship to survive, and he did.

"Soon? Why not now? I'm hungry now, you know," she insisted with defiance in her voice.

"Because I was thinking of sailing over there," he explained patiently and pointed to an island not far away. "We could have our picnic on the shore of that island, Becka. I'm sure you'd like to eat there instead of here on the deck," he continued drily. "I know I would," he muttered under his breath.

Becka looked toward the island, shading her eyes from the sun with her hand. Then, she looked at the covered portion of the deck with indecision.

"It's tempting, I won't say no," she murmured, turning back to him, "but you won't be able to moor there, so that point is moot," she said louder. "So, we can eat here, even though it is not so idyllic," she concluded, all too eager to eat. She hadn't eaten since the night before, and she had already used up a lot of her energy.

"Not really," Bryan said, still steering the yacht at full speed to the island. "There's a dock there, and I can moor my boat just fine."

His voice was always dry, and that was a sign that he was just a bit pissed off with all that fuss. He understood that Becka hadn't had breakfast, and she had already made a lot of effort that morning, but he was sure that she wouldn't have died if she had waited for a few more minutes.

The woman shrugged again. That seemed to be one of her habits, and he found it very endearing. Then, she went to sit on the bench near the steering wheel and watched the horizon.

"Are you upset or something?" Bryan asked a little unsettled by her sudden change of mood.

He didn't deal very well with women's moods, and he would usually try to get out of the line of fire when something like that happened. However, this time, he felt compelled to understand where everything went wrong. He had invested a lot of himself in that fragile relationship and didn't want to let it go to waste.

"No, why do you ask?" Becka asked, fussing around with the blanket on the bench.

She pretended she was busy folding it so she could avoid his eyes.

"I don't know," Bryan replied matter-of-factly. "It's like you're upset. You're not happy like you were earlier, and you seem in a mood. You raised your voice," he pointed out.

Becka looked at him, shocked. She had no reply for a few seconds, but then she retorted, "I'm not in a mood."

Bryan didn't say anything. He thought he'd better give her some space, hoping that she would be her usual self again after a while.

"All right," she jumped off the bench, upset. "Now you know," Becka cried out, throwing her arms in the air dramatically and stomping toward the other side of the yacht, out of his line of sight. Bewildered, Bryan looked after her. He even craned his head forward to see her better, and only after a few moments, he dared to ask, "Know what?"

Becka came back with small and hesitant steps, her hands knotted behind her and her head down. She was biting her lower lip, preoccupied with how to formulate her answer.

"I'm not at my best when I wake up, Bryan. You need to give me a little space for a few minutes, and then everything's fine again," she confessed with a small voice as if she admitted to a capital sin.

Bryan grinned, relieved that there was nothing else the matter, and he had worried for nothing after all. He reached out to Becka to pull her to him.

"Come on, baby, that's not such a big deal. As long as I know that, I can cope with it, and I can give you all the space you need."

She took his hand and came closer to him.

"I know I'm a porcupine whenever I wake up, Bryan. It's not like I want to be, you know, but...that's how I am."

"In more ways than one," Bryan said under his breath, but she heard him and looked up at him with a frown.

"What do you mean?" Becka asked.

Bryan tried to avoid saying anything more. He didn't want to aggravate her more than he had already done it. However, her eyes were trained on him and demanded an answer.

The man fidgeted for a few moments, trying to buy some more time so that he could come up with something less offensive, but there was no way out of it, so he decided to tell her the truth.

"Your hair," he waved his hand around her head. "It looks like...you're a porcupine," he finally expressed his thoughts.

Becka gasped in distress, and both of her hands shot up at her hair to tame it. However, she didn't succeed.

"Damn it, I shouldn't have skipped the conditioner this morning," she wailed, and Bryan laughed. It seemed that Becka did like her drama, and that should have made him run for the hills. Instead, he found her more and more loveable with every moment that passed, and that seemed odd.

That wasn't him, the one from before he had met her, and that was somewhat disquieting. He shook his head and abandoned that train of thought, afraid of the conclusion he might reach.

"So, if I understand correctly, you skipped using your conditioner so that you could be downstairs on time?" he remarked and not without malice.

"Okay, laugh as much as you want," she retorted, fisting her hands on her hips. "I wasn't sure I'd be ready in ten minutes, I admit. The conditioner takes about three minutes to apply," she snapped and began patting her mane of wild hair in an attempt to control it.

"Yeah, you'd have been a minute late. That's true," Bryan replied, always smiling. "Would that have been so bad?" he inquired.

For a moment, Becka stopped her frenzy movements and looked up at him. After a couple of seconds, she replied with serious eyes. "Yes, Bryan, very bad. I don't like to lose," she wrinkled her nose. Then she thought to add, "I think you'd better learn now I'm a sore loser, Bryan... Do you still want to have that picnic with me?" she inquired in a small voice.

Bryan reached for her again and pulled her into a bear hug, making her gasp in surprise. He didn't let her go, but gathered her tighter to him, and whispered in her hair.

"You're perfect, Becka, just perfect. Of course, I want to picnic with you, baby," he continued, touching his head of hers. He inhaled the fresh scent of her hair and felt content to let the moment flow.

Becka could hardly breathe, though. Bryan didn't seem to know his strength, and his hug was very tight. Yet, Becka started smiling in the folds of his shirt, happy because he wasn't put out by her mood or by her confession.

Bryan held her for a few more moments before he found the strength to let her go and return to the helm. She welcomed the reprieve and filled her lungs with fresh air.

"In a few minutes, we'll be there, Becka," he said and pointed toward the dock that now appeared to be very close.

Becka looked over the expanse of water and noticed that they headed toward a pier that appeared in quite a good shape.

"I think that dock belongs to someone, Bryan. Won't they complain if we moor there?" she glanced back at him.

He waved her concerns away and explained that the dock belonged to a friend of his, who let him use it whenever he wanted.

"The best part is that he's not even here, so we have the place to ourselves. No one will bother us for the entire day."

He kept paying attention to his driving as the shore was near now.

"He also let me use his house now and then, so if you have enough of the sun and the lake, we can go there and sit on the porch or even go inside and lie down on a bed."

Becka looked at him with doubt in her eyes but shrugged. She decided to let him entertain his illusions. She didn't enjoy ruining anyone's hopes, yet, she was sure no one would be so generous and let their friend come and go at their will.

She was close enough to her cousins, but she didn't think that any of them would welcome her in their house whenever she wanted if they weren't there as well. She was pretty sure that they would frown if she brought a friend with her and invited him into their bed.

"Do you think I should get dressed?" Becka asked him. She didn't know what to expect once they got off the boat.

Bryan shook his head. He reassured her that they were alone there, and she didn't need to fear that they would meet anyone.

He slowed down when he approached the mooring and handled the boat with a professional's ease, which made Becka beam with pride. That, he liked. He loved to see that she was proud of what he did, although it was something as insignificant as mooring the boat. Bryan also relished the times when Becka grew angry with him. To his way of thinking, that meant that Becka took the time to see him. That sounded weird even in his ears, but Bryan didn't care.

CHAPTER FIVE

BRYAN HELPED BECKA off the boat. He also balanced the food basket and a small cooler in his other hand. It wasn't a tiny basket by any means, and Becka's thoughts started racing when she laid her eyes on it. She was trying to guess what delicious things Bryan had hidden in there.

Becka couldn't wait to partake in the picnic he had prepared. She also wondered why Bryan wouldn't let her help him carry anything. From the look of things, he had too many things to take care of at the same time. The man had even draped a blanket over his shoulder. With his other hand on the small of her back, Bryan guided Becka to a cluster of trees not very far from the shore.

"I remember that it's a little meadow there, right in front of those trees," Bryan explained to her. "It's a good plot for a picnic, Becka. You'll see. We can see the lake from there. If I remember correctly, you like watching boats. However, I must tell you that not many sails come this way. The island is quite secluded. It's not in the direction of traffic. Anyway, there we'll have cover from the sun under those trees," Bryan said. He took his hand off the small of Becka's back and pointed in the distance. "They make for great shade, so I think it's the perfect spot for our picnic. And later, if you don't want to go to the house, we can stretch out on the blanket, and no one will be the wiser," he prattled on.

Becka listened to him and smiled. She couldn't help but wonder why Bryan was talking so much. He didn't look like the man to chatter at length about insignificant little things. He seemed somewhat nervous, and she couldn't understand why.

She suspected that something wasn't what seemed to be. Yet, she didn't feel that she was in any danger, so she pushed the thought aside.

Bryan didn't let her help him with laying down the blanket or arranging the food either. He just directed her to lie down under the shadow of a tree and wait for him to prepare everything.

Once he started unwrapping the food, her taste buds went in overdrive. The smell of the juicy chicken surrounded by a mound of French fries made her mouth water, and she sighed with anticipated pleasure. The Caesar salad, coming out of the basket afterward looked tasty as well but didn't hold a candle to the casserole of homemade chicken with fries, covered with grated cheese. The man had overdone himself.

Becka eyed the food with excitement and licked her lips. Bryan chuckled and shook his head.

"Come on! Let's dig in, sweetie. And keep in mind that we also have dessert, so you definitely need to save some space for it. You'll love it, Becka. I promise you," Bryan said and reached out to her to pull her down on the blanket.

Becka sat on the quilt and slapped his arm playfully. Then she picked up one of the plastic plates he had put next to the basket and topped it with chicken and fries. She had just finished piling the food on the plate when Bryan revealed a container with Greek salad. That was her favorite, so Becka forgot about the Caesar salad at once.

"Oh, I haven't left any space for that on my plate, and I want some," Becka pouted in disappointment. She eyed the Greek salad that was beaconing at her.

"Don't worry, we can both eat directly from here, can't we?" he reassured her and put the container between them. Then, Bryan crossed his legs, copying Becka's stance, and spooned some of the chicken casserole on his plate.

Becka nodded and attacked the food with enthusiasm. The aromas had made her hunger rise to new levels. Bryan took a moment or two to watch her eat, then with a smug smile on his lips, he dug into his food, as well.

"Do you cook?" she asked, tasting the chicken flavored with butter, lemon, and some herbs, she didn't even bother to identify.

The taste was exquisite, and that was all that mattered. Becka was very curious where he had found it, but she decided to go with her first guess. He must have made it.

"Yes, I do. I had to learn how to cook since I like to eat, and I got sick of so much take-out," Bryan replied with a nod. Then, he asked her, "Do you like it?"

"Oh, it's great. Amazing even. I can't cook, Bryan," she suddenly said with regret.

Bryan glanced at her, a little taken aback by her sudden confession. She was indeed upset with her admission. Her genuine disappointment with something so unimportant made him smile.

He stroked her arm and comforted her, "It's not a problem, Becka. You probably can do other things. It's not like I'd want you in front of the stove cooking away...," he said and let the words linger between them. "I want you somewhere else anyway," he mumbled, but her keen hearing didn't fail her this time either, and Becka burst into laughter, light-heartedly slapping his arm again.

"You're a naughty boy, Bryan," she managed to say through peals of laughter.

Bryan glanced at her and decided to try his luck, "Naughty, naughty, but are you against what I'm thinking?"

She looked at him for a few moments, seeming to consider his question, and finally, she shook her head. A faint blush spread over her face and made him grin. He liked to see her blush. Her innocence was refreshing and made him feel manlier, which he didn't mind at all.

After a little pause, the conversation tittered around insignificant things with long stretches of silence. That didn't bother them. They felt comfortable enough together and didn't need to fill the quietness with meaningless chatter.

Being together, sharing the great food, and enjoying the air of the lake was enough for both of them. Becka and Bryan savored each other's company, and that was what mattered. The day was growing more heated, but the shadow of the trees offered them a breather from the hot air.

In the distance, the sails of the boats spotted the surface of the lake. However, the noise of the town didn't reach them. Becka and Bryan felt wrapped in their own paradise, only the two of them. They were free to talk about anything and everything. They kissed each other whenever the mood struck. They fed each other pieces of succulent chicken now and then and burst into laughter when one of them would drop some food.

Once they filled themselves with the main course, Bryan unveiled two big slices of triple chocolate cake, and Becka's eyes widened. She had a weakness for chocolate cake, especially when it had three thick layers of chocolate. Becka tackled her dessert with a new ardor, although she felt already full.

Becka had never been able to say no to chocolate cake. It was the curse of her life or at least one of them. She couldn't pass on such a delightful dessert, and she expressed her appreciation for his taste in organizing picnics.

After a while, Bryan leaned back on the trunk of a tree. Becka snuggled up tight in his arms, and his chin rested on the top of her head.

Becka closed her eyes, and with a content sigh, she let herself drift into sleep once again, feeling safe in the strong arms wrapped tightly around her. Bryan felt her chest rise and fall under his arms, and her soft breathing lulled him to sleep as well, making him forget about the food left there on the blanket.

From a branch above, a black squirrel had watched the feast spread out on the blanket for a while. It considered that it was safe enough because the humans were out for the count, so it came down, stole a piece of the chicken, and ran away with it. No one was the wiser.

BECKA SLEPT FOR ABOUT an hour and a half and woke up refreshed and ready to attack the world again. She became aware that she was still in Bryan's arms, and she turned her head to look up at him. He was already awake and met her eyes squarely.

The change in Becka's breathing had woken him up, and he had been waiting to see what she wanted to do. He also remembered what had happened on the yacht earlier, and he didn't want a repeat of the stupid quarrel they had.

All their bickerings seemed unsubstantial, and most of the time, they were the result of misunderstandings. Bryan found them to be a waste of time, and he had proposed to himself to avoid any quarrel if possible. The stakes were too high for him, and he didn't want to miss on the chance he had gotten when he met Becka.

Becka raised her hand and touched his face with hesitant fingers. They brushed the beard that shaded his face and stroked his scar for a few seconds. She felt him tense for a second, but when her fingers continued to trace the contour of his face, he relaxed. Then, she turned in his arms, and on her knees, she faced him.

Both watched each other intently, but neither Becka nor Bryan said anything. Becka leaned in slightly and put her hands on his chest. From there, her fingers started exploring the hard planes beneath.

Bryan left his hands to rest on her hips and waited to see what she had in mind. Nevertheless, her wandering fingers had an arousing effect on his system. He could feel the fire stoking inside him.

Hesitantly, Becka leaned forward and pressed her lips to his for a brief kiss and looked up at him afterward. He was looking down at her, his eyes half-covered by his lashes.

She decided to be more forward and kissed him again. This time, her tongue traced the contour of his lips thoroughly, learning their taste and shape. That spelled the end of her initiative. Bryan couldn't take it anymore, and he pulled her forcefully into his arms. He lowered her on the blanket with care and covered her body with his. Then he kissed her with all the longing he had gathered in his heart since the day before.

It was the first time he had ever felt so much excited at the thought of holding a woman in his arms and so impatient to have her. Not even as a teenager, had he been so edgy at the idea of making love as he was now.

At first, Bryan tried to control himself and focused on exploring Becka's lips with his own. Only after he learned their texture and felt them tremble, he moved on and started exploring her entire mouth. His tongue slowly slid past her parted lips and danced against hers, filling himself with her unique flavor and texture.

Bryan took his time and tasted her leisurely. He wanted to enjoy every second and immerse himself in the pleasure she offered him.

The man's moves were measured and slow, designed to tempt and seduce. The tips of his calloused fingers stroked the side of Becka's face with reverence. Then, they brushed up and mingled with her mane that still stuck out in a frenzy of honey.

Bryan pushed himself onto her hard, and the shock of his move made her gasp, but the sound got lost in his greedy mouth. Far from satisfied, he continued to make love to her lips while his hands started wandering along her neck and arms, leaving behind little shocks and shivers.

Bryan's caresses shook Becka to the core. She trembled against him, and in one last lucid moment, Bryan raised his head and looked at her.

"If you don't want me to continue, say it now. I don't know if I'll be able to stop later, Becka," he admitted in a husky voice.

Becka nodded to let him know that she wanted him to continue with that torture of her senses. Shyness shone in her eyes and tugged at his heart.

The young woman couldn't find the words to make her wishes known to him. Becka wasn't even sure if there were still words somewhere in her mind. A sea of sensations consumed her, and besides her moans that she didn't even perceive, Becka couldn't have said anything. Her throat felt tightened and didn't work anymore. Something odd was going on inside her body, but it felt good, so Becka wanted Bryan to continue touching her with all that incensed passion that she could read in his eyes.

Bryan's eyes had lost that icy shine she had seen before. Now an unusual light had lit and darkened those cold blue irises, and she basked in that light. Becka felt proud of herself because she was responsible for putting that hot light in there.

Bryan stared at her a moment longer. He wanted to make sure that she was all right with what was going to happen between the two of them. Then he gathered Becka into his arms. Bryan wanted to let Becka feel his intense hunger for her and allow the tautness in his body to seep into hers.

He kissed her lips again and nibbled on them a couple of times before he deepened the kiss some more to satisfy his overwhelming need to become one with her.

Becka wrapped her arms around his neck and welcomed the heat of his body. Her skin tingled and longed for his touches. When his teeth nibbled at the soft skin of her neck, she sighed and let go of any coherent thought.

She had completely forgotten they were outside in the open, lying on a blanket and, maybe, a boat might sail close enough, and people might see them. She was only aware of her strong desire to have that man fulfill all her fantasies and step with him into her womanhood.

She abandoned everything in Bryan's knowledgeable hands and let him mold her body with his touches.

Bryan took off the top piece of Becka's swimming-costume and filled his hands with her breasts. Then, he rubbed his cheek on the soft skin, and Becka shivered when she felt the roughness of his beard on the sensitive spot. She arched, needing to feel him closer, and that encouraged him to be bolder. His tongue flicked out and licked at the little tip, which rose timidly into his touch, and she felt her body on fire. Becka moaned, closing her eyes. Satisfied with her response, Bryan filled himself with her scent and taste. Her body became strung like a bow, and every fiber was impatiently waiting for release.

The sensations were sharp and pleasantly painful, and Becka's yearning increased tenfold. Unable to control the tautness bottled up inside her, Becka cried out again. Powerful and overwhelming sensations assaulted her senses, and she couldn't control them. They thrust her into the eye of a tornado.

Bryan let go of the assault, and Becka breathed with relief. The tension became more bearable, but that lasted only one moment, though. He started the sweet agony all over again. Now, his fingers were playing the hyper-sensitized skin that he had already tormented with his mouth.

Becka couldn't discern what happened to her anymore or focus on a specific feeling. Her skin tingled all over. The ocean of sensations in her lower belly had turned into a volatile storm and shredded her body to pieces. The intensity of her feelings was so powerful now that she was moaning continually, and she started writhing uncontrollably underneath Bryan.

Becka didn't know if she wanted Bryan to continue, or she wanted him to stop so that she could escape the abundance of bombarding feelings that had turned her body into a mass of sensations and obliterated all thought from her brain.

Bryan's lips started their journey down, and his tongue flicked and swirled here and there, his teeth nibbling at her skin and sending piercing shivers through her entire body. Becka laced her fingers in his hair to feel more of him. She also needed some support through the storm of sensations, ravaging her body.

When she almost jumped off the blanket, Bryan's fingers dug into her hips to keep her there, prisoner to everything he had to give her. By now, Becka had drowned in a sea of piercing and coiling sensations. Her eyes were closed, and she moved under him unconsciously. Her movement made it harder for him. It was difficult not to plunge in and take what he wanted the most.

When he reached the edge of her bikini, he lowered it slowly and lavished every uncovered inch of her skin with his passionate attention. Becka let his hair go and propped herself up on her elbows. With widened, shocked eyes, she watched him, biting her lips nervously. She didn't want him to stop, but she wasn't sure she wanted him to continue his journey south. Bryan noticed her move. He thought she might back off then. Becka was excited. That was true. Yet, she was also new to all of that, and she was teetering on the edge of uncertainty.

Bryan removed her bikini with a hasty move, and then he looked up at her, questioning her intentions. At first, she didn't say anything but stared back at him. After a few seconds of hesitation, she nodded her agreement slightly only to receive a ruthless smile in return. That grin of his made her feel fearful and unsure of what was about to come.

It wasn't as if she didn't know what was supposed to happen next. She had a general idea about how that worked, but she didn't know what to expect exactly. What she knew was that she couldn't say 'no' to Bryan.

Becka did want to make love to him. She had already made her mind up the day before, and her body had responded the moment Bryan kissed her that afternoon.

Bryan pushed her back onto the blanket gently, and his head lowered over the secret place he had just uncovered. Becka blushed. She felt his face touching her thigh and became aware that he could feel her unique and strong scent.

She was happy that Bryan couldn't see her face. She was ashamed that she behaved with such a lack of sophistication, but there were some things she couldn't control.

Bryan's fingers hovered over her body for a few tense seconds. His hands slid up and down her thighs slowly, and the tender exploration stirred her nerve endings. When he felt that her arousal augmented, he pushed her legs apart gently, and stroked the inside of her thighs, starting from the back of her knees and sliding up, excruciatingly slowly, until his fingers reached the top of her legs. There, he let his fingers slide over her womanhood like an illusion, and she shivered again.

This time, the urgency of her need was much higher. Becka locked her fingers on the sides of his head, ready to pull him up to her. Yet, he had something else in mind. Bryan didn't care for her intention of bringing him back to her mouth. He burrowed his nose in the one spot he had wanted to touch all day and breathed her scent deeply, and then he started making love with her and drive her crazy.

Becka felt as if electrical shocks sensitized every nerve ending in her skin, and once more, she lost any conscious thought. She could only chant breathlessly, "Please, please, please!" over and over again.

She wasn't aware she was begging him. Becka didn't know if she wanted him to stop because she couldn't take it anymore or if she wanted him to continue his arousing torment.

Becka had already reached a point where she could only feel. She couldn't reason any more. Instinct and pleasure had already replaced thought, and somewhere in her subconscious level, she feared that she was losing herself in that uncontrollable mass of emotions. Becka felt small explosions everywhere inside her lower body.

Bryan's fingers and mouth threw her in an ocean of new sensations. When the explosions inside her became all too violent, Becka cried out, and her fingers pulled his hair. Her lower body rose entirely off the blanket instinctively, seeking more of the attention he lavished on her. Bryan raised his head and glanced at Becka, satisfied that she had abandoned herself to the pleasure he could give her. A naughty grin on his lips, Bryan dropped his head once more. He stroked her, now soothing her quivering body.

When he felt that the tension had left her body, Bryan looked up at Becka's reddened face and quivering lips. He continued to touch her thighs and abdomen with long and appeasing strokes, his fingers massaging and burrowing gently in her skin here and there.

Bryan dipped his head once more, and his lips trailed up her body with feather-like kisses and nibbles at a few choice spots. Becka exhaled noisily and moaned. Her eyes opened wide at the shock of the new sensation.

Bryan traced more kisses up her torso until his feverish lips reached her neck. There, he made a halt for a few moments and played with her silky skin, already oversaturated with sensations. She quivered again, but he continued with his sensual trail of kisses and nibbles up to her ear.

Becka turned her head to kiss him, and she was startled when she tasted not only him but also herself on his lips. The mingled scents aroused her even more, even though she didn't think it would have been possible to feel anything more.

She kissed his lips at first and bravely nibbled at them as he had done to her, and rejoiced when she felt him quiver. Payback was only fair.

Becka stroked his strong arms and tried to learn the shape of his coiled muscles. She slid her hands around him with a sense of possession that she didn't know she had. A vixen smile formed on her lips, and that uncharacteristic smile incited him to grin at her, as well.

Bryan took her mouth again in a passionate, toe-curling kiss. He rubbed his body of hers, enjoying the feel of her skin.

"Should I take my clothes off, sweetie?" he asked in a husky whisper.

"Yes, please," Becka moaned and patted his arm, more to encourage herself than him.

Bryan stood in a split-second. With hasty moves, he pulled his clothes off.

Becka stretched on the blanket, and impatiently, she was waiting for him to touch her again. Her skin wore the marks of his beard and greedy fingers, and her lips were red and swollen from their passionate kisses.

Becka looked very well-loved, but he still wanted to give her much more and take his pleasure at the same time. Bryan lowered himself onto the blanket and over her.

He braced himself on his left elbow, and the fingers of his right hand skimmed over her silky skin. He dipped his head, and his lips played with her mouth before trailing down to her neck, where he marked her again with a mild bite. Her moan amplified his desire.

Bryan hadn't thought it was possible to want a woman more than he already did. Yet, desire knotted in his belly and made him ache at a new level. He was painfully hard, and he needed Becka badly. He needed relief but didn't want to rush her.

His fingers played over Becka, ready to tease her more, but she wrapped her arms around him and pulled him over her with a strength he didn't know she had. Bryan understood her quiet message to hurry and make love to her, yet he didn't want to steal anything from her first experience.

Determined to make her enjoy their lovemaking as much as he did, Bryan leaned forward and started to pepper kisses all over her body while his hand brushed down south.

"Now, Bryan. Now!" she cried out. "I want you now. Enough with all that torture," she demanded, and at the same time, she pulled at his hair savagely.

Bryan laughed and hugged her, gathering her body to him. Then, he covered her and kissed her lips with a tenderness that was in direct contrast with the wild kisses he had given her before.

"I've never been with a virgin, Becka, my sweetie, so, you're out of luck here," he whispered with regret over her lips. "I'll try to be gentle, but..."

"You're doing just fine," she whispered back, reassuringly, "but hurry now, Bryan. I need you now," she continued with a tense voice.

He laughed nervously and found his way inside her, raising her hips with his hands. He started pushing slowly forward, but Becka had lost all patience by then and pushed up with force to meet him, only to cry out when he was all the way in.

Becka felt he was stretching her beyond her limit. The pressure she experienced inside was painful and delightful at the same time.

"Are you all right?" Bryan asked with concern, afraid that he had hurt her with his sudden invasion.

"Just perfect," she whispered and smiled at him. Her eyes had widened with wonder. "I'm pretty sure there should be much more than this," she said in a conspiring tone of voice and flexed her inner muscles.

Her words prompted Bryan's laughter again, but the squeeze of her inner muscles turned his laughter into a growl.

"Yes, there is, baby, there is," Bryan said through clenched teeth, and then he started making love to her in earnest.

Becka gasped and clung to his arms, afraid that she would get lost in the storm of sensations. She loved feeling his weight on her and that he was a part of her. She might have felt a twinge of pain for a few seconds, but she forgot about it soon.

She relished in the pressure and pleasure Bryan gave her with his body.

Unconsciously, she matched his rhythm, and pushing against him made her feel much more. The sensations were more intense.

Becka brushed her fingers along Bryan's back, down to the top of his thighs, and both of them gasped, although for different reasons.

Bryan lifted one of her legs and wrapped it around his waist. He stroked her thigh from behind her knee up to the hip, using only the tip of his fingers and awakening nerve endings that had relaxed. His rough-skinned palm slid further and pulled her body closer to him. The change in position ignited sparks through her veins, and the tension inside Becka coiled and became unbearably painful.

Now Bryan reached deeper, and stunned, Becka felt a connection with him that she had never imagined possible.

Bryan bowed his head and bit her earlobe gently. Becka cried out as her skin tingled everywhere. Then Bryan's lips trailed down and made love to her breasts, and the tautness inside Becka exploded. For a moment, she felt pulled apart in a multitude of directions, only to uncoil into a sphere of sensations that set her skin on fire.

Becka cried out once more but louder this time. Before she fell into the abyss of sensations and lost any coherent cognitive functions, Becka felt Bryan give in to the ultimate pleasure. She collapsed in the void that was calling for her. Before her mind went blank, a groan flew off Bryan's lips and touched her ears. The sound seemed distant, and Becka wasn't sure that it hadn't been only in her imagination.

Becka didn't know how long she had been out, but when she came back to the real world, she felt Bryan's lips brush along her neck tenderly. He was breathing hard, and his hands were shaking, but he still took care of her and stroked her lovingly.

"Are you all right, baby?" Bryan whispered in her ear, and then he took her earlobe between his lips and bit it delicately.

Becka shivered as the aftermath waves were still present, and his bite intensified them more. She tried to say 'yes,' but she didn't seem to find her voice anymore. Her voice was lodged somewhere in her throat, and she couldn't get any words out, so she nodded and hugged him tighter.

Bryan rolled on his side with her nestled tightly in his arms and kissed the crown of her head. He covered her legs with one of his, unwilling to let go of her and pull away yet. He continued to stroke her back and her upper thighs while rubbing his chin on the top of her head affectionately.

"Was it okay for you or...?" Bryan asked without even thinking about what he was going to say.

He didn't want to ask. Bryan didn't want to hear that it had been bad for Becka or he had behaved like a man who thought of his pleasure only, without paying any attention to hers. He didn't need to hear the lie in her voice if Becka said 'yes' when she hadn't liked his lovemaking at all.

Bryan failed to understand his insecurity around Becka. Probably he was anxious because he wanted to have with her what he hadn't wanted to have with any other woman. He might have been apprehensive because he had had the chance or bad luck to be the first man who had made love to Becka. That depended on how she felt and what she thought.

Bryan, for one, couldn't complain. He had never been with a woman that had belonged only to him. Bryan might have liked to think that he was above such caveman's thoughts, but he had to admit that he loved the idea that Becka hadn't known another man in the biblical sense.

Whatever the case, Bryan was beside himself with anger. He knew that his insecurity could ruin the best thing that had ever happened to him.

Becka kept silent and kissed his chest while her fingers brushed the curly coarse hair that peppered his skin. Then she looked up at him with a dreamy expression in her eyes and nodded, staring at him.

A smile started to grow on Becka's lips shyly, and the sweetness of the moment hit Bryan like a fist in his gut. Bryan pulled her tighter into his arms, and she objected.

"It's too tight, Bryan. I can't breathe," she said in a small voice.

Bryan became aware that he had been too rough with her and loosened his hug to let her breathe. Yet, he didn't let go of her completely. He still needed to feel her body against his.

Actually, and that was quite astounding, Bryan needed Becka again. He even thought about making love to her once more, but he decided against it. It had been Becka's first time, and he didn't want to hurt her. Bryan could have her tomorrow again if she wanted, too.

They remained entwined, both contented to be close to each other and to rest in each other's arms.

CHAPTER SIX

BRYAN NUDGED HER CHIN up with his thumb and kissed her.

"We can go up to the house and clean up if you want," he whispered in her ear.

She looked up to the hill where the big white house with blue-framed windows stood amongst trees and shook her head.

"No, I don't think so. I don't want to be an imposition."

"What are you talking about?" he frowned, not understanding what she meant.

"I know your friend said you could use the house, but that doesn't mean he'd have wanted you to bring friends in there as well. We can clean up when we get to my house, all right?" she said.

Becka patted his hand without even being aware of doing it. It was the kind of pat one would use to calm a disappointed child when he didn't get any ice-cream.

Bryan knew that Becka doubted that someone would let him use their house like that, but he had chosen not to tell her that the house belonged to him.

He had needed to play things close to the vest because he wanted Becka to like him for himself and not for his possessions.

He had had more than his fair share of gold-diggers and was sick of them. They wanted him for what his financial possibilities would offer them, and once he refused, they had always walked away.

Bryan hoped that Becka wouldn't be like that, and he wanted to impress her with other things than the size of his bank account or his material possessions. He wanted her to like him for himself, and he felt that she did like him.

However, he was painfully aware that things could change in the blink of an eye. He had met two or maybe even three women, who seemed like they had been somewhat into him. But then, once they had found out how much money he had on his name, they fell head over heels in love with him. That hadn't lasted, though. Afterward, those women proved that they loved what Bryan had in his pockets. They had no interest in his mind or soul.

Becka mattered too much for him to let the same scenario play out, so Bryan didn't know what to do. He felt guilty but still didn't say anything for a moment. It was his fault that Becka considered that she had to go all the way back home and clean up.

For a few seconds, the man was tempted to leave it at that. His sense of self-preservation advised him not to open his big mouth and say something that might not turn too good for him. Yet, Bryan thought better and decided to come clean, so he told her, "Becka, I have to tell you something."

His serious tone made her look up at him again. Becka didn't like where that was going. His tone made her fear the worst, and after everything that had happened between them, she hoped that she hadn't been wrong about him.

Becka could usually tell right away what kind of person she had before her eyes. That was one of her unique talents, even if it was raw and unrefined.

Up to that point, Bryan hadn't made her believe that he was a jerk. Nothing he had done had made her doubt him.

Bryan saw the uncertainty in her eyes, and that didn't sit well with him. He guessed what she was thinking and wanted to alleviate her fears. However, he still hesitated for a few moments because what he was going to confess went against what he had decided earlier on the yacht. Nevertheless, Bryan considered that Becka deserved to know the truth. Besides, until then, she hadn't shown any inclination toward material things.

Bryan felt a tight weight in his heart at the thought that he could nip the relationship with Becka in the bud if it turned out that she was nothing else but a fortune hunter. Bryan knew that he would suffer then, and in more ways than one because he had just realized that he wanted Becka more now after making love to her than he had wanted her before. He was almost sure that Becka was the perfect woman for him, but he was determined not to accept another relationship based only on his material status.

Bryan accepted the fact that there might not be much to him. Yet, he stubbornly clung to the thought he deserved to be with someone who wanted him, the man.

"Look, the thing is...." He started, but he couldn't continue. Suddenly, Bryan became afraid of what Becka would say, hearing his confession about his previous lie, so he tried to find the best way to explain his reasons for lying to her in the first place.

"What is it, Bryan?" Becka inquired in a calm tone of voice in spite of the anger that rose in her throat.

She had too much pride and didn't want to show him that she cared too much if he had dumped her after she had fallen into his arms like a dummy, not even twenty-four hours after their initial encounter.

"You can tell me anything. It's not a problem, you know. I can take it."

"Well, there is a problem, though... I lied to you, and..." he began, but he couldn't continue because she literally jumped up and stood above him like a vengeful goddess.

"Damn it, Bryan, are you married, or what?" she practically screeched.

Her gaze narrowed with anger, as threatening as a snake's narrow slits, ready to kill him just with that glare.

His eyes widened, and for a few long moments, Bryan could only stare at her. Becka was magnificent.

He had known that Becka would get upset, but he didn't expect that powerful anger or that she would jump to unfounded conclusions in a matter of seconds.

Becka understood then that Bryan considered her question way too crazy, and that he was rendered speechless. She slapped herself in her mind for uttering the words, but she didn't know what she could say to make it right.

It took him a few more seconds to recover enough to answer her. He stood up as well, just as angry with her accusations now, as she was with him. He looked at her incredulously with his fists on his hips.

"Of course, I'm not," he retorted with anger in his voice once he found his speech again. "I wouldn't sleep with another woman if I were married. What the hell? What kind of a monster do you think I am?" he snapped at her, even though her hard breathing made it hard for him to focus.

Her generous bust was making it difficult to look anywhere else, even if he knew it was important to look only into her eyes since he didn't want to give her any wrong ideas.

She calmed down then. "Well, if that's not the problem, then what is it?"

"I lied to you about that house," he said, pointing to the house on the hill with a nervous gesture.

She looked at the house and then at him as if she didn't understand what was going on.

"What do you mean?" she asked him after a few moments of pondering over his statement and not making any sense of it.

"That's my house, Becka. It is not a friend's, but mine. I lied to you when I told you that a friend allowed me to use it," Bryan explained again. He wanted to be sure that Becka understood his words clearly.

"Oh, okay," Becka said, utterly appeased with his words, and then she turned around to look for her bathing suit, satisfied that Bryan's confession didn't have anything that would hurt her. She also appreciated that Bryan didn't intend to move on.

Suddenly, Becka turned back to him. Her eyes sparkled with so much fury now that he took a step back involuntarily. If Bryan had thought that Becka looked sumptuous in her anger earlier, now her fierceness was much more compelling than that.

Bryan's statement had finally sunk in, and she realized what he wanted to say. One thing was clear, though. Becka didn't like it at all, and the implications of Bryan's words looked a little too ugly for her to stomach them. With a very even voice, deceitfully contradicting the wrath in her eyes, she asked him, "So why did you find it better to lie to me? Why was it so important that I didn't know that the house belonged to you?"

Bryan knew her tone was deceptive, and he was expecting that a full blow of her fury would hit him soon. Electrical current charged the atmosphere, and he could feel the twinges of tension ripping in the air.

"I had a thought, you see...," he started to explain but stopped when he noticed Becka's mutinous stance.

Becka did look glorious in his eyes with the wrath that blazed in her eyes, the spine she held straight like an arrow, and the small hands she had fisted on her hips. She resembled a pure masterpiece.

Bryan knew that Becka had forgotten that she didn't have a stitch of clothing on her, and he appreciated her forgetfulness. His eyes betrayed the hunger he felt. His gaze swept over her full figure and took in her ample breasts and narrow waist, her generous hips, and rounded thighs.

"You had a thought," she repeated, but this time her voice dripped with sarcasm.

His eyes snapped back to hers. Bryan became suddenly aware that he was in the middle of an argument, and he shouldn't lose sight of that if he wanted to solve the situation and leave the battlefield in one piece. Becka looked pissed enough to bite his head off.

"Okay, I understand how that might have upset you, but you also have to understand I had my reasons..." he said, dragging the sentence away when he saw she wasn't mollified by far with his attempt to explain himself.

"Of course, you had your reasons," she snapped, throwing her hands into the air. "How could I forget that? That makes everything all right, doesn't it?"

"Becka, come on, only listen to me, please. It's not easy to explain what I thought," Bryan tried to reason with her.

Becka looked straight at him and said with all the sarcasm she could muster, "I'll tell you what you thought, Bryan. It's a no-brainer. You thought I was a stupid bimbo, interested in a man with money, and you didn't want me to stick my greedy hands in your pockets. That's what you thought," she finished her tirade in a shout.

It sounded bad. The way she put it, it seemed very bad. Bryan felt a tinge of guilt. Her words were accurate enough, although Becka expressed his reasoning in an ugly form.

"Not really, Becka. But I had my share of women who showed interest in me only because I had money and..."

Becka stomped her foot and groaned, and her behavior stopped him from continuing. He waited to see what else she had to say.

She glanced at him, but then she averted her eyes as if she couldn't look at him anymore. Becka began to gather the pieces of her swimming costume, and in a rather low voice, she said, "I want you to take me home now."

"Please, sweetie..."

"I said now," she repeated, emphasizing her words. "I don't want to spend another moment with you. You lied to me! You thought horrible things about me!" she shouted and turned her back to him to get dressed.

He felt the pang of guilt nagging at him again, but then another thought popped into his head suddenly. Taking his pants to get dressed as well, he said sarcastically, "And you were very open with me, weren't you? You were Miss Open Book and Open Heart, weren't you?"

"What do you mean?" Becka turned back to him, stunned to hear his words. "I didn't lie to you."

"Yes, you did. You said some things yesterday, and you didn't want to expand on that. Don't you remember? When you said you didn't advise me to upset you, and when you said there were things you couldn't tell me. Well, I also had things I couldn't tell you, so we are square," he concluded.

Becka looked at him, simmering inside. She felt her rage rise like magma inside a volcano, and she couldn't hold back her anger anymore. She threw her hands in the air.

A whoosh of wind swirled around him, and Bryan felt icicles on his back. The basket flew into the nearest tree trunk, and the cooler followed shortly after it as if an unseen hand lifted them and threw them away.

Bryan felt like he was in the middle of a hurricane and watched Becka with stunned eyes. He couldn't believe what he was seeing.

Her lips started trembling, and tears welled in her eyes all of a sudden. When she closed her eyes and lowered her shaky arms, everything went back to normal. The wind stopped, and the warmth of the day chased away the chills Bryan had felt on his back.

She didn't look at him, and he couldn't do anything more but stare at her in shock. He refused to think about what had happened or to find an answer, but he knew she had a hand in it, and he didn't feel comfortable near her anymore.

It was sort of creepy, and he couldn't find a reasonable explanation for what he had experienced and felt. What popped into his mind didn't really make sense but only freaked him out more.

"I think I'll take you home now," Bryan said quietly, unwilling to go into the why's and how's right then.

Becka nodded, defeated, and started getting dressed in silence. When she finished, she went to gather the basket and the cooler. His cold voice came from behind and stopped her.

"Don't worry about those. I'll take care of everything when I come back."

Becka nodded but didn't say anything. She felt dispirited and walked with small steps toward the dock. She didn't know what to tell him, and she could see that he didn't want to hear anything from her right then.

She felt disheartened. She had been having an excellent day with Bryan, but they built that day on lies and deceit, and she didn't know how she felt about it anymore.

Bryan helped her on the deck of the boat with total indifference as if she were a woman, he had just met and extended conventional politeness to her. Any closeness, the two of them had experienced before, was now gone. They felt like they were two uncomfortable strangers thrown together in a point in space.

Once she stepped on the boat, Becka headed for the sunshade and started putting on her t-shirt and pants. At the same time, Bryan walked to the helm and started the procedures to leave the marina. He sped up as soon as possible.

Bryan didn't feel like being with Becka anymore for the moment. Yet, he imagined that his feelings would go back to normal once he had time to think about things. He felt somewhat guilty because of his omissions. But, Bryan deemed Becka's fault for those circumstances bigger than his.

Bryan didn't want to dwell on what had happened because he didn't like what he read into the facts. Despite all that, Bryan also felt regret. He already had feelings for Becka, although their relationship had developed only in the span of a day. Bryan had thought that Becka was the one for him, and it was hard to accept that it was just an illusion. He needed time to reflect upon all of that.

Becka was upset with him and with herself at the same time. She was shocked that Bryan had felt the need to keep his wealth a secret, fearing she would be more attracted to that than to him. She would have liked for him to trust her and to think differently about her.

Becka could understand that past experiences might have made him fearful about people's reasons. Still, she considered that she had been reasonably open with Bryan, and ordinarily, people didn't think that she was a person capable of taking advantage of a man.

Becka was also mad at herself because she had no control over her powers. If she got angry, she would unleash them, and she couldn't stop a thing. Becka knew that people didn't take it lightly when someone made things float in the air and brought icy swirls of wind around them. Her mother had kept telling her that since Becka was a baby and she was famous for throwing severe tantrums. Luckily, she had learned her lesson before going out into the real world.

Unfortunately, she had forgotten all those lessons today. She hadn't walked away from the fight with Bryan, and she had put herself on the spot. She had chased Bryan away because he had to be too freaked out now to want to stay with her.

She didn't like his cold and detached behavior. After they shared those precious moments, for which she had been waiting for a long time, his attitude had the impact of a cold shower.

Becka wasn't sorry that she had made love to Bryan. She would have lied to herself if she said that. However, she was sad because the aftermath had turned out so bleak and left her feeling so empty.

Becka didn't realize she was crying already, but Bryan heard her sobs and turned to her. A claw squeezed his heart.

For a fleeting moment, Bryan considered that he would better mind his business and let her cry. He wasn't of any good around a weeping woman. Bryan knew that he should let Becka reflect on everything first and try to talk to her later. However, the man couldn't keep his distance.

That woman had already had an immense impact on him, and regardless of what he was feeling that very moment, he couldn't stand idly by and let her cry without offering her any solace.

Bryan laid his hand on her shoulder, and Becka looked up. Bryan saw the tears running down her cheeks. He dried them with his thumb and pulled her up and into his arms, rubbing her back. He rested his head on hers and just held her, softly stroking her back to calm her down and make her feel better.

"It's all right, baby, You don't have to cry. It's not the end of the world, you know," he murmured.

His words made her cry harder, and through hiccups, she said, "It's the end of us, Bryan, and that's the end of the world now."

He smiled, slightly amused, and raised her head to look into her eyes. He kissed her lips softly, longing to feel her close to him again.

"I don't know if it's the end of us, but both of us have some thinking to do, Becka. Then we'll see," he said evenly.

"You want me to explain?" she asked with hesitation in her voice.

He shook his head, "No, not right now. I've got to think for a while, and then we can talk. It's better not to talk about anything right now."

"Why does it have to be on your timetable?" Becka snapped at him, forgetting about her sadness for a moment.

"It's not on my timetable," Bryan tried to be reasonable. "It's something I have to do, though. I do have to think. You can't think that I'll just put everything behind, and go on without any questions, sweetie. Believe me. It doesn't work that way," Bryan said in an even tone, although he felt like strangling her for being so dense.

It wasn't like everything that had happened was ordinary stuff. Bryan had already found an explanation, but he didn't like it, even though that possibility was nudging more and more at him. More importantly, he didn't know if his feelings were strong enough for him to continue being in a relationship with a woman who could create a small storm. He liked to have a sound balance in everything, and his relationship with Becka wasn't balanced by far.

Becka pulled away and turned her back to him. She understood that her show might have freaked him out, but she didn't know why he didn't want to talk about it.

Her family had told her never to show her heritage to strangers, but Becka thought that she would have a chance at a real relationship with Bryan, and she had to show him what she could do. It happened earlier than she had hoped, but she didn't think it was such a bad thing, quite the opposite.

She tried to console herself with the thought that, at least, she didn't invest too much in a relationship with no chance of survival.

"Becka…" Bryan started to say, but she put her hand up to make him stop.

She didn't turn back to him when she said, "Everything is fine, Bryan, don't worry. I understand your reluctance. Let's only go home and forget we've ever met."

Her voice showed more determination than she felt, but she didn't want him to stick around only because he felt sorry that she cried. If he couldn't be with her for what she was, then she didn't see a point in continuing with the charade.

"It might not be so simple, Becka. I didn't say that we should forget we've ever met. I just asked for a little time to process what happened. Maybe that time would work for you, too."

"Whatever you say," she shrugged and went to the other side of the boat to get away from him.

In a way, Becka knew that Bryan was right. It wasn't as if he had to get over a bad habit like talking with her mouth full. Yet, she felt cheated because she had jumped into an affair with him without thinking it over.

She didn't like that he had lied to her, either. Everything was too much for her to forgive right then, and Becka didn't even think that it was worth the trouble.

Becka and Bryan made the rest of the trip in total silence. They stole glances at each other, but neither of them wanted to talk anymore.

They finally got to the harbor and moored the yacht, and then they strode to the parking lot where Bryan had left the car in the morning.

The tension grew even more during the car ride to Becka's home. The car was too small to contain both their resentments and heartaches. They started to dislike each other immensely and couldn't wait to get to their destination and part ways.

Bryan had hardly stopped the car when Becka jumped out. She threw a quick good-bye over her shoulder and ran into the house. As soon as she got inside, she shut the door behind her with a loud bang. Bryan looked after her, and even five minutes later, he was still there, in front of her house, staring at the closed door. That bang had sounded like a bad omen to him.

Bryan didn't feel as relieved as he had previously thought. While on the boat, on their way back to town, he had wanted only to drive Becka home and be done with everything for that day. Now though, he had the feeling that Becka had slammed the door over the only good thing that had ever happened in his life.

The man thought about going to her door and demanding that she talked to him, but he nipped the thought in the bud. It wasn't the right moment. Even Bryan knew that although he had limited social skills when it came to love relationships.

CHAPTER SEVEN

BECKA WAS IN THE GARDEN, staring into the distance. For a few days now, she couldn't find any peace in there, although it used to be her realm of tranquility before. She had stopped attending her classes at university, and she couldn't do anything else, either, like reading one of the books she loved or talking with her cousins.

Becka used to talk with one of them once a day. Now a week and a half had passed, and Becka still couldn't pick up the phone to call someone.

Becka had avoided seeing anyone over the past week and a half since her falling out with Bryan. She hadn't felt able to go to the regular dinner with her parents, at least. She had made up a party she couldn't miss, only to get out of it.

Her father hadn't been too happy about it, but her mother had exulted hearing that her daughter finally had a social lifelike any young girl of her age. She had always thought that Becka was too introverted when it came to making friends, and she didn't like it.

It was Friday again and, this time, she knew that the next day she wouldn't be able to avoid dinner with her parents anymore. Her great-grandmother would be there, and not even her mother would find the words to apologize for

Becka's absence. When great-grandmother came to dinner, everyone had to attend. Only being bedridden in the hospital would have been a valid excuse.

Becka didn't know what she should do. She was sure that everyone would immediately see that something had happened to her, and she was heartbroken.

She had seen her face in the mirror when she brushed her teeth day after day. Becka knew that she looked just like she felt. Becka had the feeling that someone had stolen all light out of her. She couldn't get over what had happened with Bryan. She had fallen for him hard, and no matter how much she rationalized what she felt, she couldn't make those feelings go away.

She knew it was just less than two full weeks, but she was afraid that she would always think about him, and it would be difficult for her to find another man who would complete her so well.

Now, with a calm mind, she realized that her outburst about the house shouldn't have happened. They had known each other for a day only, and Bryan had the right to protect himself if he had had bad experiences before. If she hadn't reacted to that lie so strongly, everything would have turned out fine, and she could have revealed the truth about herself to him later on when he could have accepted who she was.

Unfortunately, now it was too late to think of that. Becka had managed to find a great guy and lose him on two dates. Probably that was a record.

BRYAN RANG THE BELL and waited for Becka to open the door. He had taken residence in hell since they broke up over some silly words and a little magic. He had chosen to think of what Becka had done as 'a little magic.' It just appeared easier to understand and accept.

Bryan knew that they would have to talk about that, too, but he had already decided to keep an open mind and not just give up because of what she was.

Initially, the man had tried hard to forget Becka. He owned a dojo, so that helped him to spend a few days in an intense effort. Bryan tried exercising and lifting weights at first, and then he progressed to boxing. He made a point in having a date with the boxing bag every day for hours, but that didn't work either.

After the first few days, Bryan left his friend in charge of the dojo, and he progressed to drinking. After he had got his first hangover, the man remembered why he hated drinking. He had always loathed not to be in total control, and drinking alcohol had the power of taking the reins from his hands. When he swallowed a full bottle of whiskey, his abilities to function lessened, and always Bryan despised himself after a drinking spree.

In the end, he had just wasted hours after hours thinking of Becka, and what he should have done differently, or how he should have reacted to get a different result.

Even though their relationship had had such a short span of life, it marked him deeply. He would hear her voice all the time, and he would dream of her when he finally could fall asleep.

After a week and a half, Bryan decided that he had had enough. He had to go over to her and try to fix everything so that he could bring her back into his life. He knew that he couldn't go on like that. Becka had become too vital for him, so Bryan couldn't simply forget her.

Bryan was sure that Becka had something to do with magic, but in the big scheme of things, that didn't matter to him anymore. He was willing to put up with that if Becka found it in her heart to take him back.

That was why now he was patiently waiting for her to come and open the door. The echo of the bell had already faded away, but Becka still didn't come to the door. Bryan was stubborn enough, though, and with determination, rang the bell again. He resigned himself to wait, and with his hands in his pockets, he rocked on the balls of his feet.

When a few minutes passed, and there was still no sign of Becka, Bryan shrugged and instinctively tried the knob of the door. Of course, as he expected, the door wasn't locked. He swore under his breath, thinking of the worst, and entered the house, closing the door quietly behind him.

Bryan felt like an interloper for a moment and thought of the consequences of his venture. Yet, he was determined to see that his quest had a happy ending, so he called her name.

The silence of the house weighed down on him. He didn't hear steps coming down the stairs, so he decided to go into the kitchen. The room was empty, but then again, he could see Becka through the window, sitting under the gazebo, at the other end of the garden.

The woman looked small and lost, with her hands folded in her lap. There was a faraway look on her face that tugged at his heart. Happy because he had found her, Bryan went out in the garden and walked toward her. Becka didn't seem to notice that she wasn't alone anymore. Bryan got close to her and saw the signs of her heartbreak on her face. She looked weary and beaten, and Bryan's heart hurt a little more. He knew that he had put that expression on her face and felt like a rat.

"Becka," he called her name softly when he stepped under the canopy.

She sighed but didn't say anything. Becka didn't even glance at him. That wasn't a good sign, and Bryan panicked. He thought that Becka had decided to ignore him, shut him out of her life, and not talk to him anymore.

"Becka," Bryan called her name again, more forcefully. Only then she turned to him with a soft gasp.

Her eyes widened, and he understood that she couldn't believe that he was there.

"I rang the bell twice," he said to explain his presence in her garden. "I tried the door when I saw that you didn't answer. I thought that you didn't lock it."

"I can't hear the bell from here," Becka replied quietly. "It wasn't intentional," she continued. "I mean that it wasn't like I didn't want to open the door for you."

Bryan shook his head to chase her worries away. Then he said, "I didn't think like that, sweetie. I only wanted to explain why I came inside. I don't want you to think that I'm a damn stalker."

Becka gave Bryan a small smile. However, her face didn't glow, as it would before, and he didn't like it.

"But why are you here, Bryan? Nothing changed from the last week as far as I know. You still think I'm a gold digger, I know you're a liar, and we both know what I can do."

Bryan didn't like her resigned voice, nor did he like the sadness he read on her face. He didn't care for her accusation, either. He knelt before Becka, took one of her hands in both of his, and stroked it gently.

"I don't think you're a gold digger, baby, and I never thought that. Maybe it was stupid of me to wait and see if you liked me for me at first, but I really had some bad experiences in the past, and I guess that I only needed some reassurance.

"And what about what happened when we argued?" Becka asked with hesitation. She was afraid to hear his answer. Bryan stood up, sat on the bench, and pulled her into his lap.

"Well... That was something else, Becka, I must say. Nothing I've experienced before, I am sure. Maybe you can explain it to me because...it freaked me out, Becka," he admitted in a grave voice. "I've never seen anything like that, and of course, the first thing I thought was that you are...a...," Bryan started to say, but he couldn't continue to say what he imagined exactly.

"A witch?" she asked matter-of-factly.

Bryan didn't answer immediately. He pondered on what he remembered first.

"I don't know... I thought of a poltergeist or something like that," he confessed in the end, staring at her.

"Oh, gosh, I haven't thought you'd think that," she exclaimed. "I'm not anything like that, Bryan, be serious."

Bryan narrowed his eyes and asked, "So what are you exactly? Not that it would matter, to be honest," he rushed to add.

"What do you mean that it wouldn't matter?" Becka asked him with puzzlement.

Bryan took a few moments to consider his answer. He looked over the garden and stroked her hip absently.

"All right. I'll be honest with you," Bryan said, looking back at her. "I can't function, I can't sleep, and I can't do anything, as a matter of fact. I've tried a lot of things, and nothing works. I'm thinking only of you. So, no matter what, I want to be with you. So that you know."

Bryan noticed that Becka kept her gaze trained straight on him, so he amended his statement, "If you want the same thing too, of course. I can't force you. I know that. But I hope you do want me too."

Becka stroked the side of his face with tenderness and leaned to kiss his lips.

"I want to, but I think that you do need to know everything before going any further," she said with sadness.

"Just tell me," Bryan said. "I'm sure it's not so dramatic, and anyway, I think I can live with what you are. Considering that I can't live without having you in my life, the point is moot, as you say. I know it sounds pretentious, but then again, you should know that the days we've been apart were a living hell for me."

"All right, Bryan. I'll tell you then," Becka started and then stopped.

She couldn't push the words out. She was too afraid that Bryan would run away again.

"Come on, baby. Only say it. I promise that everything will be fine," Bryan insisted.

"Huh!" she scoffed.

Her distrust was evident, and Bryan knew that he deserved it. He had already run away from her once. He chose to look at her with insistence to make her talk. Becka held his stare for a couple of seconds, and afterward, she finally went on with her explanation.

"So, how can I tell you this, Bryan? I think I should be direct," Becka murmured, and he had to prick his ears to hear her words. "All right, here it is," she started again. "I'm a witch, and unfortunately, not a very good one. I still have to learn how to control my gift. You witnessed what happens when I get angry," Becka told him, and Bryan nodded. "In general, I try to walk out of confrontations because of that, but then with you, I didn't have the space to do it. You see, when I get mad, all those intense feelings turn into icy gushes of wind, and things start flying around, and that's something I can't stop. I don't have the knowledge to do it," she explained to make him understand.

"All right, fair enough," he said. "What else can you do?" Bryan asked in a conversational tone, although he didn't feel very at ease, hearing his worst fears voiced out and knowing that he didn't have a choice in the matter.

"Not much. That thing, and...I can tell if people are all right or not. I can't tell if they're felons or killers or anything like that. I can tell, though, if they give me a good vibe or not," she shrugged.

"And I gave you a good vibe, I understand," Bryan assumed, and she nodded. "So, let's sum it up, Becka. You're a witch, and I'm wealthy. Is there anything else that should be said?"

She shrugged again and shook her head. They remained silent for a while, and then Becka decided to ask, "Should I tell you that everyone in my family is a witch?"

He looked at her with surprise in his eyes and asked, "Really? Everybody? And all of them do the same things as you?"

Becka laughed, seeing that he looked so bewildered, and answered.

"No, not everyone can do the same thing. Some can read minds, and some can heal. Everyone has a gift. Of course, we all can do basic stuff, but some of us chose not to do it anymore. I don't. It's not like I can get very far right now, so..."

"Why?" he asked, completely surprised to hear all she had to say.

"This is the part I can't tell you...or at least not right now. Not if there is a chance to be together. And if we are meant to be together, you'll find out when the time is right. I hope you'll understand and won't pressure me to..."

Bryan stopped her with a finger on her lips.

"You don't have to tell me anything now if you can't. We passed over the first hurdle, let's keep it that way. When you're ready and you can, you'll tell me, okay?"

Becka looked at him with hope, but she didn't dare to hope too much. Her heart still ached, and she didn't know if she could take another rejection from him. The first time had been enough.

"Will we be together, Bryan?"

Bryan gathered Becka to his chest and hugged her. She felt that he didn't want to let her go anymore.

"Yes, if you want to be with me and you can forgive me for the way I reacted that day at the lake, then yes, we can be together, sweetheart."

Becka nodded. Smiling, she hugged him back as hard as she could. She cuddled as close as possible to him and sighed with content.

Bryan was happy to see that Becka was so willing to get over the argument they had had at the lake and get back together. Bryan was satisfied to sit there with Becka wrapped in his arms. He leaned his head on the top of hers and listened to the silence of the garden.

The light changed, and the evening came with a pale wind, which hushed through the multitude of flowers populating Becka's garden. Becka and Bryan still cuddled together, and none of the two of them felt like letting go.

Becka's head rested on Bryan's chest, and Bryan held her tight. He rested his chin on the top of her head and enjoyed the unusual scent of her hair.

"Do you want to come inside with me?" Becka whispered after a while. "Maybe spend the night with me?"

Bryan grinned and lifted her head to see if she blushed. He wasn't disappointed. A faint blush had already colored her cheeks, and her eyes were twinkling in the twilight.

He couldn't resist and took her mouth in a kiss that held all that desire he had felt for her during the days he couldn't see her.

Still kissing her, he stood up with her snuggled up in his arms and started towards the house. Only when they got to the kitchen door, he raised his head and looked at her again, then, balancing her on one knee, he opened the door and took her inside, closing the door with his foot behind them.

"So, where's your bedroom?" he asked her, crossing through the kitchen.

"Upstairs, the last room on the left," Becka answered breathlessly, unable to believe that Bryan would carry her all the way upstairs. It was so romantic that her little heart sang.

Bryan kissed her again for good measure and carried her to the bedroom. Once inside her room, Bryan let her stand and looked for the switch to turn on the light, but Becka beat him to it. The powerful lamp burnt his eyes, and he blinked a few times.

Once his eyes got used to the light, Bryan's gaze swept the room, and he had to grin. That room spoke loud and clear about Becka. It was a room with the air of the turn of the century, cluttered with pillows and comfortable armchairs on one side. On the other side of the room, a big, antique chest of drawers took most of the wall. Becka had covered the top of the chest with photos, showing groups of people, some young and some old, and knick-knacks. All of them were representations of etheric and whimsical fairies.

Beyond0 the armchairs, a large window looked over the garden that Bryan still could see, although it was now dark outside.

He turned back to Becka and saw that she was observing him carefully as if she wanted to guess what he was thinking.

"I like your bedroom, Becka," he said. "It's got you written all over it. Too many pillows for my taste, but what the heck, it works for you."

Becka smiled brightly at him and advanced toward Bryan with her lazy stride. Her summer dress covered her legs only up to her knees, and Bryan enjoyed the sight of her shapely legs in her slow journey toward him. The two straps, holding the dress on her shoulders, didn't cover much, and he found her more enticing than if she modeled a sexy nighty.

When she reached him, Becka leaned in and kissed him softly on the lips. That fleeting kiss made Bryan burn for her even more.

He pulled her into his arms and kissed her soundly. He shaped her lips to his, nibbling at her lower lip. All the while, he stroked her shoulders and arms and her back.

Bryan gazed into her eyes again to see if Becka really wanted to make love to him. He needed to be sure because he couldn't go through another fight and another break-up with her.

When he saw that Becka was on the same page with him, Bryan unzipped her dress and lowered the straps of the dress to reveal her generous bust. He licked his lips in his hunger and lowered his head to satisfy his craving. Becka sighed and moaned and tried to keep her balance while he started the sweet torture she enjoyed so much.

Bryan led her backward to the bed and helped her lie down, and then he showed her how much he needed to make love to her.

CHAPTER EIGHT

BRYAN GOT OUT OF THE shower, whistling. He was in a rather good mood that day. He had had a beautiful night with Becka, and he had enjoyed her lack of shyness in bed, even though she was timid out of bed.

The young woman was something else, indeed. She had proved that she was everything he needed during the long night they had spent together, but also during the first part of his shower, ended with a shared passion.

Bryan realized that he was happy. He hadn't felt like that in such a long time that he couldn't even remember if he had been content before.

It wasn't just their lovemaking, although it was an interesting experience to make love to Becka. She was open to any new ideas and wanted to discover what he liked. She enjoyed making love to him. She also enjoyed the pleasures Bryan offered to her.

But more significant, Bryan had found out that talking to Becka delighted him. Becka never prattled away about fashion or other things that he didn't understand. She could touch an eclectic group of subjects and kept surprising him with her insight.

Bryan had also told her a few things from his past. Of course, he kept silent about the worst ones. He didn't want to scare Becka away, after all, but he believed that he could share everything from his past with Becka after a while. However, Bryan wanted to make Becka understand that nothing about him was only white or black. So he had recounted some of the things he had done. Bryan thought that Becka needed to know the man with whom she got involved. Ultimately, all his experiences had had a hand in making him the man he had become, and she loved.

He told her about his dojo, and she showed interest in seeing it. Becka had even said that she wanted to train with him, so Bryan had promised to take her there the following week.

Becka had also revealed her dreams, and she had told him stories about her childhood and teen years. Bryan had found out enough things about her cousins and siblings to make him understand that Becka had a close-knit family.

Becka's family members were close to each other, not like Bryan's. Bryan had admitted to Becka that he hadn't seen his father in over twenty-five years since the man took off. He couldn't live with Bryan's mother anymore. The woman's sharp tongue had weakened his will to keep his marriage together but strengthened his wish to live as far as possible from his wife. Once he left, he didn't look back anymore. He didn't even want to check on his son.

Bryan's mother was another story altogether. She was still present in his life if only to make his life a living hell whenever they would get together. She considered it was his duty as a son to visit her at least once a month, and she took great pleasure in cutting him to size, as she used to say, during those monthly visits.

Bryan had confessed to Becka that he didn't love his mother anymore. He had probably stopped loving her when he was five. She was verbally abusing everyone with an odd pleasure, and she considered that everybody was beneath her station. Her son had been good for different things over the years, but he hadn't been suitable enough to love. Yet, he had taken care of her. She had her own house and monthly alimony for a comfortable living, so he didn't feel guilty at all for not looking after her, although she did try to make him feel that way every chance she got.

Bryan dried himself with a towel and got dressed in a hurry. He knew that he would find Becka in the kitchen. She had promised to cook breakfast for him, and he was a little concerned. Bryan had proposed to make the food for both of them, but Becka had insisted. She had said that it was the only meal she could cook, so she wanted to show off her culinary talents.

Bryan smiled when he remembered the way she had sounded. He had promised himself to praise her efforts even if she laked any cooking skill.

He went downstairs, still whistling, and headed directly to the kitchen. His sweet Becka was swearing aloud. Bryan heard her from the hallway and grinned. He hadn't thought that she would know those words.

He understood that something had happened with the eggs. Becka had wanted to make sunny-side-up eggs, but the eggs refused to cooperate with her.

The grin on his lips grew wider. Bryan didn't care if he ate scrambled eggs or sunny-side-up eggs or whatever. He cared that Becka had gone through all that trouble to make breakfast for him. He couldn't remember any woman who had made him breakfast.

Bryan entered the kitchen, and for a second there, the man couldn't hide his shock. The sight overwhelmed him. Luckily, Becka was facing the stove and mumbling, so she didn't hear him coming in.

The kitchen was in shambles. Bryan put a hand over his heart and vowed that he would never allow Becka to cook again. That meant that he would have to fix the meals well into his old age, but Bryan didn't want to risk Becka's well-being.

The woman had made complete and total chaos, and that under fifteen minutes. The pristine kitchen he had seen the night before looked as if a hurricane had passed through it and turned everything upside down. Now Bryan understood why Becka's kitchen had seemed immaculate. Seemingly, Becka didn't cook at all.

"May I help you, Becka?" he asked, and Becka shrieked and dropped on the floor the spatula she had in her hand. She had been so focused on what she was doing that he had scared the hell out of her. "I'm sorry, baby," he rushed to her. "I thought you heard me coming. I was whistling so...," he said, reaching down and taking the spatula from the floor and throwing it into the sink.

"Not a problem, Bryan. You just gave me a heart attack," she said with all the dramatic flair she could muster, pressing her little hand over her heart. "I was only finishing up breakfast. Coffee is already on the table. Go and pour yourself a cup, and I'll bring the rest, okay?"

Bryan nodded, but the moment Becka turned back to the stove, he shook his head. He couldn't believe that one person could do so much damage while cooking breakfast. It was unimaginable.

In her hurry to do everything, Becka had thrown the eggshells on the counter. They laid next to the bacon package and carton of eggs that she had also forgotten there. There were breadcrumbs everywhere.

Something was burning, and Bryan assumed that probably it was the toast. He was right. The fire alarm set off, and he rushed to open the kitchen door to the garden so that the smoke would dissipate sooner.

Then he went to the toaster in a hurry and took the bread out.

By then, Becka had begun to cry. She had tried her best, and she had failed. Becka knew that she couldn't cook worth a damn. But, Becka had believed that, at least once in her lifetime, she would be able to prepare breakfast without everything going awry or starting the fire alarm.

Breakfast was the only meal she was brave enough to try. Becka was afraid that if she tried something more complicated, her kitchen would go up in flames. However, that day, she had wanted to impress Bryan. Well, she impressed him, all right. That was sure. But then, it was not the impression that Becka had wanted to offer him.

Becka sobbed aloud now. Bryan would have wanted to soothe her, but he couldn't do that at that moment. There was no time for that. He had to take care of more pressing matters.

Bryan turned off the toaster and took the toast out and then hurried to the stove where the eggs were slowly turning into a black-reddish mass. He was sure that the shrill of the fire alarm would soon rouse all the neighbors.

With efficient and measured gestures, Bryan took the pan off the stove and threw it in the sink. A look at those eggs told him that he couldn't save them anymore.

Shaking his head, he returned to the stove and turned it off as well.

Bryan looked around and picked the eggshells abandoned on the counter and tossed them in the garbage. The man wiped his hands with a kitchen towel and returned the bacon in the fridge.

After a last survey of the kitchen, Bryan washed his hands, and then, finally, he went to Becka and slid an arm behind her. He gathered her to his chest and kissed the corner of her mouth gently.

"It's alright, baby. It's not the end of the world. Believe me. Come on, stop crying now, and let's eat the bacon and toast. I think they're okay. We'll have some coffee, and everything will be fine. If you're still hungry after we finish breakfast, we can go to Timmie's and have something to eat there, all right?"

"I wanted everything to be perfect," Becka wailed, and that made Bryan grin and kiss her once more.

"Everything's perfect, honey," Bryan reassured Becka and hugged her a little tighter.

"How can you say that?" Becka shouted. "The eggs were a failure from the beginning, and that stupid fire alarm wouldn't stop..."

"It's stopped now. Look, no shrilling sounds. The smoke is gone. Look, it's stopped," Bryan reassured her anew after the last beep of the alarm faded.

"I wanted to make something nice for you," she sobbed.

Becka didn't understand why she was so emotional and why she couldn't stop sobbing. Come to think of it, she had never cried like that before the last few days, and she had never been a mass of tangled emotions.

"Come on, stop crying, Becka," Bryan shook her gently. "You did. You did something nice for me. No one has ever bothered to make me a cup of coffee, at least, so you've done more than anyone else in my life. Please, now, stop crying. It's all right," he patted her back to reassure her.

Becka hiccupped a couple of times and allowed him to lead her to the table and help her sit down. Bryan poured coffee, and they started munching on the toast, which was thoroughly black, and on the bacon, which, happily, was only partially burnt.

Both tried to ignore the crunching sounds filling the kitchen. It was as if a battalion of mice was munching at the same time.

"I do appreciate your effort, sweetie, but from now on, I'll cook, okay?" Bryan told her in between two bites. "And I do want you to promise me that you won't ever try to cook again. I'm available if you want a homemade meal. Anytime, day or night, I'm here for you. Just don't try to cook again. I wouldn't want to hear that your kitchen went up in flames," he urged her, his mind filled with horrible scenarios.

Becka nodded, keeping her eyes down, but she didn't say a thing. She felt her failure deeply, and she couldn't look him in the eyes.

She had never cared about her inability to cook before, but now she was sorry that she didn't take her Aunt Marjorie up on her offer to teach her to cook.

Bryan nudged her head up and smiled at her. He leaned over and kissed her. Then he said, "You're a real treasure, baby. Believe me. You don't have to feel ashamed. I'm sure you can do things I can't, so everything levels just fine."

She nodded again but didn't reply. They continued to eat their breakfast in silence.

"Do you have any plans for today?" Bryan asked her.

"I haven't made any plans for days," Becka confessed, shaking her head. "I didn't feel like it."

"I'm sorry that I upset you so much," he apologized, but she waved his concerns away.

"It was my fault as well, so...," she shrugged without ending her sentence. "Anyway, tonight I'm forced to go to a family dinner. Would you like to come with me?"

Bryan suddenly felt a constriction in his throat. Going to a family dinner was a big thing. He couldn't say that it was too soon because he already knew how he felt about her, although they had known each other for so little time. The week and a half without Becka wasn't something he would like to remember or relive. Yet, meeting her family hadn't crossed his mind.

Bryan looked at Becka and saw the hope in her eyes. He felt like an ogre for wanting to say 'no'. So, he agreed to go with her.

Hearing his answer, Becka jumped off her chair and directly onto his lap, peppering his face with kisses and making him laugh. He was content that she was so happy with his decision.

CHAPTER NINE

BRYAN WAS SITTING IN his idle car in front of Becka's house. He had been sitting there for almost fifteen minutes already and still couldn't find his courage to get out and ring her doorbell to let her know that he had arrived.

He was wearing his dress pants and a white shirt, although he wasn't very sure that it was the right attire to meet her entire family. He had thought of wearing his best dress suit at first, but the evening was too hot, and he didn't think he could wear a coat. Besides, he absolutely hated wearing a tie. It always felt as if someone strangled him, and he already felt his throat was a little too tight. He didn't want to add more to his discomfort.

That evening represented a first for him. In none of his previous relationships, had he made it so far. Bryan had never met the parents of the women he had dated. Maybe he hadn't cared too much about the woman he was seeing, or he had never felt that it was the right moment. There had always been reasons, and he had invariably declined to show up at such gatherings.

However, this time, Bryan knew that he couldn't reconsider. He had to go to that dinner.

The man wanted Becka in his life. He was positive about that. However, Bryan knew that having a real relationship with her also meant that, unfortunately, he had to meet the pesky parents, as well. The family represented a crucial pylon in Becka's life from what he had gathered from her, and he couldn't treat that with indifference.

Any man would have worried if he had had to meet his lover's family for the first time. But Bryan also fretted because he had to go directly into a den of witches.

Witches had never crossed his mind before he witnessed what Becka could do. Bryan had always considered such things a hoax.

That day, at the lake, he had been forced to reconsider his beliefs. Nothing else would have explained what had happened.

Had it not been for the icy swirls of wind gushing around him, he would have gone with telekinesis, which seemed to border on being a somewhat more scientific fact. He would have possibly thought of hypnosis, which also appeared a more valid theory, but then, considering the circumstances, that didn't fit. They were in the middle of a fight, so Becka couldn't have hypnotized him no matter how good she might have been.

When nothing else worked, he had to go with what might have seemed unreasonable, yet the only possibility.

Becka had told him a little about each of her family members so he wouldn't feel he was plunging into the unknown with no information at all. Yet, that didn't assuage his worries.

The idea that someone could read his mind or could turn the entire meal into a bunch of frogs had the power to render him a little more skeptical about his wisdom to make that visit. A sane man wouldn't go into something like that if he hadn't been hit over the head with something first and then dragged into the lair.

But then, he couldn't have refused her invitation if he had wanted to continue seeing Becka and have her in his life, and he did.

Bryan glanced at the dashboard clock and saw that it was almost time to go and ring the bell. He had arrived earlier because he knew that he would need some more time to reconsider everything and make up his mind or, more precisely, to pretend to do that. He had already made his decision the day before when he came to convince Becka to give him a new chance.

With a deep sigh, he got out of his car. With resolute but resigned steps, not unlike the ones of the people on their way to the guillotine, he strode to Becka's door and rang the doorbell.

Bryan was positive that he would find her door unlocked, given what he knew about Becka. However, he didn't want to make her believe that he considered that he could come and go from her house at will.

The theme of Jaws made him grin again, and he felt more at ease with his choice than he had a few moments ago. Becka's quick steps echoed on the wooden floor of the hall, and Bryan pictured her racing to open the door for him. That image in his head made his heart grow a little.

He wasn't wrong. At the sound of the bell, Becka had rushed down the stairs and left her hair down. She had been trying to make up her mind about how to fix it for the last fifteen minutes. She knew that in the eyes of her family, it didn't matter how her hair looked, but she wanted to look perfect for Bryan.

Becka had thought that her feelings for him were strong before he came back to her the day before. But then, after spending that night and half a day with Bryan, her feelings had grown much stronger.

Becka was determined to make their relationship work. Without him, she had been miserable, and life had been bleak. She didn't want to go through all that again.

Becka opened the door, a little out of breath, and beamed at him. Bryan pulled her into his arms and kissed her soundly as if he hadn't seen her for days, even though only a few hours had passed since they said good-bye.

She wrapped her arms around his neck and let herself feel his passion. Bryan's kiss made her forget about the dinner with her family and everything else she might have had on her mind. She didn't even care that someone could see them from the street. It only mattered that she was in his arms, and he seemed to love and desire her enough.

Bryan couldn't let go of her. It took him a few long kisses before he was able to pull back. Only then, he returned her smile. Every fiber in his body was alert and screamed for her.

He didn't understand how come he had fallen so hard for Becka in such a short time. However, he was in love, head over heels, something that he had never experienced before.

Suddenly, a fantastic thought crossed his mind, and he frowned.

"What's the matter?" Becka asked, seeing his scowl, and concern shadowed her face.

Bryan watched her firmly and thought about how to express his question. Only after a few seconds of pondering over the matter, he found the courage to ask Becka about what baffled him.

"Don't take it wrong, Becka, okay. But I need to know something. Is what I feel for you the result of a spell or the real thing?"

Becka scowled at Bryan and pulled back from his arms with a gasp. Then she launched herself furiously forward and punched his chest as hard as she could with her fist.

"How can you ask me something like that? You...you...you're a jerk."

Becka punched Bryan again for good measure and tried to slam the door in his face, but his arm blocked her move.

"Becka, be reasonable, baby," Bryan pleaded.

"I'll show you reasonable, you...you...you...ass!" she yelled. Then she turned her back to him and stormed out of the hallway into the living room like a little fury.

The hallway closet opened with a loud thump behind Becka. All the coats from inside flew out and swirled to the floor in a rain of colors.

Bryan only shook his head with resignation and followed her inside, stepping carelessly over the clothes that lined the floor of the hallway.

This time, he was prepared for Becka's storm and didn't mind walking into the lion's den. Bryan imagined that he would be quite safe. Becka seemed to like him enough, and he believed that she wouldn't really try to hurt him.

He did hope he wasn't wrong since he didn't know what a witch could do. The thought that he should have researched the subject a little, to be more informed and prepared, crossed his mind, but it was too late to do anything about that.

Bryan found Becka at the window in the living room. She had tears in her eyes, and his heart ached to see her so desolate. He hated himself because he was the reason for her tears, yet again.

The day before, he had promised himself that he would do his best not to make her cry anymore, and not even a day later, he did it again.

"Sweetheart," he called out to Becka in a soft voice. "Come on, don't cry," Bryan said, putting a hand on her shoulder.

He tried to soothe her, although he didn't have too much experience with soothing. He would merely go away whenever a woman started crying. This time, he couldn't walk away.

Becka shook his hand off her shoulder and rubbed her fingers over her face to dry the tears away. Then, she turned to him and looked at him with sadness but with determination.

After looking at him for a few moments, Becka said, "You'd better go, Bryan. If this is what you think about me, then it's clear that there's no chance for us to be together, so we shouldn't waste our time anymore."

Bryan felt an icy wall rising between the two of them, and for the first time in his life, he felt scared. His mind scrambled to find a way to persuade Becka that they still deserved a chance to be together. But after he struggled with ideas one after another for a few moments, Bryan concluded that he would better go with the truth.

"All right, sweetie. Here's the deal," he said.

At his words, Becka looked up at him but kept quiet and allowed him to speak. She seriously considered putting Bryan to the ground if he had said anything hurtful again. At least, she could try.

"I want you too much, baby. Now I'm pretty sure that if I like you so much, it means that I love you. The feeling is too powerful to suggest something else. Now, please, consider that I've never been in love with anyone in my entire life. And I do mean never," Bryan emphasized his words with a sharp gesture. "And what I feel for you is happening so fast," he shook his head. "I had to ask myself if you might have had something to do with it. This thing here is not like me," Bryan pleaded for her to understand.

Becka began to narrow her eyes in anger. Bryan knew that it foretold a new storm, so he hastened with his explanation.

"However, it doesn't mean that I have any bad thoughts about you. Far from that! I just wanted to make sure that it was me who loved you. Without any external interference. Do you understand?"

Becka didn't reply at first. She just kept staring at him and weighing his words. She could understand why Bryan would interpret things like that. A man of Bryan's age, who had never been in love, would have to question the validity of his feelings, and more so, if everything happened too fast. She could understand that. However, it hurt that, even for a moment, Bryan thought that his feelings were the result of a spell.

After a few tense moments, Becka nodded to show him that she could see the validity of his argument.

Then she said, "I understand what you mean. Your reasoning is valid. That's true, Bryan. But it doesn't mean that your words don't hurt. It hurts like hell," she said with a sad headshake. "Listen to me, Bryan. I am a witch, but that doesn't automatically mean that I can do whatever I want. There are limitations and boundaries. You can't step over them because there are consequences. And besides that, who the heck would want to make someone fall in love with them, only to live with the knowledge that their love is not real? Tell me!" Becka asked Bryan and slapped his chest in anger.

Bryan pulled Becka into his arms, kissed the top of her head, and whispered to her, "I didn't mean to hurt you. I only wanted to be sure that it was me."

"All right, then," Becka said. "What now? Do you want to break up with me or what? Because I don't know how I can prove that I didn't cast a spell on you. I can yell it from the top of the roofs, but that doesn't prove a thing."

Bryan pushed her at arm's length and stared at her with disbelief.

"Are you serious? How would breaking up with you make it better? There's no doubt that I want to be with you. Where do you find these ideas?" he asked in a puzzled tone of voice.

Becka shrugged again, and Bryan grinned. He did find that habit of hers charming. She looked like a naughty schoolgirl, and for a moment, the thought that she was way too young for him popped into his mind, and he struggled to fight it back.

Bryan didn't want to think of anything that might have worked against their relationship. But then, in a way, he felt like a thief. He was stealing Becka's youth. Bryan thought to tell Becka that but changed his mind at once. Becka enjoyed drama and quite a lot, and he didn't want to use up all his resources to calm her down again. Bryan was sure that he would need those while he visited with her family.

It wasn't that he didn't appreciate her dramas. Becka had a flair for a good scene, and she looked very authentic. Now, that Bryan was thinking of that, he realized that Becka was the first woman whose drama he had ever enjoyed. Before, he used to walk out of the door if a woman became melodramatic with him, so his reaction to Becka's scenes was a distinct hint that he had fallen deeply, and Bryan knew that he shouldn't bother to analyze his feelings anymore.

Bryan's gaze swept over Becka, from the top of her head to her toes. He loved how she looked in her white dress. It hugged her curves and stopped at a palm over the knees, leaving the better part of her beautiful legs in plain sight.

He appreciated the fact that she dared to wear white. Most women dressed only in black or other dark colors merely to entertain the illusion that they looked thinner. The man admired Becka and found her originality refreshing. He liked that she felt well in her skin, and she was able to see herself as beautiful as he saw her.

"By the way, you look great, baby. Your family will be stunned to see you with me. I should have worn a tie or something. Your dress is elegant, and I look like a slob. I don't have any notion about fashion or choosing clothes," he shook his head in regret.

"Be serious, Bryan," she waved his concerns away. "You look just fine. It suits you, and I want you, not the replica of a playboy. Anyway, some of my cousins will be wearing jeans, if only to drive my great-grandma crazy. We all have a bone to pick with her, and this is their way of rebelling, you know," she grinned at him.

"But not you?" Bryan inquired.

"I have the same bone to pick with her. Don't worry," she nodded. "However, I found out that wearing jeans at the dinner table would upset my mom, as well, so..." she shrugged. "Anyway, you look great, and if Matt doesn't come in his business suit, you'll be one of the best-dressed men at the table, so you have nothing to worry about," Becka patted his arm reassuringly.

Bryan nodded and pushed her toward the hallway so that they could leave. When Becka saw all her fall and winter coats on the floor, she groaned. She hadn't realized what had happened when she stormed out earlier. Bryan just grinned at Becka and patted her shoulder to show her that it wasn't a problem for him.

"It's all right, Becka. At least now that I'm prepared to see things flying around, this isn't such a big shock to my system," Bryan told her with the same grin on his lips.

Becka narrowed her eyes again. She was trying to discern whether he was making fun of her or not but chose not to reply. She started picking up the clothes. Bryan helped her, and they finished in no time, so they could finally leave.

BECKA ADMIRED THE WAY Bryan drove. He was confident, but he wasn't aggressive. He didn't want to prove anything to anyone, and he didn't care if others tried to overtake his car.

"Did you tell your parents that you were bringing me to dinner?" Bryan asked, glancing at her and taking in her posture.

Becka looked like a Madonna. Dressed all in white, she had folded her hands neatly in her lap, and her face was serene.

She nodded, "I told them that I'd come with my boyfriend, but I didn't give them any details."

He glanced at her, surprised. In his book, women would give all the details, including the ones they shouldn't. That was something very new for him.

"Don't tell me that they didn't ask any questions," he showed his skepticism to her words.

Becka fidgeted in her seat for a few seconds but decided she'd better be open with him, so she replied, "Well, all right. It seems that you know already. Mom was quite happy to hear that I finally had a boyfriend because she didn't think I'd ever get one. You know that I had the bad habit of turning all the guys away. Anyway, I think that I was right. They were too dull or too annoying. Getting rid off them was the best choice for me. Anyway, she asked just a minimum of questions, and I gave her your name and a general description. That's all. Father wanted to know more, but I cut it short. He's overprotective, and he can drive me crazy. Plus, he would send my brother your way to make sure that everything was all right for his little girl, and that would be just too embarrassing."

Bryan chuckled, hearing her gloomy tone, and glanced at her again just in time to see her pout. Becka had her moments when she resembled a teenager, but he didn't mind that either, although until the moment he met her, he had never glanced at the teenagers that crossed his path.

"You wouldn't laugh if he sent Alex your way," Becka warned him. "Alex is a sweet brother, but he can be a pain in the butt all the same."

Bryan chuckled again. He had never imagined that his sweet Becka would use such words, and it was delightful to see that she could invariably surprise him. He wouldn't have enjoyed a relationship without surprises either.

ROWENA DAWN

CHAPTER TEN

BRYAN FELT STUPID WITH a big bouquet of roses in his hand, waiting in front of Becka's parents' house.

Becka had insisted that they could go inside, but he had declined her invitation. He told her to ring the bell as ordinary people would do when they went to visit someone.

Becka mimicked a sign to show him that she thought he was crazy, but seeing his steely determination, she gave in. The woman rang the bell and waited anxiously next to him for the door to open. She wondered what her mother would say seeing her in front of the door since she had never rung the doorbell. Normally, she would merely barge in.

Bryan had impressed Becka when he took a big bouquet of roses from the back seat of the car when they stopped in front of her parents' house. She wouldn't have believed that the tough guy would think of flowers.

Now Becka was amused because she noticed that Bryan was uncomfortable, standing there with those flowers in his hand. She had to admit that Bryan didn't look like a guy who would buy flowers. It was just not him. Suddenly, a thought crossed her mind, and Becka frowned. She turned to him.

"You never brought me flowers," she accused him morosely.

At her unexpected outburst, Bryan turned his eyes to her. He stared at her as if a horn had grown right on her forehead. Her outbreak had come out of nowhere.

For a moment, he didn't understand what had upset her, and then, when the meaning sank in, with a puzzled frown between his eyebrows, he replied, "First of all, our dates have been a bit unconventional, baby. Coming to take you out to sail or coming to apologize didn't seem to require flowers. Okay, maybe when I came to apologize," he stopped for a second, reconsidering what he was saying.

Bryan suddenly realized that exactly when he came to apologize, he should have brought her flowers, but that thought had never crossed his mind.

To cover his blunder, he continued in force, "Second, what flowers could I bring you when you have that garden? How could I compete with that?"

"It's not about competing, Bryan," she dismissed his excuse with a flutter of her hand. "Look at you. You bought flowers for my mother. My mother has a garden as well, so...the question remains. Why wouldn't you buy flowers for me?" Becka asked, showing that stubborn streak of hers, although she was aware that she had chosen a man who could show romance in other ways but wouldn't bring flowers. It was just not his type, and that was just her luck.

Bryan shook his head as if he needed to clear his mind, and then he decided to answer. Exactly when he opened his mouth to reply, the door opened and a beautiful woman, in her fifties, smiled at them both, saving him from an answer that might have upset Becka even more.

He glanced at the woman framed in the door and noticed that Becka was almost the replica of her mother. Bryan smiled and thought that Becka would look great in her advanced age, considering her heritage.

"Oh, sweetheart, you're finally here," the woman cooed and hugged Becka, kissing both her cheeks after the European fashion.

She squeezed the young woman a little more, and then, she finally turned to Bryan with sparkling eyes.

"Who do we have here, dear?" she asked.

Hearing her talk, Bryan was happy that Becka hadn't inherited her mother's voice, too. The woman had one of those voices he couldn't stand. It reminded him of his mother's constant whining and recriminations. Yet, Bryan continued to smile since he couldn't do otherwise. He knew that he couldn't wince. He had to keep that phony smile on his lips, although it required a real effort. Yet, wincing wouldn't have marked a quite good beginning for his visit, and it might have had long-term unfortunate consequences.

He stretched his hand and said, "I'm Bryan, madam."

He shook her hand briefly and offered her the flowers, which were still a reason for discontent for Becka. He made a mental note to buy Becka some flowers, and as soon as possible.

Women loved flowers, Bryan remembered. They associated romance with them, although he didn't understand why. He believed in showing what he felt through what he did. Bringing flowers didn't come too high on his list.

Becka's mother, Emily, smiled at him in turn and invited both inside the house, talking steadily and making Bryan feel uncomfortable. Bryan was there for Becka, though. He was determined to make every effort not to upset Becka or embarrass her in front of her family. If he had to listen to that woman's talking all evening, he would do that.

Becka's parents lived in a real mansion, given the size of the building. Bryan had thought that his house was big enough, but compared to what he had under his eyes, it was almost nothing. From outside, it looked quite impressive and somehow intimidating, but the inside of the house seemed much more imposing.

The size of the entrance hall was on the generous side. Bryan looked around and then glanced at the floor in awe. Tiles with an intricate floral motive covered the entire ground.

Stunned, Bryan noticed that a beautiful table lined the wall on the left, and he appreciated that it came from some time in the 18th century. He wouldn't have chosen that piece of furniture for the entrance hall, and he was sure that that table had a place in a museum.

That hallway led to a circular room. There, the same tiles spread throughout the floor, but the motive was geometrical this time. The room seemed a different hallway and that perplexed Bryan. He couldn't understand the necessity of having two of them.

Once inside the circular room, several voices reached Bryan's ears. They came from somewhere on the left. The voices mingled in chatter, and he couldn't make out any words. It was just a cacophony of gibberish.

Now that he saw her parents' house, Bryan was positive Becka had never had any shrewd intentions on his wealth, and her anger at the lake made more sense to him. His accusation must have come like a blow. He imagined she had felt hurt and insulted at the same time, and she had had all the right to feel that way.

He wasn't sure if he could compare what he possessed with her family's wealth. That was by far the house of a rather wealthy family, and he wondered why his Becka lived in that small house in town when her parents were living the way they did. It wasn't like they hadn't loved their daughter from what Bryan had observed so far.

Bryan wasn't disappointed, though, since he liked to think that Becka was as unspoiled and real as she seemed. She wasn't demanding and didn't ask for expensive clubs or restaurants, and she had even enjoyed his cooking, which, in his opinion, was nothing someone could find in the restaurants en vogue.

Emily led them to the living room, which was at least ten times larger than Becka's. It was a vast space covered by several Aubusson carpets, but it still seemed to have difficulty containing all the people inside.

Bryan had the feeling that he had walked into the middle of a big party. He had thought that he would come only for a family dinner, though.

Looking around, he noticed some of the faces he had seen in the pictures displayed in Becka's bedroom the night before.

Becka sensed that Bryan was uncomfortable and took his hand. She gave it a little squeeze to encourage him. The man glanced at her, and she could read the questions in his eyes. Her fingers flexed over his again to let him know that everything would be all right. She was wrong, though.

"I told you that I have a big family, Bryan. At least, you can meet them all at once, and you get over it. I see that everybody is here," Becka smiled at him, and as always, her smile had the power to make him relax.

A middle-aged man, almost of the same height as Bryan, came to them with supple steps and hugged Becka.

"How are you, sweetheart? We haven't heard much from you for the last two weeks, I think?" he gently phrased his reproach.

"Oh, daddy, I'm fine. And I've talked to you, how can you say I haven't?" she replied, and her voice showed her love for the man.

"I've said 'not too much,' Becka. I haven't said that you didn't talk to us at all," he corrected her gently and then turned his eyes to Bryan.

Bryan noticed the older man's dislike instantly. It wasn't difficult to spot it as it was there in his eyes for everyone to see. However, Bryan didn't want to let anything ruin Becka's day, so he tried hard not to show any expression on his face. Becka was a smart woman, and she would have seen at once that something was amiss.

"So, who do we have here?" Gabriel asked in a grave tone of voice.

"Daddy, this is my boyfriend, Bryan," Becka chimed in, her happiness evident in her voice.

Bryan shook the older man's hand and lowered his head respectfully. He didn't know what to say to him, and he didn't want to get into an argument if it was possible to avoid it.

However, Bryan was as wrong as Becka. No matter what he wanted, things had a way of evolving without asking for his opinion.

More people came around them, and he began to feel crowded. Although everyone was kind to Becka, almost all of them were throwing him dirty looks as if he had come out right from the sewer. They seemed not to like her choice in boyfriends at all.

Bryan told himself he didn't care and that, in the end, they would have to accept his presence in Becka's life. He didn't intend to let them chase him away.

Gabriel, Becka's father, decided that he would be the first to begin the attack against him.

"So, what do you think you're doing with my little girl?"

"Daddy!" Becka gasped. Her father's outburst stunned her, and she turned to him with widened eyes. Her little arched mouth opened in a perfect 'o'.

"I beg your pardon?" Bryan inquired with a crisp voice, although the question had angered him. He had a pretty good idea that he wasn't part of their social class, but that didn't mean that he was nothing.

"You heard me very well, young man," Gabriel repeated. "What do you think you're doing with my girl? First of all, you're far too old for a girl like her," her father reiterated his bad feelings towards Bryan.

"Father, I think I can choose anyone I want," Becka started in a quarrelsome tone, but she couldn't go too far because she was interrupted immediately.

"Yes, sweetheart, you can, but choose someone of your age," her father replied conciliatorily.

"And maybe not a felon if that's possible, Becka. Look at his scar," Ariel chose to interfere, turning her nose up at the scar lining Bryan's cheek.

By now, Bryan's face looked chiseled into stone. He had thought about this meeting, and he had known that those would be their concerns, but now that everything was real, there, he felt chilled to the bone.

The man didn't like how things were going because it seemed his relationship with Becka was on the line.

He chose not to reply to Becka's sister, but he judged her in a second. She was one of those uptight women who had the misfortune to have had a bad hand dealt in life and took it out on everyone else.

"Becka knows what she's doing," her cousin, Jay, jumped into the melee and gained Bryan's gratitude. "You all know that she's the smartest of us when it comes to people. And I wouldn't talk if I were you," he turned to Ariel.

Bryan liked that man. He was on his side, and although he knew that Jay was a gambler, that thing didn't matter at all, right then. It was important that he took Becka's side and tried to cut Ariel down a notch.

"How dare you?" Ariel started shouting. "How dare you to say something like that to me? She's my sister, and I have to look out for her."

"Yes," Alex got involved in the general discussion.

Bryan knew that Alex was Becka's brother because she had shown him the man's picture the night before.

"You should leave Ariel alone, Jay. And, you, Becka, you should think a little better about the kind of people you get involved with."

"I should? I should think a little better?" Becka's voice increased in intensity. "How dare you talk about Bryan like that, you, moron? He's ten times better than you."

By now she was shouting, and Bryan noticed that a few knick-knacks took off and swirled to the floor, followed by a few pillows off a sofa. However, nobody cared. Probably, such scenes were usual occurrence around there.

"Becka, baby," Bryan touched her arm and tried to soothe her, but she wouldn't have it.

Becka turned to the mob. With her hands fisted on her hips, she said, "Bryan is my boyfriend, and I stress this thing. He is my boyfriend. Heed my words. You'll start treating him well, the way he deserves it, and you welcome him into our family, or I'm out of here."

Jay intervened immediately. "Don't worry, Becka. I have your back. I support you all the way. Hey, man," Jay said and stretched his hand to Bryan. "I hope you're fine. You can be sure that this is a crazy bunch. You shouldn't pay any attention to them. Everything will be just fine. Becka knows what she's doing," he repeated his earlier comment, tapping Bryan's shoulder.

Bryan shook his hand, smiling. Besides Emily, who might have only been playing the role of a good hostess, Jay's was the first friendly face he had seen in that room.

Bryan's joy was brief, though. A pretty old woman with the whitest hair he had ever seen marched to them with long strides. Everyone made way for her. She seemed to be a rather prominent part of the family, and everyone bowed to her. Bryan noticed and admired her stance. She might have been of advanced age, but she walked like a general. The marks on her face proved that she had known adversity in her life. She didn't look like a pleasant woman, but she was indeed impressive for an aged lady.

"So you're the fortune hunter, I see," the woman said in a loud voice and pierced Bryan with her hard eyes.

For a moment, silence prevailed in the room. Most of the people had thought of that. However, no one had dared to bring the subject up into the open up to that moment. They looked at each other in shock. But aside from a few raised brows and open mouths, no one moved or said anything.

Becka and Bryan stared at the woman with puzzled eyes, and then looked at each other. The others didn't get the irony, but the two of them did. Both of them burst into laughter, and Becka tumbled in his arms, laughing like a lunatic.

Everyone was staring at them, thinking that they had gone mad. No one understood what was so humorous in accusing someone of being a gold digger.

Becka pulled back a little and looked up at Bryan. She asked him through roars of laughter, "How does it feel to be at the other end of the stick?"

Bryan chuckled again and kissed her mouth soundly, which drew a few gasps from the crowd around. Bryan concluded that his behavior was not considered acceptable in that house. However, Becka and Bryan didn't care.

All the tension Bryan had felt before was gone now. Becka could have that effect on him. He wrapped an arm around her shoulders, and the two of them faced the audience.

"Well, ma'am," Bryan said politely, watching the old woman steadily and bowing his head for a second in a belated sign of respect. "Here I am. Not a fortune hunter, but I'm still here, and I intend to stay. Not necessarily in this house," he thought to specify so that no one misunderstood him. "But on Becka's side."

The old woman narrowed her eyes dangerously at him and said in a crisp tone of voice, "I don't like him, Becka. Throw him back into the pond."

Becka stared at her great-grandma in shock and shook her head. She had expected some opposition from her family, but she hadn't expected to hear things like that. Any sense of decency had disappeared, and everyone was attacking Bryan as if he were a lowlife.

"He's not a fish that I should toss back into the pond, and he's not an object," Becka said in a steely voice that Bryan had never heard before.

He thought that now he could see another side of Becka, and that one fascinated him as much as the others.

"He's a human being, grandma. He's a man, and he is mine, regardless if you like him or not. You don't decide for me. I love him, and he loves me, and that's it. Case closed," Becka declared with determination, waving her hand and tapping her right foot for good measure.

A young man, close in age to Bryan, came forward and stretched his hand to him, "Welcome to the tribe, man, even if it's a loonie bin. I'm Matt. I think that Becka chose well," he said in a sober tone of voice.

Bryan shook the man's hand. The sincerity in Matt's voice impressed him. Finally, there was another one who welcomed him among them without taking shots at him first.

"Thank you, Matt," he said. "It's a pleasure to meet you. I can assure you of that," Bryan said, smiling widely at him.

"Nonsense," the old bat retorted and took a step forward. "Put an end to this ridiculous relationship right now, Becka. He is not a man with whom you should associate. If you do need someone, we'll find you a civilized young man from a respectable family."

The woman's voice carried far in the room. She was a woman that expressed her opinions loudly, and usually, everyone listened to her. Not this time, though.

Becka took Bryan's hand and said, "We're leaving, Bryan. If my family doesn't understand to accept you, then we'll go, and that's it. I won't come to the next dinners, mother. I hope you understand," she said to her mother over her shoulder, heading to the door and pulling Bryan after her.

Becka's words shocked Emily. She cried out and covered her mouth with a shaky hand. She knew her Becka and her stubbornness. When she decided something, then nothing could make her change her mind. However, Emily didn't want to lose her youngest child.

"Becka, please," she pleaded, but Becka didn't give any sign that she had heard her mother's plea and continued her way to the door.

"If you leave this house with him now, I'll have the fund trust changed on Monday morning. You will get nothing," her great-grandma said in a flat tone of voice. "He'll leave you then because there'll be no money to feast on, but it would be too late for you to get your money back because I won't change my decision."

Everyone froze. No one had ever thought Rebecca could do such a thing. She hadn't threatened Matt when he came with Velma or Jay when he tried to pull one over her. They knew that when she decided something, she didn't revisit her decision.

Becka stopped and turned back to her great-grandmother, pulling Bryan in her wake. He could feel that Becka shook with rage, and he was sure that everything would start flying around in a moment.

Becka stopped before Rebecca, and in a clipped tone of voice, she replied, "I don't need your trust money. They come with strings attached. I don't like those strings. You can take the money and do whatever you want with it."

"Hmm," the old bat replied, gazing at Becka sharply. "And how would you live? And what about this one?" she pointed to Bryan. "Do you think that he'll still stay with you once you're penniless?" she said, turning her scornful eyes to Bryan.

"First of all, dear great-grandma," said Becka in a falsely sweet voice, "people work nowadays, and they earn the money they need. Few require a trust fund to pay for their daily expenses. I'm young, and I can work. And if you're willing, the two of us can make a bet that Bryan won't leave me," she ended triumphantly, and Bryan loved her even more at that moment.

"You think so, girl? Go ahead then. Leave the house. Let's see who'll pay for your school, and your house, and clothes and food. Do you think that he'll keep you?" Rebecca tilted her head to Bryan with disdain.

"As a matter of fact, yes," he intervened in their argument for the first time in a confident and matter-of-fact tone of voice. "I can take care of Becka's expenses with the school and house. She deserves it. Actually, Becka merits much more than that. I mean to see that she receives everything she wants," Bryan concluded.

Marjory came forward and spoke for the first time. "Grandma, you've done a lot of things to all of us along the years, and no one has ever said anything. I think it's time you thought of others as well. It's not always about what you want and the way you think that things should be. I must tell you that you're not always right. Becka is a smart girl. She may be smarter than many in this group," she said. Marjorie looked around at the people surrounding them. Then she continued, "She found someone she loves, and it's clear to me that he loves her, too. I think you'd better let them be."

While Marjorie was talking, Gabriel glanced at his wife and noticed that she was desolate at the thought of losing her daughter. He didn't feel too comfortable with that, either. Becka was the apple of his eye, and he hadn't taken into consideration that he would lose her because of his stubbornness.

He still believed that Bryan was a little too old for Becka, and he was concerned about his scar. That scar might have been an accident. He couldn't know for sure. However, it might have been the outcome of a life outside the law, and that worried Gabriel a lot.

"Son," he said to Bryan, "I see that my daughter is determined to be with you, and I know very well that I can't do a damn thing about it. She must live her life as she wishes and probably make her own mistakes. However, I don't want to lose my youngest child, so I think that I'll have to welcome you into my home," he said and extended his hand to shake Bryan's.

Bryan shook Gabriel's hand. He understood it was hard for Becka's father to accept him. In a way, Bryan admired the man that he was able to put his daughter first and push his feelings aside.

However, Bryan wasn't naïve, and he didn't believe the man took a liking at him all of a sudden. He knew that he would always be a reason for discord in their family.

Emily was so happy that her husband had decided not to shun their daughter that she started crying in earnest now. She went and hugged Becka as if she had returned from a very long trip, and she had been away for years. After she cried over Becka for a few moments, she also went and hugged Bryan, shocking him effectively with the expression of affection coming from her.

However, not everyone was happy. Bryan could hear murmurs around them and see a few unfriendly faces. The old bitty, Rebecca, was watching everything with an evil eye.

The most unfriendly face, beside Rebecca's, was Ariel's. She didn't like how the story was evolving, and she decided it was high time she had done something about it.

"Father, you can't accept that. Becka's a child and has no idea what she's doing. You have to make her see that she is wrong."

"And I say that she does know what she's doing," Matt intervened.

"Could you let your bitterness and jealousy aside for a moment, Ariel, and be happy for her? It's obvious that she loves him, and we shouldn't trifle with love," Matt scolded Ariel.

"You can't know that she loves him," she retorted. "Your talent is not developed, Matt. You can't be positive about Becka's feelings. And if you tell me that you do, then you're lying," she shouted, pointing her finger to him.

"I don't know what she feels because I've read her mind," Matt replied in a calm tone of voice. "I haven't even tried to read her thoughts. But it's obvious. Doesn't anyone else see it?" he turned around, and his eyes swept over the others. He couldn't believe that everyone was blind.

"What do you mean?" Adam, his grandfather, asked. "If you haven't read her mind, then you can't be sure that she truly loves him. No one can. She might only want to rebel against the family, which is perfectly normal at her age," he added, shaking his head.

"She was angry just now," Matt pointed out. "You could see her shake with rage. Has any of you seen anything flying around? Have you?" he repeated more strongly, glancing at each of them.

Everyone was surprised, including Becka. She hadn't even realized that nothing happened, although she had been pretty furious. She had controlled her gift unconsciously.

Thrilled that she had been able to restrain her powers, Becka jumped up, pumped her hand in the air, and yelled, "Yay me." Then she hugged Bryan. Seeing her so happy, he chuckled, although he didn't understand the reason for her happiness or what Matt wanted to say.

"I did it, Bryan, I did it!" Becka exclaimed in a cheerful tone of voice.

"Yes, baby, you did. You rock," he replied, still laughing. He lifted her and swirled around with her, kissing her soundly.

The others were watching them, unable to believe their eyes. Some of the people from the younger generation were jealous that little Becka had been the first one to beat the odds and get control over her powers. However, Jay and Matt were happy for her and only watched the couple with broad smiles on their faces.

Once Bryan finally put Becka down, Matt hugged her, "You did it, little girl. More power to you," he said, kissing her cheek loudly.

Marjorie hugged Becka and turned to her grandmother, "Becka did her part. Now, you have to do yours. You have to give her the trust money. That's the right thing to do."

Rebecca smirked at her granddaughter and replied, "In your dreams! Becka might love him. She might have committed to him, but he definitely doesn't love her. We'll have a meeting with the trustees, and they will see what's what."

A few loud expressions of approval came from the others, who didn't like to be left behind by the youngest of the bunch.

Becka turned to Rebecca and told her, "I was serious when I said that I didn't need your money. So, the meeting with the trustees is unnecessary."

"Hmm, I see that you're afraid of what the trustees are going to say. They'll observe at once that this man doesn't love you, and you can't face the truth," Rebecca chuckled, satisfied to have been vindicated.

"No, it's not that. I'm not afraid because I know the truth, and I don't need anyone's confirmation. I don't see the point in having Bryan paraded in front of them only to satisfy your sadistic pleasures," Becka replied.

"Baloney," Alex intervened with sarcasm. "If you don't want to meet with the trustees, it means that you know that Bryan doesn't love you, and you're afraid of what you'll hear."

"All right, all of you just calm down," Bryan intervened in a stern tone of voice. He had noticed that Becka was getting angrier, and he thought that he had listened enough to their drivel for one evening. Bryan wanted only to end their absurd discussion. "What are they talking about, sweetie?" he asked Becka.

"Bryan, it doesn't really matter because I won't take her money," the woman answered with stubbornness.

"You don't need her money, Becka, and if you don't want it, then you won't take it. That's not an issue. But there's more to this thing than that, Becka. So, what is it?"

Becka looked down and didn't want to answer his question. In fact, she didn't know what to do. It wasn't that she didn't trust Bryan's feelings. Becka didn't believe that the two trustees would tell her that Bryan didn't love her. However, Becka worried that if Bryan discovered the purpose of the meeting with the trustees, he would get upset, thinking that she didn't believe in him.

"I'll tell him, sweetie," Matt put a soothing hand on Becka's arm. "So that you understand better, Bryan, our great-grandma here," he said, pointing to Rebecca, "thought that it would be clever to get her vengeance on her philandering husband by putting a curse on the next generations."

Rebecca gasped, hearing Matt's disrespectful tone. "I thought you loved me," she accused him.

Matt waved her concerns away. "I love you. That's not the issue here. That doesn't mean, though, that I'm not upset for being your Guinea pig, great-grandma," he told her and then turned to Bryan. "Anyway, Bryan, this is how things are. None of us can refine and control their powers until we fall in love for real, and we commit to the person we love. Now, let me explain to you what's with the trust money. We can access it only if the person we love also loves us in return and commits to us. And that's determined by a pair of trustees, who are mind readers," Matt finished his explanation.

"Oh, I see," Bryan said, nodding. "So, those trustees would be able to see if I also loved and committed to Becka. That's the bone of contention here," Bryan concluded and then turned to Becka. "I understand that you don't want her money, and I support your decision, Becka. I don't want it, either. Is this the only reason you don't want to see the trustees, though?" he inquired, staring at her intently.

"Well, not really... I don't know how you'd feel to have someone read your mind," she admitted.

"So, it's not because you don't trust my love," Bryan looked for a clear answer, staring into Becka's eyes steadily.

"Of course not," she snapped at him.

"All right, then," Bryan said and then turned to Matt. "This mind-reading thing, are there any consequences to that?"

"Consequences?" Matt asked, confused.

"Yes, you know, like you could lose some of your mental capabilities, or you might be persuaded to do something you don't want to...," Bryan explained.

"Oh, that," Matt dismissed his concerns with a wave of his hand. "No, there's nothing like that. Don't worry. The only downside to it is that the mind readers can see what you think."

"Well, if they're not concerned that I might swear at them, I don't mind," he said and then turned to Becka. "Sweetie, I know that you don't want the money, and I strongly advise you not to accept it. I have enough for both of us, and we won't starve or have to cut down on too many things. However, if this will bring peace of mind to your parents, I'm willing to do it, all right?"

Everyone stared at him with disbelief. For a few moments, no one was able to do or say anything.

Only Becka hugged him and whispered, "For them, it would be great. But you don't have to do it if you don't want to. I trust you, and that's what's most important."

"I know, baby," he whispered back. "But if we can make them feel at ease, why not?"

Becka nodded and hugged him with more force. She couldn't believe that he would do something like that for her, and she loved him even more for his thoughtfulness.

"Do you think that you can fool them?" Ariel asked Bryan with contempt. "Jay tried that, and it didn't work. So you won't succeed, either," she told him.

For a moment, Bryan looked at Ariel as if she lost her mind. But then, his gaze only swept over her. The message was clear. She didn't matter. That annoyed Ariel even more, and she left the room in a huff.

"Why don't we invite the trustees here now?" Rebecca asked Bryan sweetly. "There's no better time than the present. They're two of my dearest friends, and they won't refuse me. I don't want to wait until Monday only to hear that something happened, and you couldn't make it to the meeting," she said to Bryan.

"That's just fine with me," he replied to her. "Invite them over. Maybe we can have a drink while we wait," he said to Emily. "My throat is a little dry after so much talking." Bryan didn't doubt that Emily viewed his behavior as tawdry. However, he really craved a strong drink and didn't care about Emily's opinion of him at that moment.

"I'll bring you a glass of scotch," Matt said. "I'll take one for me, as well. I do need one after all this ruckus," he continued and left for the table covered with several bottles.

Becka took Bryan's hand and pulled him to a love seat. She didn't intend to let anyone come close to him after they had behaved so horribly with him. They sat down, and Bryan stroked her arm to soothe her.

"It'll be over soon, love, and then we can go home," he said.

"Where's home, Bryan?" she asked him with wide eyes.

He took a moment to think, but there wasn't much to mull over. Bryan knew that he needed Becka with him all the time, and even though their relationship was so young, he didn't need time to see where it was going. He didn't intend to let Becka go anyway.

"It's up to you," Bryan answered. "I know what I want, and that's being with you. Now, if you want to wait and see how things will be between us, we can wait for a while and see each other every day. However, if you feel the same as I do, then we can choose to live together. We can stay either at your house or mine. Of course, my house is there on that island. That means that we have to sail to town every day if you need to go into town."

Becka squeezed his hand and replied, "I'd say that wherever you want is fine with me, but that would be a lie."

Bryan froze, hearing her answer. He couldn't believe his ears. He had never expected Becka to crush his hopes.

"I knew that you wouldn't continue with this charade, Becka," Ariel said with glee.

Becka and Bryan had been so focused on each other that they hadn't noticed that Ariel, sneaked upon them. At the sound of her voice, they looked up at her. Ariel watched Bryan with triumph in her eyes, and her face shined with delight.

"What's going on?" Matt asked, returning with the drinks.

"Not much," Bryan muttered. "I'll probably have to go now," he said and tried to rise, but Becka pulled him back on the seat next to her.

"What do you mean? Why would you leave?" Becka asked Bryan, and he noticed the pain in her eyes.

"You said that..." Bryan started to say, but Becka interrupted him.

"I said that I preferred to stay in town. You know that I don't like waking up early in the morning. Coming from your island to the town in the morning would be awful. Of course, we can spend our weekends there. It is a wonderful place, Bryan, but I don't see myself living there permanently. That's what I said."

"No, it isn't," Ariel snapped. "You were very clear that you didn't want to live with him," she pointed out.

"No, I wasn't. I might not have phrased my thoughts with enough clarity, but I meant that I wanted to live in town. So you can stop being so delighted," Becka snapped back at her.

Ariel put her hands on her hips and repeated stubbornly, "No, Becka. You said that..."

"Shut up for a second," Bryan barked at Ariel, and the fierceness in his voice disconcerted Ariel. The woman couldn't continue speaking.

Bryan took advantage of Ariel's surprise and turned to Becka. "Becka, let's clear things here. Do you want me to stay with you at your house?"

"Yes, of course. That's what I want, and you said that I could choose," Becka replied in a stubborn tone of voice.

"Yes, you can choose. That's not the issue here. As long as you don't ask me to leave from your life, I'll agree to anything," Bryan said, taking her hand with tenderness.

The icy block that had begun to form inside him started to melt. Bryan was relieved that he hadn't been wrong about Becka.

Becka hugged Bryan. Kissing his lips, she whispered, "Don't be silly. Why would I want you to leave when I can't function without you?"

Happy, Bryan hugged her tight and kissed her hair in relief. He didn't notice that Ariel left in a huff, and he didn't actually care about what she was doing. After holding Becka tightly to him for a while, he let her go with regret and took the glass from Matt's hand.

"You don't know how much I need this now, man," he said to Matt.

"I can imagine," Matt murmured. "You do look like a man in need of something strong, indeed."

Bryan raised his glass and swallowed half of the whiskey at once, and he felt less tense afterward. He tapped Matt's shoulder and said, "Thanks, man. Good stuff, by the way."

"Yes, Uncle Gabriel always has good stuff handy. He's the most generous of the uncles," Matt said, elbowing Bryan. "Keep that in mind. If you go to visit Uncle Michael, you're out of luck. He doesn't put out the good stuff for guests. That's only for him."

Bryan laughed and felt included in the inside stuff. Matt was indeed the good man that Becka had described to him. Bryan thought that Matt would also make a good friend, besides being one of his few allies in that house.

Bryan chattered with Matt for a while. Most of the time, Becka remained next to him, hanging on his arm. However, some of the time, Becka took off to talk to her cousins or aunts.

Tall and fit, Bryan looked quite impressive. Still, he was looking around as if he were lost, trying to find Becka in the sea of people crowding his aunt's living room, and that amused Matt a lot.

The arrival of the two trustees didn't surprise anyone. All of them knew Rebecca's reputation, and they expected nothing else. The chatter stopped when the mind-readers entered the living room, and the family members glanced from Becka and Bryan to the trustees. All of them were impatient to hear the verdict.

Bryan started to sweat. A thought had crossed his mind a few seconds earlier and was still nudging at him. He had wondered if the old bitty had the trustees in her pocket because, in that case, they would say what she wanted to hear. Bryan was sure that Becka would believe them. They were witches, after all, and they could read minds. His word against theirs might mean close to nothing.

Gabriel came with the two trustees and introduced them to Bryan. "This is Mr. Thompson, and this is Mr. Jones."

Bryan shook their hands and expected to see what they had to say. Becka had come next to Bryan and slipped her arm around him as if she wanted to comfort him. Bryan wrapped his arm around her shoulders, as well, and looked inquiringly at the two older men.

No one was talking anymore. Bryan glanced around and saw different expectations on everybody's faces. Only Rebecca's face was expressionless, although her hard eyes tried to intimidate Bryan.

Bryan shrugged and turned to the two men to see what they wanted from him. Once his attention was on them again, he felt a light probing inside his mind and frowned.

"He can feel it," Mr. Jones whispered to Mr. Thompson. "Did you see?"

"Yes, I see he can," Mr. Thompson replied. "Well," he said, turning to Rebecca, "You know that I don't lie, Rebecca. I understand what you want me to say, but the truth is that Bryan does love Becka, and he's committed to this relationship."

Mr. Jones approved his friend's words with a nod, and Rebecca frowned. Everyone in the room waited to see what Rebecca would say. They didn't have to wait for too long.

"Very well, Becka and Bryan," she said. "If this is the case, then you have my congratulations. I won't lie and say that I like you," she said to Bryan squarely. "However, I'll welcome you to the family for as long as you're faithful to Becka."

Bryan nodded. He understood her feelings, even though he didn't agree with her. He imagined that it wasn't so easy to accept the fact that a man like him would date a young woman like Becka.

"On Monday morning, come to my office, and I will make the transfer of your funds," Mr. Thompson said to Becka.

Bryan intervened right away, remembering her stubborn refusal of the money. "Do you want that money, Becka? Because I do have enough for both of us."

Becka took a moment to think. Finally, she shook her head, "No, I don't. I didn't like what happened here tonight because of that trust fund, and I don't want to have anything to do with it."

"Oh, my God! Are you stupid?" Ariel shouted. "How can you reject so much money? Didn't you want to open that silly shop?"

"Calm down," Matt admonished her. "Becka, I understand your feelings in this matter, but the money is yours, and you should take it."

Becka shook her head, and Bryan gathered her to him.

"If Becka wants a shop, I'll take care of that," he said. "I think we can skip dinner tonight, Becka. What do you think?"

She nodded and said, "Mom, Dad, we're leaving now, and we'll talk later, all right?"

Emily teared up again and hugged her daughter. She was happy that Becka had found her true love, but she was also sad that her little daughter wasn't so little anymore. She hugged Bryan, as well, for good measure, and he hugged her back with stoicism, although he wasn't used to such gestures.

EPILOGUE

ELEVEN MONTHS LATER

"GABRIEL, YOU HAVE TO come now. Now, I said," Bryan yelled into the phone.

"What the heck happened to you that you're in such a state?" Gabriel's voice boomed at the other end of the line.

"She's mad. That's what happened. Becka's lost her mind," Bryan shouted again.

"What do you mean? What's going on there?" Gabriel snapped at Bryan, worried for his little daughter.

"Becka lied to me. Do you hear me? She lied, and now, I don't know what to do," Bryan replied in a near shout.

"Okay, calm down, son, and tell me what the problem is. What could Becka have done to make you lose your calm like this?"

"She's giving birth now!" Bryan answered.

"What do you mean now?" his father-in-law asked, scared witless.

"Becka hasn't said anything about being in labor all day, and now she's telling me that she's ready to give birth. I asked her to go to the hospital, and she said that it wasn't time and that she planned it that way. Becka told me to call Marjorie, but no one's answering the phone at their place, and I don't know what to do. I've never assisted in a birth. I haven't even watched a birth in a movie. Damn it! I've always walked away when there was a scene with something like that. What the hell am I going to do?" Bryan lost his calm completely.

"Okay, okay, let's see. Calm down first! Marjorie is here. We'll come at once. I'll have her call you from the car so that she can assist you by phone if...if... You know," Gabriel ended in a weak voice.

"No, I don't know. I don't want to know. It's Becka we're talking about, and I don't know anything."

A few murmurs came to him through the phone line, and Bryan understood that Gabriel was talking to someone.

"All right, Bryan. Marjorie said that you have to calm down. She'll call you from the car."

"But..."

"No buts, man. Just wait," Gabriel replied and hung up on him.

Bryan couldn't hear anything, but the background static on the line.

"A GIRL AND A BOY, BRYAN," Marjorie said. "Congrats to both of you. And you've done a good job helping Becka to bring the boy into the world. Have you thought of any names yet?"

Becka nodded exhausted, and Bryan stroked her forehead lovingly. He turned to Marjorie and told her with pride, "He's Sean, and our daughter is Lea." He looked at his wife again with love and kissed her, "You have to rest, baby."

She nodded and closed her eyes. The little ones were sleeping soundly, as well, but Bryan felt like he had climbed Everest.

MATT'S DILEMMA

BOOK 2

To Simona and Andrei

THE WINSTONS FAMILY

REBECCA'S CHILDREN

    Adam (m. Anna)

    Evelyne (deceased)

    Adam's children

    Marjorie (Twin, m. Jonathan) – children: Matt (34), Maggie (28), Jay (28)

    Michael (Twin, m. Amelie) – children: Josh (26), Lily (26)

    Gabriel (m. Emilie) – children: Ariel (32), Alex (32), Becka (19; m. Bryan; twins: Lea and Sean)

CHAPTER ONE

"BECKA, MOVE YOUR BUTT upstairs now," Bryan's voice boomed and made Matt smile.

Matt knew Becka's policy of not locking the front door. He also knew that Bryan didn't have much success in making her heed his advice.

That was why Matt didn't even bother knocking. He just came inside. After all, he felt there like at home. Becka and Bryan were some of the kindest in the family, although their couple was strange by far.

"I thought you liked my butt," Becka shouted from the study and then stormed out of the room.

She missed Matt by an inch. She didn't even notice him and started taking the stairs two at a time.

"I love your butt, and you know it. But right now, bring it up here. Lea levitates, damn it, and she won't listen to me," Bryan's harangued voice came from somewhere above, and Matt burst into laughter.

Matt's imagination wasn't very active, but at least, he guessed how stressed Bryan felt, having two gifted children.

As an outsider in the Winston family, Bryan had to put up with a lot of things. However, no one could say that he shrunk his responsibilities.

Even if he didn't have a clue what to do in some circumstances, he dug his feet in the ground and took everything in stride. Now, though, he seemed overwhelmed with his one-and-a-half-month daughter, who inherited her mother's family's heritage.

Only whispers came from upstairs, so Matt decided to go there and visit with his niece and nephew. He knew his apparition would make Bryan roll his eyes. He would understand that Becka had failed to lock the door again, and he would probably give her hell after Matt left.

He wouldn't say a thing in front of Matt. No matter how upset he was, Bryan never said anything to Becka in front of others. He thought they had judged her enough for marrying a man twelve years older, and she didn't need to hear any 'I told you.'

Matt knocked on the nursery door, and Bryan looked up, concern edged on his face. When his eyes fell on Matt, his tension eased away, and he smiled, shaking his head.

"You haven't locked the front door again," he said in a resigned voice, glancing at Becka.

"I forgot," she shrugged, and patted his hand. "Don't worry, no one will come in, but Matt. Hi, Matt, what's up?"

Matt couldn't hide his amusement. His younger cousin was always a delight, and he enjoyed seeing Bryan struggle both with his concern for Becka, and his ineffectiveness in making her understand the dangers of the city.

"Just passing by. I've got an hour to kill and thought of coming and seeing you two. And the munchkins."

Matt came inside and went to Becka, who was holding Lea in her arms. He kissed Becka's cheek, and then, he stroked the baby's head and put a kiss on the top of her head.

"She's already causing problems, I hear," he turned to Bryan, who raised an eyebrow inquiringly. "I heard you when I came in," Matt confessed, and a naughty smile appeared on his lips.

Becka blushed. She remembered what Bryan had shouted to make her come upstairs. She speared him with a pointed look, and Bryan just grinned.

Matt chuckled. He loved both of them, and his heart burst with joy whenever he thought how good they were together. Yet, he was jealous of them sometimes, because he couldn't have the same thing.

"So, the problems started, I understand," he said, nodding to the little bundle in Becka's arms.

'Yep, and it scares me shitless, to tell you the truth. Thank God, Sean hasn't manifested any powers yet," Bryan replied.

"He will... In time," Matt told him, putting a reassuring hand on his shoulder. "You'll manage, don't worry. You've never struck me as a man who can't handle everything."

Bryan scowled but didn't reply. He glanced at Becka, ready to say something, but she shushed him, putting her finger to her mouth.

"She's asleep again," she whispered, and Bryan came to her to take his daughter and replace her in her crib.

Becka and Matt started to the door, expecting Bryan to follow. When Matt looked back, Bryan was still watching his daughter sleep, and his expression was priceless.

Matt had liked Bryan since the moment they met. Yet, once he got to know him, his respect and feelings for the man evolved.

Bryan was a devoted husband and father, and it crushed Matt to see that hulk of a man so deeply in love with his family.

Matt followed Becka downstairs and found her in the study. She was typing something at her computer while checking a pile of papers at her elbow.

"What are you doing?" he asked her.

"I have to finish an essay. I have two more lines to write, and I've done it," Becka replied but didn't look at Matt.

Matt leaned on the doorjamb, crossed his ankles, and kept silent so that Becka could finish her work.

A minute later, Bryan came downstairs, as well. Bryan waved to Matt, inviting him to the kitchen. Even before stepping into the kitchen, the aroma of a beef stew reached Matt's nostrils. The scent pleased him, and his belly growled. Bryan, who close behind Matt, chuckled.

"Ready for lunch?" he teased Matt.

"I suppose that you cooked," Matt inquired in a dry tone of voice.

"You suppose well," Bryan replied. "I wouldn't let Becka in the kitchen. She's a walking disaster," he shrugged, and going to the stove, he picked up a wooden spoon to stir the stew.

"Am I?" Becka bristled from behind Matt, and Bryan winced.

"Come on, sweetie. You know that you can't boil an egg," Bryan replied. However, Matt didn't discern any reproach in his voice.

"And we're fine, aren't we? It's no need for you to cook when I can do it very well," Bryan added.

He came to her, took her head in the cradle of his palms, and kissed her lips tenderly. Matt turned to look out of the window. The tender display touched a yarning in his heart. Matt thought that he had squashed that feeling long ago.

"Hungry, everyone?" Bryan asked. He turned off the stove and went to take the bowls out of a cupboard.

"I'll set the table," Becka intervened.

"What's there to set, baby?" Bryan wondered. "Just take a seat, and I'll bring everything to the table."

"But I want to help," Becka retorted with annoyance.

Matt knew that she didn't want him to think that she wasn't doing anything around, but he knew better. Bryan didn't allow Becka to do much.

"You've had enough to do today, Becka," Bryan stroked the side of her face and kissed the tip of her nose. "You had to go to school, and you forgot to lock the door in the process," he thought to add. "And you worked on your paper for the last couple of hours..."

"Yes, and you cooked, cleaned, and took care of the babies," she replied. "And in a couple of hours, you'll have to go to the dojo for your afternoon and evening classes, so..."

"I can do it. Don't worry," Bryan waved her concerns away, at the same time, leading her to the table and helping her to sit. "You're a new mom, and you must rest as much as possible," he pointed out.

"I was a new mom a month and a half ago, Bryan. I'm perfectly fine now," she replied stubbornly.

"And that's how you have to remain," he pushed on her shoulder when she tried to stand up. "Come on, Becka, only take a seat. I can carry three bowls to the table myself," he said in a frustrated tone.

Becka just shrugged but didn't try to stand up again. Matt, who always enjoyed their sparring immensely, watched her. She was biting her lower lip, annoyed with something.

"What's the problem, pumpkin?" he asked quietly.

"He won't let me do anything," she snapped. "As if I were fragile."

"I never said that you were fragile," Bryan's voice came from a few feet away.

Becka and Matt turned to him, and Matt immediately stood and helped Bryan to put the heavy tray on the table. Bryan had filled three bowls to the rim and also sliced fresh homemade bread.

"I'll tell you, man. You cook as well as my mom," Matt sniffed the stew and grumbled in satisfaction.

Proud of Bryan, Becka smiled. Aunt Marjorie was the best cook she had ever known, and Matt's praise meant something. Then she dipped her spoon in the stew but fidgeted a little in her seat before carrying it to her mouth.

"Out with it," Bryan said. "Something's bothering you," he added, looking at Becka sideways.

Matt already knew that Becka couldn't even sneeze without Bryan getting concerned.

"Well," she started saying hesitantly, "if you want to know, I don't think it is right that you do everything. It's already been a month and a half since I gave birth, so I am perfectly able to..."

Bryan stopped her, touching her hand.

"Don't worry about it, Becka. You do more than enough. You have to wake up at night and breastfeed, and..."

"Huh!" she snorted inelegantly, and Matt had to hide his smile.

"Huh?" Bryan asked. "What does that mean?"

"Whenever I wake up, you wake up too. So don't try to sell me on that stuff," Becka shrugged.

"I might wake up, but I don't breastfeed," Bryan retorted, miffed.

Matt couldn't hold it anymore and burst into laughter. "You two are comical. You're the first couple I've seen quarreling because the other is doing more," he shook his head.

"You eat and shut up," Becka snapped at Matt. "I'm serious, here. Yes, I breastfeed. And yes, I go to school. That's the sum of my accomplishments," she sulked.

"I wouldn't say that," Bryan murmured. "You keep me happy, Becka," he said, taking her hand and squeezing it with tenderness. "And don't worry so much. Your mom will send Rosa's daughter here tomorrow. She'll clean and do the laundry, and I won't have much to do."

"Finally," Becka said, relieved. "At least, you won't do those anymore."

Matt grinned. He knew that Becka wouldn't accept Bryan's hard work for long. Now at least, she knew that someone else would take up the brunt of the housework because Bryan would have never accepted her help.

It wasn't easy to hire help in their houses, though. They needed to keep the family's secret, and they couldn't hire just anyone.

Luckily, their hired help worked for them generation after generation. Rosa was Becka's parents' housekeeper and Uncle Michael's housekeeper's daughter.

"So, will she start tomorrow?" Becka asked.

Bryan just nodded and spooned more stew. Matt knew that the man must have been exhausted. Bryan had started doing everything by himself long before the birth of his children, and he had also respected his training schedule.

They savored the beef stew in silence for a few minutes, and then Becka looked at Matt. Her glance held a lot of questions.

"What?" Matt asked her.

"I was only wondering if you had any news," she shrugged and took another slice of bread.

"What news are you expecting?" Matt asked Becka, and following her example, he helped himself to another slice of bread.

Bryan did know what to do in the kitchen. Matt imagined that Bryan knew what to do in almost any situation. Bryan, his cousin by marriage, was one of the most resourceful and talented men in their family.

"You know, Matt," Becka insisted. "It's May 19th already."

"And?" Matt asked with dismay. He knew where the conversation was going and didn't like it. Only Bryan looked from one to the other with curiosity.

"In July, it's your birthday," Becka doggedly continued. "On 27th," she thought to specify.

"So?" Matt asked, feigning disinterest. "Are you planning a party for me, or what?"

"Don't try to play games with me, Matt Winston," Becka snapped, and her small fist hit the table. Bryan's eyebrows shot up. "You know very well what I'm talking about."

Matt shook his head, scooped more stew, and chewed.

"Not really," he replied. "I was thinking of taking a cruise or something. That's true. I haven't made my mind yet, though," he shrugged.

Becka stared at him with disbelief. Then she took a breath, ready to launch herself in a lecture. Bryan touched Becka's arm and calmed her.

"Matt," he said. "I see that there's something the matter here, and I really don't want Becka riled up. So what is it?"

"Why don't you ask her?" Matt replied in a stubborn tone of voice. "I don't know what she wants from me," he answered with indifference and continued eating.

He didn't regret coming to their house. He liked watching Becka and Bryan interact and loved the little ones. Moreover, he always ate well in Bryan's kitchen.

"Okay, sweetheart. What is it?" Bryan asked Becka. He understood Matt wouldn't give in.

"He'll be thirty-five on July 27th," Becka pointed out.

"And?" Bryan insisted. He knew that there must have been much more to that than Matt's birthday.

"He'll lose everything then."

"What will he lose?" Bryan asked again, feeling like he was pulling teeth.

"His powers and trust fund," Becka said

"Oh, I see, now. So that thing has a deadline," Bryan nodded when the truth dawned on him. He turned to Matt, expecting that he would say something. Yet, Matt only continued eating, uninterested in expanding on the story.

"Come on, Matt," Becka said. "You still have a little over a month and a half."

Becka's words made Matt's hand freeze with the spoon halfway to the mouth, and his baffled eyes locked on her. After a few seconds of deafening silence, Matt put the spoon back in his bowl and asked, "Are you for real?"

"What now?" she asked, throwing her hands in the air.

Bryan mused. Becka had a real talent for drama sometimes.

With regret, Matt pushed the bowl away. He did want to eat that stew. A frown appeared between his eyebrows, and he stared Becka down.

"So far, I haven't found a woman that I could love, Becka, but you seriously think that in the following month and a half, I'll find one," Matt shook his head. "Bryan, your wife has lost her mind. I'm really sorry for you," he said, turning to Bryan.

"Nah," Bryan replied. "Becka's smart, and you should listen to her. It doesn't always take years to fall in love. It took me a day and a half, maybe less. And you still have over forty-five days, I think," Bryan shook his head, chastising Matt.

"Okay, I see it now. You're nauseatingly happy, both of you, and you see everything through pink glasses," Matt concluded and started to stand up.

"Maybe that's true," Bryan replied to him. "That doesn't mean that you can't finish your stew. Both Becka and I," he said, throwing a meaningful look at Becka, "will refrain from talking about this matter anymore. Am I correct, sweetie?" Bryan said to her, and after a brief hesitation, Becka nodded.

Undecided, Matt looked from one at the other, and, in the end, his hunger won. He sat back on his chair and pulled the bowl back in front of him.

"So, how's your schedule these days?" Bryan asked. "You said you'd like to come by my dojo for some training," he observed.

"Not today, though," Matt said with regret. "I have a late meeting. An ugly divorce case," he specified. "Are you there tomorrow? In the morning, for instance? I have a couple of free hours then."

"Yes, I am. It's Becka's day off school, and she'll be staying with the brats. See, sweetie, you do things, so don't complain anymore," Bryan turned to her.

CHAPTER TWO

TENSION FILLED THE conference room, yet Matt didn't appear affected. He leaned back in his chair, his ankle over his knee, his papers forgotten on the table. Matt never needed to refresh his memory. Files represented props for him, and he used them to intimidate. He never checked them, either in a conference room or in court.

Matt's client sat on his left at the table. In his thirties, Paul Willow looked too stylish, and Matt didn't like him. However, Joshua, Matt's partner, had accepted the Willow case. When Joshua suddenly married and went on an extended honeymoon, the Willow divorce had fallen in Matt's hands.

Something didn't seem quite right with that Paul Willow, but his divorce case didn't present any difficulty for Matt. The facts didn't leave any loophole for the opposing counsel.

"So, let's recap here," he addressed to the opposing lawyer, Fred Rhoades. "Mrs. Willow signed a prenup before marriage. It is a straightforward document. We all agree with that. If she cheated, she'd get nothing. We have four men willing to testify that they slept with her on several occasions. They might not be outstanding citizens, but their bad reputations will make our case stronger. Plus, Mr. Willow is willing to pay for a DNA test to prove Mrs. Willow's son is not his," he said very matter-of-factly and stopped to gauge their expressions.

The lawyer seemed annoyed and started cleaning his glasses. Her client, Nora Willow, soon to be Nora Barnes, had paled, and the shadows under her eyes swallowed almost half her face.

Matt didn't feel any pity for her. He couldn't stand cheaters and gold diggers, and according to the file he had on the table, that woman was both.

Interesting though, although she had paled and her fingers were shaking, she didn't flinch under his stern eyes. She returned his look squarely as if she didn't feel any remorse or shame.

"Now, we can go to court. We can't lose. Everything is cut and dry. Of course, by the end of the proceedings, we'll have your reputation in tatters, Mrs. Willow, and your son will find out the truth about his mother," he told her directly, his scorn evident, both in his voice and eyes.

"I'll sign the agreement," she said to Matt in a calm tone of voice.

Matt had never seen such a composed woman in a divorce case as the woman before him. She didn't react verbally to anything. She didn't attack or tried to push the guilt on her ex-husband's shoulders. The only sign that Mrs. Willow felt anything was the shaking of her fingers.

"It's not like I'd have wanted a cent of his money anyway," she continued. "And Paul's contribution to the house was indeed much higher than mine. So, of course, I couldn't demand that I receive the house. However, I should ask for the money I invested in it," she pointed out, and Matt decided to pay more attention to her.

He didn't believe that Nora would give up the money if she thought that she had the right to get it. Matt's eyes narrowed, and he tried to use his mental abilities to read her, but he didn't succeed, and that puzzled him. His mental-reading powers hadn't entirely matured, but usually, he could see something in people's minds.

"What I want, though, and this is not negotiable," Nora warned Matt in a steely voice, "is that he signs a document to surrender any parental rights. Paul has stated that my son isn't his, so he must sign the papers," she concluded, and the inflections of her voice warned Matt that she wouldn't budge on that score.

Matt lifted his left eyebrow, pensively. The woman had a lot of guts for a woman painted as a slut. She kept surprising him, and he didn't like it.

He turned slightly to his client with an inquiring look. The man only shrugged.

"I don't care about parenting the brat. You can prepare the documents, can't you?" Paul Willow asked Matt.

Matt nodded briefly and stood up. "I'll be back in a couple of minutes. May I hope you won't start fighting while I'm gone?" he asked.

The woman's behavior wasn't natural. Nora didn't chide, accused, or pleaded, and Matt feared that she would explode while he was away.

Nora just nodded. Entirely indifferent in her future ex-husband or the lawyer, who sat next to her, Nora picked up her mobile phone off the table and began reading text messages or emails. Matt shook his head slowly. That woman befuddled him.

Then he left the room to ask his paralegal to prepare the documents and bring them to the conference room.

He didn't dare to stay away for long. His instincts told him that something was wrong, and he wanted to avoid any ugly events.

He returned to the conference room, and silence greeted him. Only his client was drumming his fingers on the tabletop. Fred Rhoades was checking an agenda, and Nora was standing near the window, admiring the square at the back of the building.

She turned her head when he returned, but when he told them the documents would be ready soon, she preferred to remain near the window.

The following fifteen minutes felt like hours. Matt tried to make small talk with his fellow lawyer, but Rhoades's monosyllabic answers annoyed him.

His client started texting back and forth with someone and seemed to have the time of his life. His soon to be ex-wife didn't leave the window until his paralegal had come with the papers.

Then, she approached the table, took her reading glasses out of her handbag, and after she read the documents carefully, dignified, she signed them.

When she finished, she collected her things silently, ready to leave.

"Mrs. Willow," Matt stopped her, but when he saw the mocking glitter in her eyes, he corrected himself, "I apologize, I wanted to say Ms. Barnes. My paralegal brought these papers to you. You have info about how to change your name and everything. As Mr. Willow renounced his parental rights, you can also change your son's name, if you want to," he specified.

"Do I have to?" she asked, and for the first time, she sounded fearful.

"No, you don't have to," Matt answered softly.

"Thank you," Nora said and stretched her hand to him.

Matt shook her hand briefly. Her skin was freezing cold, but that didn't bother him. The brief electrical shock did. He had his eyes focused on her face, and the surprise in her eyes told him she felt it as well.

Matt stepped back, bowed his head, and started gathering the files. The door clicked behind her, but he didn't even turn.

CHAPTER THREE

MATT HAD A NEWSPAPER under an arm and an umbrella in his hand. The phone rang, and he stopped under the overhang of a newsstand shop.

The weather channel had announced frequent rain showers and thunderstorms for that day, so Matt had left the house prepared. The forecast hadn't been wrong. It poured, and lightning lit the sky, covered with heavy clouds.

Matt took his cell phone out of the pocket. He looked at the screen and frowned. Becka rarely called him so early in the morning, so he feared the worst. Matt had seen Becka two days before, and then everything seemed fine.

"Hey, pumpkin. Is everything all right?" Matt asked Becka.

"I need your help," Becka replied breathlessly. She sounded as if she ran for her life.

"What happened?" Matt inquired, his heart beating frantically, and his fingers clenched on the umbrella handle.

Becka perceived the panic in Matt's voice, so she hurried to reassure him. "Oh, no, Matt. Nothing happened. I've merely run to take cover. It's pouring, you know. And I couldn't call you from home. I need your help to buy a gift for Bryan. Of course, I couldn't call if he could hear me," she chastised Matt.

Matt breathed relieved. He hadn't even realized that he was holding his breath.

"Thank God, Becka. You scared me," he confessed. "When do you want to buy that gift?"

"Are you free now? I'm in town, not far from your office," she replied.

"I'm not in the office. Do you know the shops across from my office? I'm there. I came to buy a newspaper, and I thought to go for a coffee or something."

"Oh, Matt, it's perfect. Can you make it to the mall? I'm already there. Most of the shops will open in half an hour. We can have a snack together before going shopping," Becka said with enthusiasm.

"Won't Bryan get upset if you eat now and then skip the lunch he cooked?" Matt asked her maliciously, his eyes wandering along the road.

"Nope. He'll cook dinner today, but not lunch. Bryan knows that I'll have lunch at U of T, and anyway, he will be at his dojo. Mom came in the morning to spend time with the babies. She'll stay until I get back at three," Becka explained.

"Okay, Becka, you've got yourself a deal. See you at Timmies in about fifteen minutes, all right?" Matt gave in.

"Great, Matty. I knew you'd help me," she replied enthusiastically and disconnected the call.

Matt sighed and resigned to walk through the rain to the mall, so he opened his umbrella. He strode down the street, whistling a merry tune. At the traffic lights, Matt crossed to the other side of the road so that he could head right to the mall.

Matt didn't see many people in the street. He imagined that most had already taken cover from the rain. Anyway, he was happy because he could move at ease.

Suddenly, the wind intensified and almost blew his umbrella away. He grabbed the handle better and angled the umbrella against the rain pour, which came sideways now.

He pushed ahead mulishly, his head down, and mumbled to himself. Becka had chosen the wrong day to go shopping.

He heard an anguished cry and looked up. A few meters away, a woman with a toddler in her arms was fighting the wind. Her umbrella had broken, and her bags had fallen to the ground. She shielded the child, as much as she could, and now was trying to collect her things.

Matt rushed up and picked her bags fast. He started to hand them to her, and only then, he saw her face and practically froze.

Nora Barnes looked at him warily. The rain had plastered her long red hair to her face, neck, and shoulders. Her wet summer dress left little to the imagination. It showed every single curve of her body and outlined her underwear. Her arms, full of a fidgeting toddler, Nora tried to balance everything in the other hand.

"So, we meet again, Ms. Barnes," Matt drawled.

"Yes, it seems so," she replied in an indifferent tone of voice, yet her eyes betrayed her nervousness.

Nora tried to take back her bags from his hand, but Matt pulled them to him. She frowned, and her lips parted. Her entire face showed that she was puzzled. Matt's actions didn't make sense to her.

"Why are you with your child out in this rain?" Matt inquired, his voice far from friendly. "This is an irresponsible action for a parent," he observed. Matt came closer to Nora so that he could hold the umbrella above the toddler's head and shielded Nora, as well, although he didn't like it.

"Well, parents can't dictate the weather, Mr. Winston," she replied sarcastically. "And parents do need to go to work and leave children at daycare when there's no one to watch for them at home."

"Huh! I wouldn't have thought you'd get a job so soon," Matt said maliciously.

He didn't think that that type of woman would look for work. Generally, someone like Nora would immediately look for another sucker to pay her bills.

"Not that's your business, but I've had this job for over seven years," Nora replied, peevishly.

She would have preferred to keep her mouth shut and let him think whatever he wanted. Yet, she was afraid that Matt would consider that she wasn't a good mother, and he had the means and power to make her lose her child.

Matt scowled. He couldn't believe that she had had a job for the last seven years.

"I'm not one of your swains, Ms. Barnes, and I don't believe everything someone's telling me."

She just shrugged, and said, "That's your prerogative. I apologize, Mr. Winston, but I do have to get Nathan to daycare. I have several things to do before my shift today, and I really cannot spend the entire day here in the street with you."

Long eyelashes shadowed Nora's green eyes. Raindrops clung on them and distracted Matt. The green of her pupils reminded Matt of the lush meadows he had seen in Scotland a few years before.

"Mr. Winston," Nora repeated more forcefully, "We do have to go."

"Hmm, I apologize. I spaced there for a few seconds," Matt replied. "Where are you headed?" he asked.

"Just told you, daycare," she said through tight teeth.

Nora didn't understand what was going on with him, but she didn't have the time to ponder upon his bizarre reactions. She had too many things to do that day. She had just cleared the appointment she had with Nathan's doctor, but she hadn't finished her errants.

"I got that," he snapped. "But where? What direction?"

"None of your business," Nora replied.

"I'm afraid it's my business, Ms. Barnes," he answered sternly, and his unnerving eyes disconcerted her.

Afraid, Nora pointed toward the entrance of the mall.

"We need to take the train."

"Good, I'll take you there," Matt said.

Without surrendering her bags, Matt slid an arm around Nora and her child. He gathered them under his umbrella and herded them to the entrance of the mall. A slight tremor crossed her body and vibrated in his hand, which was also holding the umbrella over them.

Nora didn't protest, although she was pretty angry. She was furious because of the rain and because of him. She was angered with herself because she was foolishly afraid that Matt would do something to take her son away.

"Why are you doing this?" she asked, frustrated.

"Because I can," he answered calmly.

Nora stopped in her tracks, shocked by his crisp answer, and Matt merely nudged her ahead.

MATT ARRIVED AT TIMMY'S, where he found Becka seated at a table in the corner of the shop.

As Matt noticed that Becka had two cups of coffee and two breakfast sandwiches on the table, he didn't stop at the counter but headed directly toward her. Lost in her thoughts, Becka didn't notice Matt's arrival.

"Hey, there, pumpkin. Why the long face?"

"What long face?" Becka smiled at Matt. She rose and gave him a warm hug. "I've got no reason for a long face. I have just been thinking," she assured him. With a wave of her hand, Becka invited Matt to take a seat. They attacked their sandwiches, and after the first bite, Becka started grilling him.

"Why did it take you so long to get here?"

He shrugged, "I met someone I knew, and we exchanged a few words, that's all."

"How come you're not wet?" Becka wondered, checking him out. "You don't have an umbrella. I got wet even with the umbrella," she observed, showing him the wet patches on her shirt.

"I had an umbrella, but I gave it to that someone," he waved her question away as if weren't very important.

He had foisted that umbrella on Nora. They had fought back and forth for a few minutes for that darn umbrella, Matt remembered.

For such a small woman, Nora could be very stubborn. In a way, she reminded him of Becka, but Becka had a sweetness, which Nora lacked.

Matt didn't know if it was the difference in their age, but the woman seemed hardened somewhat. Matt knew that Becka would never be that way. With Bryan on her side, Becka would always keep her serenity and a certain innocence.

Becka sipped her coffee, her eyes on Matt, pensively. Matt's dark hair, the shadow of his beard, and his dark-blue eyes, as well as his impressive built, made him a favorite with the ladies.

Yet, lately, he didn't even date. Becka had an idea why, but she hoped that she was wrong. She didn't understand why Matt would sabotage himself.

"Are you all right, Matt?" she asked, touching his hand with hers.

"Yeah, why?" he looked up at her. For a moment there, Matt had got lost in his thoughts.

"I don't know. It's something about you, you know. And you haven't even shaved…"

"Ah, that," Matt grinned mischievously. "I don't have to meet clients today, pumpkin. So, I indulged. Don't read more into it than it is," he reassured Becka, patting her hand.

Matt finished his sandwich, drank his coffee almost in one go, and then asked Becka, "So, what were you saying about that present for Bryan? What's the occasion?"

"Ah, that," Becka said and started to gather the wrappers. "On 23rd, it's Bryan's anniversary, so I wanted to give a party for him, but Bryan refused. Then I asked Bryan if I could invite at least a few of the cousins. Bryan said that I could if I wanted to have some company, but not for his birthday. Bryan doesn't seem comfortable with having guests, especially for celebrating his anniversary. I think that no one has ever celebrated his birthday, you know?" Becka said ruefully.

"Then you could celebrate it with him. I mean, only the two of you. You could organize a romantic evening and have something to drink," Matt said. "Oh, sorry, you can't drink, I forgot," he smiled at Becka remorsefully.

"I know, but I could have a drop of champagne, I think. Merely to toast for him," Becka added in an insecure tone of voice.

"Yes, you could do that. It won't harm either your babies or you. I am sure of that," Matt reassured Becka.

"And I want to buy a present for him," Becka confessed to Matt. "I thought to get something practical, you know, something he'd use, and something whimsical, just for the fun of it. But I don't want to buy a shirt or a tie," Becka said and shuddered. "Oh, gosh, imagine Bryan with a tie!"

Matt chuckled. However, he knew that Becka was right. Bryan didn't wear a tie. Ever. He had wanted to wear one for their wedding, but Becka had refused to have him uncomfortable that day. Bryan was probably one of the few grooms who didn't wear formal attire at a big wedding.

Matt thought a little and then said, "I know what you could do for him, Becka. You could organize a small gym in the basement. You have that room next to the laundry. You can put a boxing bag, a treadmill, and a home gym. I saw one of those. You can try about thirty different exercises with it. Bryan would be set for the days when he can't go to the dojo."

"You're a genius, Matty," Becka jumped off her chair and smacked a kiss on his cheek. "I thought of buying something like that but didn't know exactly what. You know that I don't have any experience with that," she admitted.

"Yep, I know," Matt grinned. He remembered one of Becka's visits to his house a couple of years ago. She had wanted to try the treadmill. Becka fell and practically flew away off the treadmill. Matt had had a hard time to explain Becka's bruises to her father. For over half a year, Gabriel had forbidden Matt to come to their house.

"I know where we should go to buy everything you'd need. Now the problem is how to set everything up without Bryan's knowledge, of course," Matt said.

"Well, if we hurry," Becka said, checking her watch, "we'd have about five hours per total. That means to do the shopping and arrange the gym. Would it be possible?" she asked him, her imploring eyes fixed on Matt.

"Yes, of course, we can do it. If we don't waste time looking for that funny thing that you want to buy," Matt explained to Becka and stood up.

Becka waved her hand, and then she snatched the tray before Matt could take it.

"I'll take care of this, Matt. And no, I won't buy that thing today. I don't need advice for that," she explained.

"Then, we can do it," Matt concluded, and after Becka took care of the tray and wrappings, he took her hand to lead her to the shop he had in mind.

CHAPTER FOUR

WHEN THE ALARM RANG off, Matt woke up, mumbling. Then he growled and stopped it with a violent slap. Matt sat up and rubbed his face, trying to dislodge the sand that scratched his eyeballs. He ruffled his hair, running his fingers through it.

Matt glanced at the clock and scowled. He had slept only three hours, and the lack of sleep had left his brain in a dense fog.

He got out of bed and went to the bathroom, wondering where the days when he didn't need more than an hour or two of sleep, had gone.

He leaned on the washbowl and dared to glance at his reflection in the mirror. He regretted it at once. Oh, man. He almost didn't recognize the man who stared back at him.

When, the heck, have I grown so old? Lines marred his forehead, and black shadows outlined his eyes. His one-day stubble hid the civilized man that he liked to show to the world.

Matt shook his head in puzzlement. Not even six years ago, he could party all night and then go to court the following day with a clear mind, able to focus on the case without problems. Of course, he hadn't partied so hard ever since.

Pondering that mystery, Matt turned on the faucet and picked up his toothbrush. He brushed his teeth and thought that he was fortunate enough that day. At least, he didn't have a court day that morning, and if he remembered correctly, which could have been questionable, considering the blur in his mind, he didn't have any pressing appointments.

His eyes narrowed to slits. *Why, the heck, did I wake up? I could have slept a couple of hours more.*

Yesterday, Bryan had been so happy with Becka's present that he had caved in and accepted her party proposition. Becka hadn't invited many people, only Jay and Matt, and a couple of Bryan's friends.

Yet, the party lasted until four in the morning, and Matt got home and in bed only after four-thirty. Matt shouldn't wonder for his bloodshot eyes and the dryness of his mouth. The mirror didn't flatter him that morning, either, and his thirty-something body protested vocally to the lack of rest.

Matt remembered he used to feel that way only when he had a hangover. Yet, he knew he hadn't drunk anything else but a couple of beers and a glass of champagne the night before. He could drink a bit more without getting wasted.

Brushing his teeth refreshed his mood enough, so he took a long shower, which made him feel almost whole again. He considered shaving but pushed the thought to the back of his mind with disgust.

He didn't have anyone to impress and didn't enjoy the thought of wasting ten minutes just for that. He could do with that beard for another day. *I heard beards are trendy again, so ...*

His stomach protested, and Matt opened the fridge, thinking that he could use a sandwich or something. His gaze fell on a lonely tomato, forgotten on a shelf. *Worse than Sahara around here,* he scowled and slammed the door.

He didn't remember when he had gone grocery shopping the last time. A quick search through the cupboards depressed him and made him grab his car keys, determined to head for the first Timmy he could find.

MATT HAD STOOD IN LINE for over fifteen minutes. The line moved slowly, and Matt's need for caffeine grew more and put a metallic shine in his eyes. With narrowed eyes, he willed the cashier to move faster.

Matt understood that the man was in training and had his limitations, but he refused to understand the logic of using a trainee at peak hours. *What smart ass thought it would be good for business? A location to avoid in the future,* Matt thought and remembered that he could find a Timmy's not far from his office.

Everyone in the shop was annoyed. People were in a hurry to get to work, so lots of disagreeable comments flew around. The annoyance escalated more but didn't worry any of the shop employees that were milling around without an apparent goal.

Matt's tiredness and hunger made him less charitable toward the young man, who moved with the lightning speed of a turtle. Matt still had two more customers before him and started to jingle his car keys impatiently.

After five more agonizing minutes and a string of sweet words, addressed to the young employee mentally, Matt finally succeeded to give his order and got his coffee.

Then he moved to the side to wait for his sandwich. Matt already relished the thought that he was going to taste the black coffee for which he had waited for so long.

Matt had barely sipped from his coffee cup that the cell phone vibrated in his pocket.

What now? Matt mumbled.

They could have waited for him to enjoy that coffee first.

Resigned, he took the phone out of his pocket and checked the screen: St. Michael's Hospital. He frowned at first, and then, the implications hit him square in the chest. Someone close was hurt. He forgot about the coffee instantly.

"Hello, Matthew Winston speaking," his grave voice announced.

"Mr. Winston, I'm officer James Preston. Do you know a Nora Barnes, sir?"

Matt clenched his fingers on the phone. Yes, he knew Nora Barnes, but he didn't understand why the police would call him.

"Sir?" the officer's voice sounded inquiringly on the line.

"Yes, I know a Nora Barnes," Matt found his voice. "Why?" he asked.

"Would you be able to come to St. Michael's?" the officer avoided giving him a direct answer. "I'd be at the emergency room entrance," he specified.

Matt disliked the officer's underhanded manner but couldn't refuse to go to the hospital. He had a bad feeling about the reason for that call.

"I should be there in about ten minutes," Matt confirmed and disconnected the call.

Matt was about to leave, forgetting about his sandwich when his number got called. Matt shrugged and went to take his sandwich. Then he strode out of the coffee shop.

He hesitated in front of the shop for a moment and pondered the wisdom of taking his car from the parking lot. Then, he thought better.

I doubt there's any parking space there. Better I leave it here, he thought and went to add some more money for the parking.

MATT ENTERED THE HOSPITAL full of anxiety. He loathed hospitals and made a habit not to visit any if none of his family members were in there. Then, he didn't have a choice.

Officer Preston, a solid forty-something man, was waiting near the entrance, talking to the security guard. He had probably made a joke because the guard was laughing loudly, with no respect for the sick people, waiting not even a few feet away from them.

"I'm Matthew Winston," he said, closing the space between him and the two men. "You called me," he said to the police officer, who was watching him as if he'd been an exotic exhibit. Matt thought that it was probably because of his beard.

"Oh, yes, Mr. Winston," the officer greeted him. "Let's go to that corner and talk without interference," he proposed pointing to one side of the waiting room.

Matt gritted his teeth. He wanted to hear why he was called and didn't give a fig if anyone had heard them.

"I understand that you know Ms. Barnes," the officer stated.

"Yes, I do. I've already said so," Matt replied, his fingers clenching into fists.

He had worked with police before, but that specific officer didn't have any consideration about wasting his time.

"You know she's a paramedic," the officer assumed, and Matt nodded.

He didn't know anything of the kind, of course. He hadn't been interested enough to check Nora's background, but he wanted the officer to continue and didn't think that his denial would help speed up the conversation.

"We were called to a scene this morning. The person who called said that they needed the police, but also an ambulance because people were hurt," the officer explained and rubbed his mustache. "Ms. Barnes and her colleague got there a few minutes before the police cars. The shooter hadn't left the scene yet, you see," the man continued, "and both of them were shot."

Matt's blood ran cold, and he shoved his hands into his pockets. They were shaking, so he clenched his fists to control them. His dark-blue eyes had turned metallic.

"Now," the officer continued, "Jack Nolan, Ms. Barnes's partner, wasn't hurt very bad. The bullet missed the artery. He was still conscious when we got to the scene and was trying to get to Ms. Barnes. She wasn't so lucky," the police officer said flatly. "Two bullets in her chest, one in her left leg, and one in her left arm. The shooter was furious because of a woman. That one had run away, so he took his anger out on Ms. Barnes," Preston said without inflection.

Matt swallowed hard and brushed his forehead with unsteady fingers. He might not have liked Nora Barnes much, but only two days before, he had seen her, and she was fine. He couldn't imagine that young and composed woman, lying on a slab in the morgue.

"Has she died?" Matt managed to ask through tightened teeth.

"No, don't worry yet. Ms. Barnes is still alive. She's in surgery but alive. They reserved the prognosis yet. Anyway, we spoke to Jake Nolan. And he mentioned two things. First, Ms. Barnes has a son," the officer said, counting on fingers.

"Yes, Nathan. He's about three," Matt replied in a hoarse tone of voice and rubbed the root of his nose.

"Yes, that's what Nolan said," Preston nodded in agreement. "Now, it seems that Ms. Barnes is a valuable employee and has some leeway. She works some modified shifts or something like that. She'd arranged with her manager to leave work at eight-thirty to take the kid to daycare. Ms. Barnes hired a neighbor to stay with her kid after her departure for work at five-thirty in the morning. However, the babysitter must also go to work at nine-fifteen or something like that," the officer said and looked at Matt meaningfully.

"I see," Matt replied because the police officer seemed to expect an answer.

"Nolan says that Ms. Barnes has no one to help her out. In the past, she told him that she had to make it home in time because the neighbor was quite clear that she wouldn't wait. Nolan also says that Ms. Barnes is adamant not to have the kid taken by social services, you see," Preston confided.

"Yes, I see," Matt replied dutifully, wondering where the man was going with all that prattle.

"We talked to Nolan, who, by the way, is with my partner right now," Preston thought to specify, and Matt only stared at him.

Matt didn't know why the officer would think that Matt had any interest in Nolan's company. He didn't know Nolan but imagined with malice that he was probably one of Nora's conquests. Matt felt raw and mean at the same time.

"Nolan implored us not to let the child go to social services, and the doctor also said that if Ms. Barnes survived, it would be good if she didn't stress out. This thing with the child would stress her, guaranteed," the officer nodded.

Matt kept staring at him. He didn't understand what the man wanted from him.

"So?" he asked, a migraine drumming in his temples.

"Nolan didn't know anyone close to Ms. Barnes. I understand that her parents passed away. She's completely estranged from her ex-husband. That man considered that the child wasn't his, so he didn't want to have anything to do with the boy."

"Yeah, so?" Matt asked more forcefully. His patience already clung to a thread.

"Well, Nolan remembered that she had mentioned you, Matthew Winston, two days ago. He said that Ms. Barnes had complained of your domineering demeanor. She told him that you had made her take your umbrella and stuff like that. So, Nolan thought that you might be her boyfriend," the officer said, and Matt's eyes widened in shock.

"We looked through her bag and found some papers with your letterhead, so we called your office. They gave us your phone number, you see," the officer explained.

"Yes, I see," Matt said in a tired tone of voice. "So, what do you want me to do?" he asked matter-of-factly.

Yet, his heart cringed in his chest, and the air, suddenly, seemed in short supply.

"I knew we could count on you," Preston slapped him on the shoulder and chuckled.

CHAPTER FIVE

THIS TIME, CONTRARY to his custom, Matt didn't burst into Becka and Bryan's house. He didn't even think to check and see whether the door was locked or not.

Matt was still in shock and couldn't behave normally, so he pushed the bell and waited patiently for someone to come and open the door.

Matt's mind was in turmoil, and he couldn't focus on anything specific. His world had turned upside down in a matter of hours, and he could do nothing more but keep a façade of calm. Matt was far from being calm, though.

Bryan opened the door, a smile on his lips. His smile stopped when his gaze fell on the bundle in Matt's arms. Bryan saw only a mop of brown-reddish hair, sticking everywhere on the head of a toddler, whose face hid in Matt's shirt.

"Hey, there," Bryan greeted them in a soft voice and with a small smile, although he had already noticed the storm brewing in Matt's eyes. "Would you like to come in?" he asked when Matt didn't answer.

Matt, unable to speak yet, nodded curtly and passed by Bryan into the house. Bryan shook his head and then closed the door behind him.

"Let's go out on the patio. We've decided on a brunch today," Bryan explained to Matt, only to fill in the silence. "Becka doesn't have school today, and I took the morning and half of the afternoon off," he continued.

Matt didn't seem to hear a word.

Aware of Matt's strange disposition, Bryan didn't want to push him. He had always known that Matt was a man with very profound feelings, and his calm was a mere fabrication.

Bryan always believed that Matt would explode one day, and he had proposed himself to be far away when that would happen.

"Look who came to visit, Becka," Bryan told his wife in a cheerful voice, stopping next to Matt.

The toddler still held on Matt's neck and didn't dare to look around. Bryan saw the stuffed leg of a plush toy coming from between the child's body and Matt.

"Hi, Matt," Becka said softly, standing up and coming to him.

She touched his cheek, looked straight into his eyes, and shook her head.

"Why don't you two take a seat?" she invited them. "And maybe you can introduce us to your little friend."

Matt nodded and sat down. The child always clung on him. With a few whispers, he convinced the boy to sit in his lap and face his cousins.

"This is Nathan, Nat for short," Matt told them. "Nat, these are my cousins, Becka and Bryan. They're fine, so don't worry," he said, stroking the toddler's head.

"Would you like a cookie?" Becka asked Nat. "Bryan bakes the best cookies in the land," she continued cheerfully and made the child smile shyly.

When she presented a plate with cookies to him, Nat chose carefully and started nibbling on the chocolate cookie immediately.

"You'd like some milk, too," Bryan guessed and poured milk in a cup, which he handed to Matt.

Matt took the cup but halted for a moment. Bryan held Matt's gaze, and slowly, Matt got to something close to normal and helped Nat drink some milk.

When the boy pushed the cup away, Matt chuckled. A white mustache lined the child's upper lip.

"How old are you?" Becka asked Nat.

The boy considered her thoroughly and then showed three fingers.

"Oh, you're already three," she exclaimed cheerfully again. "You're a big boy, not a baby," she said with exaggerated wonder.

Nat nodded earnestly, and Matt stroked his head. "Do you want some more milk?" he asked the child, who had finished the cookie already.

Nat shook his head and then looked around.

"Would you like to run through the garden?" Matt asked. "It is okay, isn't it?" she asked Becka.

"Of course, it is," she said. "It's all yours, Nat," she invited the toddler to take control of her savage garden.

The boy's face lit with delight, and he squirmed in Matt's lap. Matt lowered him to the ground, and Nat shot as fast as his short legs allowed him to the first bunch of colorful flowers. On his haunches, he touched the petals with awe, yet he never let the teddy-bear under his arm go.

"Should we talk now or...?" Becka asked Matt.

Matt shook his head, his eyes on the boy.

"He has to sleep soon, I think. Toddlers sleep during the day, don't they?" he asked, turning to them.

Bryan smiled at him and shrugged, "Not something I'd know. I haven't had any experience with any other children, but my own. And they have a long way till they become toddlers."

"We can call aunt Marjorie or mother," Becka proposed, but Matt shook his head.

"No way. I don't want them to know anything right now. If later it's necessary, I'll tell them, but not now," he repeated stubbornly.

"Then we can check the Internet," Becka said.

"That's a good idea," Bryan said. "I'll bring the laptop," he announced, going inside.

Becka and Matt waited for him in silence. Nat was muttering something to a flower, but no one understood what he was saying. The regular breathing of the twins came through the monitor, Becka had put on the corner of the table earlier.

Bryan returned with the laptop and a notebook to take notes.

"I imagine you'd like to know more, not only if he sleeps during the day," Bryan explained the notebook. "We can make notes of what's important. It's a good lesson for Becka and me, as well."

Becka and Matt nodded, and the three adults started their research about a toddler's timetable and routines, all the time glancing at the child, who had a lot of fun talking to the flowers and insects he found.

Half an hour later, Nat came to Matt and nudged him.

"Yes, pal. What is it?" Matt asked.

"You read," the boy said.

Matt seemed confused for a few seconds, but Becka intervened.

"I think that Nat wants you to read to him. That's what you want, Nat. Yes?" she asked the child.

Nat nodded vigorously, stretching his arms to be taken up, and Matt sighed. He stood up, took the boy in his arms, and told Becka and Bryan, "He asked me to take a few books with us. They're in the car. I'll be back in a moment."

"Don't trouble yourself," Bryan stopped him. Give me the keys, tell me where the books are, and I'll bring them."

"That's a much better idea," Matt agreed and handed the car keys to Bryan. He sat back with Nat on his lap.

"Bryan will bring your books, and you will choose one. But only one," he said in an authoritative voice when a greedy light shone in the toddler's eyes.

His eyes focused on the child when Becka's musical laughter reached his ears. He looked at her. She had fun at his expense.

"Becka!" he warned her.

"Come on, Matt, you're so funny. And I can see you'd be a good daddy," she added gravely, and Matt paled at her words.

"Don't even joke on that subject, Becka. It's a forbidden topic," he argued.

"If you say so," she shrugged.

CHAPTER SIX

"HE'S FINALLY ASLEEP. Thanks, guys, for lending me that monitor," Matt said, pointing to the second monitor on the patio table.

"Don't sweat it," Bryan answered. "No big deal. We bought four to be sure we had one working if anything happened, so..."

"Anyway..." Matt started, but Becka stopped him, touching his hand.

"Forget about that, Matt, and spill the beans," she insisted, and Bryan smiled.

He liked it when Becka reacted with authority. Her attitude was in such a contrast with her small frame that it amused him to no end.

Matt explained about Nora and what happened that morning.

"I had to go and get the child. That woman didn't have a conscience, man. I got there exactly when she was coming out of the door. She didn't care that she left the boy alone," Matt said, and his voice shook with anger. "And she did ask me to pay her for the time she stayed there. What kind of mother leaves a child with someone like her?"

"Maybe a mother who had no other choice," Bryan replied softly. "Did she mistreat the child?"

"No, but..."

"And probably Nora intended to be back on time," Becka reminded him. "I understand that she arranged her shift so she could have plenty of time to go and get Nat before that woman would have left."

"But she should have thought she could get hurt," Matt insisted mulishly. "With her type of job..."

"Not necessarily, Matt," Bryan disagreed. "It's not like she's in the line of fire all the time. Probably, it was the first time something like that happened, you know."

"I think," Becka said thoughtfully, "you resent her because of the way her ex-husband portrayed her during the divorce."

Matt stared at her for a few seconds and shrugged.

"It was true, you know. Nora didn't fight back and didn't say that he was lying about her being a serial cheater."

"Serial cheater? Really?" Becka asked, and her eyes narrowed. "Why? Because her ex, who, apparently, has enough money to buy witnesses, says so?"

"She didn't defend herself, Becka," Matt replied in a very matter-of-fact voice.

"What would have been the point? Does she have money to fight you?" Bryan inquired in a quiet voice.

"I don't know," Matt admitted. "But she could have said something."

"If it had been pointless," Bryan shrug, "I understand why she didn't. Did you verify the facts yourself?"

"No, of course not. Everything was in the file when it landed on my desk."

"Then," Becka said, poking Matt with a finger, "you can't know what's true or not, so don't throw rocks, Matt. I thought that you were more ethical than that," she scolded him.

"But she didn't defend herself," he bellowed. "Don't you get it?"

"You have to figure it for yourself," Bryan shook his head and slapped him on the shoulder. "We can talk till we're blue in the face, Matt, but only you can uncover the truth. Anyway, what now?"

"I don't know," Matt admitted. "There's no one who can take care of the child. If child services take him, she'll face some serious problems to get him back," he said, and his face darkened.

"So?" Becka insisted.

"So, for the moment, I'm stuck with the kid. The problem is that Nora and Nat live in a rather small apartment. One bedroom, a tiny living room, and a kitchen. The bathroom has a tiny shower. I wouldn't even fit in there. I thought to move him and his stuff in my apartment," Matt said pensively.

Becka approved his decision with a nod. Bryan merely smiled, enjoying Matt's thinking process.

"I think I could take care of Natt," Matt said, although his voice didn't sound very convinced. "I mean, I have the time. We have cases on the roll now, but I have three young associates, and they could handle them. I can lend them a hand now and then, without effectively going to the office.

I'd have to take time off, you know," he told them, glancing from Becka at Bryan. "I don't know where Nat's daycare is, so that's out. I will have to go grocery shopping," Matt shook his head. "This morning, I discovered that I had only one tomato in my fridge and half a box of cereals in a cupboard. Nothing else, not even a box of coffee or tea," he opened his arms in exasperation, and the other two smiled.

Matt paused, and a frown appeared between his eyebrows.

"I don't know how to do with the cooking, though," he admitted. "And I don't want to involve my mom. Would it be bad if I buy fast-food?" he asked, and both Becka and Bryan nodded vigorously.

"Don't worry," Bryan said. "First, did you look into Nora's fridge?"

Matt closed his eyes with a scowl on his face and slapped his forehead.

"I didn't even think of that. I should go and do it, I think. God knows how long she'll be in the hospital. She wouldn't like to find living beings in her fridge when she comes back home."

"Definitely," Becka said, laughing.

"We'll go and check it together, all right?" Bryan said. "And then, knowing what's there, I can start making some food for you. It's no big deal," he put his hand up when Matt wanted to interrupt him. "I'll make enough for two or three days. When you finish it, you have only to let me know, and I start a new batch."

"Oh, my God. How long do you think she'd be in the hospital? If she survives, I mean, because it wasn't very sure that she would," he clarified in a bleak tone.

"Don't worry, she will," Becka stroked his arm.

"The boy should sleep at least two more hours," Bryan said. "Let's go and take his things from that apartment. We'll also check the fridge. We'll go grocery shopping on the way back here. Becka can take care of Nat if he wakes up, and Marissa's here if Becka needs help. Is it all right with you?" he asked his wife.

"Sure," Becka said. "I'll manage. Don't worry. Just go," she pushed them out of her garden.

"SMART OF YOU TO MENTION that fridge," Matt told Bryan. "All those vegetables and fruit would have gone to waste."

"Told you. From what you said, Nora seems a very devoted mother, Matt. I don't know why you can't see it. Anyway, I was sure that she'd have a lot of good food for the child. We need to buy only a few things for you – coffee, tea, things like that, and you're good for a few days. I'll make you a few casseroles for today and tomorrow, at least, and you can easily warm them in the microwave."

Matt shook his head and said, "You can't imagine how grateful I am to you right now."

"Matt, you are a smart guy, and you can also read minds. Read mine, already, and stop bothering me with your gratitude. We're family, man. You were there for me when I needed you. I'm here for you now," Bryan said quietly, arranging the things in the trunk.

He had insisted on taking his car because he didn't like how shaken Matt was. Bryan didn't want to risk him behind the wheel.

Matt, even staggered, decided to probe Bryan's mind. He avoided doing it, as a pattern, because he didn't like to intrude in people's thoughts. Yet, he wasn't always successful in holding back. As he didn't have enough control over his gift, Matt picked random thoughts now and then even if he didn't want to pry.

This time, though, he felt compelled to pry. Bryan's thoughts leveled him. Indeed, the man didn't think that Matt should be grateful and was willing to do everything in his power to help him.

The day had been a roller-coaster of emotions and shocks for Matt. The man tried hard to recollect himself when tears pricked at the back of his eyes.

He longed for his usual self, but it seemed more and more afar and difficult to reach.

The two men returned to Bryan's house just after Nat woke up. Tears welled in the little boy's eyes.

The thought Matt had also left scared him. He didn't understand why his mommy wasn't coming to take him, and he clung to Matt as if he'd been his last resort.

"Come on, munchkin, let's eat a banana," Matt said, "and stop crying. I won't leave you. You won't get rid of me so soon. We'll go to my house to live until mommy comes home, all right."

"Mommy says no stranger," the boy replied and looked at him with big eyes.

"I'm sure she did," Matt said, "and she's right, Nat, but I'm no stranger. You saw me talking to your mommy."

Nat rubbed his eyes and pondered over his words, then he nodded.

"Banana?" he asked.

"Yes, you'll have a banana," Matt confirmed and sat him on a stuffed pillow, he'd previously placed on one of the garden armchairs.

"Do you want me to slice it?" he asked Nat after he made sure the child was secure.

"I'm not a baby," Nat countered. "I can eat a banana," he added, and the mutinous expression in his eyes warmed Matt's heart.

Matt smiled and shook his head, "Yes, you're not a baby. Here you are," he handed the banana to Nat and then watched the child peeling it thoroughly.

The kid was focused on his task and didn't pay attention to them. Becka leaned toward Matt and whispered, "Have you noticed that he doesn't talk like a small child?"

"Is that bad?" Matt straightened, with a glint in his eyes.

"No, don't be ridiculous," Becka laughed. "Natt's only very smart. Someone took excellent care of his education. I'm sorry that I have to point it out to you, Matt, but the woman you described wouldn't have done that. I think that you should collect all the information before judging Nora," Becka shook her head at Matt in disapproval.

Matt watched the child and thought that Becka was right. His eyes turned pensive, and Bryan slapped him friendly over the shoulder, "You'll straighten everything up, Matt. I count on you."

Marissa came out with a fresh pot of coffee for the adults and filled their cups, making small talk with them. She left them with their coffees, and went inside, brushing her fingers through Nat's hair. Nat laughed.

"He's a very sociable child," Matt noticed. "I expected problems, you know. Especially because he saw me only once, and even then, I quarreled with his mother."

Bryan waved his hands, "All's good, Matt, you'll see."

He hadn't even finished reassuring Matt that Matt's cell phone rang. Taking it out of his pocket, Matt verified the screen and winced.

"What?" Becka asked.

"The hospital," Matt said and took a few steps away from the child so that Natt wouldn't hear what he was saying.

"Matthew Winston's speaking," Matt answered the phone, and both Becka and Bryan kept their gaze on him. They noticed that Matt looked frustrated and upset. Matt paced with nervous steps. He ran his fingers through his hair and rubbed his nose.

"I'll probably be there in half an hour," Matt replied to something and then listened to some more, nodding. "All right, I understand. Of course, I'll come," he added and turned off the phone.

"Guys, I'll have to go to the hospital. Nora's awake and frantic. The police had told her that I have..." Matt said, pointing to Nat.

"Not a problem," Bryan said. "Nat can remain here until you come back, Matt."

Matt nodded and thanked him. Then he knelt in front of Nathan and said to the child, "I have to run an errand, Nat. You'll stay with Becka and Bryan here, and I'll be back in no time."

"No," the child replied. "I won't stay. I'll come with you."

"I'm sorry, munchkin, but I can't take you to the hospital. I promise to be back. You'll have fun here, Nat. You can make cookies with Becka and..."

Bryan interjected immediately. "God forbid, Matt. Becka has a red light in the kitchen. If Nat makes any cookies, it will be with me."

Becka didn't appreciate the dread in Bryan's voice. "Come on, Bryan. Do you really have to..."

Bryan stopped her with a finger on her lips, "Sweetie, you know that I do. Imagine the fire alarm raging and the babies waking up. No, love, you won't touch anything in the kitchen. I thought that we had an agreement," he said in a very grave tone of voice, and Becka reluctantly agreed.

"Yes, Nat, you'll make cakes with Bryan, and afterward, we'll draw something together. Is it okay?" she asked him.

The child continued to stare at Matt.

"I promise to be back this afternoon," Matt repeated, noticing the rebellious expression of the child. "I won't leave you."

The boy considered Matt for a few more seconds and then agreed with a nod. Matt hugged him, laughing, and turned to leave.

"Take a cab, Matt," Bryan suggested.

He feared that the visit to the hospital would shake him more. Matt had already had his share of shocks that day, and Bryan didn't think it was smart to let him drive.

"I'll call you one right now," he said and went inside.

Matt had to give in. Bryan's thoughts had been too loud for Matt not to hear. Matt understood that the man worried for him, and he didn't want to repay Bryan's kindness with callousness.

CHAPTER SEVEN

THE NURSE BUZZED MATT into the intensive care unit immediately after his arrival. Her stern and reproachful face made him uncomfortable. He felt as if he were a teenager again, called to the principal's office for one of the pranks for which he had been so famous.

"Nora's been frantic, but she refused a sedative. You need to calm her down. Her fever spiked, and that's not good," the nurse explained to Matt.

Matt nodded and followed her to Nora's ICU room. He looked at Nora through the glass before opening the door. The bed seemed to swallow her whole, and his heart cringed.

"Try to calm her down, not to agitate her," the nurse warned him again, in an authoritative voice.

"Of course," Matt replied, although he doubted that he wouldn't agitate Nora.

The nurse left him there, and Matt gathered his courage to open the door. He knew that his visit might cause Nora much more anguish, and even though he didn't like her, he didn't want to make more problems for her than she already had.

The moment Matt entered the room, Nora turned her head to him, and he felt the intense gaze of her green eyes right in his chest. Nora watched him with something akin to hatred.

Matt was a few feet away, but even from that distance, he noticed the tears that clung to Nora's lashes. Matt felt the impulse to console Nora, so he balled his hands into fists, afraid that he would react stupidly.

Nora looked paler than he remembered, although the fever, which glimmered in her eyes, had flushed her cheekbones. The dark shadows under her eyes had expanded and swallowed almost half of her face.

Under his scrutiny, Nora made an effort to wipe the tears off her face, but she had one arm hooked to the IV unit, and she couldn't make use of the other, although she tried.

Nora seemed determined, though, and afraid that she would hurt herself more, Matt rushed to the bed, quieted her movements, and wiped off her tears with his thumbs. The gesture felt extremely close. Uncomfortable with that closeness, Matt hurried to step back.

Nora had shivered under his touch, and Matt's eyes searched her face to see if she was afraid of him. The emotions that Matt read in Nora's eyes didn't reassure him.

"I want my son back," Nora articulated with accuracy. Her voice was hard, although Nora looked vulnerable.

"Don't worry about that right now," Matt replied quietly. "Just..."

"I want my son back," she practically shouted, interrupting him.

"As soon as you get out of the hospital, you'll have your son back," Matt said in a steady tone of voice. "Right now, I don't see how you could keep Nat here with you," he circled his hand around the sterile hospital room.

"I won't let you take Nat away from me," Nora continued as if Matt had never said anything.

Matt sighed, bowed his head resignedly, and ran his fingers through his hair. He needed patience with Nora, no matter what. The nurse had already bad-mugged him, and he didn't want to be the recipient of her black gaze if he failed to reassure Nora.

"Look, Nora..." Matt began to speak anew, but of course, she interrupted again.

"I won't let you," she said in a stubborn tone of voice. "You've struck my dignity, insulted me in any possible way, and made everything in your power to leave me penniless. And I'm talking about the money that belonged to me, not to that sorry excuse of a human being that was my ex."

Matt noticed that Nora gathered more steam along with her declaration, and the flush of her cheeks intensified. He worried that her fever would go up and decided to end that stupid discussion.

He stepped next to the bed and leaned over her. He hushed her with his hand, which covered half of her face. Her eyes widened, and again, he wondered whether he frightened her.

"Now, I want you to keep silent until I finish what I have to say. I don't want to hear one word from you, Nora," he warned her in a stern voice. "Do you understand?" he asked her.

He waited a couple of seconds, but she didn't answer. She just kept staring at him with those shimmering green eyes, which pierced him straight into his soul.

"I've asked if you understand," he repeated, sterner than before, trying not to think of what he felt.

After a second, she licked his palm, and he practically jumped out of his skin. He took his hand off her mouth immediately and watched her, shocked.

"You wanted an answer," she shrugged. "Well, with that shovel over my mouth, I couldn't have answered. So..." she explained, a quirky little smile in the corner of her mouth, and Matt had a glimpse of the naughty girl she must have been a few years back.

"But you'll keep your mouth shut and listen," Matt concluded after taking a deep breath to calm his senses.

That lick had reached deep inside him, and all his nerve endings stood to attention. Matt didn't doubt that Nora would see the proof of his arousal if she looked closely, and he prayed that she wouldn't. He would have had a hard time to explain that.

Matt tried to pry on Nora's thoughts but came back blank, and that stunned him. He might not have had full control of his abilities, but still could read something from everyone.

"For the moment," Nora nodded with hesitation. "But make it fast," she warned Matt, and her eyes narrowed. "If I don't like what I hear, the entire hospital will know it. Do you understand?" she finished in a menacing tone of voice.

"Little girl," Matt smirked, "never make threats you can't carry on," he advised Nora and tweaked the tip of her nose.

Nora scoffed in indignation and opened her mouth to refute him. Matt only touched a finger to her lips and shook his head. That made Nora keep quiet.

"Now, maybe I can speak in peace for a moment or two," Matt said. "So, that Nolan guy was concerned about the kid. By the way, you've found a 'great' baby-sitter, Nora. When I got there, she was getting out of the door and stopped for only enough time to ask me for money. What kind of woman leaves a small child alone in an apartment, huh?" Matt asked, and a frown appeared between his eyebrows.

"I always..." Nora started, but Matt's finger came back on her lips to silence her.

"I'm talking now. And I wasn't talking about you. I imagined that you'd have made it in time if the shooting hadn't happened. I wasn't accusing you. So, let me finish," Matt ordered.

"Where's my son now?" Nora asked as if his finger didn't touch her lips, and Matt didn't ask her to keep silent.

Matt groaned and bowed his head in mock resignation. Matt shook his head, and with a faint smile on his lips, he looked back at Nora. "You can't stop talking if your life depended on it, huh?"

"Where's my son?" Nora repeated doggedly. "I see that you don't have him with you. Have you already delivered Nat to child services?" she asked, and her voice shook. Now, fear was evident in her voice.

"No, of course not. If I'd had that intention, I'd have let the police call child services in the morning, and I'd have finished with this issue."

"So, where is he?" she asked stubbornly.

"He's fine," Matt replied.

"Not what I asked," she retorted peevishly, and stared him down, a nasty light shining in her eyes.

"Maybe not, but I thought to let you know that Nat was fine. He's with Becka and Bryan," he replied.

"I don't know any Becka and Bryan," she observed and lifted an eyebrow interrogatively.

"They're my cousins," Matt answered. "At least, Becka's my cousin, and Bryan is her husband."

He took a few steps to the window to gather his thoughts. He had a few questions for Nora and didn't know how to ask them. He came back and observed that her eyes had never left him.

"We couldn't determine if you knew someone who could take care of Nat. A relative or a friend," he inquired quietly.

"I don't have relatives, at least not in Toronto," Nora admitted and moved her fingers agitated. "I have a cousin and an aunt somewhere in BC. Friends..." she started to say and turned her eyes to the bed.

Matt waited a few moments, but she didn't continue.

"Yes, friends, Nora. Do you have any friends?"

She shook her head and then looked up at him.

"I know a few people from work, but more like acquaintances, you know. There's no time for friends, with work and a child."

Matt noticed that she avoided his eyes, so nudged her chin up with his thumb. Surprised, Nora looked at him, but Matt had already seen that she looked uncomfortable, having to confess her loneliness to him.

"I understand things like that, Nora. You shouldn't be embarrassed."

A shadow crossed her face, and she looked down again.

"What now?" Matt asked, turning her face back to him.

"It's not like you believe me anyway," Nora shrugged and then hissed.

The movement of her shoulders had sent ripples of pain through her entire body, and she bit her lower lip not to yelp. Tears gathered in her eyes, turning their green in an intense glimmer.

"Stay still, baby," Matt soothed her, tenderly stroking the side of her face.

Nora's puzzled eyes came back to him. Matt didn't seem aware of the appellative he had used, but Nora had felt his tenderness profoundly.

"Don't make unnecessary movements for a while, okay?" Matt advised her and then straightened.

Nora missed his touch immediately and turned her eyes back to the functional blanket that covered her up to midriff.

"I believe that you don't have time to socialize," Matt reassured her but noticed the ironic smirk that appeared on her lips again. "What now?"

"Mr. Winston," Nora drawled, "you thought that I was a femme fatale with a string of lovers to shame a call girl. I doubt that impression changed in the span of a few hours."

"My name's Matt," he replied in a sterner voice than he wanted, but Nora's words had touched a sensible cord.

Bryan had sowed some grave doubts in Matt's mind. Now Matt worried that he didn't have the correct the facts when he worked on the Willows case. Matt had decided to verify everything again, although he knew that it was too late to do anything about the results of the divorce. Nora had already signed the settlement.

"I think," Nora said with hesitation in her voice, "that we lost the thread of conversation. You were telling me about my son..."

"Yes, let's get back to that," Matt conceded.

Matt wanted to return to safer ground. He didn't want to touch the matter of her divorce right then. Matt needed to find some answers first, and then he could either apologize or show Nora that he wasn't naïve.

"I took him with me," Matt said and put up his hand to stop her when Nora opened her mouth. "I'd have preferred not to take him from his environment, especially now because he has to put up with your absence, as well. But I couldn't have taken even a shower in your apartment. It's like a tiny dollhouse, for God's sake," Matt exclaimed. "We've spent the day with Becka and Bryan so far, as I've told you already, but we'll go back to my apartment tonight. Bryan helped me to gather Nat's things and empty the contents of your fridge," Matt said to Nora and smiled. "I thought that you wouldn't like to find it full of alien beings when you returned from the hospital," he looked at Nora for confirmation.

"You thought well," Nora gave him his due.

"That's good," Matt grinned. "Anyway, we've done some research..."

"What research?" Nora narrowed her eyes.

"About toddlers, of course," Matt answered, nonplussed. "It's not like I've been around many, and Becka and Bryan have got only babies. They've got twins. The babies are a month and a half old."

"Oh, my God! Those people are so busy, and you left my child in their hands..."

"As I said before, calm down, Nora," Matt snapped at her. "They're fine. Becka relates perfectly to children, and Bryan is the embodiment of patience. Plus, Bryan will cook for us, enough for two days..."

"Bryan?" Nora asked, not sure that she heard him correctly.

"Yes, why?" Matt looked at her inquiringly.

"Bryan will cook for you," she repeated, to make sure that she understood what Matt said.

"Yes, specifically for Nat. Our research showed that fast food wasn't very good for him, and I don't know to cook at all," Matt explained.

"But how come that Bryan is... Never mind," she decided to drop the subject.

Matt finally understood why Nora was so astonished.

"I get it now," he laughed. "You wonder why Becka won't cook. It's simple. Bryan won't allow her to step into the kitchen. No, no, it's not like that," Matt rushed to explain when he saw Nora's frown. "In the kitchen, Becka's only a disaster waiting to happen. Even if she tries to boil an egg, freaky accidents happen. So, in their family, Bryan's the cook."

"Oh, he's a cook," Nora said, relieved.

"No, he's not. He's a kick-boxing and Brazilian jiu-jitsu trainer," Matt said, and when Nora's face fell comically, he grinned.

"You're pulling my leg," she accused him.

"Nope, I'm telling you the truth," Matt shook his head. "Bryan is...a very unusual character, I'd say. I like him, you know. You'll like him too," he said quietly and looked at her with a strange intensity that she felt down to her belly.

Matt kept quiet for a few seconds and then continued, "Look, I think we should do this. I won't bring Nat here," he said, and seeing that Nora wanted to say something, he stopped her. "No, don't take it wrong. I won't bring Nat here as long as you're in the ICU. I don't think that you want him to see you like this," Matt said, looking at Nora inquiringly.

Nora shook her head. "Of course, not. Nat might not understand what's going on and get upset."

"Exactly," Matt approved. "As soon as they move you into a reserve, I will bring him there to see you. All right?"

"I might get a semi-private room. I think that my insurance covers that," Nora said pensively.

"Don't think about it now," Matt waved Nora's words away.

Matt had already decided to ask the hospital to put Nora into a private room, and he would pay for it from his pocket. Matt didn't want to bring Nat into a room that Nora shared with someone, afraid that another person might frighten the child.

"Meanwhile, if you want, you could talk to Nat over the phone," Matt proposed to Nora. "I think that this solution would work for a maximum of two or three days. If you're good enough, you'll get better by then," Matt grinned at her, and Nora scowled at him in response.

"It's not up to me, you, loggerhead," she observed.

"Oh, yes. It is," Matt insisted. "It's up to your mind, Nora. You know the saying: mind over matter," Matt explained to Nora.

"That's bullshit, and you know it," Nora replied crossly.

"No, actually, it isn't," Matt answered in an earnest tone of voice. "Your state of mind will help you recover sooner. Anyway, do you want to talk to Nat now or not?" Matt asked Nora, and tears welled in her eyes. "What now?" he asked with exasperation, opening his arms.

"Nothing. I'm only happy," Nora answered in a shaky voice. "So, you won't take my son from me," she asked Matt for reassurance.

"Don't be stupid," Matt's dry answer came, and he took his phone from his pocket and dialed Bryan's number.

He listened with half an ear to the conversation Nora had with her son. He was thinking about how to organize everything and made mental notes to get in touch with his personal assistant that evening and rearrange his schedule for an entire month. Matt knew he had a few appointments he needed to keep, but hoped to get rid of everything else.

He was more interested in the conversation Nora had with Becka and Bryan. She surprised him by smiling a few times and even laughing heartily at something one of the two said.

When she finished her conversation, she handed the phone back to Matt.

"Thank you, Matt. I won't ever forget that," she told him, and her eyes shone with gratitude.

"No big deal," he replied with indifference, although he doubted he would ever be at ease when she trained those eyes on him.

He couldn't understand how she could affect him when he didn't like or respect the woman.

"Does Nat have any allergies, something I need to know?" Matt asked Nora.

"No, no allergies. Nat's a very healthy kid," she smiled at Matt. "About the daycare now. I know that you could leave him there, but they won't give it back to you," she said with a brief hesitation and bit her lip. "Maybe, if I call tomorrow and see what they need, we could arrange something."

"Don't bother with that," Matt waved her offer away. "Is it important for Nat's development to go there?" he reconsidered.

"Not really," Nora shook her head. "Well, he plays with other children," she added.

"But couldn't I take him to a park and have him play with children there?" Matt inquired, shoving his hands into his pants pockets.

"Yes, you could. But don't you need to go to work?" Nora asked Matt, and her voice showed surprise.

"I'm the boss," Matt replied dryly. "I decide when and if I work," he explained. "I'll have to go to the office for some meetings, and I do have a couple of court appointments scheduled, but Becka and Bryan promised that they'd look after Nat when I can't, so don't worry about it," Matt continued, balancing on the balls of his feet.

Nora and Matt assessed each other in silence for a few seconds, and then, Nora said, "I can't thank you enough, Matt."

"You don't have to," Matt replied, always in a dry voice. "Everything will be fine, and, no, you owe me nothing," he thought to add for good measure.

Nora looked at him with disbelief and then huffed, "Yeah, sure. You rearrange your entire life around my kid, and I don't owe you..."

"No, you don't," Matt repeated forcefully. "So, are we good now? Can you get back to sleep so that you recover sooner?"

Nora closed her eyes, shook her head, and said, "Yeah, why not?"

"Good, then I'll see you tomorrow," Matt hurried to say and left the room.

Nora looked after him aback. *That's one weird man, Nora. Something's not right with him.*

MATT LEFT THE HOSPITAL after he discussed the possibility of covering the costs for a private room, once they moved Nora into a regular hospital room.

Matt made sure that they understood he didn't want any fuss about who paid the bill, and he persuaded them. He explained to them that Nora was a proud woman, and it wouldn't do her any good to have her riled. Matt pointed out that Nora would be upset if they told her that he covered the costs.

In the cab, on his way back to Becka and Bryan's house, Matt questioned the reasons for his actions. He was a rational man, after all. Matt had never done anything without weighing the pros and cons carefully.

However, this time, he hadn't even stopped to think. Something pushed him to do things he would have refused if he had given himself time to ponder about them.

It wasn't about the money, of course. Mat was far from wanting any. Yet, his behavior was beyond his comprehension.

Matt couldn't even say that Nota had bewitched him. He had first-hand knowledge about that. He knew a witch when he saw one, and Nora wasn't it.

Now, there was one question that persisted. What did Nora have that Matt's behavior changed when he got close to her?

What the heck? I've changed my life for her entirely in one day, and willingly.

When he realized that, Matt froze.

CHAPTER EIGHT

MATT WOKE UP WITH A little bundle of joy, bouncing on his stomach. He liked sleeping on his back and enjoying his kingsize order-made bed. Almost 6.2 feet tall, Matt needed all the space he could get.

He rubbed his face with one hand and steadied the kid with the other. It had become routine already. Every single morning, during the last four days, he had woken up with Nat jumping up and down on him, and he wondered if the child did the same thing with his mother.

Matt thought about the differences in size and muscles between Nora and him. He wondered how she fared after such an episode. She was just a slip of a woman, no match for the energetic bouncing of the child.

His training with Bryan had defined Matt's abs some more, and he was in great shape. However, the child's bouncing still felt like a mule kicked him in his stomach.

"All right, munchkin," he said. "I see you're up already."

Nat nodded vigorously and showed Matt all his milk teeth. All in all, Matt observed with satisfaction that Nat was a very balanced and happy kid. He took everything in stride and didn't get riled easily.

"What made you so happy this morning?" Matt asked, setting the child aside and getting out of the bed.

"You promised that I could go to Becka," the child enunciated correctly, almost jumping on the bed. "She promised we'd go to the park. She promised you'd take me sailing on the lake on Saturday. And I can see my mom today again," the child talked a mile a minute, and Matt smiled.

"I see Becka promised a lot at my expense," he joked, but when the child glared, he hurried to add, "Now, don't worry, we'll do everything she promised, okay?"

Nat smiled happily again and jumped out of bed. He followed Matt into the bathroom, and like every other morning, Matt helped him to clean his teeth, wash his face, and comb his hair.

Matt had already found out that the kid liked to choose his clothes and get dressed by himself, so after he had his shower, Matt went directly into the kitchen to prepare breakfast for both of them.

Matt had a long day before him, starting with leaving Nat at Becka's so that he could go into work. He had a court appearance in less than two hours, and he couldn't be late for that.

SOMEWHAT TIRED, MATT came to take Nat from Becka a little after three. By that hour, Nat must have finished his nap, and now, he was probably ready to go.

Matt also hoped to get some lunch from Bryan because he hadn't had the time for a bite since morning, and his stomach had been grumbling since noon.

Matt didn't bother to ring the bell. He doubted Becka had locked the door after he left in the morning. He knew that Bryan didn't have any plans to go out that day, and that meant that he couldn't have discovered his wife's forgetfulness.

He went directly into the house and for a second there, froze. His great-grandmother raised voice came from the back of the house. When she wanted, Rebecca's voice boomed in a way that would have made a drill sergeant proud.

"I can't accept it, young man," she bellowed.

Matt immediately rushed through the kitchen and out onto the patio. It wasn't a stretch to think that Rebecca was chastising Nat, and he couldn't allow it. The child was in his care, and he wouldn't have permitted anyone to shout at him.

Rebecca wasn't a mean and unfeeling woman, but she did like to have her way every single time. Yet, this time, Matt couldn't let her.

Once outside in the garden, Matt stopped suddenly. Baffled, he stared at the scene before his eyes. For a moment, he was sure that he hallucinated.

Rebecca held Nat in her lap, one arm around his midriff, and she pointed a bony finger to Bryan, who was sitting in a lawn armchair not far from her. Bryan tried to keep a stern face, but a stubborn smile fought to appear in the corner of his mouth.

"What's going on?" Matt asked in a voice far from mild.

Nat immediately turned to him and shouted, "Matt."

Nat held his arms up so that Matt could take him in his arms. Matt realized that he had become the child's anchor since his mother's shooting, and curious enough, he didn't mind it. He actually enjoyed the pure joy on the kid's face whenever Natt saw him.

"Hush, now, young man," Rebecca told Natt with authority. "You must finish eating your snack first, and then you can go to Matt."

Obedient, Nat immediately snatched another biscuit off the plate on the table and stuffed it in his mouth. Everyone smiled, and Matt ruffled the boy's hair.

"Where's Becka?" Matt inquired, glancing at Bryan.

His great-grandmother waved her hand, "Becka's in the study. She had to take her mother's call," she explained.

"You see," Bryan intervened maliciously, crossing his arms over his chest with indifference, and stretching his legs in front of him, "Rebecca thought a double-front attack would be in order. Becka's mother would nag her, while Rebecca would bellow me into submission."

"Submission for what?" Matt asked. He hadn't heard any problems or complaints related to his favorite couple lately.

"For taking the trust money, of course," Rebecca snapped at him. "I've waited long enough. I've hoped that they'd come to their senses sooner or later, but it's been almost a year. I won't take his refusal for an answer," she ended with obstinacy and pointed the same bony finger to Bryan.

"Sweet great-grandma," Brya began to say, but Rebecca interrupted him with a smirk.

"Don't take me with sweet great-grandma," she retorted. "I know that you don't mean it, and I won't have it."

"Don't mean it?" Bryan inquired with puzzlement.

"Of course, you don't mean it," Rebecca huffed. "I've seen you, and I know how you think. You hate me, and that's why you won't let Becka have the money," she explained in a bitter voice.

"Now, there, you're wrong. I do think you are sweet in your own way," Bryan replied.

When he noticed that Rebecca intended to contradict him, Bryan stood up and put a hand on her shoulder.

"You don't show it, Rebecca, but you're not as mean as you want people to believe. About the money, sorry," he said and shook his head, "but I don't need it, and Becka doesn't want it, that's all. Don't take it personally. I won't say I'm sorry she doesn't," Bryan shook his head and patted her shoulder as if he wanted to sweeten the blow.

Bryan thought for a moment and leaned over Rebecca and kissed her parchment-like cheek, which stunned her. Then, he started back to the house, throwing over the shoulder, "I suppose you're hungry, Matt. I'll bring you something, only take a seat."

Pleased, Matt smiled and sat next to Rebecca. Bryan was always considerate, and if he told someone how domestic Bryan had become, no one would have believed him.

Matt shook his head, amused. Then he felt Rebecca's eyes on him and turned to her to meet her assessing sharp gaze.

"How have you been, grandma?" Matt asked her politely.

He had to make some conversation with her. He couldn't ignore Rebecca forever.

"Don't grandma me, Matt," Rebecca retorted. "You've got some explaining to do, young man," she said, looking at him pointedly.

Matt shook his head and replied quietly, "No, I don't have to explain anything."

"I care to differ, and the proof is in my lap," she snapped, and Nat looked up at her.

"Me?" Natt inquired shyly, and Matt wanted to shout at his great-grandmother for not considering the child's feelings.

It wasn't something new coming from Rebecca. However, Matt still hoped that she would change. At least her age should have mollified her enough.

"You're the proof, kiddo, but in a good sense," Rebecca ruffled the boy's hair. "Now finish eating if you want to play," she ordered in a voice that didn't allow any more inquiries.

Nat immediately snatched a slice of orange and shoveled it into his mouth. Satisfied, Rebecca smiled at him and stroked his head.

"So, when were you going to tell me that you had a son?" she brusquely asked Matt.

Matt merely stared at her. He would have liked to answer something, anything, but his mind went blank in shock.

"You're my daddy," Nat said in awe, and the adoration in his voice humbled Matt.

The glimmer in the child's eyes shook Matt, and he came back to reality.

"Thanks, grandma," he said sarcastically. "How can I now..." he started to say but couldn't finish.

"You take care of Nat. That means that you're his dad, I don't care who fathered him," Rebecca replied. Then she shrugged as if everything were quite simple.

"You're my daddy," the child repeated, and Matt groaned.

"Should I congratulate you, Matt?" Bryan's dry voice came from behind him.

Matt looked up and noticed the stern expression on Bryan's face. He didn't need his mind-reading gift to know what his friend thought.

Matt raised his arms helplessly and asked Bryan, "What should I do now?"

"It's not for me to know," Bryan replied curtly and set a tray with a bowl of soup and a sandwich before him.

"What kind of question is that, Matt?" Rebecca huffed and lowered the child to the ground. "Now you can go and play," she told Nat and slapped his behind, jokingly, and making him laugh.

But then, Nat didn't go to play immediately. He looked up at Matt and said, "You promised that I could see mommy today."

"Of course, you will see her," Rebecca answered at once. "We'll all see mommy today."

Rebecca's words shocked Matt, and he chocked. A jet of soup came out of his mouth, but Bryan jumped back, and the stream didn't get him. However, Rebecca wasn't so lucky because she was right on the path of the liquid, and both her face and blouse took the brunt of the spray.

"Matthew Winston!" Rebecca bellowed and threw her arms in the air with exasperation.

Rebecca hadn't expected something like that from Matt, not in a million years. Matt had proved the most balanced of her grandchildren and great-grandchildren by far.

Nat and Bryan started laughing like hyenas, but Rebecca gave them the evil eye, with a huff. She needn't do more. They smothered their hilarity at once.

Nat chose to run to Becka's flowers, which fascinated him, and where Bryan had set up his outdoor toys. Meanwhile, Bryan gathered napkins to help Rebecca clean up.

Matt only stared at her with widened eyes. Matt couldn't consider that he had spat on his fastidious great-grandma. But then, Matt couldn't believe Rebecca's nerve, either. Rebeca had utterly invited herself somewhere she had no business to go, and Matt decided that he would be damned if he merely submitted to her orders without taking a stand.

Rebecca huffed again and snatched the napkins from Bryan. She started wiping her face vigorously, still frowning.

All the time she made use of the napkins, she muttered, "I've never...never...never thought you'd do that to me. How, the heck, am I going out now? Huh?" she ended her muttering, with a shout from the top of her lungs, and she bad-mugged Matt again.

Matt still couldn't say a thing. His tongue was in knots. He would have liked to say a lot of things, but none was appropriate for his great-grandma's ears.

Bryan intervened immediately. He noticed that Rebecca was ready to slap Matt silly. Although he would have liked to see how that would go, considering that Matt was much taller than his great-grandma and outweighed her by at least 80 pounds, Bryan didn't think that the show would have been good for the kid.

"I'm sure you can borrow something from Becka," Bryan tried to soothe Rebecca, in a quiet voice. "It isn't the end of the world, you know? I know. You are taller. It's true, but Becka's rounder, and it will compensate," he explained.

"Are you saying that I look like a scarecrow, young man?" Rebecca changed her target suddenly and rallied against Bryan, gathering more steam.

"Far from me, Rebecca," Bryan replied.

His voice was always calm. Bryan didn't need another shouting match that day, and Rebecca had given him enough grief that afternoon.

"Then, are you saying that Becka is too round?" Rebecca snapped at him, ready to defend her great-granddaughter.

"She's perfectly round," Bryan observed very matter-of-factly. "So, let's not get into an argument here."

"I think that I should go," Matt finally found his voice.

He thought to take advantage of the sparring match between Rebecca and Bryan and sulk away with Nat. Yet, Matt thought wrong.

Rebecca immediately turned to Matt and barked, "Eat your lunch and keep your mouth shut. And maybe, this time, you can eat your soup without sprinkling me again."

Matt's worry escalated. He thought that he knew Rebecca, but he didn't understand her game now. Matt only knew that he would have a horrible fight on his hands if he wanted to make Rebecca remain there, at Becka's house, or go home, but not to the hospital with him.

"Grandma," Matt started to speak, but Rebecca didn't have any of it.

"I said, have your lunch," she snapped more forcefully. "You'll have enough time to talk to me this afternoon and evening," she observed.

Her words had the effect of a cold shower for Matt and strengthened his resolve.

"What do you mean?" he asked in a dry voice, pushing the tray away, definitely not hungry anymore.

"I decided to borrow a top from Becka, so you won't get rid of me so swiftly, Matt," Rebecca scowled at him. "I'll be ready in no time at all."

Matt frowned at Bryan because he was the one who had had the idea to offer one of Becka's blouses. Bryan only shrugged, disinterested in Matt's anger.

"This is your battle, Matt," Bryan said.

"What battle?" Becka's voice came from behind him, and Bryan turned his head to her.

He smiled at his wife and informed her, "Rebecca needs one of your tops, sweetie. Matt showered her with soup," he grinned.

Rebecca slapped his arm, unamused with his antics.

"Try to find one that goes with my skirt," she ordered Becka. "How did it go with your mom?" she asked slyly.

"We had a nice conversation, grandma, and no, I didn't accept the trust money," she said. "How come Matt sprayed you with the soup?" she asked, sitting in her husband's lap with fluidity.

"Don't change the subject, young lady," Rebecca snapped at her. "I want you to reconsider," she slapped her palm on the tabletop, vexed that the Becka hadn't bent down.

"Sorry, grandma, I can't," Becka shrugged, and her voice showed no remorse. "If you hadn't conditioned that money, things might have been different," she observed.

"You know why I did it," Rebeca defended her decision.

"I know, and I understand your reasons, really," Becka replied, and leaning forward, she stroked her grandma's arm. "But that doesn't mean that I agree with you. The way you treated Bryan..."

"Sweetie," Bryan intervened, but Becka hushed him, with a shake of her head and a finger firmly put on his lips.

"What did you expect me to do when I saw a man like him with you?" Rebecca countered, waving her hand in Bryan's direction.

"A man like him?" Becka jumped off Bryan's lap, ready to do battle, and the air vibrated all around them.

Becka controlled her fury now, and things stopped flying around all the time. Yet, the air still vibrated whenever she grew angry, and her husband knew that he had to do something.

Bryan attempted to intervene and pull her back in his lap, but she slapped his hands away.

"No, Bryan, she won't get away with insulting you once more," Becka said ferociously. "Once it was more than enough," she observed, and her eyes thundered to her great-grandma.

"But I didn't insult him, Becka, don't be stupid," the old woman said in a very unemotional voice, which contrasted with Becka's white fury. "I just said he's so imposing and severe, and I couldn't see you with a man like him...at that time," Rebecca thought to add when Becka practically growled. "I thought that he'd stifle your exuberance and youth. Now I know better," she shrugged. "You don't have to get in a huff, young lady. People make mistakes. Just wait until you get to my age. Then tell me that you haven't made any," she challenged Becka.

Becka didn't have the time to answer because Matt chose that moment to stand. He braced his palms on the table and reclaimed Rebecca's attention.

"I want to know what you plan to do," Matt demanded with authority and watched his grandma with steely eyes. "You've played enough with me already," he raised his voice.

Matt slapped the tabletop, finally losing his temper and making a few eyebrows raise. Matt never showed if he was rattled or furious, and his outburst was uncharacteristic enough to astonish them.

'Now, I'm starting behaving like a loony bin,' Matt thought, his eyes always fixed on the old woman. He knew that she plotted something, and he didn't like the direction of her actions.

If he could have gone back to the early hours of the morning, Matt would have made different plans for Nat that day. He would have never taken the chance of letting Rebecca know what was going on.

"I'm planning to see your young lady, Matt," Rebecca said very straightforward, unimpressed with his temper. "With or without you," she pointed out.

Matt's eyes flashed with anger. He even had to step back so he wouldn't be tempted to knot his fingers around the old bird's neck.

"There's no such thing like my young lady, grandma," Matt said squarely, unwilling to attract Nat's attention.

"Who are you kidding, Matt?" Rebecca mocked him, waving her fingers to him. "Humph! No man takes over the care of a child just out of the kindness of his heart," she waved the assumption away, with a flutter of her hand.

"There was no one else, that's all," Matt groused.

"Sheesh!" Rebecca puffed. "You have enough money to pay someone, Matty. You are a kind man, I'll give you that, but kindness only goes so far. So, I want to meet the woman..."

"You won't meet anyone," Matt snapped, interrupting her in a rude tone of voice. "You'll stay here or go home, whatever you want, but you won't interfere in my business. Is it clear?" he practically growled at Rebecca.

"I don't like your tone," the old woman straightened her back and stared him down.

"I don't care," Matt answered. "You don't know when to stop. You tried to control everyone's life from the beginning, and it simply killed you that you couldn't control mine. Well,

I don't care," his fist made contact with the tabletop. "I won't have it," he thundered to the old woman. "You can do whatever you want, great-grandma, but do it as far as possible from me and my business," he said in an icy voice now, aware that he had lost his temper and made a show of himself.

Then, he turned to Nat and stretched his hand toward the boy, "Nat, we're leaving to see your mom now. Come on, munchkin."

Nat ran to Matt, forgetting about the yard toys with which he was playing. Matt had bought him a crabbie sand table three days ago, and Becka and Bryan had set it next to the flowerbed the child liked the most.

"You promised that Becka and Bryan could come too," Nat took Matt's hand.

"I know I promised, Nat. But you that they've got guests right now. Becka and Bryan could come with us tomorrow," Matt said with a smile and ruffled the child's hair.

"It's not necessary," Rebecca intervened. "We can all go with you now. I only have to change my top, Nat, and we'll be on our way."

Rebecca had already understood that Matt didn't want to say anything wrong in front of the child. So she took advantage of Matt's weakness. She knew how to play her hand and succeed in her plans. Rebecca didn't know anything about pity. People needed a steely back to survive, and Rebecca had learned early not to show kindness when she shouldn't. She never backed down when she wanted something.

This time Matt effectively saw red. He let go to Nat's hand and turned to Rebecca. Matt's expression revealed that now he was ready to say everything he wished to say, no holds barred.

Becka whispered fearfully, "Bryan, do something."

CHAPTER NINE

BRYAN'S INTERVENTION spared both Matt and Rebecca of a total break up. Matt left Becka and Bryan's house with the kid and Becka in tow. Bryan remained to deal with the old witch, as Matt called Rebecca in his thoughts now.

Matt rarely had evil thoughts about his great-grandma. He understood why her heart had grown cold and why she wanted to control everything and everyone, even though he didn't like it.

Rebecca and Matt had butted heads over the years, sometimes more, sometimes less. The worse had been when Matt brought Velma with him to introduce her to the family. Yet, even then, Rebecca hadn't made him see red, ready to lash out at her and spit out all the resentments he had gathered over the years.

This time Rebecca hadn't just stepped over boundaries, but she had blown them up entirely.

Matt was beyond furious because Rebecca had made all those comments in front of the child. If Nat had repeated any of them to his mother, and that was a strong possibility, Nora would have been sure that Matt wanted to steal her son.

And just like that, Matt would go back to square one with Nora. Over the last few days, Nora and Matt had found somewhat common ground. Nora was less cautious and fearful of Matt, and some of the barriers had come down between them. Matt loved that.

When the doctor moved Nora into a reserve, Matt had begun to bring Nat to visit her. The child had helped with Matt's interactions with Nora, and she had opened more to Matt.

The glimmer of resentment and hatred had disappeared from Nora's eyes, and that relieved Matt. That Nora was also well on her way to recovery now could only add to his satisfaction.

Matt thought that Nora would follow her way, and he would go on his soon. He told himself that the situation satisfied him, but Matt knew that he was lying to himself. There was something there between them, although Matt didn't know what for sure. He had never been so confused in the head when it came to a relation with a woman, and Matt didn't know whether he wanted to see more of Nora in the future or not.

Their conversations had become less strained, and Matt had learned that Nora was an interesting woman, far from the materialistic and cheating female he had considered her before.

Matt still couldn't glimpse into her mind but didn't belabor over his inability to read her thoughts and took everything in stride. He discovered things about Nora in the same way a regular person with no paranormal powers learned about the people around. That seemed to be more satisfying than just reading someone's mind.

Matt had also hired an investigator to dig into Nora's past and her ex's past and present. He hadn't forgotten what Bryan told him, and he wanted to see whether he'd been duped.

Matt found out that Nora had been on her own for most of her life, and It saddened him to hear that. Nora's parents had moved to Florida when she was barely eighteen. They died there, in a break-in, a few years later.

The investigator researched the divorce evidence and came back empty. He had established beyond any doubt that the four witnesses couldn't have had an affair with Nora. Not only had they never met her, but at the times of the alleged dates, Nora was always working.

What the detective found was evidence against the ex-husband, though. Paul Willow had had two girlfriends on the side, and for some time already.

Matt had sworn never to accept a file again without checking the evidence himself. He knew that he had done a terrible injustice to Nora and had been the instrument of her humiliation. Whenever he remembered how he had talked to her, he gnashed his teeth in frustration.

"Are you alright, Matt?" Becka touched his arm.

Matt glanced at her for a second and then looked at the child in the back seat.

"Yes, I'm fine. Only a little raw after... well, after, you know."

Becka nodded and glanced out of the window. "You know, Matt, I don't think that anyone has ever stood against Rebecca, and that's why she thinks that she can do everything she wants," Becka remarked pensively.

"I don't give a...fig," Matt censored his language, both for Becka and Nat's sake. Matt felt cold and nasty, and he needed to swear. "I've had enough of her meddling in my business and of her demands," Matt slapped his hand on the steering wheel.

"I know. But Rebecca's old, and in her way, she does love all of us. Everyone knows that Rebecca loves you more than anyone else," Becka pointed out to Matt.

"As if I cared," Matt shrugged, a scowl etched on his face. "I'd prefer that she didn't love me at all."

"I like her," Nat's voice came from the back of the car, and Matt's brows climbed on his forehead.

"Really? How come?" he asked the boy.

"She barks. She doesn't bite," Nat replied.

"Where did you hear that?" Matt asked Nat, surprised that the boy could say something like that.

"Mom says that about dad," Natt explained.

"Did your dad shout as well?" Becka asked and turned in her seat to look at Nat.

"At mom," the child said. "He doesn't see me."

"How the... how come he doesn't see you?" Matt asked with disbelief, editing his words again.

"He says... I don't exist," the boy explained, and both Becka and Matt snarled.

"Maybe you didn't hear correctly," Becka tried to console him.

"No," Nat replied. "He said so. Many times."

"Bastard," Matt grumbled. "Someone should teach him a lesson. With their fists."

Becka heard him and smiled. Matt had always been willing to protect the underdog and dole the necessary punishment.

"Mommy needs flowers," Nat said suddenly.

"I beg your pardon?" Matt asked, surprised, stopping at the traffic lights.

"Flowers. She needs flowers," the child insisted.

"How do you know that?" Becka asked.

"Yesterday I saw people with flowers. People bring flowers in a hospital," Nat repeated stubbornly.

"Okay, don't get your pants into a twist, pal," Matt laughed. "We'll buy flowers, buddy. Look, right there," Matt said, pointing to a flower shop. Then he signaled to the right and changed lanes.

MATT ALLOWED NAT TO choose the flowers he liked, so they made their entrance in Nora's room with a large basket. To Becka's delight, the toddler had chosen one full of Alstroemeria. She knew that the flower symbolized devotion, prosperity, and fortune.

Nora's gaze fell on the basket, which supposedly Matt and Nat carried, and her eyes widened. Matt had persuaded the boy that they should both carry it. He doubted that the boy had the strength to hold it in his tiny hands.

Nora accepted the flowers gracefully, although she shook her head to Matt, chastising him for spending so much. Nora had seen baskets like that while window shopping, and she knew that they cost over $150. She couldn't believe that Matt would spend so much only to humor a child.

Her gaze was on Nat and Matt, so Nora nearly missed the short blond woman, who was standing near Matt. When she noticed Becka, Nora's heart cringed for a second. But then, Nora chased away the sadness she felt and smiled at Matt's companion.

"I'm Becka," the woman said to Nora. "I'm Matt's cousin, and I bear fruits," Becka showed a bag, where she had stuffed a few oranges, bananas, and apples. "Some stuff you can eat without cutlery," Becka explained and placed the bag on the nightstand next to Nora's bed.

"Becka's my friend, mom," Nat boasted. "She plays with me every day. She let me touch her babies. They're funny. They have no hair or almost no hair. And they sleep all the time, or they cry," Nat rushed to say, tripping over his own words.

The adults smiled indulgently, and then, Nora turned to Becka.

"You can't imagine how grateful I'm to you for all the help..."

Becka interrupted her by touching her arm and shaking her head.

"You don't need to be grateful. It's a good experience for my husband and me. My babies won't be babies forever, you know," she laughed.

Nora nodded and laughed, as well, "Don't I know it! It's like now they're in the crib, just sleeping and asking for food every few hours, and, suddenly, you have a small typhoon on your hands."

"Should we put the flowers on that stand there?" Matt asked, suddenly unwilling to be left out of the conversation.

"Yes, I think it's perfect there," Nora replied, a strange shyness in her voice.

Matt's left eyebrow hiked up his forehead. He had never seen Nora shy.

Nora invited them to sit. She had two chairs in the room, and she took Nat on the bed with her. She kept touching the child and brushing his hair, a sign that she had missed him terribly.

"So, you're good with Becka, Nat, yes?" she asked the little boy.

"Yes, and with Bryan. And I met their great-grandma today. And she is funny," the boy announced with exuberance.

Both Becka and Matt looked at the child as if he had lost his mind. There were lots of things one could say about Rebecca. Being funny wasn't one of her traits, though.

"What?" Nora asked, noticing their puzzlement.

"Great-grandma is anything but funny," Matt replied in a dry voice. "Not even when I was of Nat's age, I thought differently," he explained.

Becka merely nodded. She agreed wholeheartedly with everything Matt said.

Feeling Nora's curious eyes on her, Becka explained, "Great-grandma is... let's say, unusual. And she's good to take in extremely tiny doses. Today, both Matt and I have had a little too much of her presence," she laughed.

Matt just growled and ruffled his hair with nervous fingers.

"She said that Matt's my dad," Nat announced proudly, jumping on the bed.

All three adults froze. Matt looked at him with widened eyes, Becka covered her mouth – she didn't know if she wanted to scream or laugh, and Nora watched Matt in shock.

"What did she say?" Nora asked in a small voice, afraid that she would hear the same thing again.

"Matt is my dad," Nat repeated, nodding vigorously. "And I agree," he let them know that there was no doubt in his mind about Matt's identity.

"Say something, darn it," Nora snapped at Matt.

He shrugged, "I am at a loss of words."

"How can you be at a loss of words?" she rebuked him. "You're a lawyer, for God's sake. You don't do anything but talk all day long."

He scowled at her and groused, "That's what you think lawyers do all day? And what the heck do you want me to tell him? He's three. What will he understand?"

"I don't know," she threw her hands in the air. "But you need to say something, and soon," Nora pointed out.

"Why me and not you?" he retorted furiously. By now, his eyes glinted, and he spoke through tight teeth.

When Nora didn't have anything to say to that, Becka intervened, "If you two don't mind, maybe it's better to leave it like this for the moment. There's enough time to…"

"When? After he's convinced that Matt's his father?" Nora pounced on her.

"Hey, I'm not the enemy here," Becka thought to mention and put her hands up. "Yet, Matt still has to take care of Nat for a while, and I don't think that antagonizing…"

"He's my father," Nat interrupted her furious. "Great-grandma said so," he said, and everyone noticed tears in his eyes.

"No one says differently, kiddo," Becka replied, ruffling his hair. "Just adult talk," she laughed.

"Becka," Nora said, staring at Matt. "Would you mind taking Nat with you to the coffee shop downstairs and buy me a latte or something? I'd owe you one."

"Buy one for me too," Matt said, taking money out of his pocket. "And Nat, they have cookies, I hear. See what you want."

"I have money, Matt Winston," Nora tried to push his hand away so that Becka couldn't take his money.

"And so do I," Becka said and exhaled loudly. Then she took Nat's hand and pulled him with her. "We'll buy you some cookies and some white chocolate for me," she explained to the boy.

"I want white chocolate, too," the child scowled.

"Then you shall have it," Becka laughed. "Nothing wrong with that once in a blue mood," she told him in a conspiratorial voice, and they left the room.

Nora looked after Becka and Nat. Matt didn't need to be a mind-reader to know that Nora was furious.

"Look," Matt started to say, but Nora stopped him with a shake of her head.

"You need to straighten things up when they come back," Nora insisted.

"You're right, but your timing sucks," Matt replied, and she glared at him. "I know you're upset, Nora, but the child must live with me for at least another week, if not a little more. I won't have him unsettled. In time, he might transfer his wish of having a father upon someone else. I don't know, okay? However, I know that I can't upset Nat now. It's enough that he misses you. Don't you think?" Matt tried to soothe Nora, stroking her arm, but she jerked away, and Matt tightened his teeth in frustration.

"Yes, I know, but when I get out, and he won't see you, Nat will think that it's my fault, and I have to live with him for a much longer time than you do," Nora said, and her finger poked Matt in his chest.

"Is it absolutely necessary that Nat doesn't see me anymore?" Matt asked Nora.

Matt's question came like a blow and stunned her, so Nora couldn't do anything more but stare at him.

The silence stretched for almost a minute. Matt ran his fingers through his hair anxiously and then said with sarcasm, "I see that you glow with glee at my proposition."

Nora shook her head and replied to him, "You only... astonished me. I'd have imagined that you couldn't wait to get rid of us."

"Nat is great," Matt pointed out. "Why would I want to get rid of him?"

"Me, then," she groused, hurt by his words.

"I've never said that. I...like you...I think," he shrugged. "I thought that...we should try at least. I mean...we should see how it works...if it works. We haven't seen each other in the best light until now, you know. We might be surprised with what might be," he continued wistfully, and his eyes swept over her.

The day when she moved into the private room, Matt had brought her a set of sweats at her request. They hang loose on her but didn't hide much of her shape.

Nora's eyes glimmered, taking him in. Then, she closed her eyes for a couple of seconds, clenched and unclenched her hands a few times, and afterward, she looked straight into his eyes.

"Right now, I have a phobia about any relationship with a man."

"I know you've just divorced and I don't want to pressure you,"

Matt took a step toward her, but she stopped his words and his advancement with a gesture.

"It's not the divorce, Matt. The divorce was the end. It's been about a few years of resentments and upset...and... I know I'm unfair right now, but I lump all men in the same category – unworthy, untrusty, and better gone from my life."

"I see," Matt said quietly. "I think... I won't bother you then. Once you've recovered and can take care of Nat, I'll remove myself from your life, don't worry," he replied bitterly.

Nora watched Matt thoughtfully. Then she came to him and touched his chest. "No, I don't think I truly want that. Maybe we can try and see how it goes, but you should know that Nat goes where I go. I don't have anyone to stay with him when I am away, so..."

"Don't worry," Matt replied, taking her hands in his. Hope glimmered in his eyes, and his tone didn't have the same resigned and bitter sound. "I don't mind having Nat around. And maybe, now and then, he can stay with Becka and Bryan for a couple of hours, to give you some respite," he smiled at her.

"Definitely," Becka's reply came from the door.

Both surprised and not only a little guilty, Nora and Matt turned to her, and Becka smirked.

"I think that's a great idea, Matt. And I am sure that Nat believes the same. Don't you, Nat? Don't you like spending time with Bryan and me?"

Nat nodded vigorously and then said, "And Bryan even cooks. Like you, mom. His food is pretty good," he said and licked his lips, making the adults laugh.

"So, you're a good cook," Becka concluded. "That's just perfect. Matt can't cook to save his life," she shrugged. "A lot like me. Matt, do you think we've got a gene missing in our genetic code or what?"

Matt chuckled and nudged Becka's chin with his thumb, "Oh, kiddo, you're so funny."

"By the way," Becka told Nora, "on Saturday, Matt will take Nat sailing."

Nora frowned and turned to Matt, "I don't think it's safe."

"Oh, yes, it is," Becka contradicted Nora and patted her on the shoulder to smother any upset. "Matt is the best and most careful sailor you'll find. Besides, he insists that guests wear life-saving vests, so Nat won't be in any danger."

Nora seemed a little reluctant, but the imploring face of her son made her turn to Matt, "Are you sure you can take care of him while sailing?"

"Of course, I can," he responded, offended by Nora's lack of faith in him.

"And if I convince mom to take care of the babies, Bryan and I can accompany them," Becka chimed in.

"And we'll come to visit you in the afternoon, so you'll see that Nat is in one piece," Matt joked. However, he regretted that immediately when Nora scowled at him.

"By the way," Becka said, "I am sorry, but tomorrow, Nat won't be able to come to visit. I bought tickets to a puppet show, and it's exactly after his nap," she apologized. "I hoped you wouldn't mind..."

Nora shook her head immediately, "No, it isn't a problem. I can survive without visitors for one day," she smiled, but her smile was sad.

"You'll still have me," Matt rushed to say.

Becka burst into laughter at the look on his face when he realized what he had said.

"I mean, I'll still come," he rephrased his statement, bad-mugging Becka.

CHAPTER TEN

MATT COULDN'T WAIT to have a visit with Nora only for himself. He had enjoyed watching her interacting with Nat, and he had been quite pleased to see Nora getting along with Becka.

However, Matt longed to be alone with Nora. He wanted to further the relationship he had told her about, and that wasn't going quite smooth when there were witnesses in the room.

He drove and left Nat and Becka at the puppet show, promising that he would be back for them before it ended. He hurried to the hospital afterward, and on the way there, he stopped to buy a potted orchid for Nora.

Matt remembered Nat's words. People brought flowers when they came to visit someone in the hospital.

Matt thought a little further ahead and decided to buy some cookies for Nora to nibble on, a couple of magazines, and a new book. He had already brought Nora a couple of books the day before, but Matt didn't think that she had too much to do in that hospital room. He would have crawled on the walls, had he been in her place.

He wasn't very sure about the magazines, but he decided he couldn't go wrong with a National Geographic and a Reader's Digest.

A KNOCK ON THE ROOM'S door brought a smile on Nora's lips. Matt was early, but she wasn't sorry that he was there already.

Nora had been thinking about that visit since the day before. Once Matt had planted the idea in her head, she had been thinking of nothing else.

She left the book that she was reading on her pillow and said, "Come in."

The door opened, and to her surprise, it wasn't Matt the one coming into the room. An older woman, well in her eighties, if not more, entered her room with the gait of a general. Her white hair rendered her black eyes more compelling, and those eyes zeroed in on Nora as soon as she stepped into the room and closed the door behind.

Although she could see some resemblance to Matt, especially in the way the woman carried herself and the shape of her eyes, nose, and mouth, Nora remarked, "I'm afraid you have the wrong room."

The woman gave her the chills. Her piercing look and the smile perched on her lips didn't reassure Nora at all.

"I've got the right room," the woman replied and advanced into the room. "I'm Rebecca, Matt's great-grandmother. I think it's high time we met," she observed, stretching her hand to Nora.

Nora politely shook her hand but replied, "I haven't even thought that we should have met. I'm nothing more but a passing acquaintance of Matt..."

"Balderdash," Rebecca retorted, and Nora's eyes widened. "Passing acquaintance, my foot. My great-grandson doesn't make a habit of caring for people's children. I don't even think that he'd spent more than a couple of minutes with a child before meeting you," she waved her hand dismissively.

"Probably, he had his reasons," Nora said softly and indicated a chair to the woman to sit down, even though she would have preferred to send her on her merry way.

Rebecca sat on the chair while Nora perched on the edge of the mattress. Rebecca's visit made her anxious, and her nervousness increased with every second.

Nora supposed that the old woman had come to tell her '*shoo away and leave my great-grandson alone,*' and she wasn't sure how she should react.

She had pondered everything carefully since the previous afternoon and felt that she wanted to get to know Matt better. She didn't welcome Rebecca's interference, but for the moment, she decided to wait before reacting.

"I brought you some chocolates," Rebecca said and took a box of sweets out of her large handbag.

Nora thanked the woman with half a voice and put the chocolates on the nightstand next to the flowers she had received from Nat and Matt.

Both women assessed each other in silence for a couple of minutes, and then, Rebecca began her attack.

"So, you're the woman who bewitched my Matt," she said. The tone of her voice implied that she had already judged Nora and found her wanting.

A warning light shone in Nora's eyes. She proposed to herself to be polite with the woman. Rebecca was old, after all, and Matt's great-grandma. However, Nora didn't want to let Rebecca humiliate her.

Nora knew that she was somewhat average. Her hair was just a touch too fiery, her skin rather pale, and her green eyes looked big on her face. Even her height was average, barely 5.4. Nonetheless, Nora had a fullness of her hips, thighs, and bust that was far from ordinary.

"I must say that I was dying of curiosity to meet you," Rebecca continued, not bothered with Nora's attempt to warn her off. "Matt has never been unkind, but he's never gone so out of the way to please someone. He'd arranged his personal and professional life around you and your son," she remarked.

"Let's leave my son alone," Nora asked in a mild voice, yet the underlying steel was there, and Rebecca chuckled.

"Let's not," she retorted, and Nora's eyes flashed with storms. "I like the little imp. He's smart and energetic, a good child. Someone took good care of him," Rebecca gave Nora her due. "Anyways," she fluttered her hand, "the idea is that there's something with you, and you reeled my Matty in," the woman continued.

Nora looked at her with disbelief. Yes, Matt showed some interest, but he didn't seem hooked on her. He only expressed some interest in exploring a possible relationship. That didn't mean that he was bewitched, as Rebecca claimed.

"Don't look at me like that, young lady," Rebecca snapped. "I know my boy, and I know that he's infatuated with you."

"If he's just infatuated, you don't have anything to worry about," Nora remarked very matter-of-factly.

She was sitting, her back ramrod straight and her hands quiet in her lap. Yet, inside, she seethed.

How dare you come here and judge me? What makes you think that you're above me?

"I'll worry if I want. Now, I want what's best for my boy," Rebecca continued as if she'd discussed the weather. "You're good, probably, given how Nat turned out, but..." she paused for effect, "you're not the best."

For a second, Nora couldn't breathe. She knew the old bat would say that, and yet it surprised her.

"Why are you here again?" she asked with nonchalance as if she hadn't been insulted already.

"It's pretty simple, girl," Rebecca replied. "You need money. That's no doubt there," she continued, and irony sounded in her voice. "I already know everything about you. That's how I traced you here," she waved her hand, showing the hospital room. "Now, you need to tell me how much you'd need to let Matt go. His future is somewhere else," the woman concluded in a demanding voice.

Nora looked at her in shock. She'd expected a dress down, more insults, threats, possibly. She didn't expect to have to name her price.

She needed only a few seconds to recover, though, and then, she jumped off the bed and started bellowing.

CHAPTER ELEVEN

AN ICY FOG CLAIMED Matt's mind when the nurse told him Nora had an older woman visiting with her. He knew who that woman might be.

He needed a few seconds to react and gather his thoughts. Then, in a hurry, he threw a '*thank you*' to the nurse over his shoulder and practically ran to Nora's hospital room.

He perceived a raised voice coming from the room just before opening the door. He didn't waste time knocking but threw the door open. He stopped in the threshold, his nostrils flaring and his eyebrows almost knotted in a terrible frown.

Nora was looming over his great-grandma, and he couldn't stop admiring how good she looked in warrior mode.

"Is it clear?" she continued, without noticing his arrival. "I don't need your money or your approval. You can shove both where..."

"Young lady," Rebecca stopped her. "Your language is deteriorating," she observed with icy contempt.

"So what?" she replied. "I don't care about your opinion about me, and you cannot buy me."

"Of course, not," the old woman remarked. "It's not like you'd accept less when you know Matt's financial worth now. You wouldn't, would you?" she sneered.

"I don't need his money or yours," Nora stressed out. "I make what I need. What I want is for you to get out of here and never come back," she shouted.

Then, she turned to the door to open it and throw the old bat out. She went cold all over when her eyes fell on Matt.

He was watching her with impenetrable eyes. He looked good, although slightly harassed, and regret nested in her heart.

She was a practical woman, though, so she squashed any regrets and feelings, and said, "You're just in time to show your great-grandmother to the door. I'll ask for a discharge tomorrow morning, so, yes, I apologize, but I do need you to watch Nat for me tonight. Tomorrow, though, I'll take him out of your hands." By the end, her voice shook, although she had started calm enough.

Matt didn't answer at first. Her flat voice sounded strained to his ears. He looked into her eyes and found them dull. The light he had seen there yesterday was gone.

"Yes, I'll show great-grandma to the door, and yes, if you want to leave the hospital and it's safe to do so, I'm all for it. What won't happen is to make me go away," he pointed out.

Closing the distance between them, Matt touched her faintly rosy-colored cheek with his fingers. Anger had powdered her skin, and her lips were trembling. Without thinking, he leaned down and lightly touched his mouth to hers. His fingers lingered on her face for a few more moments, and then, he straightened.

Matt stared at her a little more and then handed her the bag with the things he had brought her. "Hold onto this, Nora. I have to take care of my great-grandma," he mentioned sarcastically.

He turned to Rebecca and asked, mildly interested, "Are you going out on your own steam, or do you need my help?"

Both women gasped. Nora couldn't believe her ears. She had thought that Matt would leave, and that would be the end of it.

Rebecca was even more stunned. She had never imagined that Matt would take action against her. He would grumble, maybe, but in time, he would resign to her way of thinking.

She had tried to wedge a rift between Nora and Matt the day before when she told the child that Matt was his dad. She liked the boy well enough, but she didn't think that Matt should be with someone only because of his sense of duty. Rebecca wanted something more for him.

"How dare you talk to me like that?" she pounced on him.

"I asked whether you leave by yourself, or I needed to have you removed," he rephrased his previous statement and stared Rebecca down.

The woman huffed, and the color raised in her face. Nora felt sorry for her when she saw her lips quiver.

"Matt," Nora touched his arm hesitantly. "Maybe you shouldn't..."

"I should have done it long ago," Matt contradicted her in a steely voice. "Excuse me, honey," he said and moved her hand from his arm.

He stepped closer to Rebecca, and unnervingly, he asked her again, "So what'll be, great-grandma?"

"If you think that Marjorie won't hear about this..." Rebecca threatened, but Matt put up his hand and stopped her.

"I don't give a... fig," he blue-penciled his language. "Mother will understand," he shrugged. "Now, I want you to leave," he said in an even sterner voice.

Rebecca had had enough. She straightened and replied in the most authoritative voice, "You understand that you'd never get your hands on the trust money."

Nora gasped lightly. She hadn't intended to make Matt lose his money or put him in the crosshairs with his family because of her.

She rushed and touched his arm again, "Matt, I don't want you to..."

"But I do," he replied, always watching Rebecca with flinty eyes.

Rebecca realized he wouldn't back down, and she glared at him. She turned on her heels without a word and left the room.

Matt observed her glare and knew what Rebecca would do first. He turned to Nora, caressed her face with his fingers, and said, "I'm sorry, but I need to let mom know that Rebecca will park on her doorstep."

"Oh, my God, your mom will hate me, if only for that," Nora cried out with dismay.

Her chances with Matt became thinner and thinner, and she admonished herself for not listening to her reason. She knew that she shouldn't have gotten involved with anyone. She had other priorities in mind, and again, she had set herself up for disappointment.

"Be serious," Matt replied. "Mom's not like that," he explained to her and helped her sit on the bed.

Then, he took the phone out of his pocket to call his mother. He intended to call Jay afterward and ask him to go and take Becka and Nat from the theatre and bring them to the hospital.

CHAPTER TWELVE

NORA WATCHED MATT TALKING to his brother, Jay, over the phone, and envied the easy camaraderie between the two. She had never had such an open and warm relationship with anyone in her family.

The conversation with his brother relaxed Matt. He had been tensed and furious before. She had felt his tension. The man was hopping mad, and all that made her nervous as well. However, Matt slowly came back to something close to his usual peaceful self.

Matt had surprised Nora a second time that day when he called his mother in her presence. She had assumed that he would leave the room so that she couldn't hear his explanations.

The call hadn't lasted long. Matt had succinctly explained to his mother that he had a girlfriend, and that befuddled Nora even more. She hadn't known that he was thinking of her in those terms. Not that she minded. Nora was a practical woman. However, she liked to daydream now and then. She had fantasized about Matt a lot and in a surprisingly short period.

Matt had also confessed to his mother that his choice didn't meet his great-grandma's expectations, and consequently, she had done her best to sabotage him. That, he couldn't abide. He hadn't gone into details but warned his mother that Rebecca was probably on her way to her house. She would want to complain that Matt had turned to be an ungrateful brat.

Nora hadn't been able to hear his mother's replies, but Matt's words and behavior had astonished her. He had even chuckled a couple of times, and in the end, he had resignedly accepted an invitation to dinner on Nora's behalf for when she would leave the hospital.

Jay needed much fewer explanations than Matt's mother. Matt just told him that he had quarreled with Rebecca because she interfered in his relationship with Nora and asked Jay to go and take Becka and Nat from the theatre and drive them to the hospital afterward. Matt didn't want to leave the hospital before he had had a chance to speak to Nora, and Bryan was watching the babies that afternoon.

Once he had organized everything to his liking, Matt shoved the phone into his pocket and turned to Nora.

"I think I need to apologize for my great-grandma's behavior," Matt said. His stance showed that he wasn't very sure about what to say.

Nora looked at Matt pensively for a few seconds. Then she walked with difficulty toward the bed and sat down. Nora had been standing and listened to his calls. Besides, all that commotion and the roller-coaster of emotions and thoughts had exhausted her. Her stiff and painful legs barely supported her. The doctor had advised Nora to use crutches, but her chest hurt when she tried to walk with them, so Nora preferred to limp.

Nora looked at Matt thoughtfully again and replied, "You know your grandma thinks that I refused her money only because I thought that you'd have more."

"And why would you care?" Matt asked her. "You didn't seem so concerned with what people thought of you a few days ago," he alluded to the day in his office.

"I didn't care about what you thought then," Nora admitted with a shrug. "But I seem to care now."

"And why do you care now?" Matt closed the distance between them and sat on the bed next to Nora, taking her hand.

He felt her fingers quiver. '*She's not indifferent to me. Far for it,*' Matt thought, a satisfied smile perched on his lips. He squeezed her fingers with tenderness.

"Because it matters," Nora replied quietly, staring into his eyes. "You must think that I'm a fortune hunter, especially because of what you know about me," she continued ruefully.

Nora remembered very well the words said in that conference room in his office. She didn't forget what Matt had said to her when they met in the street, either.

"I know better now," Matt replied and brought her fingers to his mouth.

Nora glared at him and reclaimed her fingers, "What do you know better now?"

Matt heaved a deep sigh. He had known that he would have to tell her one day, but he had hoped that wouldn't be the day. There had been enough turmoil for an afternoon, and Matt was afraid that Nora wouldn't respond well when she found out the truth.

Matt needed emotional distance to do it, so he stood and sauntered to the window. There, he leaned on the windowsill. His eyes roamed over Nora, a strange light shining in his dark-blue pupils. His gaze lingered over some choice spots, and his nostrils flared. Then, he became serious and looked straight into her eyes.

"I've done what I should have done before you'd signed those divorce papers," Matt finally confessed.

Nora drew a long breath. She felt like she couldn't get enough air. She couldn't look away from him. Matt's eyes were very compelling.

"What does that mean?" she asked for clarifications.

"It means that I hired an investigator," he replied quietly, watching her thoughtfully. He didn't want to miss any of the reactions that played openly on her face.

"What for?" she flashed out at him, and her eyes narrowed.

Nora had her suspicions, and she didn't like them at all. After finding out that Rebecca had checked on her, hearing the same thing from Matt made her seethe.

"Because during the last few days, I got to know the real you, and what I read in that file before the meeting didn't match what lay before my eyes," Matt shrugged, to excuse himself.

"So, you wanted to make sure that I didn't try to dupe you," Nora replied in a quarrelsome voice.

Matt didn't say anything for a few seconds and only stared at her. He just knew that what he was going to say might spoil his chances with her.

"Wouldn't you have done the same?" he asked quietly. "I mean that I read that file, and I thought I had the correct information before my eyes – for which, by the way, I'm going to kill my partner when he comes back from his honeymoon," he groused out. "He should have done his homework and not accept such a case. I mean, we're lawyers, and sometimes, we do defend people who don't deserve it, but not in such situations, like yours," he said furiously, clenching and unclenching his fists.

Matt needed a few seconds to calm down and then continued, pointing to her, "Then, there you were. I got to know you, and nothing I saw matched the image I already had in my head. Wouldn't you question your instincts, Nora?" Matt inquired softly.

'*Especially when you've already got burnt,*' he added in his mind caustically, always his steady gaze trained on her.

"Maybe, yes," Nora admitted with a noncommittal shrug.

She understood in a way, although she wasn't very comfortable with him knowing so much about her when she knew almost next to nothing about him.

"You know, we're not equal in anything," she pointed out.

"What the... heck, do you mean?" Matt groused, finding himself again in the situation of changing what he wanted to say in mid-sentence.

His language had worsened during the last few days, and he knew where to place the blame.

"Well, let's see," Nora tapped a finger to her lips, suddenly feeling mean.

The day had strained her, and it wasn't over yet. She needed to release some of the pent-up pressure, and she chose him to be the recipient. She knew that she wasn't fair, but that very moment, being fair seemed overrated.

"You seem to know everything about me, while I know next to nothing about you," she pointed out.

"You know plenty," Matt replied, pushing away from the window.

With heavy steps, he came toward her.

"Come on, Nora! We've spent together a good part of a few days already. You must already have some knowledge of me. I know that there are other things you need to find out, and you will," he said.

Matt inhaled deeply to calm sudden doubts. Few people would accept his loony bin family, and particularly their unique skills.

"There might be things you'll dislike, or which will make you run for safety. I know that, but I won't hide anything from you," Matt stated with determination.

Now Matt loomed over Nora, uncomfortable with his decision to be completely open with her. Matt had never been that honest before but always kept something secret, even from his parents and siblings.

"You have money. I have only got a paycheck," Nora pointed out. "I haven't got any savings left, you know. I made the down payment for that house that my ex husband got in the divorce," she explained to Matt in a sad tone of voice.

"Yes, I know. It was the money you should have received after the divorce, and I made it impossible. I know," Matt nodded, in a bleak mood now, his nervous fingers running through his hair.

"Don't gloss over what I'm saying here, Matt," Nora snapped at him. "I didn't say that I lost money because of you. I said that you have money while I don't."

"Unimportant," Matt waved her argument away.

"How can you say that it's unimportant? Rebecca already labeled me, and the remaining part of your family will soon follow suit," she said with exasperation.

"Some will," he admitted and sat next to her.

He took her hand in his again. Now, a smile played on his lips and drove Nora crazy.

"How can you be so unconcerned about that?" she cried out. "Matt, I'm talking to you," she poked him when she saw that he was more concerned with her palm than what she was saying.

"I know you are," he looked up into her eyes, suddenly very serious. "I can guarantee there will be family members who will try to undermine your position and say vile things about you. It would have happened even if you'd had a fortune, or blue blood, or whatever. Bryan went through all that, you know. If Becka and Bryan survived, we will too. I promise you."

"I have a child," she reminded him.

"So what? I can't see any problem there. The little imp is smart and sweet. And he is yours, so I have no issue with that."

"But others will," Nora replied quietly and touched his face. "I might not be the best choice for you, Matt, even for a brief affair."

"First, I don't need a brief affair, Nora," Matt replied dryly. "If I merely wanted that, I wouldn't be here. Second, I don't care about the best choice," he said, watching her intensely. "I care about my choice."

Matt leaned over Nora, kissed her lips briefly, and then rose to walk his frustration.

"All right, we might break up today, tomorrow or next year. Or we might end up together," Matt said. Annoyed, he turned back to her. "What will be, it will be. We can't change it, Nora. But I'd be damned if I let some hypocrites dictate my actions and my choices," he boomed, and Nora's eyes opened wide.

"Very well said, son," a melodic voice came from the door.

CHAPTER THIRTEEN

BOTH SHOCKED, NORA and Matt turned like one. Someone had entered the room, and they hadn't noticed. A hushed cry flew off Nora's lips, but Matt's hand on hers reassured her that everything was fine.

Marjorie Winston and her husband Jonathan stood just inside the door, holding hands, as always. Pride for her firstborn had brought tears in Marjorie's eyes.

Jonathan grinned at the younger couple with delight. Once, the man had been in the exact sore spot where his son stood now, so Jonathan understood better than anyone what Matt felt.

"Mother," Matt exclaimed with exasperation. "I thought we arranged to see each other when Nora came out of the hospital," he scolded her.

"I know, I know," Marjorie waved her hand. "I also know you'd have found a way to keep me away, afraid that I'd try to meddle in your business, like grandma," she admonished him, waving her finger under his nose. "You should know me better than that, my firstborn," she rebuked him. "Plus, I needed a reason not to talk to grandma. She came when we were leaving. We apologized because we were in a rush and

331

left her there," Marjorie said. Then, pensively, she continued, "I hope she won't still be there on the door stoop when we get back home. She didn't take it well, I must say."

Nora glanced at Matt, and the blush spreading on his face and neck surprised her.

"Care to make the introductions, Matty?" his father asked, amused, and his smile reflected in his dark eyes.

Curious, Nora studied Matt's parents. Matt didn't take it after only one of them. He had his mother's eyes and his father's coloring.

His mother seemed very serious, and his father easy-going. Matt's temper was a combination of the two.

Matt sighed and glanced at Nora. He shrugged, took her hand, and brought her in front of his parents.

"This is Nora, my girlfriend," he introduced her. "Nora, this is my nosy sweet mother, Marjorie Winston, and this is my father, who, if I know him well, and I do, has surely been dragged here. He's Jonathan Winston."

Nora barely kept her laughter in check. However, his father chuckled and slapped his son over the shoulder.

Marjorie scowled at Matt and then took Nora's stretched hand. Yet, instead of shaking it, she pulled the younger woman into a hug.

Now, that astounded Nora. She had expected a different welcome from Matt's parents. They certainly must have had higher expectations for their son, not a single, almost broke, mother.

She didn't even know what her financial situation was right then. Matt had helped her to fill in the forms for a disability claim two days before, but she still had to wait for an answer.

Nora awkwardly hugged Marjorie back. No sooner had Marjorie released her that Jonathan enveloped her in a bear-hug. As tall and well-built as Matt, Jonathan didn't bother to control his strength, and she yelped at the sudden pain.

Immediately, Matt pulled Nora in his arms, and with a ferocious scowl, bellowed to his father, "She's hurt, damn it." Then, Matt led Nora to the bed as if Nora had come unglued before them and nudged her to lie down.

"I don't want to lie down in front of your parents, Matt," Nora hissed. "I'm fine. It was only a twinge, really," Nora attempted to convince him, but Matt didn't have any of that.

"Who are you kidding now? If I didn't know the extent of your wounds..." Matt shook his head.

"I'm very sorry, Nora," Jonathan came and caressed her arm. "I haven't realized you were hurt," he explained.

"Why would she be in the hospital if she weren't?" Matt growled, and everyone looked at him as if he lost his mind.

"It's not like I knew the circumstances of her hospitalization," Jonathan reproached to his son.

"Don't worry about it," Nora waved Jonathan's sincere concern away. Then, she turned to Matt, and in a soft voice, she said, "It was just a twinge. I'm fine. I'll even talk to the doctor to discharge me in the morning," she explained, stroking his arm to soothe him.

"Allow him to worry, pumpkin," Marjorie said to Nora.

She came to the bed as well and wedged in between the two men. Gently, but with steel determination, she helped Nora lie down, which made Matt very happy.

"You have to give a man his due, now and then. Their pride is a fragile thing, I'm afraid, and you need to appease them," Marjorie said, brushing Nora's hair away from her forehead.

"Hey!" an entire chorus of male objections came from around the room.

Nora peeked past Marjorie and chuckled. Both Matt and Jonathan were scowling. Then she noticed the scowl of a third man, who had come with Becka and Nat. It was a darn convention gathering in her room.

Unruffled, Marjorie patted her hand and turned to the others. She said with insouciance, "It's true, you know."

Then she noticed the new people in the room and greeted them, "Hi, Becka and Jay. I haven't seen you there."

"We've come just in time to hear you, auntie," Becka grinned. "And I undoubtedly agree with you," she nodded vigorously.

"Not you, too," Jay complained.

"Who do we have here?" Marjorie looked at the toddler, who was clinging on to Becka's hand.

Nat hid behind Becka shyly, and Nora tried to jump off the bed, only to be stopped by Matt.

"Easy, honey. My mom won't have him for dessert," Matt attempted to joke, but her glare told him that he wasn't funny.

Then Matt eased her up in a sitting position.

"Stay here," he ordered, and Nora frowned.

Matt didn't pay attention to her frown but called Nat to him. The boy came from behind Becka and launched himself at Matt, hugging his legs.

"Easy, Nat," Matt said in the same voice he had used with Nora. "Look, these are my parents," he turned the boy around, pointing to Marjorie and Jonathan.

That was all it took for the boy. He forgot about his shyness and greeted Matt's parents with a smile.

Marjorie showered him with compliments and made him feel important, and Jonathan shook his hand. Nat beamed with pride.

After a few minutes of inane chatter, Marjorie turned to Nora, "So, tomorrow, you want to get out of the hospital. You know you can't go home alone, especially with Nat. I doubt you could manage by yourself."

"I will manage, don't worry," Nora dismissed Marjorie's concerns.

She didn't want Marjorie to believe that she would be a burden to Matt, and she would cling to her son.

Matt didn't even bother to tell her she was wrong. He only rode rough-shod over her words.

"Of course, she won't be alone. She and Nat will stay with me until she recovers. I understand it might take a few months."

"Matthew Winston," Nora glowered at him and pushed him so that she could stand. "I won't have you tell me what to do," she poked him in his chest with her finger.

"She has the same bad habit, mother, like you. She likes to poke," Matt chuckled.

Jonathan and Jay joined in his hilarity, which didn't endear them with the two women.

"Yep, that she does," Jay said and came next to Matt and elbowed him, a grin on his face.

However, neither Nora nor Marjorie seemed amused with them. Nora raised a brow and stared Matt down, while Marjorie merely gave them the evil eye.

Becka thought she would better save the remaining part of that visit. The men seemed oblivious of the detrimental currents, and the other two women were seething.

"I think Nora's correct if she wants to make the decisions about her recovery, Matt," she said, and Matt glinted his eyes at her. "And I'm very sure she'll decide to live with you and take advantage of your help with Nat. After all, we all know that she loves Nat above all."

Nora knew that Becka's words trapped her. She couldn't stubbornly insist that she would live by herself. She knew she had physical limitations for the moment, and didn't want to endanger her son. Yet, it didn't seem right to only move in with Matt.

Nat kept looking from an adult to another. He was confused because of their behavior, but he understood just fine that Matt wanted them to live with him.

"We'll go home with Matt, mommy, right?" he asked Nora, putting her on the spot again.

She sighed deeply and said, "We'll see, sweetie. Mommy will have to think it over, all right?"

CHAPTER FOURTEEN

NORA SAT ON THE CUSHY pillow laid on the wide window sill, watching the marina. Matt's apartment had a superb view of the harbor, and Nora had already learned to enjoy it.

The morning after meeting Matt's parents, Nora persuaded the doctor to discharge her. She promised him that she would take it easy and start physiotherapy after two weeks. It helped that Matt supported her and assured the physician that Nora wouldn't overtax her body. Of course, Matt took her to his apartment directly and started doing just what he had promised.

During that afternoon, she spent with Matt's parents, Nora had accepted to go home with Matt for Nat's sake. However, she wasn't sure that it was a smart move.

Whenever she thought of the encounter with Marjorie and Jonathan, Nora shook her head with dismay. That had been one of the most confusing afternoons she had ever lived, and she wasn't sure that she had entirely understood what had happened.

Nora feared that everything would crumble to her feet in no time. She had had her doubts when Matt came to take her from the hospital the morning the doctor discharged her.

Some of those doubts didn't disappear during the following two days, although Matt had been very considerate, in his way, ever since.

Matt offered her the third bedroom available in his apartment. That brought some relief. Nora had been afraid that Matt would nurture certain expectations. She didn't think that she could live up to them, not so early in their relationship anyway. Her ex-husband might have painted her in harlot's colors, but at heart, Nora was an old-fashioned woman. Aside from her ex-husband, Nora had been in a relationship with only one other man before her marriage. That relationship had lasted for almost three years.

Nora wasn't entirely at ease in Matt's house, though, in spite of Matt's efforts to make her feel welcome. Not used to be underfoot and waited for, hand and foot, Nora worried that one day, Matt might feel crowded or view her or her son as an imposition.

Living in the same house with him gave her more insight into the kind of man he was. She found out new things about him all the time, and she liked more and more the man she discovered. Yet, one thing distressed her: Matt was overbearing. He didn't allow her to do anything, not even to carry her cup to the sink or dishwasher. He would jump to his feet at once and nudge her to sit or lie down. Matt expected her to accept his order of not lifting a finger and rest as much as possible. If she didn't, discussions would arouse.

Even when it came to Nat, they had arguments. She couldn't complain that he tried to separate them. He was all for her to spend as much time as possible with her son, but only if she didn't try to take care of the boy's bath, for example, or prepare his food.

Bryan still supplied them with meals, and that embarrassed her to no end. Yes, she had a hard time standing and walking, but she could do most of the cooking sitting, in her opinion. Of course, Matt turned a deaf ear to any argument.

The thought he was so bossy drove her crazy. As a result, they butted heads all the time, and they hadn't spent seventy-two hours together yet.

Matt lectured Nora whenever they had a discussion. He would speak in a calm voice as if he tried to soothe her. That tone of voice riled her more than if he had shouted at her.

She had eyes and could see the twitch in his jaw or the flash of his eyes when she turned to be very stubborn. Yet, he pretended he wasn't upset and left the impression that she had overreacted, and he had to calm a child's tantrum.

The buzz of the intercom interrupted her ruminations. She glanced at the door, surprised. Matt had left with Nat for ice-cream half an hour ago, but Nora doubted that he didn't have the key.

For a moment, she thought to ignore the intercom, yet the person calling was stubborn enough and kept punching the code. With her heart in her boots, Nora tiptoed to the door.

The intercom went finally silent, and she sighed, satisfied with the respite. She turned to go back to her favorite spot when the beeps began again, and she jumped up. The sudden move jarred her leg, and Nora hissed at the piercing pain, tears welling in her eyes.

Now, her temper flushed, she pushed the key and asked in a belligerent voice, "Who's there?"

"Finally," Marjorie's melodious voice came, and Nora froze. "We were concerned that something happened to you. I've just spoken to Matt, and he said that you were alone at home," Marjorie said, and then, she sighed with relief. "Buzz us in, Nora, dear," she asked.

Nora closed her eyes in defeat. She didn't even want to know who that '*us*' was. Far too many people were around Matt all the time. During the last few years, she had learned to be content with Nat's company. She didn't have a family or a string of friends to visit her.

She pressed the button to open the door downstairs and unlocked the apartment door. Then, she leaned on the wall, waiting for the group to come upstairs.

A few minutes later, a knock sounded on the door, and she opened it. Stunned, she looked at the people crowded on the landing. She knew most of them. At least she had already met most of them.

Marjorie and Becka beamed at her and came in, leading the way for the others. Marjorie took one of her arms, and Becka the other. They both helped Nora to get to the sofa without allowing her to put much weight on the injured leg. The others followed, chatting with each other and carrying bags in their hands.

Nora couldn't understand that family. They baffled her. Ironically, she understood Rebecca. Her behavior was predictable. Theirs wasn't. She couldn't believe that they would visit with her and not scold her for laying her hands on their golden boy, Matt, as Rebecca said.

Marjorie sat next to Nora with a whimsical smile on her face and patted her hand as if she knew what thoughts crossed the woman's mind.

"This is my husband, Bryan," Becka motioned a tall, well-built man to come and make Nora's acquaintance.

Nora's eyes swept over the strong shoulders and prominent cheekbones. She noted the scar on his left cheek but didn't react. She beamed at him, grateful for everything Bryan had done for her son and herself.

"Nice to meet you," he said, shaking her hand. "I'm going to put the food in the fridge," he winked at her. "You'll have enough for about three days now. Some of it will go into the freezer, but Matt is capable enough to microwave it," he grinned.

"Jonathan, take our bags to the kitchen, as well," Marjorie asked her husband, in the voice of a general.

He just saluted her jokingly. First, he came to Nora, kissed her cheek, and asked, "Is everything fine? Does my boy treat you right?"

Taken aback, Nora couldn't formulate an answer and just nodded.

"Good, then," Jonathan approved, patted her shoulder, and sauntered in the direction of the kitchen.

"Have you cooked, as well?" Nora asked Marjorie with dismay.

"Of course, dear. I mean that I knew Bryan cooked for you, but I had to contribute with something," Marjorie explained with a shrug. "What kind of mother would I be if I let others take care of my children, huh?"

Nora didn't know how to answer, and wide-eyed, she just stared at her. For a moment, she thought that Marjorie had taken a pot-shot at her because she did let someone else take care of her son. Marjorie rubbed her arm and beamed at her some more until Nora thought she would scream.

"Now, let's see... You know Jay already," Marjorie continued as if she didn't notice Nora's confusion and distress.

Jay waved at her, and the grin on his lips told Nora that he knew what she was thinking. She wondered what he would say if she wiped that grin off his lips with a well-aimed fist. Those Winstons played with her mind.

"This is our daughter, Maggie. She's Jay's twin," Marjorie specified, the ghost of a smile in the corner of her mouth.

Nora understood why. Maggie and Jay looked anything but alike. Jay had inherited his father's eyes, and his hair was dark blond, while Maggie had her mother's eyes and her father's coloring like Matt. Anyone would have guessed that Maggie and Matt were siblings. Jay was more challenging to place in the family if someone didn't know his mother, as well.

"Hey, there," Maggie greeted her with exuberance, almost hopping in place, her curls going this way and that way.

At the tone of her voice, Nora winced inwardly. She just knew that Matt's sister was one of those women with an excess of energy, busy all the time. They never stopped to rest or smell the roses. Nora wasn't a slacker herself, but people like Maggie exhausted her only with their presence.

Nora merely waved back with a shy smile, and Maggie, her dark hair bouncing in thick and silky curls, tucked her legs under her on the carpet, next to the armchair Jay had already claimed.

"This is Lily," Marjorie presented the other young woman in the room. "Lily is my niece, and Matt's cousin," she explained.

Lily shook Nora's hand with warmth, but she didn't have Maggie's enthusiasm. Nora's eyes took everything in - the tall and slender silhouette, the short curly red hair, and dark blue eyes. Lily looked very different from Nora, although she seemed of the same age or maybe a couple of years younger than Nora.

"I'll take care of cakes and snacks. I'll take them out of the bags," Lily said, looking at Marjorie, and then she attacked the bag close to her.

Except for the bags Bryan and Jonathan carried into the kitchen, the others lay next to the coffee table. Nora imagined that the family had been shopping. The thought that they had brought cakes and snacks for their visit didn't cross her mind.

"I should be offering you coffee or cakes," Nora suddenly realized.

She tried to stand up and go search in Matt's kitchen. It was true that Nora wasn't in her house, but she lived there for the moment, so she had to play the role of hostess.

"Don't be silly," Marjorie stopped her. "You may hold with a ceremony when you have friends or acquaintances in the house, but we're family. Matt would never talk to me again if I'd let you go through all that trouble," she shook her head at Nora.

"You only have to get used to having a large family," Becka laughed.

"It isn't easy, believe me," her husband replied. Bryan had just come back from the kitchen, carrying two platters with hors-d'oeuvre. "By the way," Bryan said to everybody, "Jonathan is making coffee. I boiled some water to make some tea for you, Becka," he said to his wife, who thanked him with a nod.

"But you're the guests in the house. I mean that... I...," Nora started stuttering. The idea that they might think that she was the guest in that house swiftly dawned on her. She couldn't contradict them. They were right.

"We are the guests, Nora. That's true," Maggie said. "But you are in convalescence, and that gives us the right to change roles," Maggie waved her worries aside.

"I didn't mean," Nora tried to explain, but Jonathan, coming with coffee and cups, interrupted her.

"But you should," he said, putting everything on the table. "If I know my Matt, you have the right to think that you're in your house, and we're mere guests here."

"No, no, no, I didn't mean..."

"Don't trouble yourself," Marjory took her hand. "Matt will be here in no time, and I don't want to explain to him why you're agitated and how we upset you."

"Matt's stubborn enough not to talk to us for a year," Jay remarked, and Nora stared at him. Everyone could see the disbelief and shock that marked her face.

Matt and Nat chose that precise moment to arrive.

CHAPTER FIFTEEN

WHEN NAT LEARNED THAT they had guests, he didn't want to linger in the ice-cream shop anymore but insisted on going back home at once.

Matt didn't argue with him. He needed to be there as well and shield Nora from any possible attacks, so they rushed back home.

Now, Matt glanced at Nora and noticed the shock on her face. Matt had already fretted, but instantly he became furious. His eyes narrowed, and his nostrils flared. Matt asked in a stern voice, "Now, who upset Nora and why? What did you say to her?"

Matt had thought that he would get excuses or explanations, but none came.

Jay and Maggie burst into laughter and howled like hyenas. Nora tried to say something and opened her mouth, but nothing came out. His mother glared at him and shook her head in disapproval.

"Now, Matt, is this the way to talk to your parents?" Marjory chided him.

"If you distressed her..." Matt started saying, but his father came to him and slapped his shoulder.

"Call back the troops, son," Jonathan said with a chuckle. "Nobody declared war here. Nora merely can't believe that we take care of our people, and we consider her part of the family now. No need to blow a fuse over that," he shook his head to his firstborn.

Matt looked around and felt ashamed. He picked a thought here and there and realized that his father was telling the truth.

He had made a lot of wrong assumptions. No one was guilty of anything and were openly making fun of him.

"Come on, brother," Maggie said from her spot near Jay. "Lighten up. We're not here to upset Nora, but the opposite. And we brought gifts, by the way," she mentioned and pointed to the snacks Lily was still setting on the table.

Lily knew Matt and took his outburst in stride. Matt always jumped to defend people who couldn't protect themselves. She imagined that he had seen Nora as the sacrificial lamb when he found her in the middle of his close-knit family.

"So you're all right," Matt said to Nora, although he didn't sound very confident.

Nora only nodded and stretched her hand to Nat, who came to her immediately.

"We bought ice-cream for you too, mommy. Matt asked what you liked best and bought you pistachio," he said, although his tongue knotted around the word '*pistachio.*'

Everyone smiled, and Nora kissed the top of his head. "That's awesome, baby. I can't wait to taste it."

"Not before you try my pastries, I hope," Marjorie intervened.

"You're in for a treat," Lily said, finally finishing fussing with the food. "Aunt Marjorie is the best when it comes to baking."

"I wouldn't sell Bryan so short," Becka contradicted Lily, a scowl on her face. "You should know that his pastries are heavenly."

"Thank you, sweetheart," Bryan said with a self-deprecating laugh. "That's what a man wants to be praised for—his pastries."

"Come on, Bryan. Everyone knows how macho you are," she blew off his concerns.

"That's true," Jay noted. "Don't worry. One look at you and no one would give a thought to your pastries, Bryan."

"What do you mean?" Becka asked in an icy voice, measuring him.

"Becka, Becka, Becka," Jay shook his head. "The man rivals a mountain. One look coming from those steely eyes of his, and no one would dare to say anything to him."

"But Rebecca," Bryan corrected him, and another round of laughter burst out.

"Oh, man, I won't ever forget what happened when she met you that first time," Jonathan slapped his knee. "Matt, you need more seats around here. How come I didn't notice that before?" he wondered.

"Because you've never come in groups," Matt observed dryly. "I'll make sure to add more furniture shortly. Now, let's borrow the chairs from the breakfast table and..." he frowned, thinking what else to bring in.

Matt thought of the bar stools in the kitchen, but they weren't very cozy for a chat in the living room. He also had a chair in his den, but nothing else.

"I'm okay," Bryan said. He left the tea he had brought for Becka on the coffee table and then pulled Becka up. He took her seat, and then he lowered her in his lap.

"Nat will seat in my lap," Marjorie demanded.

She waved to the boy, calling him to her, and Nat came immediately—another surprise for Nora.

"I'm good," Maggie said to Matt from where she sat on the carpet.

Matt knew that she was. Maggie rarely sat in an armchair or on a sofa. She was happier when she could sit on the floor with her legs tucked under her. Many made fun of her. They called Maggie the family gypsy.

"So, you need only two chairs," Lily made the math for him. "One for me, and one for you," she waved her hand around to the others who were all seated.

"Right, two chairs coming up," Matt attempted to joke to lighten the mood in the room. Matt felt awkward because he had accused his family of nefarious endeavors. Then, he brought the chairs from the breakfast table.

NORA LAY DOWN ON HER bed, sated with food, and laughter, and fun. She had felt out of her element when Matt's family came to visit. That changed once everyone was pushing food on to her and recounted stories of a much younger Matty.

She had felt included. She was the center of attention, although sometimes, either Matt or his mother fanned too much over her.

A couple of times, she even rolled her eyes, and that baffled her. She hadn't done that since her high-school years.

Some of the stories they told had been very touching, but she enjoyed them all. Nora also enjoyed seeing Matt blush a few times. Seated across from her, Matt couldn't touch her. However, Nora was aware of his intense gaze all the time. She even felt the caress of his dark-blue pupils all over her skin whenever his eyes swept over her.

Sometimes, her heart would trot faster, and she wondered how Marjorie didn't hear it. At the same time, she got hotter and hotter under that intensity and the waves of desire coming from him. Those raw sensations, which she didn't want or afford to feel right then, bothered her a lot.

Despite Matt's opposition, Marjorie and Jonathan shared their memories about Matt as a toddler. Sometimes, Nora laughed hearing about his antics, but mostly, her feelings for Matt grew a little more.

His siblings and cousins told stories about him as a teenager. They were so good at recounting those times that she could almost see Matt, as a teenager, always chased by girls or ready to play a harmless prank, which would land him up in the principal's office.

Maggie's stories were the most outrageous. Some of the things she related shocked her parents. They were completely unaware that such things had happened in their children's lives during their adolescence. Jonathan laughed heartily, but Marjorie had to fan herself a few times.

Once, Matt growled and threatened his sister, promising serious payback if she didn't stop. Maggie just laughed at him, and high-fived Jay, who supported and contributed to all her stories.

For Nora, it had been a magical afternoon and evening. She had never experienced so much camaraderie between family members. Her family had never shared such joyful and touching moments.

Yet, something bothered her. Sometimes someone would begin to tell a story, and suddenly, all eyes turned to them in a warning. Immediately, they would change their story in mid-sentence. She even surprised a few subtle shakes of the head. Bryan grinned with irony every time that something like that happened as if he knew a secret that eluded Nora.

She was sure that they hid something from her. She didn't know what but intended to find out. She felt it was something very significant and decisive for the evolution of her relationship with Matt.

Light knocks on the door drew Nora back to the present. She hesitated a fleeting second, but then she said softly, "Come in."

Matt opened the door and stopped. He had mussed his hair again, undoubtedly by running his fingers through it. Nora had noticed that habit of his several times and found it charming.

Dressed only in dark slacks and a white shirt that defined his shoulders and was open halfway down, Matt looked good to eat. Too bad that Nora was on a strict diet.

He looked her over, and his dark-blue eyes turned darker while sweeping over her sleeveless nightie. The cotton hugged the curves of her body in the right places, and unaware, Matt licked his lips.

He looked his fill. Then he said, "I saw that your light was still on. I imagined that you were still awake, so I thought that we could talk, maybe. I don't feel like going to bed already," he explained with some difficulty.

Matt massaged the base of his nose. It wasn't like him not to find his words, but his world had changed dramatically lately, and he felt like walking in a haze.

"Yes, of course," Nora replied and sat up carefully. Her movements didn't pain her so much now. Most of the soreness was gone.

Nora leaned back on the headboard. His eyes followed the fall of the thick red mass of hair over her shoulders.

With a pat on the bed, she invited Matt to sit, and he closed the door and hurried to do so. It was more than he had expected when he decided to come to her room.

"I hear if Nat wakes up, don't worry," Matt thought to assure her. "Are you pretty tired?" he asked, and concern showed in his eyes.

"I know a lot of people visited tonight, and you're still in convalescence. I saw it on your face, you know. The exhaustion, I mean. It was evident that you were tired."

"Oh, that's why you rushed everybody out," Nora guessed, and he nodded.

"You shouldn't have," she said, shaking her head. "Yes, I felt a little tired now and then, but that's because I'm not used to such gatherings, Matt," she stroked his strong forearm with a featherlike touch, and a shiver rippled through his body. Nora thought that she had only imagined everything and continued, "But everybody had fun, including me."

"I'm glad that you enjoyed their company, Nora. I love the others in the family, even Rebecca sometimes, but the people who were here tonight are the ones I love the most. If you feel good in their company, then it's perfect," Matt said, half-facing, and playing with her fingers and looking intently into her eyes.

He had stroked her fingers several times by then. The first time, his touch had surprised her. Nora would have thought that the skin on a lawyer's fingers and palms was smooth. Yet Matt's wasn't. His skin was rough, and every time he slid his fingers over hers, Nora felt it deep in her core.

"You do some physical labor, don't you?" she asked Matt before she was even aware that she had opened her mouth. Nora cringed when the meaning of her own words dawned on her, and Matt chuckled when Nora closed her eyes in dismay.

"You know, you can ask me anything, Nora," Matt said to her in a soft tone of voice. Then, his fingers touched her wrist and slid up on her arm.

Nora shook her head and licked her bottom lip. Then, she opened her eyes and said, "You're touching my hands and arms all the time."

"I'd love to touch all of you all the time," Matt admitted, and her eyes rounded. "Don't worry, Nora. I know that you need time, and not only to recover physically. I know you're not ready to open yourself to me emotionally now," Matt said very matter-of-factly and stroked the side of her face. "But a man still can hope," he chuckled with self-deprecation.

"What if I'm never ready?" Nora inquired in a whispered voice.

Matt shrugged and bowed his head. His gaze followed the finger he slid up and down on the inside of her arm.

"I'm a grown-up, so I'll survive, Nora," Matt shrugged anew. "It's not as if I could force you to like or love me, and I couldn't blame you, of course," he replied.

"I like you just fine, Matt," she said and brushed the hair off his forehead.

Matt, always watching her intently, leaned over her and touched his mouth to hers. She sighed and cradled his face in her hands, opening her lips for him.

Matt braced on one arm on the bed and then kissed her softly, his lips learning hers. His kiss was hesitant at first but became more confident.

He didn't hurry. Matt kept his kiss sweet, taking his time to savor her taste. Matt didn't want to arouse Nora, but to help her recognize his body as her mate. Yet, he could feel her tremble next to him, and that satisfied his male ego. His fingers slid over her right arm, in a hypnotic rhythm, leaving goosebumps on her skin in their wake. Matt changed the angle of his kiss. His fingers reached to her waist, resting on the roundness of her hip for a few seconds.

"Would you lie down to be more comfortable?" Matt asked Nora, his lips almost touching hers.

Nora felt the words, forming over her lips, and the heat inside her spiked. She shimmied down, almost without thinking.

Her fingers burrowed into his forearms for support. Her nightie hiked up on her thighs, and Matt breathed deeply when his gaze swept over her legs.

Braced on his elbow, Matt stretched next to her, his head in his palm. His other hand lazily stroked the side of her face and then cupped her chin.

He leaned down until his mouth was a hair's breadth away from hers. Then Matt whispered, "I'd love to kiss you some more, Nora. But only if you're comfortable with that." He searched her glimmering eyes, but they didn't reveal anything. Then, Matt tried to read her mind and see for himself what she thought. As always, he came out blank.

"Yes, please," Nora replied softly, and Matt felt her breath on his lips.

Now, more than anything, he needed to kiss her. His hand slid from her chin and caressed the side of her neck.

His lips settled on hers, and he sighed. Nora swallowed the sound and answered with a sigh of hers. Matt felt a jolt of awareness in his lower body.

While his lips shaped hers, his fingers stroked her shoulder and arm, down to her wrist. His fingers intertwined with hers, while his kiss became more daring and deeper.

Matt stopped kissing Nora when both of them needed to breathe. Both breathed hard, and Nora's lips looked rosy and slightly puffy. His fingers still closed on hers, and his thumb stroked the inside of her wrist.

Matt's eyes locked on Nora's face. She still had her eyes closed, but then, when her respiration quieted, she opened them slowly. The heat in her pupils kicked Matt squarely in his chest.

"I'd love to touch you everywhere, Nora, but I don't dare. I think I'll try not to think of that for at least another week, baby," he confessed.

Nora didn't do anything more than look at him. After a few seconds, she blinked and licked her lips.

"You know you're killing me here, honey," Matt said with a chuckle, yet his voice didn't sound as confident as usual. "You never say anything, and I don't know what you think."

"Oh, I think plenty, Matt," she replied in a dry voice. "The problem's that everything confuses me right now. I know that I want you, and I can feel that you want me, but I don't know if it is all right, or it is too soon, or if you want only that," she shrugged.

"Wow, all that," Matt laughed. "You know you don't have to make up your mind right this moment. About anything," he assured her, smoothing her hair.

Then, he took a thick lock between his fingers, lifted it to his face, and brushed it to his cheek.

"No, I can't make up my mind now," she replied ruefully. "I need time, and probably more than a week," Nora warned him.

"Sweetheart, you can take a month or two, or as long as you need," he said and kissed her forehead.

They lay in silence for a few minutes, Matt always braced on the elbow, his other hand stroking her arm, her hip, and in a very daring moment, her thigh. Nora kept watching his face, and the emotions she could see in his eyes captivated her.

"You want something from me," she suddenly said, and his gaze turned to her eyes swiftly.

"How can you tell?" Matt frowned.

"I can see it on your face," Nora replied. "It's hard to miss it."

"I see," he said. "I thought you read my mind," Matt replied in a mild tone of voice.

Nora giggled at his words, and that surprised him. He had never heard her snicker and didn't think that she would be the woman to do it. "Come on, Matt. I'm a grown woman. I don't believe in fairy-tales and paranormal things. I do believe that there's an explanation for everything," she stressed out. "Like now," Nora said. "I knew you wanted something because I could see it in your eyes. No one can read minds," she shook her head with determination.

"If you say so," Matt accepted her explanation, although he felt a sort of hurt. Yet, he couldn't come out and say, *Hey, I can read your mind*. Quite inaccurate. He couldn't read her mind.

"So, what do you want?" she asked again.

"I don't know what you'd think," he started hesitantly, "but I was thinking..." he said and stopped.

"Come on, Matt, don't be shy. You've been anything but shy until now," she laughed.

"I was wondering if you'd like to sleep with me," he snapped, uncomfortable with what he had to say and annoyed with her amusement.

"Smooth," she said gingerly and touched her upper lip with her tongue.

"I didn't mean... I'm talking about sleeping, you know, that activity people do at night, to regenerate or whatever," he clarified his idea, miffed by her comment.

"Oh, I see," she smiled. "Really? Do you mean only sleeping? Why would you want that?" she suddenly frowned.

"Because I want to feel you next to me," he admitted. "And because we might feel more emotionally comfortable afterward, or... I don't know why," he admitted. "But I know I do."

"So, to be clear," she said, turning on one side to face Matt, and held her head with her hand, copying his posture. "You want to sleep next to me, to hold me in your arms, and nothing more," she said, and her voice showed her bafflement.

"Yes, that's what I want. I told you that I wouldn't touch you otherwise, even if you wanted it. You wouldn't enjoy anything right now, anyway, considering your wounds."

"Probably not," Nora conceded. "Do I have a minute or two to think?" she asked him, in a playful tone.

"Take as long as you need," he murmured, and his hand rested on her hip.

Nora closed her eyes and touched his chest with her palm. Matt knew that she was pondering the pros and cons because a serious frown formed between her eyebrows. He wanted to reach out and smoothen her frown away but fought the impulse. He knew that it wouldn't have been fair to touch her and confuse her mind. But, for a moment there, Matt didn't care about what was right.

Her fingers drummed on his chest, and each touch drove him mad. Blood pulsated in his temples, and his arousal increased tenfold. He clenched his teeth and thanked God Nora had her eyes closed.

After something that felt like hours, Nora opened her eyes, smiled at him, and said, "All right. Nothing wrong if we share a bed and body heat," she explained her decision.

"Romantic," he noticed dryly. "I don't know about the body heat," he continued. "It's summer already if you haven't noticed."

"Yes, I noticed, Matt," she snickered and patted his chest. "I was merely joking. I hope you know that," she suddenly looked up, straight into his eyes, and he saw genuine concern.

"Yes, I know," he grinned at her.

"And how do we do that?" she asked.

"I thought you'd never ask," he joked. "Let's take my bed," he proposed. "I had it order-made, and I am comfortable in it. This one here is only a regular king."

"You mean to say that you gave me the low-quality bed?" Nora pretended that she felt affronted.

Matt laughed and flicked her nose.

"You're a laugh a minute. Do you know that?" Matt replied. "No, smarty-pants, your bed isn't low-quality, but you're tiny, so it's big enough for you. Anyway, you'll share my bed now, so you can't complain anymore," he said.

With a fluid motion, he rose and took her hand. "Come on, let's see how you like my giant bed," he grinned at her and helped her stand.

Then, Matt knelt, and finding her slippers, slid them on her feet. She giggled again. Although Matt had abhorred giggles before, he liked how she sounded. Now, though, Matt put his finger on her lips, "Shush, Nora, you'll wake Nathan."

Nora pretended to zip her lips, and he chuckled. Their fingers intertwined, and he pulled her after him. They moseyed to his bedroom, Matt always taking care to match her slow gait.

When he opened the door, she stopped and looked around in awe.

"My God, this is much more than a bedroom," she whispered.

His bed was broad enough for at least four people to sleep without touching each other. A thick carpet, in warm autumn colors, stretched from wall to wall. Two armchairs and a small table hid in a niche in the corner of the room.

"I gather you like it," Matt said dryly.

"You could say that," Nora nodded with enthusiasm. "Much better, more colorful, and with more personality than the other one," she added and grinned at him.

"Now, you share it, as well," Matt shrugged. "The ensuite bathroom is that way," he showed her a door on the right. "Tomorrow morning, I'll bring your things from the other bath so that you could use this one. After Nat, of course," he grinned. "I'm sorry, but he always uses my bath in the morning."

"Yeah, I noticed," Nora said. "I expected him to come to me in the mornings, and to be honest, I felt somewhat betrayed when I noticed that he came to you instead," she replied.

"Better me than you," he remarked, and her eyes widened.

"What do you mean?" she glared.

"I imagine that he likes to jump on you in the morning too. I haven't had a morning without him bouncing up and down on me. With your wounds, that wouldn't be what your doctor recommended," Matt pointed out, an eyebrow hiking up his forehead.

"Oh, I forgot about that habit," Nora laughed briefly and then grimaced. "How could I forget?"

"You've had to deal with enough things. Let's hope Nat continues to choose my body for his morning amusement," Matt said and stroked the side of her face with the back of his hand. "Now, are you ready to turn in?" he asked her.

Nora nodded hesitantly, and then, shyly, she headed to the bed. "What side do you prefer?" she asked without turning to him.

"Any of them is good for me," he replied.

Matt helped her climb onto the bed, and then, after Nora lay down, he covered her with the bed linen.

Matt turned off the light and crept into bed next to her. He slid his arm around her, and, gently, he pulled her to him. Once they settled, he opened his fingers on her abdomen, and a satisfied sigh sounded in Nora's ear.

Nora felt her skin burning under his fingers, and long-forgotten sensations ran through her body.

It felt good in Matt's arms. His body almost surrounded her. To her surprise, Nora discovered a sense of security in his arms that she had never felt before. "If you need to sleep more tomorrow, you can," he whispered, his lips nearly touching her ear, and Nora shivered. Matt pulled her closer, thinking that she was cold.

"Becka said that you'd promised we'd go sailing tomorrow," she whispered back, and her hand rested on top of his on her belly.

"I know, baby, but that will be at eleven. We won't stay long on the lake tomorrow," he promised her. "Just a couple of hours. We'll spend more time when we go to that get-together to Bryan's house on the island, okay? I don't want you to overdo it right now," Matt explained, and his concern touched her.

"That's fine with me," Nora replied and caressed his fingers.

"Good," Matt said. "Now, sleep baby," he asked her, and his lips touched her face.

CHAPTER SIXTEEN

THAT WAS NORA'S FOURTH outing on Matt's yacht, and she had started to wait for those trips with impatience. Nora loved the feel of the wind in her hair and the smell of the water. Everything was different there, the light and sounds, the air and silence. She couldn't wait to see Bryan's house on the lake, which Becka had praised so much. She was as giddy as Nat whenever she thought of that Saturday.

Maggie and Lily had taken an exuberant Nat to the bow. They chatted and laughed together. The boy kept asking questions, barely giving them the time to answer any of them, and that amused the women to no end.

Nora smiled. Those days, Nat could ask questions faster than anyone could answer. More than that, the lake fascinated him, and he was curious about everything. He had already expressed the wish of becoming a sailor one day. Nora was just thankful that that day was far away.

Before the shooting, Nora had taken Nat on a stroll on the shore now and then. However, she had never had the time to linger. Nora had always had too many things to do and didn't have the luxury of longer outings. She always felt guilty because she couldn't offer Nat such luxuries, but Nora had promised herself that she would do that one day. Now, with the lake always in their sight from Matt's windows, her son had become crazy about it. Nora couldn't deny that she had also fallen in love with the lake.

Seated near Nora, Marjorie and Jonathan had chatted with her a little. Now they whispered to each other.

Nora looked at the men who handled the yacht, and her mouth watered at the show of powerful muscles on their backs and arms.

Jay and Josh looked good enough, but they didn't hold a candle to Matt. Matt was taller and brawnier, and his dark coloring made him look quite dashing. Nora couldn't look away from him.

A seagull speared the sky and cried out, startling Nora from her reverie. She shadowed her eyes and looked in the direction of Bryan's power yacht, which was also full of people.

His in-laws had joined them for the get-together. They were on the deck, fanning over the babies, and the corners of Nora's mouth lifted in a crooked smile. Nothing like a baby to make grown-up people sappy.

Nora had met Emilie and Gabriel a few days ago when they came by Matt's apartment for a brief visit. It was evident that they had come to ogle her, and that had made her very self-conscious.

She should have gotten used to it by then. Lately, it had been a constant parade through Matt's house. One evening, Matt even observed dryly that his apartment had never seen so much traffic in years.

Beyond Bryan's yacht, the sail of his friend's sloop was visible. Bryan had invited Max to spend the day with them, not only because he needed another boat for all the people coming to his lake house. Max was his partner in the dojo and his best friend, and they got along very well.

Nora caught a glimpse of Ariel's straight blond hair, flying into the wind. She stood alone at the bow, looking into the distance.

Nora had noticed Ariel was slightly uncomfortable with Max, and she suspected Max was making Ariel jumpy and all too aware of her being a woman.

Alex and Max worked together, handling the yacht, and Michael and Amelie huddled on a bench on the deck.

Nora liked all of them, although Ariel and Alex had seemed somewhat cold and reserved toward her. Nora didn't know whether they disliked her or were more introverted than others. She shrugged – she didn't care one way or the other.

Nora had gotten to know Maggie and Jay better, and she had made fast friends with Becka and Bryan. They were warm and friendly, so it wasn't hard to relate to them.

She had already spent over two weeks in Matt's apartment. Although she felt better now, and she had even started her physiotherapy, Nora found it difficult to broach the subject of her leaving his house. She had gotten used to being around Matt, and the thought of not seeing him again made her sick.

Not that Matt seemed willing to give her an opening to discuss her imminent leaving. Whenever he asked about her health, he always changed the subject before getting to the point where she would claim that she would manage by herself and had to move back home. She didn't know how, because her disability pay covered only the rent, but she had to find a solution.

Nora had spent all the nights in his bed. Matt would hold her, always careful not to give her any reason for discomfort. Yet, he always seemed to envelop her completely.

She didn't recall to have ever had such a restful sleep in her entire life. Matt made her feel protected and cherished.

He never asked anything from Nora and never went beyond a few kisses—all right, quite hot kisses. He truly intended not to rush things and demand anything from her, and his consideration baffled her. It was clear that he wanted more, but he never pressured her.

Nora turned around and brushed the hair off her face. She sighed deeply. She knew that everything would change once she moved out of his house. That feeling of well-being and security would disappear. Nora also wondered if Matt would still take the trouble to come and see her when she wasn't underfoot.

"Anything the matter, Nora?" Matt asked, sliding his arms around her from behind and brushing his lips on the side of her face.

"No, not really," Nora smiled, looking up at him and covering his hands with hers. "Just enjoying the surroundings."

"Yeah, sure," he replied in that dry voice she loved so much. "That's why you're sighing, right."

"No, really. I do enjoy being on the lake," Nora said, leaning her head back on his chest, her eyes always on his.

"That I know," Matt said.

He stared intently into her eyes first. His eyes always seemed to harbor mysteries and secrets Nora couldn't imagine. Then, he looked at her lips, and his fingers burrowed unconsciously in her midriff.

"How come you know?" she said lightly.

"It's on your face, baby," he answered, pushing his chin forward. "It's not like I can read your mind," he mumbled, and she laughed.

"Good to know," Nora said. "You might run for cover if you read my mind," she teased Matt.

"I doubt that very much," he said and leaned over her to steal a kiss.

It was almost over before it started, but her lips still tingled, and her fingers quivered on his hands.

"Later, baby," Matt whispered. "We're almost there," he explained, kissed her again, and left.

Nora turned to see if they had arrived at their destination, and her gaze fell on Marjorie and Jonathan. The two of them were smiling at her with deep satisfaction. She had completely forgotten about them, and now a blush spread all over her face.

Jonathan laughed heartily, and Marjorie, smacking him for his lack of subtlety, told Nora, "Don't mind us, Nora, dear. We only love to see you and Matt like that."

She patted Nora's leg and left it at that. She turned to her husband and began lecturing him in an undertone.

Nora couldn't understand Matt's parents. They should have been infuriated that she had insinuated herself into their son's life. Matt was a renowned attorney and had amassed a fortune. She was just a paramedic, who, right then, was paid a little over half her salary, because of her health issues, and that would continue for at least half a year, as her doctor warned her.

Nora shook her head and gave up understanding their reasons. She went back to watching the men. They were busy with the approach maneuvers.

CHAPTER SEVENTEEN

THE PARTY HAD BEEN going strong for several hours already. Nora wondered that the people weren't exhausted yet. She had sat on a blanket most of the time and still felt a little tired.

They had arrived at Bryan's house a little after ten, and the first thing, they arranged the food on a few folding tables. They spread blankets under the trees, in the shadow, and ate heartily, laughing, talking, and teasing each other.

Nat had his nap inside Bryan's house. Marjorie and Jonathan, but also Michael and Amelie, and Gabriel and Emilie rested in the house with the children, while the younger generation played volley.

Jay invited them to a card game, which made everyone throw something at him. They laughed while egging him, but Jay still seemed somewhat hurt.

Nora didn't understand why, and no one offered to explain. Feeling bad for Jay, she told him that she would play with him, but Matt stopped her.

"You know I don't like to say you can't do something, baby. But, I have to do it in this matter. You'll never play cards with Jay," Matt said in a stern voice.

"But why?" Nora asked with exasperation, taking exception to his arrogant manner. "Why everyone is reacting like this? Does he cheat?" she asked.

Jay groaned loudly, as if she had just stabbed him in the back, and covered his face with his hands, bursting into laughter.

Matt smiled whimsically and shook his head.

"No, he doesn't cheat, but you still won't play with him. I know you're probably bored out of your mind, but if you want to play cards, you can play with me," he offered, a crooked smile on his lips.

"I'm not bored," Nora replied through tight teeth. "You can go and play," she shooed him away.

"You won't get rid of me so easy, sweetie," Matt countered and lay down next to her on the blanket.

He had noticed that Nora was annoyed, and he had already spent too much time away from her. Matt had been painfully aware of Nora and gazed at her all the time. But he had to play with his siblings and cousins for a while. Otherwise, he would have never heard the end of it. They would have ragged him and said that he was besotted. That was the truth, of course. However, Matt didn't feel like being the butt of their jokes.

Nora shrugged and turned her head to the group of young people. They had gone back to having fun. Ariel took off her shirt and shorts. Underneath, she wore a black one-piece swimsuit, which hugged her body like a glove. Nora snickered when she noticed Max's eyes bulging out.

"What's so funny?" Matt asked and looked in the same direction. He immediately saw Max's reaction and scowled. "Ariel will make mincemeat out of him," Matt grumbled, unsure whether he liked Max's attention for his cousin or not.

"Why?" Nora turned to him with curious eyes.

"Ariel is fastidious by far. She doesn't even like Bryan. She merely tolerates him," Matt shrugged. "Imagine how she feels about this guy."

When he saw that Nora didn't like how it sounded, Matt hurried to explain.

"Don't take me wrong, honey. I love Bryan. He's like a brother to me. You've seen it. And I have nothing against Max. I know him well. Heck, I've sparred with the man, and we went out in a group a few times. I like him just fine. He's steady and honest. But I don't see Ariel go for his ponytail or goatee," he shook his head. "And that might be her loss," Matt remarked. "Max might be the right man to mollify her a little. She's too stiff by half."

Nora leaned on Matt, and he took her in his arms.

"Maybe she'll try to know him better," Nora said quietly, watching Ariel. The woman was heading to the shore for a swim.

Matt observed Max taking off his shorts and following her. Max's thoughts were loud enough, and Matt snickered.

"I think I'll put my money on him," Matt said, and his fingers burrowed underneath Nora's shirt.

Everybody had carped at her to take the top off. It was a hot and sunny day, and it must have been uncomfortable to wear it. Yet, self-conscious, afraid that her scars would draw eyes, Nora had refused.

Her abdomen quivered under his palm, and a grin lifted the corner of his mouth. His mouth found the hollow between her neck and shoulder and kissed her.

"Matt," she panted for breath and tried to still his hands. "We're in the open. Everyone can see us."

"So what?" he groused.

His lips trailed the column of her neck up until they found the sensible spot Matt had already discovered behind her ear.

"I don't care. The family must have guessed we're together by now. If they haven't, then I've been wrong about their intellects all along," Matt whispered.

His tongue touched her earlobe, and Nora shuddered. A faint moan reached his ears. Satisfied, Matt started nibbling at her. His fingers gently touched and massaged the skin on her abdomen. Then they slid up until he reached underneath the soft curve of her breasts. He didn't dare to continue his journey. He had been continuously aroused for two weeks now, and he didn't think he could behave himself if he went into forbidden territory.

Matt breathed deeply and put his chin on the top of her head. He could do with holding her for the moment.

Not even five minutes later, Nat ran out of the house like a tornado and came to them. "I'm up, mommy. Matt, we must go swimming. I woke up," the boy reminded him.

Matt chuckled, kissed the top of Nora's head, and told her, "Sorry, honey. Duty calls."

"You'll take care of him, Matt," Nora said. Her voice sounded inquiring.

"You can trust me. I won't let anything happen to Nat," Matt replied to Nora in an earnest voice and kissed her briefly. "He'll also wear a safety vest, so don't worry."

"I should come too," she said, nibbling at her bottom lip.

"And do what?" Matt asked in an irritated tone of voice. It wasn't as if she could jump into the lake and save Nat if anything had happened. However, Matt noticed that Nora was irked and changed his mind. "All right. I'll spread the blanket right there on the shore so that you could keep an eye on us," he offered.

"I can spread the blanket myself," Nora retorted, but Matt didn't want to hear a thing. He pulled her up, picked up the blanket, and moseyed with her to the shore. Nat was hopping, happy to get into the water at last.

Nora sat on the blanket, her legs tugged underneath her, and she watched them. Matt was teaching Nat to swim, and she wondered at his patience. She didn't hear him raise his voice once. Sounds carried on the lake, and Nora could overhear his patient instructions. Matt even repeated things several times. Matt never got tired.

From farther away, Ariel's harsh replies to Max's words clashed with the quietness of the lake. It seemed that everything Max said rubbed Ariel the wrong way.

After almost an hour, Matt took Nat back to the shore. The boy still had energy, but Matt knew that he needed to have his afternoon snack.

They returned to the others, and Nora noticed fresh food on the tables. Her mouth watered when her gaze fell on the famous pastries that both Marjorie and Bryan had baked. Nora understood that a quiet competition was going on between the two of them.

Lily had already filled her plate with everything on the tables. Nora suspected Lily's metabolism was very active. Nora had seen Lily eat, and she couldn't have been so slender otherwise.

Nora smiled until her eyes fell on the cup with hot chocolate that Lily had left on the table. Her eyes widened when she saw the teaspoon stirring the liquid. Lily didn't handle it, and that shocked Nora.

She gasped and blinked hard. Matt immediately realized what Nora had seen and grumbled, "Lily."

Lily looked their way, and suddenly, the teaspoon stopped moving. Nora looked from the cup to Lily and then to Matt. He pretended to watch his brother, who was teasing Alex. Nora thought that she had imagined things and decided to let the matter drop.

"I might have a sunstroke," she said in a faltering voice. Nora couldn't find any other explanation for what she had witnessed. She rubbed her eyes with shaky fingers.

Matt took her hand, kissed it, and then said, "Let me take you under the trees. You need some shadow. All right? I'll fill a plate for you with everything," he assured Nora and spread the blanket under a tree.

He helped Nora sit, and to his astonishment, Matt discovered that he could read her mind and feel her turmoil now. He had tried to read some of her thoughts during the last few weeks and couldn't. Matt probed her mind a little, happy to be able to do it. Then, he blocked her thoughts, feeling like a voyeur.

Matt shook his head, overwhelmed with the significance of the event. After making sure that Nora was comfortable, Matt returned to the food with Nat, to fill plates for all of them.

Nora still looked suspicious, unsure whether she had imagined things or not. However, her logical mind didn't allow her to dwell on improbable things. Nora assumed that Lily might have stirred the hot chocolate before they came to the table, and the teaspoon continued to move because of inertia. '*This is the only reasonable explanation,*' Nora nodded and decided to leave it well alone.

CHAPTER EIGHTEEN

EVERYBODY GATHERED on blankets, close enough to carry a conversation. They talked about everything and nothing.

Marjorie mentioned a few fundraisers she organized, and everyone offered their time and money to help out. Matt's mother was a good organizer, and she chose the neediest causes to support.

Ariel spoke about a few experiments she had made with grafting some different species of plants. She was passionate about horticulture, yet, she didn't like her present job. She felt smothered and unchallenged. Nora understood that Ariel would have loved to own a nursery one day.

Becka spoke about her classes, and Bryan seemed to know everything about it. Nora couldn't believe that such attentive husbands existed. In her experience, men were egocentric and narcissistic.

Everyone shared something, and they tried to make her share as well, but she didn't have anything to share.

She was afraid to let them know about how things had evolved with Matt, and nothing else had happened in her life lately. She just recounted something Nat had done, and they seemed to be content with that.

After a while, they broke into groups and moved a little farther. Becka, Ariel, Maggie, and Lily were playing with the babies and entertained Nat.

The older generation gathered on one blanket and shared their concerns about their children in hushed voices. Yet, now and then, something reached Nora's ears, and she wondered why all of them seemed concerned about a specific task that the young people had to complete. She intended to ask Matt later and hoped that he wouldn't mind her nosiness.

The men started playing football. Just Matt remained with her, always holding her in his arms and whispering some nonsense words in her ear.

The afternoon trailed along. The sun was bright, and a light breeze ruffled Nora's hair. Everything was just perfect.

Nora breathed the salty smell of his skin, and her body reacted immediately. Yet, she still fell asleep and dozed for a while, lulled to sleep by Matt's endearments and the heat coming from his body.

When she woke up, her eyes searched for Nat immediately, and she smiled when she found him. He was still with the women and babies.

Maggie played hocus-pocus for children, and Nora had to admit that she was very good at it. Maggie had produced a little bird out of thin air, and Nat almost laughed his heart out. Then Maggie snapped her fingers, and a small chocolate bar appeared in her hand. She handed it to Nat, and he looked at her adoringly.

Nora was in awe. She had seen shows before, but Maggie was smoother than any other magician Nora had ever seen. As a rule, Nora could guess how the magicians did what they did, but there was no way to say with Maggie.

Nat turned to Ariel and said something, and Ariel smiled. She snapped her fingers, and a red apple appeared in her palm.

Nora frowned in confusion. The apple was big, and she didn't see where Ariel could have hidden it. She still wore her swimsuit only. Just a few moments ago, Nora had wondered how Ariel didn't melt under Max's hot stare. The man's eyes zeroed in on her, and he practically didn't blink.

The baby in Lily's arms raised his arms, and the toys on the blanket beneath them floated in the air.

That was too much. Scared now, Nora jumped out of Matt's embrace and shouted, "What the heck's going on here?"

Her words stopped all activities. Even the men who were playing football forgot about the ball. The football kept rolling to the edge of the water. No one paid any attention when it went under the surface of the lake.

Nora felt that all eyes were on her, but now she didn't care. She was scared. She couldn't find any reasonable explanations for what she had witnessed, and her fear escalated. Her chest heaved. Nora was breathing hard, and her head felt light. Then, she fainted.

"Damn," Matt grumbled and rushed to catch her.

"I am sorry," Becka said, coming toward them.

Bryan followed her with his eyes and then asked Max to follow him inside the house.

Max understood something was happening, and his friend didn't want him to witness it. He respected Bryan too much not to heed his call.

Becka sat on Matt's blanket and stroked Nora's hair.

"I still can't stop the babies if they choose to play," Becka explained to Matt. "Sean has just discovered that he can move objects. Imagine how titillating it is for him," she apologized. "They're too young to understand when they may do some things and when they shouldn't. I imagine it will take a few years..."

"Don't worry, sweetie," Matt said. "Nora had to find out somehow. She's a very rational woman, and I'd have had a hard time to make her belief if she hadn't witnessed everything by herself," he pointed out.

He brushed his lips over Nora's and then whispered, "Come on, Nora. Come back, baby. Wake up."

After a couple of attempts, Nora opened her eyes. Confusion glimmered in her green pupils, and her eyes searched Matt's face for an answer. She sat up in his arms, rubbed her eyes, and then turned to him.

"I think I'm hallucinating, Matt," Nora confessed with a small voice. She still sounded scared.

Matt shook his head, his eyes on her face.

"What do you mean?" Nora asked, and her breath caught in her throat.

"You aren't hallucinating," Matt answered her in a very matter-of-fact tone of voice.

"Impossible, Matt. Do you know what I thought I saw?"

"Not really, but I can imagine. However, if you give me a second and allow me to read your mind, I can answer."

The color disappeared from Nora's face. Her lips quivered, and her fingers shook on Matt's forearm.

"What do you mean?" she asked.

"I mean that I can read your thoughts, baby, but I won't do it if you don't allow me," he answered quietly.

Nora scowled at Mat for a second, and then she taunted him, "All right, read away."

He looked at her intently for a few seconds and then chuckled.

"First of all, I didn't know you had such a colorful vocabulary, Nora," he jokingly chastised her. Then, he became serious, "Right now, you're thinking that I'm playing with you, but in the back of your mind, you still wonder what's going on. I understand you saw Sean lift the toys off the blanket, Nora. It's no big deal," Matt started to say, but Nora interrupted him.

"What do you mean when you say that it's no big deal, Matthew Winston?" she asked in a very firm voice. "And how come you knew what I was thinking?" Nora thought to ask when the reality dawned on her.

"What Sean did it is called telekinesis. If someone has that gift, it is not difficult to achieve. So far, Becka, Lily, Alex, Josh, and now Sean have that gift," Matt explained, and her eyes widened in shock.

"What Maggie and Ariel did?" Nora remembered their exploits and asked in a fearful voice.

"That's mere... witchcraft," Matt said and winced. He imagined how that would sound in her ears.

Nora pushed away from Matt, scrambled a little farther, and stared at him. Then, she looked around at everyone. "What do you mean?" she roared now.

"Well, I'd say..." Matt started to say, but Alex spoke first.

"Come on, Matt, you're a wuss. Things are simple, Nora," Alex turned to Nora, although Matt tried to stop him. "We're witches. Well, most of us are, except my mother, Matt's father, Becka's mother, and Bryan. The rest of us inherited several talents. Some have one talent. Others have two or three. Some of us cultivated them, and others didn't. That's all," Alex shrugged.

Nora merely looked at him at a loss of words. She couldn't accept what Alex had said. "What?" she asked, dizzy already.

"By God, Matt, you said she was a smart woman," Alex grumbled with disgust.

"Shut up," Matt bellowed at him. "And leave, now," Matt ordered, angry with his cousin. Alex didn't have any tact at all, and he didn't care if he insulted anyone.

Marjorie came to Nora and took her hand. "Pumpkin, it's not like we're a horrible family. We only have a few gifts. That's all. As some people can play an instrument, I can do automatic writing and read emotions. Matt reads minds and feelings, but that shouldn't scare you, Nora. Ask Jonathan if you want. We've been married for thirty-seven years now, and he's never had anything to fear. Right, Jonathan?" Marjorie turned to her husband.

Jonathan approached Marjorie, took her hand, and kissed it. Now Nora understood then where Matt had learned to do that.

"I have had only one fear, my love," he said, a whimsical smile on his lips. "That I wouldn't give you the happiness you deserved."

Marjorie's eyes shimmered with joyful tears. She turned back to Nora, patted her shoulder, and said, "You'll see that you shouldn't worry about anything. Think only of what you know about Matt. You'll make the right choice, pumpkin. I'm sure of that."

Nora stubbornly looked away, and Matt sighed. "I think we should go back home," he suggested, and everybody agreed.

They had started to pick up everything when Nat came to Matt and asked, "What's a witch, Matt?"

Nora froze in place.

CHAPTER NINETEEN

NORA FELT FROZEN INSIDE. The cruise over the lake didn't calm her, as it had happened before. When Matt transferred everything into his car, she just waited aside, her thoughts churning in her head.

Everyone came to say their good-byes, but she seemed aloof, and they didn't linger.

Matt helped Nora in the car after he secured Nat in the child's chair in the back. He leaned over her and locked her seatbelt when he noticed that she only stared through the windshield.

Suddenly, Nora turned her eyes to him and said, "I want to go home."

"We're going home," Matt nodded quietly.

She grabbed his hand and said through tight teeth, "My home, not yours."

Matt shook his head, and instinctively, leaned over Nora, and kissed her hard. "I'm sorry, sweetheart. I can't drive you to your apartment. You're not a hundred percent, and you can't take care of yourself and Nat the right way," he denied her requests, shaking his head.

When he saw that she wanted to interrupt him, he touched his fingers to her mouth, shaking his head again.

"I know you'll try, Nora. You're strong and stubborn enough to try. But your body won't let you. I have to take you home with me," Matt repeated mulishly, and the tone of his voice didn't leave room for arguments.

"I won't sleep with you," she lashed out at him.

Matt remained still, hurt visible in his eyes, but then, he nodded, "All right. You'll sleep in the other bedroom if that's what you want."

"That's what I want," Nora replied in a nasty tone of voice. "You lied to me and..."

"I've never lied to you," Matt contradicted her quietly. "I merely haven't revealed everything about me." With those words, he closed her car door and jogged to the other side to get them home.

The drive home didn't take more than five minutes. When they got upstairs, Nora wanted to take Nat with her in the empty bedroom. Nat didn't understand why he couldn't spend the remaining of the afternoon with Matt and started crying.

Emotionally exhausted, Nora left them alone and went to her room. Regardless of everything, she still trusted Matt to take care of her son.

Lying in bed, Nora kept turning things in her head. The shock hadn't worn off yet, and she still couldn't believe that the Watsons were witches. She knew that there wasn't such a thing as witches.

Then, Nora thought about their paranormal abilities, although she had discounted them in the past. She still didn't reach any conclusion, and after a while, worn out, she fell asleep.

Later, Nora woke when Matt brushed his fingers over her face. Confused, she blinked and looked at him. Matt had turned on the lamp on the night table, and Nora realized that it was already dark outside.

"Hey, there," Matt said softly. "I didn't know if I should let you sleep or not. It's late, though, and you haven't had any dinner yet. Do you want me to bring it here, or do you think you could stand having dinner with me?"

His eyes revealed his insecurity, and her heart cringed. Matt was a kind man, and Nora didn't want to hurt him. However, she couldn't just gloss over what had happened.

"I could have something to eat," Nora mumbled.

"Do you want me to bring you a tray here?" Matt offered again.

"No," she replied, sitting up. "I'll be in the kitchen in a couple of minutes."

"Do you need my help with anything?" Matt asked her, straightening up.

"I'm pretty sure I can go to the bathroom under my own steam, Matt," Nora replied. "I don't need your paranormal powers to support me."

Her voice sounded spiteful. Nora felt raw and didn't feel like cutting Matt any slack.

Matt took in her bad mood and nodded. He locked his hands at the back of his head, and he left the room. The feeling of defeat was gnawing at him, and Matt didn't know how to stop that train wreck.

WHEN NORA CAME INTO the living room, Matt was seated at the breakfast table and watched the lake. He had already laid everything out on the table.

Sensing her arrival, Matt turned to her and stood up.

Always the consummated gentleman, Nora thought, and then she scolded herself. Matt had always been considerate and respectful toward her. Nora was only lashing at him now because of what she had uncovered that afternoon.

Nora moseyed to the table and sat down. Matt held the chair for her, and then, he sat down again.

He started serving Nora with salad first, and then, he added a large grilled chicken breast and stir-fried vegetables on her plate. Always in silence, Matt filled his plate, and with a gesture, invited her to eat.

They ate in complete silence for a few minutes, and then, Nora looked up at him and asked, "Did you ever intend to let me know?"

"Yes," Matt answered.

She didn't like his brief answer and scowled at him.

"Yeah? When? Sometime in the next twenty or thirty years?"

Nora sounded like a shrew, and Matt's left eyebrow hiked up his forehead. She blushed slightly, but her expression didn't change.

"Actually, no, Nora. I knew that I had to let you know before we'd become more involved."

"Really?" she asked mockingly. "How more involved should we have been for you to spill the beans?"

His eyes turned hard. Matt had hoped that they could discuss things reasonably without attacking each other.

Matt understood that Nora felt betrayed somehow. He didn't try to read her mind, though. Matt didn't think that he could do it without her permission. However, her emotions were extremely compelling, and no empathic person could have stopped the emotional waves.

"Definitely, before taking you into my bed and before asking you to be my wife," Matt replied silently.

To mask his concerns, he cut a piece of chicken and stuffed it in his mouth. He didn't taste it but chewed carefully before swallowing.

Nora's eyes widened, and a faint blush colored the top of her cheeks. Her fingers shook on the fork, which clanked on the plate. The sound resonated in their ears, and Nora put the fork down. She leaned back and measured him.

"You've already taken me into your bed," Nora observed with sarcasm.

"Not the way I want to," Matt replied with a shrug. "I love cuddling with you, and I need sleeping with you," he admitted. "But I do need much more than that."

"I see," Nora said quietly and crossed her arms over her chest.

She stared at him a little more and then said, "You know that you could have had something more for some time now."

"Maybe," Matt shrugged again and forked some vegetables. "Eat your food, Nora. It's getting cold."

"How, the heck, do you think I can eat now?" she scowled at him.

"The same way I do," he replied and nodded his head toward her plate to nudge her to eat.

"I'm not as insensible as you are," Nora said through her teeth, and Matt stilled.

Then Nora realized what she had said, and recalling how careful and attentive Matt had been with her, she wanted to slap herself silly.

Nora reached out and touched Matt's hand, "I'm sorry, Matt. You don't deserve that. I'm only pretty confused and scared, you know."

"I can imagine," he groused.

"No," she replied with a self-deprecating laugh. "You can read my mind. You don't have to imagine anything."

"But I do. As I said, I'll never read your mind without permission. Your emotions, though...," Matt shrugged.

"What about them?" she inquired.

"I can't block them. I'll always know what you feel. I mean that I know if you're happy or sad or if you're scared or hurt. You know. I don't know if you love or hate someone. I'd have to read your mind for that," Matt explained to her, and waved his hand again, inviting Nora to continue eating.

This time, Nora took her fork and played around with her vegetables, pensively.

"When you didn't allow me to play cards with Jay," she said and looked up at Mat, "was it because of his talents?"

Matt nodded and continued to chew. It took him a few seconds to swallow. Then he reached out to Nora and interlocked their fingers. He turned her hand, palm up, and his thumb started drawing circles on her smooth skin. Nora felt his caresses everywhere inside her body and swallowed hard.

"Yes, Jay has got an extra-sensorial perception, ESP, if you want. He can see what cards you have in your hand. For the moment, he can't control the gift, and as a result, he can't stop using it. Playing cards with him is a farce, if you want," Matt shrugged.

"I see," Nora said. "Outside the family, does anyone else know what you can do? I mean, you and your cousins. You understand what I mean."

"No," Matt answered. "There are people who'd consider us freaks. Others would want to take advantage of what we can do. So, no, only the people in the family know about our talents. Of course, the ones marrying into the family are told beforehand so that they could choose. So far, none of them backed out," Matt said in a very soft voice.

For a few seconds, Nora and Matt gazed at each other.

"You said that you wanted to have me in your bed and marry me," Nora said in a hesitant voice.

"Yes, I do. Both," Matt nodded.

"Why me?" she asked, and Matt blinked.

"Come again?" he asked, confused.

"Why me? Why would you want to marry me?" she repeated more forcefully. "Because I found out what the Winstons can do?"

"Don't be stupid," Matt replied in a harsh voice. "I wouldn't marry for such a trivial reason, Nora."

"Then why me?" she repeated stubbornly. "Why would you be interested in marrying me?"

His eyes rounded, and the intensity of the dark blue took her breath away. Matt shook his head and stood up to pace, lost in thought.

After a few minutes, he came back to her.

"I can't understand. You're a smart woman. I've seen proof of your intelligence on many occasions. How can such a smart woman ask such stupid questions?" Matt asked, shaking his head.

"Look here," Nora stood at her turn. "I'm not stupid."

"That I know," he agreed with her. "I don't know how you can't see it, though."

"See what?" Nora asked with exasperation.

"That I love you," Matt replied. He registered the shock on her face. Nora fell back on her chair, looking at him with disbelief.

"Yeah, I can see you're overwhelmed with joy," he said dryly. Matt took his plate and the platters on the table into the kitchen. He cleaned them and put them into the dishwasher. Nora was still watching him with skepticism.

"Finish your dinner, Nora," Matt invited her, quietly. "Leave everything on the table. I'll take care of the dishes later. Good night," he added and left the room.

Nora remained at the table, looking out of the window, yet her eyes didn't register anything. In a way, she was happy to hear Matt's words. However, they also scared her. Nora didn't know whether she loved him too.

Later, she realized that her food was cold and her body stiff, because she had been sitting in the same position for too long. With difficulty, Nora stood and slowly made her way to her room.

CHAPTER TWENTY

NORA WAS SITTING ON the window sill bench, watching the lake, when the intercom beeped. She grimaced and abandoned her place to answer the door.

Being Canada Day, Matt had taken Nat to see some shows on Harbor Front, together with Marjorie and Becka.

Although she had some apprehensions about the abilities running in the Winston family, she trusted Matt and his family with her son.

The last two weeks had been awkward. Matt had always been polite but withdrawn, and Nora had spent time mostly by herself.

They took their meals together, and Matt took Nat to visit Becka and Bryan regularly. Matt took Nat to the park, but Nora always declined to go out.

Nora didn't know how to react around Matt anymore. She knew that she had been mean and spiteful, and she didn't know how to take her words back. Her former marriage had left her unprepared to fix the situation.

Nora was exhausted. Her mind churned around her feelings for Matt and what he had told her.

She also worried about moving back to her apartment. As she suspected, her disability pay covered the rent, and she had only about two hundred dollars left in the bank after paying it.

She could solve that problem only if she returned to work, which seemed out of the question. The doctor didn't want to sign off. She had asked him just that when she had her medical appointment the other day, and he refused.

Yet, she knew that she couldn't take advantage of Matt anymore. Matt was testy now. Nora believed that Matt left her and Nat to remain in the apartment only because of his upbringing.

Nora pushed the button to the intercom and unlocked the door without asking who it was. She didn't really care. Nora felt so lonely that she would have welcomed anyone, even Alex, who didn't seem to like her much.

When she heard the knock on the door, Nora opened it immediately and found herself before Bryan. She sketched a shy smile and waved him to come inside. She knew that she would feel awkward to see someone after the fiasco at the lake, but she didn't expect to feel so bad.

Bryan entered, watching her thoroughly. He leaned over and kissed her cheek. "You seem awfully tired and depressed," he noticed. "Is everything fine?"

"You flatter me, Bryan," she replied in a dry tone of voice.

"Not my intention, Nora," Bryan shook his head. "I've brought something for us," Bryan showed the bag he had in his hand to Nora.

"Go and take a sit on the sofa. I'll put everything on a platter and come to join you."

"I can put everything on the platter," she replied stubbornly and snatched the bag. "Now, you can go and sit on the sofa," Nora said and gave him a push in the direction of the sofa.

Bryan didn't budge at first. Then he laughed, put his hands up to show that he surrendered and sauntered to the sofa. He could see Nora in the kitchen, trying to locate the platters.

He chuckled and told her, "Try the last cupboard down on the left. That's where Matt keeps the platters. I see that he still doesn't let you in the kitchen," Bryan observed.

"You know that he doesn't," Nora replied ruefully. "Either you or Marjorie provide the food. I'm not allowed to do anything around here, and it drives me crazy," she confessed, arranging the pastries on the platter.

"Have you told him that?" Bryan inquired mildly, always watching her, judging her reactions and emotions.

Nora shrugged but said nothing. She carried the platter to the coffee table and asked, "Would you like some coffee, coke, or beer?"

"A beer would be good," Bryan answered with a shrug. "Don't bother with a glass, Nora. I don't need one," he thought to mention, as he never bothered about etiquette.

Nora returned to the kitchen to bring the beer, and Bryan noticed with satisfaction that she moved easier. Nora hadn't fully healed, and from what Matt had told him, Bryan knew that she might remain with a slight limp for her entire life. That didn't bother Matt at all.

It was good that Nora was on the road to recovery. Now, only if Bryan could help to heal her other wounds.

Nora returned with a beer for him and a coke for her. She sat in an armchair and sighed.

"Tough day?" Bryan inquired.

"A tough couple of months," she replied with a nod.

"I can see that. So, why haven't you told Matt that you'd like to do some work in the kitchen?"

She looked away. Then, she leaned forward and picked a piece of pastry.

"You're avoiding my question," Bryan observed.

"Of course, I'm avoiding your question," she snapped at Bryan.

"Why?" he insisted.

Nora sighed deeply, and then, she gave in.

"Because Matt and I are not precisely talking, you know. Matt asks if I'm okay or if I want to eat something or watch a movie. He also asks permission for taking Nat with him, but nothing else," Nora shrugged.

"Since when?" Bryan asked.

"Like you don't know," she scowled at Bryan. "Since that blasted day at your lake house."

"So, you're upset with Matt for what had happened there and what you found out," Bryan concluded.

"I was then," she thought to specify. "Come on, Bryan, don't tell me that you wouldn't have been surprised if something like that had happened to you," Nora lifted her brows in disbelief.

Bryan shouted with laughter and slapped his knee. His eyes sparkled with amusement.

"What's so funny?" Nora frowned, not understanding how Bryan could laugh in such circumstances.

"You, Nora, you're funny."

"Because I was surprised and scared when all that happened?" she asked with dismay. Nora hadn't expected that coarse behavior from Bryan. He didn't seem the kind of man to make fun of someone just for the sake of it. '*How wrong can I be sometimes,*' she thought.

"Of course not. I wouldn't laugh at you for that, Nora," he scowled at her.

Bryan had hoped that Nora knew him better than that by then.

"I'm laughing because you assume that I've never been in that position," he hooted again, shaking his head.

Nora just looked at him, her eyebrows up to her forehead. She had never seen Bryan in such a state.

"Imagine," he said, "I took Becka exactly to the same spot. We made love for the first time, one of the most beautiful moments in my life, by the way. And then we quarreled," he said. "You'll certainly hear why," he added with a wave of his hand. "I won't waste our time going into those details. Pretty soon, someone will find great joy relating the events to you. I've been the butt of their jokes ever since," he flapped his hand with disgust. "Anyway, at the time, I didn't know anything about her family, and to be perfectly honest with you, I didn't believe in such things," he explained.

"I know what you mean," Nora said. "I had the same ideas, and everything came as a shock."

"Yes, I know. It was the same with me. Anyway, at the time, Becka couldn't control her powers, you know. She got so upset with me that the wind started gushing around us, and things flew into the air," he shook his head, chuckling.

"Imagine, a big cooler just flying around, past your head. Oh, boy, that did scare me," he confessed, although he was laughing.

Nora listened to him with astonishment.

"What did you do?" she asked breathlessly. She'd have run for cover and waited there until the coast would have been clear.

Bryan ran his fingers through his hair, gulped from his beer, and then, looking straight into her eyes, he said, "I was an ass, the biggest possible ass. I treated Becka as if she'd been a freak. I hurt her and deeply."

"Oh, my God. How come that she took you back?" Nora asked, and her eyes widened. She knew that she wouldn't have been able to forgive something like that.

"I think that I was lucky. I went to Becka a few days afterward. I had in mind to beg and grovel, you know. I thought to do everything possible to make her forgive me. But Becka forgave me immediately, and she didn't feel the need to punish me."

"I see," Nora murmured. Yet, she found it hard to believe that a woman could merely push something like that aside and forget about it.

"Now, let me tell you something, Nora. If I could accept things flying around and winds and storms, then you can accept Matt's talent. His, at least, doesn't scare you. You know that he can't hurt you, like by hitting your head with a cooler, for instance," Bryan said, laughing.

"Matt has asked you to come and talk to me," Nora concluded, clenching her hands together.

"Oh, no, Nora. Don't even tell him that I talked to you about this. He'd skin me first. I'd love to remain in good relations with Matt. He's one of the good guys, you know. I don't want to lose his friendship, Nora. But I know that he pines over you, and if I were to guess after seeing you today, you pine over him too. Why don't you cut some slack to both of you, and try to talk to him? I understand that Matt's afraid that you don't want to listen to what he has to say, and he hurts," Bryan said, finishing off his beer.

"I'd like to talk to him, but I don't even know where to begin. I'm also afraid. Matt might think that I'm only trying to take advantage of him because of my present situation, and that's even worse," Nora confessed, leaning forward. "He knows that the doctor won't sign me off for work, and I'm in a bad financial situation."

"Then allow him to read your mind. That should banish any doubts and suspicions. I assure you that the process is painless. I tried it," Bryan said in a matter-of-fact tone of voice.

"Easy for you to say," she snapped.

"I know it's easy for me to say," Bryan nodded. "It's always easy to give advice. I know. But if you don't do something, you'll both lose. Matt won't ever pressure you, and if he thinks that's what you want, he'll leave you alone, no matter how much he hurts," Bryan explained to Nora.

Nora closed her eyes and bit her bottom lip. Bryan practically could see the little wheels turning round and round.

"May I ask something more from you, Bryan?" Nora suddenly opened her eyes and trained her shiny green eyes on him.

"Of course, you can," Bryan nodded.

"Would you and Becka keep Nat overnight today? Or maybe, you'll take Nat with you tomorrow if it isn't possible today," Nora hurried to say.

"We can keep him with us today. It isn't a problem. It will be fun," he grinned. "Let me call Becka and tell her. She's with Matt and Nat right now. She can take Nat directly home, and you and Matt can have the apartment to yourself tonight," Bryan winked at her and took his phone out of his pocket.

He dialed Becka's number and explained everything as fast as possible, warning her from the beginning not to say a thing to Matt.

CHAPTER TWENTY-ONE

MATT DREADED AN ENTIRE afternoon and evening alone with Nora. He longed to be with her, and yet, knowing that Nora didn't want to talk to him made his chest ache.

Becka had asked to take Nat with her until the next day and assured Matt that she had cleared everything with Nora. Matt still checked with Nora, and that made Becka growl at him, which cheered Nat considerably.

They were just about to go home, and the boy didn't want to go inside. He would have preferred to run along the harbor.

Marjorie had wanted to accompany Matt at home. He had sensed it. Yet, Becka took her hand and invited Marjorie to see the twins. Matt couldn't compete with the twins those days. Soon, his mother sauntered to Becka's car and left with her.

Matt resigned himself to another afternoon of silence. The thought that Nora was in the same apartment with him, so close, and yet, so far away, killed him slowly.

Matt groaned, but he didn't have anything else to do, so he drove back home.

To his dismay, he didn't encounter any traffic stops, any traffic jams, anything. He got there in no time. With a sigh, Matt parked the car and leaned his head on the driving wheel for a few seconds.

'*Start cracking, scaredy-cat,*' Matt mumbled and got out of the car.

His apartment was on the twenty-seventh floor, and sometimes, the trip by elevator seemed to take forever. Of course, not that day. It felt as if the elevator had transported him to his floor in the blink of an eye.

Matt headed to his door with dread, breathed deeply, preparing himself for another silent treatment, and then unlocked the door.

As expected, the apartment was quiet. Matt knew that Nora wouldn't welcome him, as she had done in the past.

Suddenly, a painful thought popped into his head. Nora had left, and her request to Becka was just a decoy. She would be waiting for Nat at Becka's house, and head with him to her apartment afterward.

"No," he bellowed, and his fist punched the wall with all the force Matt could muster.

Matt wanted his chance, and he couldn't just lie down and have it slip through his fingers. He couldn't let Nora go without a word.

He practically tore the door down when he pulled it open. Matt didn't care that his knuckles were bleeding, or he might destroy the door.

He had barely got out of the door with a purposeful stride that Nora called from behind, "Matt, where are you going? What's happened?"

Matt staggered on his feet. He slowly turned around, and his eyes fell squarely on Nora.

Wide-eyed, Nora looked from him to the hole in the wall and back. She paled when her eyes zeroed in on his bloody knuckles.

"That's what I heard," she whispered. "You punched the wall," she said louder, shaking her head.

She couldn't believe he'd done that. Matt was always calm and composed. He wasn't a hothead, and she couldn't reconcile the image she had before her eyes with the man she knew.

Nora stared at him for a few seconds and then bellowed, "Are you out of your mind? Why, the heck, would you do that?"

Matt flapped his hand, tried to say something, and then scowled at her. He didn't find the courage to admit why he had done it.

"What's the matter? What made you so angry?" Nora asked again in a calmer voice this time.

Nora would have never thought that something could make Matt lose his temper. He was invariably so patient and understanding that his present behavior astonished her.

'*What made me so angry? The woman is clueless, damn it! She's just torn my heart apart, and she's asking what's the matter,*' Matt shook his head.

Then, he cleared his throat and looked away for a few seconds. Reaching a decision, Matt closed the door behind him. He threw the keys in the bowl on the table near the door, and only then, his gaze came back at Nora.

Matt felt stupid for what he had done, and he knew that he had to say something and explain his behavior. Lying to Nora wasn't a choice.

"I thought you left," he said with a sigh.

"I beg your pardon?" she replied, and her eyes widened.

"I thought that you left the apartment. You left me," Matt repeated, "and you asked Becka to take Nat, so you could go to her house and take him with you," he explained louder in a rebellious tone of voice. He sounded like a petulant child, justifying why he had done a stupid thing.

For a few seconds, Nora couldn't answer. Her green eyes showed bewilderment at first, and then anger.

"Really? Do you think I'd be so cruel, Matt?" Nora asked, hardly keeping her temper in check.

He sensed that his words had offended her and tried to apologize, "I'm sorry, baby. I didn't think. I just reacted," he opened his arms, at a loss of words. He didn't know what to say and make her hurt less.

"You should know me better than that," Nora said, morosely.

"I know you better," he admitted. "I've just lost my common sense for a moment."

Nora looked Matt over, and then, she took his hand and pulled him after her.

"Where are we going?" Matt asked, and then he slapped himself in his mind again for asking stupid questions. As long as she wanted him with her, he didn't mind where they were going.

Nora turned her head toward him and smiled, "Just in the living room for the moment. Right after we've cleaned those knuckles and stopped the bleeding," she thought to add.

"The bleeding's stopped, don't worry about it," Matt waved the matter away, as unimportant.

"Come on, Matt, humor me. Let's clean those knuckles first, and we'll see afterward."

Matt gave in and let her fuss over his knuckles. When she finished, Nora led him into the living room and invited him to sit on the sofa. Satisfied that he was doing her bidding, she moseyed to the kitchen.

"By the way, Bryan passed by this afternoon," Nora said, disappearing into the kitchen. "He brought some pastries for us. I asked him first if Nat could go to their house for a sleepover, and then he called Becka," her voice came from the kitchen, and Matt leaned sideways to see her through the alcove.

"Why did he come?" Matt asked, and suspicion rang in his voice.

Nora returned with a tray in her hands, and Matt immediately jumped to his feet and rushed to relieve Nora of the burden.

She tapped her foot on the floor, furiously.

"I'm not frail, Matt Winston. I'm able to carry a tray," Nora grumbled at him.

"No, baby, you're not frail. But you won't carry a tray before another month or two. We'll see how it goes," Matt shrugged, without promising anything.

"With you, I won't be allowed to carry anything for the rest of my life," Nora glared at Matt, putting her hands on her hips.

Matt shrugged and grinned at her. He was smart enough not to go into an argument with Nora right then.

"Come here and have a sit," Matt invited her, laying the platter on the coffee table in front of the sofa.

Nora decided to choose her battles and let that one go. She didn't see that she would win it anytime soon.

She sat on the sofa. Leaving her slippers on the floor, she tugged her legs under her. Nora leaned forward to take one of the plates on the tray and a pastry, but Matt immediately stopped her and prepared a helping for her. Nora huffed but didn't comment.

She waited until Matt also helped himself to a pastry and sat in an armchair not far from her.

During the last couple of weeks, before the event at the lake, Matt had bought two more armchairs, a few ottomans, and pillows, and he had spread them through the living-room.

It seemed necessary because guests came almost every day at that time. They usually came in groups and always commented about the lack of furniture.

After her melt-down at the lake, the group visits ended, and some visits stopped altogether. Probably, people were wary of her.

"I think we should talk," Nora said, after biting into the pastry.

Matt was about to carry his pastry to the mouth, and his hand froze in mid-movement. His eyes darkened, and he didn't dare to blink.

"You don't need to worry," Nora said, with a small smile tucked in the corner of her mouth. "Or better said, I hope that you won't worry. You said that you could read my mind if I allowed it," Nora continued in an inquiring voice.

Matt just nodded. He put the pastry back onto the plate and left the plate on the table.

"I allow it," Nora said softly. "Knock yourself out," she tried to lighten the mood, but Matt didn't feel so relieved.

"Are you sure?" he asked in a faltering voice.

She nodded with determination and closed her eyes. Nora didn't know what reading her mind involved, but she had already decided to take Bryan's advice and didn't want to back out.

Matt stared at Nora, and then, seeing that she didn't change her mind, he closed his eyes and let himself slide in her thoughts. He didn't need more than a few seconds to have tears in his eyes.

He left the armchair, and pulled her in his arms, forgetting about his earlier worries, and hugged her tight until she said a soft 'ouch.'

"Oh, baby, I am so sorry. I didn't mean to hurt you," he said in a rush and pulled himself at a distance.

"I know, Matt. You just held me too tight. Otherwise, you, touching me, that's not a problem," she said and touched his face with her fingers, tracing his stubby beard.

Nora closed the distance between them and slid her arms around him. She leaned her head on his chest and breathed contentedly.

Matt hugged her again, not so tight this time, and kissed the top of her head.

"I'm ready now," she whispered.

Matt became so still that Nora feared that he had stopped breathing. She looked up at him and felt as if the intensity of his eyes had swallowed her. The dark-blue of his pupils had turned darker.

"Do you mean that you're ready for me?" Matt asked, unsure of himself.

"Yes, if you haven't changed your mind, of course," Nora replied.

In a second, Matt scooped her up in his arms, and with long strides, he headed to his bedroom.

"Not in this lifetime, Nora. Sorry, baby, not in this lifetime."

Once in his bedroom, Matt laid her on his bed and stepped back. He just stared at her, happy to see her lying in his bed once more.

Then, he turned back and closed the door as if he were afraid that the world would intrude upon them.

CHAPTER TWENTY-TWO

WHEN THEY ARRIVED AT Marjorie's house, Nora couldn't believe her eyes. Her future mother-in-law hadn't spared any expenses.

Flowers covered every corner and every surface available. The buffet was decadent and in an array of colors that caught people's eye and watered their mouths.

Matt held her hand and chuckled at her surprise.

"Mom always knows how to give a party, baby," he brushed his lips on her cheek.

"I can see that," she replied in awe. "I've never seen anything like that. But she needn't have gone to so much trouble..." she shook her head.

"Honey, you have to understand something," Matt whispered in her ear. "I'm her firstborn. She's been waiting for this moment for thirty-four years. We must let her have her way," he advised, and Nora nodded.

Nat, who was holding her other hand, shouted, "Mommy, look, Becka's here."

Immediately, he pulled his hand out of hers and ran to Becka, his most favorite person in the world after Nora and Matt.

Becka welcomed him with a tight hug and a kiss on the cheek.

"Wow, you look so handsome," she praised him.

Matt had refused to have him dressed in a suit for the party. He had insisted that Nat was a child and needed to feel free to move around.

In the end, all parties involved had reached a compromise – Nat wouldn't wear a suit for the engagement party thrown by Marjorie for them, but he would wear one for the wedding.

Once the word that they had arrived spread out, everybody came to congratulate them. Marjorie and Jonathan beamed with pride and hugged both Nora and Matt several times.

People admired Nora's dress, and she blushed. Matt had weakened her resolve with a constant attack for a week and made her accept it. He bought it himself and presented it to her as a gift, together with all the necessary accessories.

The emerald sleeveless silky dress hugged her body, without being snug. It stopped just at her knees. Her eyes shone stronger, reflecting the color of the dress.

Considerate, Matt bought low-heel shoes for Nora so that she wouldn't overtax her leg and a small bag. He had already worried that Nora would overdo it during the party, so he had lectured her about not standing for too long. He asked Nora to let him know when she got tired. By the end of the lecture, she had rolled her eyes several times, but she promised to let him know if it became too much for her.

She remembered what Marjorie had said about giving a man his due. Matt was always attentive and attuned to her needs. The least Nora could do was to respect his wishes in that concern.

Nora and Matt moseyed through the guests, holding hands, chatting about inconsequential things, and answering questions.

They had to go different ways when men took Matt aside to discuss the bachelor's party that he had initially refused. Nora had convinced Matt to accept it. It was like a coming to age ritual, and she didn't want him to miss out on anything.

Nora went outside onto the patio with Lily for some fresh air. Marjorie had outdone herself, but Nora still felt smothered in large crowds.

"I understand that the wedding will be at Bryan's house on the lake," Lily said, sipping from her glass with champagne and eying Nora's dress.

That color would have worked for her, too, but she needed it in another model. She didn't have Nora's curves.

"Yes," Nora smiled at her. "Becka will be my matron of honor, you know. We decided to have only one matron of honor and one best man. Otherwise, we wouldn't have had any guests or almost any," Nora laughed, and Lily shared her hilarity.

"Yep, you're right. I remember Becka's wedding. Only the older generation played the role of guests. We were all bridesmaids and groomsmen. It was hilarious," Lily giggled.

"What was hilarious?" Maggie sashayed to them and toasted Nora.

"Becka's wedding," Lily explained. "With all of us part of the wedding party, remember?"

"Oh, yes," Maggie made a face. "I hope you won't do that to us," she implored Nora.

"Don't worry," Nora replied, laughing. "Just Becka and Bryan. Everyone else will be considered guest."

"Phew, thank God, Nora!" Maggie wiped off her forehead, theatrically, and the other two women laughed at her antics.

"So, I see you grabbed him, eventually," Rebecca's voice came from behind Nora.

Nora turned stiffly to the older woman. She hadn't seen Rebecca since the day when she came to the hospital. Nora couldn't say that she had missed her.

Rebecca sneered at her, and, suddenly, Lily turned on her heels and rushed to the house.

"Hello, Rebecca," Nora replied calmly. "I don't remember to have ever grabbed a man," she said and sipped unhurriedly from her glass.

She tried to hide any sign of distress. She knew that Rebecca would pounce on her if she saw any weakness.

"Great-grandma," Maggie intervened in a bored voice, "I think Matt did all the grabbing in the end. I can vouch for that. I witnessed almost everything," she flapped her hand.

"I'm sure that you have something else to do, young lady, so get lost," Rebecca snapped at her.

Maggie seemed to reflect a moment, then she shook her head, "No, sorry, grandma. Nothing to do. I was doing something," she pointed out. "I was talking to Nora. But it's not a problem," she patted her grandma's arm. "We can include you in our conversation. Right, Nora?" she asked and winked at Nora, who couldn't stop a crooked smile in the corner of her mouth.

"Girl, your manners are lacking," Rebecca snapped at Maggie again. "You don't know when you're not wanted somewhere. Now, get lost."

"I know that you don't like that I'm here, but Nora does, grandma. Don't you, Nora?"

Nora assessed the older woman before her eyes. Rebecca's annoyance with Maggie was escalating, and Nora didn't want to be the instrument of a rift between the two of them.

"It's okay, Maggie. Rebecca seems determined to tell me something, so we'd better let her do it. Meantime, would you mind filling me a plate with desserts? I saw them earlier and couldn't take my mind off them," she asked Maggie and stroked her arm.

"Are you sure?" Maggie asked, but she seemed unconvinced.

"Yes, I am," Nora replied and smiled at Maggie.

Yet, Maggie read a fierce determination beyond that smile.

"All right, grandma, the scene is all yours," Maggie bowed mockingly, and Rebecca's eyes thundered at her.

Maggie glided toward the house, giggling.

Rebecca watched her leaving and then turned to Nora. She stared her down with hard eyes, but then, Nora didn't back down either. She squared her shoulders and looked straight into Rebecca's eyes.

"Do you know that you ruined all chances for Matthew?" Rebecca asked in a disdainful voice.

"I don't know what you mean," Nora shook her head.

"He could have had everything," Rebecca replied and threw her hands in the air.

Nora heard the sudden rustle of leaves and felt the gushes of cold air surrounding her. Her heart skipped a beat when she remembered Bryan's story, but she told herself that Rebecca wouldn't kill her in Marjorie's house. She matched her look for look.

Rebecca scowled and threw her fist into the air. A black cloud appeared, and rain started to pour over Nora.

Nora didn't move or show distress. '*A little rain didn't kill anyone*,' she thought.

Suddenly everyone came out on the patio and began thundering at Rebecca, and Matt's voice roared the loudest. He ran and hugged Nora to his chest.

"If you ever, and I mean ever, touch her, even with your thought, I won't recognize you as part of my family," he bit Rebecca's head off, and she gasped.

"You'd do that for her?" she asked with outrage.

"She's the woman I love and will be my wife in a week. You either respect her and my decisions and wishes, or you can forget that I exist," Matt glowered at Rebecca and then took Nora with him.

Passing by his mother, who looked utterly shocked, Matt asked her in a calmer tone of voice, "Could you help Nora with something to wear, mother?"

Marjorie nodded and joined them on their way inside.

Everyone looked at Rebecca with astonished eyes. She had been vocal in the past but had never attacked anyone.

"Why?" Bryan asked her quietly. "You weren't so malicious to me, and I, at least, did look like a ruffian," he said.

"Bryan," Becka shouted at him. "How dare you to speak like that about yourself?"

"Calm down, sweetheart. We need to know why she hates Nora," he stroked Becka's arms to soothe her.

"You hate my mommy?" Nat's voice interfered, and the grown-ups groaned.

"If Matt finds out that he knows, it will be hell," Jonathan whispered to Amelie, who was closest to him.

Amelie immediately came forward and took Nat's hand. She said soothingly, "No one hates your mommy, Nat. You saw we all love her."

"But she doesn't," the boy said in a stubborn tone of voice, pointing to Rebecca.

"I don't hate her," Rebecca replied to the child. "I hate that some plans can't come to life. That's all," she said and tried to ruffle the child's hair, but Nat stepped back.

He stared at Rebecca for a few more seconds and then looked up at Amelie, "May I have another slice of cake, auntie?"

Amelie nodded and smiled, relieved that they averted the crisis. Besides, she loved it when the boy called her auntie.

Marjorie had told Nat that Matt would marry his mommy, and consequently, he would become his daddy. That news made Nat happy. Nat already loved Matt because he always made time for him and never scolded him. Then, everyone told Nat to call them auntie or uncle, and, suddenly, the boy found himself in the middle of a huge family where everyone tried to make him happy and paid attention to him.

NORA, MARJORIE, AND Matt returned after fifteen minutes. Nora had refused a dress from Marjorie but accepted a pair of pants and a shirt.

She had to explain to Matt several times that she didn't hold him responsible for what had happened, and no, she hadn't changed her mind. She would marry him the following Saturday.

Matt was seething. He had always known that his grandma was a cold woman, who put her wishes and thoughts above everyone else's. Yet, Matt had never imagined that Rebecca would use her abilities to hurt someone, and especially, the woman he loved.

Rebecca was still there when they arrived on the patio, and Matt saw red before his eyes. Determined to get to her and throw her out, he lengthened his stride, but Nora squeezed his fingers and pulled him back. Matt looked at her over the shoulder, and she shuddered at the black intent in his gaze.

"No," Nora said quietly. "You won't do anything to tear your family apart."

"She hurt you," Matt growled.

"Not really. Rebecca just doused me," Nora shrugged. "It's no big deal, Matt. A little rain never killed anyone."

"I don't care," Matt barked again.

"But I do," Nora replied quietly, and he closed his eyes.

"All right, I won't throw her out, but she must not touch you. Ever."

Nora nodded, and then both joined the others.

Rebecca pierced Nora and Matt with a black look. She fisted her hands and advanced toward Matt.

"You're making a mistake, Matt."

"It's mine to make," he replied in an icy voice. "And I don't see any mistake from where I stand," Matt pointed out.

"You won't get all your powers and your money," she snapped.

"Sorry to disappoint you, grandma, but I do have the powers. And I do have money. You know that I have no reason to complain about that," Matt snickered.

"You can't," Rebecca stepped back, horrified. "You're with her just because you're a kind man and feel sorry for her," she pointed toward Nora.

"I told you not to insult Nora again," Matt started toward Rebecca with angry steps, but Nora, pulled his hand, and he stopped.

"Nora, she's maligning you," he complained.

"So what?" she replied. "It's not like I care."

"But do you care you cost him his abilities and his money?" Rebecca asked her in a nasty voice.

"What is she talking about, Matt?" Nora asked, a frown between her eyebrows. "Have you lost something because you're with me?" she raised her voice.

"No, baby, quite the opposite," he assured her. "Because of our love, I finally have all the abilities I should have had from the beginning."

"I don't understand," Nora complained.

"Let me explain," Bryan said, striding toward them, a smile in the corner of his mouth. "As an outsider, and once in your shoes, I might make more sense, Nora," he told her and came closer.

Rebecca gave him the evil eye, but he just smiled at her.

"You see, because of two tragedies in her life, great-grandma cursed all generations to come. They can't reach their full potential and use their abilities until they've fallen in love and committed to someone," Bryan explained.

He stretched out his hand to Becka, and she immediately linked her fingers with his.

"For instance," he continued, "Matt's love for you helped him to control his mind-reading skills and other extra sensorial perceptions," he said. Nora looked at Matt, and he nodded, then leaned over her, kissed her lips, and whispered, "You see, you brought me much more joy than I could have ever dreamed."

Nora blushed, and Bryan chortled.

"Now, to continue, Nora. Rebecca also set up trust funds for her grandchildren and later for her great-grandchildren. But they can't get that money until they fall in love, commit to someone, and that someone commits to them. Of course, there's a set of trustees – mind readers, you see, who can check if someone tries to cheat. I understand that someone did it in the past," he chuckled, looking at Jay, who scowled at him.

"Why everyone has to bring me into this discussion?" he asked with disgust, throwing his hands into the air.

"Because your story is funny," Bryan answered and winked at him.

"Then," Nora said hesitantly, "I don't see what Matt has lost by being with me." She looked at Rebecca inquiringly and then at Matt.

"That's the idea, love. I lost nothing, but I got everything," he said and lifted her hand to his lips and kissed it.

"Yeah?" Rebecca snickered. "Then prove it."

"The only thing we have to do is prove it to each other, grandma," Matt shook his head. "We don't have to prove anything to you."

"You're afraid," she said with an ugly laugh. "You know that the trustees will see through this sham, as I have already done."

"You wear blinds, grandma, so you don't see anything that's not directly before your nose," Matt replied.

"The children love each other, Rebecca," Marjorie intervened. "Leave them be," she urged her.

"You're stupid, Marjorie," Rebecca lashed at her.

"You won't talk to my wife like this. I told you so in the past, and I won't repeat it," Jonathan came to support his wife.

"I see," Rebecca said. "Nora and Matt fooled you all. They thought that I'd give them the money immediately if they came and gave me a teary story about love. I'm made of sterner stuff than that, Matty boy," she snickered at Matt.

"Maybe I wasn't clear," Matt repeated dryly. "I don't want the money. I already have here everything I want," he said, lifting Nora's hand.

"You know what I think?" Rebecca said with satisfaction. "I think that you are afraid. If you weren't, you'd accept to have the trustees read her mind."

"Nora offered me her thoughts, so I know very well what she thinks and feels," Matt replied, unconcerned. "I don't need your trustees to tell me what I already know," he shrugged.

Bryan put a hand on his shoulder, "Matt, in the long run, it helps that thing with the trustees. I've been there and done that, you know."

"I don't want them to read her mind," Matt dug his heels in the ground, glaring at Bryan.

"But I do," Nora replied in a calm voice. "I know that you know how I think, but maybe it's better if everyone is sure that we don't try to pull the wool over their eyes," she told Matt, stroking his arm.

Matt closed his eyes in defeat.

FINAL CHAPTER

THE SUN SHONE OVER the island on the day that Nora married Matt. She wore a princess sleeveless white dress with little pearls all over the torso. The dress hugged her chest and waist but flared around her legs.

Nora had had some reservations about wearing such a virginal dress at first. She had been married before, after all, and it didn't seem right to wear a white dress.

But then, she had discussed it with Marjorie, who, together with Becka, Lily, and Maggie, insisted on going with her to buy the dress.

Her future mother-in-law patiently explained to Nora that she was wrong. Nora hadn't had a white dress for her first marriage. She had married at the Town Hall. Besides, that was Matt's first and only marriage, and he would have loved to have his bride dressed all in white.

Matt's eyes shone with unshed tears when Nora started moseying toward him. His gaze roamed all over her face and body, and pride flashed in his dark-blue pupils.

He surveyed her advancement toward him, but, for the first time in his life, Matt lost his patience. He dashed down the aisle that Marjorie had fashioned by throwing a white carpet between the rows of chairs. Matt didn't stop until he reached Nora, entwined his fingers with hers, and kissed her lips lightly.

"What are you doing, Matt?" Nora whispered, and her widened, confused eyes zeroed in on his face.

"I made a mistake, baby. We should have had this ceremony in our living room, under five minutes flat, and then leave for our honeymoon immediately. I don't know if I have the patience to go through all this. I want to be alone with you right now," Matt whispered back, and for the first time since her accident, he didn't think of the wound in her leg but urged Nora to hurry and get before the pastor faster.

His action shocked everyone, and they couldn't react at first. Marjorie covered her mouth, and tears trailed down her face.

Becka and Bryan looked at each other. Becka seemed taken aback, but Bryan wore a broad and knowing grin on his lips.

Nora had explained the ceremony to Nat, and now he didn't understand what changed and kept asking his aunties, "What's going on?" Yet, no one was able to give him an answer.

When Matt slid his arm around Nora's waist and rushed her before the pastor, they recovered and burst into laughter.

Jay and Maggie high-fived each other, as they would usually do, and the others elbowed one another, and even the older generation chuckled.

"He's got it worse than I had," Jonathan whispered to Marjorie, and she nodded, a smile on her lips, despite her tears.

Nora blushed to the tip of her ears, but Matt had only one care in the world. He only wanted to get married and be on his way to the cottage he had rented on the shore of a lake in northern Ontario.

Matt and Nora had already arranged and discussed things with Nat, and the child had declared that he would be happy to live with Becka and Bryan for a couple of weeks, while his mommy and Matt enjoyed a brief honeymoon.

Everyone enjoyed the brief service – Matt's stipulation because he didn't want to waste any time before the *I do's*.

Matt had invited Rebecca to his wedding only because the women in the family insisted. Nora had also lobbied for her coming. Matt had turned ice-cold toward Rebecca and didn't want to talk or see her.

The engagement party had ended with inviting Rebecca's trustees so that they could ascertain whether the young couple was really in love.

Matt had been entirely against that, but Nora didn't want to cause any discussions between Matt and his family, so she had insisted.

When the trustees acknowledged Nora and Matt's love and commitment, Rebecca had felt like fainting. She had been wrong once more.

She had tried to approach Matt, but he didn't bother to discuss anything with her. He just announced the trustees that he didn't want or need the money, and then, he gathered Nora and Nat, said their good-byes, and left.

Now Rebecca watched the couple making their vows, and a shadow crossed her face. She knew Matt, and she knew that it wouldn't be as easy to get back in his graces as it had been with Bryan.

Matt was a kind man, yet he didn't forgive or forget. He had already told her in unequivocal terms to stuff her money where the sun didn't shine. Nora had supported his decision, although she asked Matt to express it in more pleasant words.

Some of the family members still talked to Rebecca, but not all of them. She didn't need their pity, but that fiasco had decided her to find another way to get what she wanted.

Her gaze fell on Ariel, who tried to fight off the persistent invitations of Bryan's friend, Max. Rebecca shuddered. That was a man she didn't want in her family. Thank God, the girl seemed to have brains!

AUTHOR'S BIO

ROWENA DAWN writes romance, reads thrillers, and watches comedies. She likes walking through the woods but insanely loves the sea. She has a love-hate relationship with her writing and drives her dog crazy whenever she doesn't stop writing to take him out.

OTHER BOOKS BY ROWENA DAWN

Thank you for taking the time to read *The Winstons Book One*.

If you enjoyed it, please, consider telling your friends or posting a short review.

Word of mouth is an author's best friend and much appreciated. Thank you,

Rowena Dawn

Contents

ROWENA DAWN

Don't miss out!

Visit the website below and you can sign up to receive emails whenever Rowena Dawn publishes a new book. There's no charge and no obligation.

https://books2read.com/r/B-A-SAED-SOIS

BOOKS 2 READ

Connecting independent readers to independent writers.

Did you love *The Winstons Book One Becka's Awakening &
Matt's Dilemma*? Then you should read *Jay's Salvation*[1] by
Rowena Dawn!

*Jay was just looking for fun. What he got was losing his
heart and peace of mind.*

Jay is not a very good guy. He can read minds - even
though not very well and not all the time. Yet, he uses his
ability to play cards and win the pot.

He plays once too many times. He loses his money and
hardly escapes with his life and that only because he has a
guardian angel.

---

1. https://books2read.com/u/mvKp5z

2. https://books2read.com/u/mvKp5z

Now, he needs to decide if what he feels for his angel is love or gratitude.

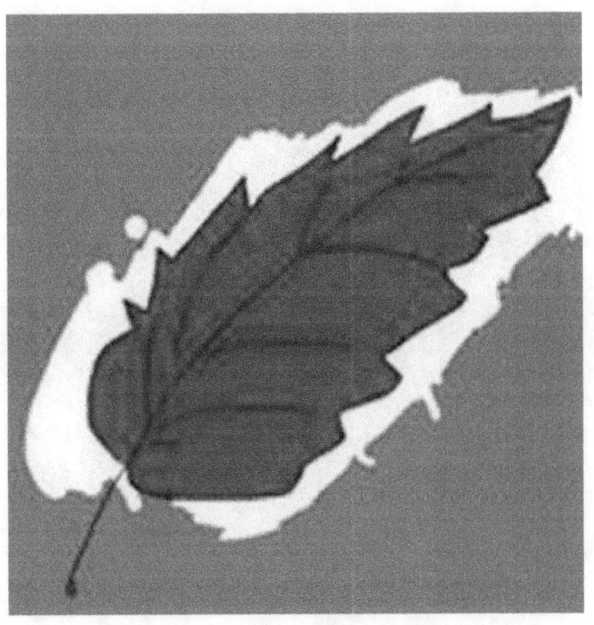

About the Publisher

It is based in Toronto and brings to public various books:
poems, novels, short-stories, children's books, language study
books and non-fiction. It publishes the literary review:
Scarlet Leaf Review: www.scarletleafreview.com

Our mission is to help emerging authors and poets to
make their works known to the public.

Contact   email   address:
scarletleafpublishinghouse@gmail.com